Also by Meyer Levin

Meyer Levin

THE ARCHITECT

1612 – July 1991

Simon and Schuster
New York

Copyright © 1981 by Meyer Levin, Eli Levin, Gabriel Levin,
Dominique Quignon-Fleuret and Mikael Levin
All rights reserved
including the right of reproduction
in whole or in part in any form
Published by Simon and Schuster
A Division of Gulf & Western Corporation
Simon & Schuster Building
Rockefeller Center
1230 Avenue of the Americas
New York, New York 10020
SIMON AND SCHUSTER and colophon are trademarks of Simon & Schuster
Manufactured in the United States of America

1   2   3   4   5   6   7   8   9   10

Library of Congress Cataloging in Publication Data

Levin, Meyer, 1905–1981
The architect.

1. Wright, Frank Lloyd, 1867–1957—Fiction.
I. Title.
PS3523.E799A88   813'.52   81-13622

AACR2
ISBN 0-671-24892-8

The author gratefully acknowledges permission to quote from the following:

"A.D. Blood," from the book *Spoon River Anthology*, new edition with new poems, 22 printing, 1957, copyright 1915, 1916, 1942, and 1944.

"Chicago," from Chicago Poems, *Selected Poems of Carl Sandburg*, edited by Rebecca West, copyright 1926, Harcourt Brace and World, Inc. and copyright 1954, Rebecca West.

My very special thanks to
Edgar Tafel
who gave so unsparingly of
his expertise and time

Part One

The Cave and the Treehouse

AFTER THE big Sunday family picnic in Uncle Matt's grove, the men now having their pipes, and the women cleaning up with the girls helping, leaving only cider jugs on the spread blanket, Andrew Lane knew that the solemn family powwow over his mother's sudden situation was about to take place. Why shouldn't he have a say-so? But Mother was certainly not going to move back here to the valley from Madison. Not with the ideas she had for him.

The big cousins, young men and grown girls, were piling onto a wagon, laughing their own kind of jokes, and of Andrew's size no one was left except his cousin Susan, though she really could have gone along, she was more than two years older than he, and today she had on a long dress below her ankles, a real ground-sweeper like a real woman, and she had arrived with her hair done up. But after a while she had let it down loose. Sue busied herself putting hampers back in her family's wagon, but Andrew guessed she was maneuvering to maybe catch a few words of the serious talk that was coming. His sister Tess too was lingering around, by the big oak, pushing Susan's little brother Chester on the swing.

"Why don't you and Andrew go up to the cave, take along Chester, you know how he loves it," Aunt Allison said to Sue, and added, surveying the field, "Why don't you take Tess along, too?"

Tess gave them a look between fury and defeat, and left Chester swinging in midair, going off to the riverbank to read her *Little Women*. She took herself for the artist one, and was always drawing sketches of people, just a bit comical.

Mother and Aunt Nora were already settled under the crabapple tree; no doubt Nora was trying to persuade her, since Father had walked out, to give up the house in Madison and come back here to River Valley and teach. Now the rest of the elders were joining the talk. Aunt Tabitha —don't dare call her Tabby!—let down her broad frame in sections, the left side, then the right side, then smoothed her big apron over her dress. Andrew even found himself reflecting, inappropriately at this moment, that some women, you could feel the lightness of their forms within their garments as the voluminous clothing swung around them, but with poor Aunt Tabby, clothes and body were one great solidity. He knew, of course, what the female form was like; even as a tyke, when Father was a preacher in Weymouth, he had been led by his mother through the Boston art museum, but his speculation now, maybe to avoid what was really important, shifted to the very nature of clothing, of different kinds of materials, some following, some solidifying a shape, so that if you didn't know, you could think women had no legs.

Uncle Matt now took his place at the head of the blanket, alongside Aunt Tabby. With streaks of white in his spade-shaped beard, Uncle Matt, the oldest of the Daniels brothers, was acting as head of the family since Grandfather Enoch, past eighty, no longer came to the picnics, especially on the Sundays when he preached.

Aunt Allison now called out impatiently to Chester to

skedaddle, and so, with Susan letting Chester get a head start, the three of them made it a race toward the bald top of the hill. After sprinting ahead of Sue a bit just to show he was faster, Andrew let her catch up, and they ran side by side, her loose hair flying.

The climb was easy enough, the rocks like huge steps. Chester was already mocking them from above. Slowed by that long skirt, Sue waved a "you win" to her little brother, and climbed more like a lady.

Reaching the wide ledge, you at once imagined Indians squatting in front of their cave, keeping watch over the valley.

The cave dwelling had an almost perfect arched opening, high enough so at its center a man wouldn't have to bend. A stream of light reached inside. Though the walls were obscure you felt the dome shape; around the smoke hole you still could make out smudging, though mostly the walls were defaced by scratched initials, names, and double hearts. Chester began to scrape and kick with his shoe for old arrowheads, though none had been found here since before he was born. Then he went out to climb to the top.

Andrew squatted with Sue, near the opening. Imagine yourself an Indian, the hunter home from the hunt. . . . No matter what they decided down there in the family conference, Andrew knew what he was going to do, he was going to quit high school right now and get a job. Maybe construction work—get the feel of it in your hands. Come back here to the Five Farms this summer only if really needed by his uncles for the harvest. Oh, right this minute they must all be advising Mother to move back here with him and Tess, there was a district high school in River Valley, and Mother could teach in Nora's private school. But in Madison at least you already felt you were in the world.

Sue said, "You really don't want to come back and live here?" And added, "I love it here. I never want to leave."

The way Susan acted toward him had always been even-Steven, no matter about her being older. Perhaps she already—as girls did—chose to seem younger than she was, though up to eighteen they were supposed to want to seem older than they were. Last summer Andrew already had known Sue was as good as spoken for, by a husky half-Swede from hereabouts.

Now they drew farther inside, settling on the floor with their backs curved to the wall, her skirts tucked under, the two of them nearly touching but not, they were the same cousins who had, when he came aged ten from Madison for his first farm summer, lugged full milk pails without spilling a drop, or played spies, she with her boisterous whoop when she tracked you down, and the two of you wrestled a bit on the straw.

Right now, Andrew was aware, Susan wished she magically could hear the secret private things being said down there. What happened between a man and a woman when they broke up. And for this, Andrew was now the one who knew more than she, knew about life.

"But you mean your father just went, just like that, he just put on his hat and walked out of the house?"

Andrew was silent. He didn't feel ready yet, or know how he could talk about such a thing, even to Sue.

"Didn't they even have a fight? Did they holler?"

Imagine his father hollering. Or his mother, for that matter, though she could at times raise her voice.

"You know they'd never holler."

Sue smoothed her dress to hug her knees the way women did, as though this cleared their thoughts. "But they did have an argument? A dispute? Weren't they talking about something?"

How could he explain that it was the opposite—they didn't talk at all. Not for a long time did Andrew remember his mother and father just talking to each other, much less having it out, as he used to wish they would, whatever it was. Father had become increasingly silent, except that he could go off and deliver a long lecture, talking to a women's society about the ancient Egyptians, or other such subjects, since in Madison he didn't have a church and preach.

14

Only, at home he'd come to the table at meals, say grace, hardly enter into the conversation except with a yes or a no concerning factual matters, like if Mother asked whether Adella Kitteridge's parents had paid for her music lessons. No. Should she mention it to Mrs. Kitteridge? No, he'd rather not just yet, they'd pay. Then Mother's look of strained patience. She might remind him of unpaid bills of their own, always money talk it seemed, until, saying thanks to the Lord for His bounty, he folded his napkin and rose and went back behind his closed door. Soon they'd hear the chords. It always sounded like from the hymnal, though they knew that the music was his own. Long since were the times when he would call them in to hear his new song, even to try to sing it, the whole family together. "Thou shalt sing unto the Lord a new song . . ." That was one Andrew remembered because his sister Tess had burst out, "Doesn't sound new to me," and Mother had to turn her face away before she could reprove.

"No, they didn't holler at each other," Andrew replied to Susan. "It was more the other way. Father didn't talk at all, lately."

"Oh?" Susan said thoughtfully. But smiled to herself as one who fits a piece of a puzzle into place. "That's my mother's trick sometimes when they have a fight, not speaking to Father, only she can't do it for more than a day, she's so talkative it hurts her more than it hurts him. Pretty soon something happens like a sick calf, so she forgets she's not talking to him, and he pretends the fight never happened, and the fight is over." She gazed at Andrew. —Was it more complicated than that?

How could he tell her? His mother and father were always polite to each other, if only as good breeding, but these last few years it was more and more as if his father wasn't there. Of course when he was working at his songs you could hear, but there would come lapses of silence, long silences; you knew he was writing or reading. Or— Andrew had to utter a small laugh—the other way that you knew he was there: Andrew made a sniff.

He *smelled?* She was incredulous. The well-groomed, meticulous Pastor Lane?

A certain glue. The old man had a new ambition lately, he was going to discover the secret of the Stradivarius, and so he kept cooking up pure animal glue for those fiddles he was making. Smelled up the whole house. Drove Mother frantic.

And over that smell, the two of them had had words.

Andrew, indeed, had been intrigued by the violin making, and once before supper he had knocked and gone in. It had been almost like boyhood days in the East when his father would show him things he was doing, like how to write musical notations and read them at the piano. Now, at the neat side table for the violin work, Father gave him a lecture on the way a sound box vibrated, something of course that Andrew already knew. The glue was one of the important secrets of the Italian violin makers, but another great secret was the varnish, which had to be flexible with the vibration.

On the worktable lay an almost completed fiddle, the spruce still pale and naked, the color of human skin; clamps were holding the box together as the glue dried. On his desk, Father had open an ancient-looking book with engravings showing violin construction. Whoever could find the secret of the Stradivarius would not only bring something beautiful into the world but also make a tidy bit of money, which was not to be scorned. That was how he always spoke about money, with a faint rather aloof smile. But Father was sure that the money was not what Signor Stradivarius and the other great craftsmen of his day were most concerned about. They thought of creating something beautiful. And just for an instant a rather wistful bit of smile lit his father's face, and it was as though there came a vibration between them, a single-string vibrating.

And just now, sitting beside Susan, the cave engulfing them, Andrew understood something about his father's musical compositions, about all his father's efforts: his father was no genius. There was no originality. He was always trying to do something that was new for him, but it was not new, it was something that had been done before, like these violins. And that also was why all his songs were as though you had heard them a thousand times before. —Yes, they sounded nice. Mother always said that, very nice. To please him. And other people said it, too. When he preached, yes, it was fine, excellent—but it was just like the hymns, you had heard it before. Yet now Andrew recalled a certain look, almost fugitive, a kind of pain within his father's polite acceptance of the praising remarks. And Andrew knew: his father had hoped, each time, that he had done the real thing: struck fire.

And as Andrew thought about his father, trying to explain his father's leaving home, to Susan, to himself, there came back to Andrew a certain moment when the family had returned from the East and was moving into the house by the lake, in Madison. A moment with his father.

For, gazing out now over the valley and its broad stream, Andrew recalled that earlier time, and another vantage point over a body of water—from his treehouse. That was the younger time with his father, when Tess was a baby, arriving at the new place, the new house, in Wisconsin where Mother's family lived, coming here from out in Father's New England.

The Madison house was right beside the lake, and almost before running through the rooms upstairs and down Andrew had spotted the great oak whose branches reached out above the water. An easy climb, branch to branch like stairs circling the trunk, and then out along a solid limb that didn't even feel his weight, out straight over the water.

At once, both parents were below, though not ordering him down. A boy must climb trees, his mother would have declared, it was a natural thing. Only nevertheless as he balanced himself edging out on the branch there came a "Careful, not to the end," from her. Even if he were to fall he'd only get a ducking, like a high dive, but Andrew already had got the idea of what he would do up here—a treehouse! He announced it to their upturned faces. "I'm going to build myself a treehouse!" There were the crates arriving, Father's books, Mother's harp, her weaving loom. Andrew had helped his father nail up his precious library, and taking the crates apart would provide him with a perfect floor and walls and even a roof if he wanted—no, it should have no roof, just the branches above. Or maybe a half-roof, for winter, if he wished to sit up there like Neptune commanding his stormy sea.

That memory was maybe the best. He and his father drawing the nails out carefully, straight, so Andrew could reuse them. And after everything was carried into the house, there was his father himself actually coming up the tree, pushing aside twigs that tangled in his fine soft beard, and Mother waiting below to help them haul up a whole section from the harp crate, to be Andrew's treehouse floor. Now, on what, his father asked, was the floor and the whole contraption going to be supported? Why, on this heavy branch, Andrew said. Nailed down with spikes. "You'll have a seesaw, not a treehouse!" his father jested. When he was in good humor he could be humorous. Then Andrew had another idea: at either side were somewhat higher branches almost parallel. He would nail uprights from his floor edge, for support, and also he could then use those side branches for benches! Natural seats! Well, now, that was an idea! his father agreed.

Mother, below, shouted up her worry: wouldn't the main, central branch snap off? If Andrew planned to have friends coming up there, a whole club? They'd fall and crack their skulls! Andrew had to laugh. How could that thick branch snap? Why, it was like a strong arm, stuck out. And he really felt it, like a law of nature—the tree had an outreaching strength as from muscles in the body.

To test the construction with a man's weight, Preacher Lane edged to the end of the floor, and nothing swayed a hairbreadth. A sturdy oak. Andrew had a hunch his father was even a bit envious of his treehouse.

Already that afternoon as he hammered away, three

boys, two of them bigger ones, were hovering below; one of them offered a door from an old chicken coop.

A treehouse club is all right for smaller boys, but once he'd be thirteen or fourteen . . . Andrew even thought of then rebuilding it into a real study, with an added perch higher up, a seat like on a schooner's mast, high up enough so you could feel the tree sway deliciously as you contemplated the stars.

Thus now, up here on the hillside ledge, one might imagine a lone Indian contemplating the valley, the river, the sky. Behind, the cave evoked a different vision, the warm hollow shelter to enter into, with its fireglow beneath the smoke hole, and its spread of buffalo hides.

How much older was he than Andrew's mother? Susan was saying.

Andrew had never exactly calculated. Of course, much older. "Maybe about twenty years?" she said. That much? But older for a man was all right. And his father wasn't like an old man, if that was what she meant, he stood straight and walked vigorously. His hair was gray but in a thick wave back from his forehead.

How old was he now? she wanted to know.

Why did that matter? "He's fifty-nine," Andrew said. His last birthday.

"Not yet sixty," she said. "But still that's getting old."

Susan was trying to find out something from him, woman-man, like when someone questions a child, about man-woman things the child still doesn't understand. Andrew felt a touch offended, yet uncertain.

Susan spoke of her own mother and father. When they got a real mad on, sometimes her father slept in the barn, in the hayloft. So when Andrew's father and mother weren't talking, did his father—

No, Andrew said, they used the same bedroom. But they didn't go up together. Father would stay late in his study. But for a long time now, even when they didn't have words, his father stayed late, and went up afterward alone. Andrew would hear the steps in his sleep.

Was Sue getting at—could his father be too old to do it anymore? This question had not occurred to Andrew, and he supposed it had had to come from a woman's inquisitiveness. Well, Sue was still a virgin, of course, but even if a woman hadn't gone through it yet, girls seemed to have a way of knowing more about these things than you did.

"Well, they weren't exactly lovey-dovey," he said, and hadn't been for years, but . . .

And the scene at the dinner table was before him, should he tell her? This time Father's silence weighed heavier and heavier. Tess got up to serve the coffee, as Mother was teaching her, and as she filled Father's cup you could barely hear his "Thank you." She put the pot hastily on the stove as though her hand was scorched, said a quick "May I be excused?" to Mother, and without waiting ran up to her room.

That was when Mother said it. "Why don't you just leave us, Mr. Lane, why don't you take your hat and go your way?"

Father took a long sip of the coffee, and set the cup down. "If that's what you want, I will, then."

She didn't reply. He folded the napkin, put it beside his plate, moved back his chair as he always did, with care that it shouldn't scrape. He went to his study, plainly to pack his music, his personal things.

To Andrew, his mother said, "Don't you have your geometry to do?" and he went to his room. Each person all shut away from the other. He heard his father on the stairs coming up, and after a short time going down. Should he go down himself, to say goodbye? And where would Father go to, exactly, in the night—to a hotel? Or perhaps he meant tonight to sleep downstairs on his sofa, and say goodbye in the morning?

"What I mean, your mother is still a young woman . . ." Susan was flushing. "Perhaps she still has needs —that he doesn't."

A woman's needs. Of that kind. This somewhat star-

20

tled Andrew. But he didn't let on, didn't ask. A man's needs he knew, already for a few years, how the damned thing tormented you until you had to do a disgusting thing to get relieved, hoping your mother wouldn't find any trace on the sheet. But that a woman also—? He couldn't quite understand. Yet even though there was an honesty between him and Susan, dear cousins with no secrets, he could not bring himself to ask her, and he let the moment pass as if he knew what she meant by a woman's needs. Affection and kisses, he supposed.

But as to her hints about the age of his father, could it be that just as there was a time in young boys before the terrible need began, there came a time in older men when it ceased? Had this happened to his father? Was that what Sue meant?

They were now standing in the cave mouth, gazing, both he and Susan gazing speculatively out over the valley that lay so quiet and sun-drenched in the length of the afternoon. Slowly, then totally, a feeling of oneness came over them, as though they were gazing out over their entire future lives, maybe not to be lived together, she was already going to marry her young man, promised, as good as engaged; yet without even holding hands it was as though they were welded entirely together, breathing together, one. Andrew experienced a sense of untroubled love; Susan would always be this unity for him.

Their faces turned toward each other, and then again to the valley, to the world, as though they had meanwhile exchanged the most profound secrets and pledges through what they had been probing in the troubles of men and women.

Quietened, he told her the rest, how when he and Mother and Tess came down the next morning his father had already made himself an early breakfast; the portmanteau and handcase of papers stood ready; he kissed Tess on the brow, and then at Andrew's turn held his hand, a long moment, placing the other hand on his son's shoulder. "Be a good man, Andrew. Realize your dreams." And with a look at their mother, a brief look, not hostile, not loving, not sad—you couldn't tell anything in their faces—he said under his breath, "Goodbye, then, Marta," and took up his grip. Tess made a half-start to open the door for him, but he did it himself, then closed it carefully behind him, and through the window they saw him walking straight-backed down the street, to the railway station was what they guessed. Their mother called them to breakfast.

After Andrew had told Susan that last part, there was again the sense of closeness, of oneness, not even really broken when her little brother, whom they had just about forgotten, scrambled down from above the cave shouting, "I found one!," showing a fragment of flint that could with imagination perhaps even be a chip of an arrowhead. Chester started down, but Andrew and Susan remained for a bit, watching him almost like mature people amused at their child. Sue squeezed his hand. "It'll work out all right, Andrew."

"I'm not going back to high school, I'm getting a job." He hadn't, as yet, even announced this to his mother.

They stood thus together, and even more totally the ineffable calm came over him. A unity. Would he—but surely he must one day find such a peace as this, in his lifelong mate.

2

DECISIONS HAD been made. His mother would not close the Madison house; she would manage, she said, with her kindergarten.

Andrew declared he would quit high school and get a job, but Marta patted his hand; he must go on with his education. There was really no need to worry. He guessed that the uncles had insisted on helping. At least with as much as Father had been bringing in, which hadn't been much at all.

Perhaps during this summer, as he was so eager for experience in construction, his uncles could get him work with the River Valley carpenter and sometime barn builder, Neil Hagedorn, and in the big harvest when needed Andrew could come to the farms.

He worked with Hagedorn, adding on a porch. Hagedorn really knew about wood—what would hold, what would crack. And he scorned measurements—he could measure with his eye to a thirty-second, carrying a folding rule in the back of his overalls to prove it. He hated spikes, you would think they were going into his own flesh, and

Andrew got to feel the same way, for Neil Hagedorn's mortice-and-tennon joints were virtually imperceptible.

Andrew stayed at Uncle Peter's; after supper he might walk over to Uncle James's. Sometimes Susan's intended husband came over in his trap. Her face glowed when Gus came in, true enough, but they were not as moony as Andrew had imagined an engaged couple would be, they were cheerful and easy with each other, and they sat by the lamp planning their house. The house was going to be built right after the crops were in, so when the wedding was held the couple could move at once into their home, and Gus would have his twenty head of cattle already in the barn.

Susan and Gus had drawn out a kind of floor plan which she now showed to Andrew, as he was after all destined by his mother to be an architect, another Christopher Wren.

The engaged couple bent their heads over their plan, while Susan unblushingly discussed how many children they were going to have, and when. For the upstairs where the children would be after infancy, Andrew suggested, why not save on the usual giant-high ceiling, and bring it down, to, say, seven feet, enough for even a tall man like Gus, still save a lot on lumber. And kids would feel cozier. Now, that made real sense, Gus said, and he was all for it. Then, the floor plan downstairs. They had Franklin stoves, but why not in the sitting room a big old-fashioned fireplace? Nothing in a house gave the home feeling you got from a hearth.

What did he mean, to go back to a log cabin! But Andrew drew it for them, even with a little boy lying on a hearthrug, also an inglenook with the mother sitting knitting, the father reading, and Susan began to see it. Then she asked could he draw the whole house, and Andrew said he would draw them a rendering, which meant what a building was going to look like. He extended the eaves downward for protection over the side porch, so the thing didn't look anymore like a Swedish crate, and Gus even asked if Andrew had some ideas about the cow barn. The first idea Andrew had, thinking of howling winter mornings, was for a covered walk connecting the kitchen door of the house to the cow barn. And while he was at it, Andrew rendered the house and barn together, with the low eaves on the cow barn as well. The first creation of Andrew Lane!

Susan was so pleased with the picture that she awarded him a big smacking kiss on the forehead, while Gus grinned.

At summer's end, Uncle Peter paid him twice as much as ever before. Andrew understood this was intended to help Mother. And his spinster Aunt Nora repeated her persuasions for his mother's moving back here to join her in her school. With the new generation of Danielses, she now had over twenty-five pupils. Indeed, several youngsters from "outside" were coming to board. Nora's cherished plan was to build a "home school." The daring idea of Aunt Nora was that her "home school" would be for boys and girls together! After all, they would grow up to be men and women together! Surely Marta, with her advanced ideas in her kindergarten, should be interested in such a school!

His aunt even took him to the site, across the river from the farms. Nora owned an entire hill, next to the cave hill, and there she intended to build her Home School, and she wanted Andrew to start thinking about it, he was so talented and from his birth her dear sister Marta had known he would be a great architect.

Standing, absorbing the shape of the hill, the top a perfect mound, he could see a crowning element like a circlet of flowers on a woman's hair—a circlet on this mount, of little log cabins, each for a grade?

A lovely idea, but she would need more teachers, Aunt Nora said; if only Marta would come back!

His mother and Nora had been so close as young sisters, and both had become teachers in the River Valley school. There had come a need for a county superintendent, and thus Mr. Lane had been brought out: a Harvard graduate, son of a minister, himself a preacher as well as an educator—every qualification. A widower, too! And presently teacher Marta Daniels was in love with him and married him. And so Andrew Lane had come into the world. By then, Sanford Lane, deciding to try the ministry again, had moved with his bride to Ohio. And on eastward.

And Aunt Nora had started her own school.

In the house in Madison nothing was changed, Father's study was the same except the desktop was bare. Mr. Lane had not sent for his books, was Mother's only remark; she believed he was out West somewhere. Andrew's summer money she accepted in part, with her way of compressing her lips, so she too considered it the family's way of giving her a little added help. But Andrew must not think of leaving his schooling to take a job so as to bring in money!

Finishing high school was a waste of time! He had to get started!

She would like to send him to M.I.T., to the best. Unfortunately at the university here there was no school of architecture.

He already knew; there was a school of engineering, which in these days, with iron construction coming in strongly, was maybe at least as good for a start.

His mother had thought of this. Luckily, she taught weaving to the wife of the head of the engineering school, Professor Emil Gamsey. Andrew must go and see him.

WEARING THE new collegiate suit Mother had bought him for his birthday, Andrew walked into the red brick building. Professor Gamsey's office was open, but there was nobody there. On a large slanted drafting table, under a tracing sheet, was a plan of girders. On the side wall hung an engraving showing long rows of slaves building the Egyptian Pyramids, pulling up huge quarried stones by use of a primitive hoist. Also, there was a cross section of a Greek column, he must be sure to remark to the professor it was Doric. And then a large photograph of the Crystal Palace in London all glass over a spidery iron dome.

The professor, in a velvet jacket, came in. He was more Mother's age than Father's. Sandy-haired, with a Vandyke. "Well, now, let's see what we can do."

He even dropped a few words about "in the circumstances," meaning wanting to help Mother. Again, like being a poor relation. At least, once Andrew got started working, maybe that would stop!

The professor now stood over the drafting board remarking he didn't suppose Andrew had had any training in draftsmanship, but did he think he could do tracings? And to show him, Professor Gamsey picked up from a velvet-lined coffer on the table, marked "Keuffel and Esser," with all kinds of slits for compasses and dividers and mechanical drawing pens—a beautiful set such as Andrew had seen in the display window of the university supply store—a mechanical drawing pen with the little knob that regulated the thickness of the line. From the special stopper of an India-ink bottle, he slipped some ink into the cleft of the pen and then, leaning over, drew along the T square, on the tracing paper, then handed the pen to Andrew. Andrew continued the line, but so lightly that nothing came out of the pen. "You have to press down a little." Andrew got the feel of it. "Good," the professor said. Only now did Andrew look at the detail plan under the tracing paper—a zigzag iron truss. Must be for a span across a wide floor area, probably the gymnasium they were going to build. Seemed to him, just to support the roof, the iron beams were overheavy. "Are there upper floors?" he ventured. "Not as planned," but with a sharp glance—the professor had caught Andrew's thought.

"Ever tried lettering?" The professor handed him a snubnosed lettering pen. In high school, Andrew had sometimes lettered instead of using handwriting, just because he felt like it. Already, he had his rapid touch. Watching him, the professor wore a little smile.

Then Professor Gamsey sat down behind his desk and gave Andrew a kind of lecture. In modern construction, the line between engineering and architecture was disappearing. Look at the Brooklyn Bridge! Look at London's Crystal Palace! . . . He would get Andrew special permission for a few university courses, and advised him to study French, the Beaux-Arts was still the best place for architecture. . . .

He was being taken on, he had a job!

Marta had been sure Professor Gamsey would recognize Andrew's great promise. The pay, of course, would be a real help. If there was something he wanted for himself . . . He wanted to make things easier for her with the house expenses, Andrew said. —Did he know what she would like to do? She was going to use part of the money to start Tess on harp lessons!

Andrew would not let himself feel resentful. Indeed, this meant they were not as badly off as he had thought. Many times he had heard his father say there was no instrument so appropriate for the home as the harp. A woman playing on a harp was a delight to behold. Even as a little boy, Andrew had felt he shared exactly what was meant—a woman, Mother, in her fine dress, and the harp strings outlined against the fireplace flames as her arms made magical movements.

His mother had gradually given up playing the harp, no longer accompanying Father in his songs. She was always busy looming, and teaching children, with her Froebel kindergarten things, those bright-colored triangles and oblongs, and the blocks and structural forms that she felt sure would become a great architectural influence on Andrew.

Thus, alongside his father's image of the woman by the fireside playing the harp, there was for Andrew the

28

gentle domestic image of his mother sitting at her weaving, the color stripes growing on the fabric as her arms and hands passed back and forth in their magical movements.

Like Penelope in the *Odyssey*.

Perhaps a woman always believed a man would come back.

Then was this why she should want to give Tess lessons on the harp? Was it some sign that Mother perhaps dreamed Father would one day walk in, and there he would behold his daughter playing the harp?

But there came a contrary sign. For on the day after Andrew handed his mother his first weekly wages, he came home to see on her face that particularly pleased look that meant she had done something for her son. The door to the study was open, and there, covering Father's desk, Andrew beheld a large tilted drawing board, with T square and triangles. And beside it lay, in an open green case, a gleaming Keuffel and Esser drawing set.

His mother was really done with Mr. Sanford Lane.

3

THE IMPORTANT uncle was the youngest, Bruce, who was making the name of Daniels count in Chicago. Just a step older than Mother, he had been a cannoneer in the Civil War, after which the older brothers had decided that Bruce should have a full theological education in the seminary in New York. Clear-eyed, with magnetic vitality, Reverend Bruce Daniels not only had built Chicago's wealthiest and largest Unitarian congregation, but was soon on the regional and then on the national board.

With the new River Valley generation marrying and begetting, the Danielses had put together money to build a proper house of worship. Uncle Bruce had brought a design by a Chicago architect, the local builder Anton Siebert had put up the structure, and Uncle Bruce, coming to plan the dedication, stopped first in Madison to see Marta.

It was quite a dinner, with Marta's blueberry muffins, and broiled fresh trout from the lake. Aunt Nora had come, and Bruce got them all laughing with his tales of Chicago's newly rich, and his neat way of extracting special contributions out of them by knowing what parvenu wanted to meet which socialite, and then putting them on a committee together. Never, Andrew guessed, had Pastor Sanford Lane been up to such wise tricks. Perhaps that was why his father had never made a go of it.

Now it was Aunt Nora who wanted practical advice from Uncle Bruce, for her Home School. Did he think she might expect resident pupils from Chicago?

"Do you mean, will I send them!" he boomed with his easy laugh. Oh, he'd speak of her fine school. "You must make it exclusive. Be slow about accepting one or two. Then get them to come to me to use my family influence to have you take them in!" They laughed like real conspirators. Meanwhile, with Mother reminding her, Nora brought out the sketch Andrew had made, for the hilltop circle of cottages.

"Well, Andrew, excellent!" Indeed, he would take it back and show it to his church architect, Mr. Allen Olmstead. A real professional rendering!

Andrew held back a retort: wasn't he working professionally for Professor Gamsey!

In Chicago, building was going on at a great rate, said Uncle Bruce. When Andrew completed his college work in a few years, he must come to Chicago.

That sounded better. But in the next moment his uncle, studying the hilltop plan, judiciously offered some thoughts. The circle of cottages was charming, but wouldn't a single building housing everything together be more economical? And going from one cottage to another in the cold weather . . .

The cottages could be connected to each other with covered passages, Andrew quickly suggested. A linked ring, like a circle of children holding hands.

Aunt Nora smiled. What a pretty idea.

"Yes, that's a very pretty idea you had there, Andrew, and it ought not to be lost," said his uncle. Someday Andrew would be a full-fledged architect, and he ought to start now collecting a whole bag of ideas. Just in this same way, said Uncle Bruce, ideas for sermons sometimes came to him, not quite right for the moment. Into the idea bag they went, and invariably the occasion came to reach in and pull out a good idea.

But Uncle Bruce went on with another thought. Little groups under separate roofs were one thing, but all the pupils living under one roof would give them a sense of community. Thus a structure itself, the form of a school, a home, had its effect on what people were and would become. He beamed on Andrew. Architecture could indeed actually shape people's lives. Andrew forgot his resentment; why, this was a real thought. Until now, he had thought simply of the way a structure looked. Now was added the idea of how it made you live. Uncle Bruce maybe understood things, after all.

He was brought back by Aunt Nora pleading, wouldn't he try to design a building with the classrooms, the dormitories, even her own quarters, all under one roof? She was sure Andrew would do something really beautiful!

The next morning Nora drove them all to River Valley. The new church looked like a cozy residence, entry porch and all; Andrew recognized the fashionable Queen Anne style, seen even in Madison. Plus this chapel had a low square tower topped by a modest spire. The structure indeed had a kind of charm, so while Uncle Bruce was conferring about the ceremonies, Andrew got out his sketchbook.

Emerging, Uncle Bruce admired the drawing, could he have it? And made Andrew sign it. "Andrew Lane"— well, something more, so he added "Delineator." To show to the architect, Andrew expected.

A few weeks later there came a letter from his uncle in Chicago, with a printed proof of his chapel drawing as it would appear in the Unitarian journal. "Andrew Lane, Delineator."

"Your first appearance in print!" Marta exclaimed. She wanted to frame it. He was pleased, of course, but said he could really draw much better. The architect, Mr. Olmstead, wrote Uncle Bruce, had been impressed with the delineation and was sending a copy to the *Midwest Builder*.

But he was getting nowhere here. Professor Gamsey had him supervising the gymnasium structure, crawling out on the trusses to make check measurements. Once he nearly fell. Pulled himself back up to the beam, but never told Mother.

Nor could he get anywhere with his few classes at the university. The idea had been to learn French, just if he could get to the École des Beaux-Arts in Paris. All the big architects had gone there, Richardson of Boston, and Sullivan of Chicago. But to these collegians with their classroom sprawl, French was for when you tour abroad and parlez-vous, ha-ha! He had to get out, go to Chicago and start real work in an architectural office!

For just when Andrew had thought he had a chance, with Gamsey getting the courthouse to build, Gamsey had taken on a designer. True, the fellow had graduated M.I.T. Smoked aromatic cigarettes from a fancy case. His name was Craig Kogan, he sported a blond pompadour, and Andrew suspected the fellow was a Jew. Not that Andrew was anti-Semitic. He just couldn't stand fake.

Mr. Kogan produced the usual courthouse thing, Greek Revival porch, Roman columns, false, and inside, a high rotunda with more imitation-marble columns, upholding a dome.

Staying on, Andrew would be stuck here with the construction dog-work, and with this M.I.T. genius bossing him, and no real chance at doing architecture.

First, he tried to persuade Mother. He had to go, get started in Chicago. Her eyes already took that look of distress. But—his college degree!

With his handful of credits, it would take years more to get a degree, and even then what use would it be for architecture? And meanwhile he'd be watching her hunting pupils for her kindergarten, her weaving lessons, and in the evening weaving lengths of fabric to earn a few extra dollars. Marta's mouth, her whole face, becoming always thinner and more resolute. No, the few dollars from Professor Gamsey hardly helped pay the grocery bill. Andrew couldn't stand it the way each time before going out to shop she counted over her change to the last penny and snapped shut the small purse, with that pinched mouth for making do.

He went on arguing and she merely kept shaking her head. At least he must finish out the term, get his credits, just a few more months. No, she would not hear of his leaving.

When he had written to Uncle Bruce, "Absolutely no!" replied Uncle Bruce. A nefarious habit of never finishing anything—not high school, not college! All youth was impatient, but etc.

On Saturday morning, when Mother and Tess had gone off for Easter shopping, Andrew undid the mink collar and carried it, with his father's tooled-leather-bound volumes of Emerson, to the pawnbroker. Ten dollars was all. Ten dollars to get to Chicago and find a job. Strictly on his own. Not after that scolding letter was he going to ask Uncle Bruce for introductions.

A note to his mother: "I feel I must make my own decision." She was not to worry. He would be in touch as soon as he was settled in Chicago.

4

THE SOFT hills of Wisconsin rolled themselves out, lesser and lesser, and presently were down to flatland, prairie, black earth fields with a plowman now and again. Isolated gray farmhouses, track crossings with a few wagons waiting, children waving as the train passed.

The crossroad towns became more frequent, and presently, strung-out street ends, lines of two-story frame houses, and then, his pulse beating like the train rhythm, he saw smokestacks, grimy yet somehow exhilarating. Railyards, with long strings of freight cars standing. Already there arose a smell of iron, a swallow of iron seemed to be entering into your blood.

He checked his bag and portfolio.

The station as he emerged was a massive overgrown French château, thrusting a clock tower into a smoke cloud. Andrew had to restrain his first impulse of admiration—simply at the size of it. All around, factories with sky-piercing brick chimneys. Then the river, flanked by high grain elevators with diagonal chutes, must be for scooping up wheat going directly from flatcars onto boats. The river itself was crammed: high-masted sailing ships, tugboats towing chains of barges, scows, a fireboat. Blasts, steam whistles, bells. Through a tumult of horsecars, carriages, wagons, Andrew crossed the bridge to what must be the downtown business area; already he could see amidst the solid blocks of four-, five-story structures several new high buildings, like giraffes craning among a herd of sheep, twelve stories, and going higher.

Horseless cable cars. He had read about them. A few feet below street level ran a heavy belt chain, endlessly circling from a central engine house. On the end platform of each car stood a brakeman, and through a floor slit he could engage the car's lever into a chain link, thus the car was pulled along. The carmen all looked foreign, husky, and kept ceaselessly clanging their bells: get out of the way.

The downtown streets were filled with Saturday-afternoon shoppers, droves of women, most of them smartly dressed in fresh spring colors, their faces lively and somehow fresh-skinned despite the city's grime. Within a few blocks he had come to Chicago's "pride," the new City Hall, a full square block. It looked like three kinds of structures one atop the other, lower piers of granite blocks, and atop them thirty-foot columns in pairs, Corinthian, supporting nothing whatever but ornate statuary that you couldn't really see from the sidewalk; above rose two more floors, the roof line interspersed with Greek Revival pediments. What a stew!

But then Andrew found himself before a new corner office building, one of the tall ones, that stopped him. The facade absolutely clean. Not a false column, not a protrusion. Eleven stories, each marked by a modest string course continuing from the windowsills. The whole topped by a small cornice, with a few medallions for decoration. You could perhaps say it was still a layer cake, but he noticed that the frontal midsection protruded a few feet forward, all the way up, providing a verticality. Over the entrance was the name: Hartford Insurance Company. Andrew approached, and found the architect inscription. Burnham and Root. Among the most important firms in Chicago. He backed off again, and this time realized that a slight, Egyptianlike forward curve at the base started the eye upward. This building he really could admire. With every foot of downtown space worth a fortune, they had dared to set back the side sections from the building line. Maybe he would have a try at their office on Monday. Which should he ask for, he wondered, Burnham or Root, which had had this idea?

But there was another aspect to all these lofty buildings, and this returned on him as he was jostled. These downtown business streets with their cable cars and the shopping crowds, the clutter of carriages and dray wagons, the people in droves trying to cross the streets to the big stores proclaiming Easter sales, what would happen if the buildings sprouted higher and higher, the crowds and the vehicles multiplying, masses of clerks coming to work in cubicles up there—why this density? Wasn't there room enough to spread out, in America? Twelve-, fourteen-story buildings already poked up among the walkups, and he had seen projects in the architectural journals for eighteen-story structures in the high "Chicago style." Some builders used cast-iron beams, bolted together into a framework, for carrying much of the load, but still added wide stone pier supports. These were so thick that shop windows were narrow. And, above, there was little office light. But now there was a new method that Professor Gamsey had said was sure to sweep the cities. The steel companies were getting into the game. Railway rails were being adapted as structural beams, instead of cast iron. No more thick supporting masonry. Wider windows. At least if they were going to crowd working drones into these honeycombs, let the drones have more air, more light.

Just in the next block Andrew saw a structure going up, a gawking crowd around the fenced-off area. Himself among the gawkers. Several stories aloft on a structural platform was a blacksmith at a forge. With huge tongs he pulled a red-hot rivet from the fire and swung it, setting it flying—a red streak against the sky. The riveters, a sure-footed team, were out at the upright. One of them with a pail caught the flying rivet, the crowd gasped in awe, the second ironworker seized the blazing bolt in his pincers and inserted it into lined-up holes in the joining plates, and the third man, with a sledge, wonder he didn't lose his balance up there, gave a mighty blow and smashed flat the projecting end of the rivet. A sigh of achievement all around. Girls gave pleasurable gasps. "Wonder he doesn't fall off!" "Oh, they're trained, like acrobats!"

There would be no limit to man's upward thrust, Professor Gamsey had predicted.

And what about people? Andrew found himself wondering. He almost felt like breaking through his shyness and expostulating to a bright-faced pair of young girls who were oohing and aahing, but when they exclaimed at the physique of the sledgehammer wielder up there he held back.

But why be opposed? After all, great aesthetic possibilities could be opening!

Already, with the use of bolted cast iron, exciting structures had been designed and built—what shapes would not be possible with riveted steel? The breathtaking iron-ribbed Crystal Palace in London. And right here in Chicago he had meant to see a new building, also by the firm of Burnham and Root, called the Rookery, and now found it. Yet Andrew had to smile at the building's name, for indeed that was what people were coming to—pigeons in roosts. Still, once he walked into the lobby, his critical mood vanished. A vast translucent-domed space, like a covered courtyard, with the offices rising around it. The courtyard dome was supported by high openwork iron trusses and arches, with intertwinings of decorative wrought iron, but most striking was a double stairway like two upstretched arms, arching together at a projecting platform that gave access to a second-floor circle of shops, and also served as an observation point—indeed, it reached out like a giant pulpit over the busy lobby. What freedom in space! And the wrought-iron balustrades, in curved, inter-locking designs.

Yes, wondrous things were being done! It was the moment for him to have come, he was right not to have waited another day!

Up and down the stairs went messenger boys, and men in gray toppers, plumed women visiting the fine shops, trim young typewriter girls working in the financial offices, hurrying out early on Saturday.

Andrew walked the whole downtown, not letting himself be overwhelmed, but absorbing, indeed as though physically taking it in. One structure, also read about, he asked his way to, the Marshall Field Wholesale Store, for it was the work of the American master Henry Richardson, summoned from the East by the magnate Marshall Field. Now Andrew paced all around the building, a solid city block, granite masonry, a fugue, as he described it to himself, of Romanesque arches, the perfection of the Richardson style. A structure like music, the lower row of wide windows forming the base notes, and then the double windows in rows of half notes above, surmounted by a row of quarter notes, and the topmost layer, eighths. All at once Andrew saw a page of his father's music. For a long while he hadn't thought of his father. Didn't even know where he was.

Then a thought came to him: At this moment nobody in the whole world knows just where I am.

And that other excitement of the city was upon him: the anonymity. Not one person at home, or here in Chicago as yet, or anyplace, knew where he was, what he was up to, and this thought gave him a peculiar sensation of self-power. Not even Mother knew. His first absolute freedom. Even if he would do nothing more than roam the streets and sleep at some modest hotel.

Letting himself drift with the shoppers now, he found himself on the street of the department stores, the renowned State Street, the shop windows filled with bright spring costumes. Andrew stepped into one of the stores, only for the sensation of it. Droves of women, with a kind of avidity, even anxiety now, making their last hunt for Easter—why weren't they gay, happy?

He pushed his way out. At a cross street, with the sun behind him, he saw, only a few blocks away, the lake, glowing under the downgoing sun. Andrew went to the edge. It made him feel he had reached a destination, a body of water. Like the lake at home, only here he stood on Chicago's elegant Michigan Avenue. One side of the street was built up, the other side was open to the lake except for a single monstrous structure, a convention hall.

On the built side, amidst the fine shops, stood the Art Institute, of heavy granite blocks and round arched windows, and it, again, was by Burnham and Root. John Wellborn Root, what a fine name to have: Wellborn.

Alongside was a taller building, ten stories, the shop windows showing antiquities, Oriental vases, fashions. Elegant women stepping out to elegant carriages, with shop boys behind them carrying beribboned parcels.

And then, just after that, an enormous excavation was in progress. Suddenly Andrew knew he had not wandered here at random. This was to be the new opera house that he had read about in architectural journals, the winning design pictured—by Adler and Sullivan, they had won over Burnham and Root. A vast structure, biggest cost ever, three million dollars. The opera auditorium to be flanked on the lake side by a grand hotel, and on the west side by office floors, all under one roof and with an office tower atop, raising the building's height to twenty stories, the highest in the world! The spirit of Chicago!

Down in the foundation hole, wagons in an endless chain were being filled with excavated earth, then, pulling up a ramp, the teams crossed to dump the mud-soil at the lake.

Andrew peered down. The hole, as every rubberneck remarked, seemed already halfway to China. For this vast structure was to be of solid masonry, Professor Gamsey had remarked on it, probably the last.

What a foundation it would need, to hold all that stone weight! Andrew peered at the swarms of laborers filling wheelbarrows, rolling the barrows on planks, to be hoisted and emptied into wagons.

At the far end of the excavation, already leveled off, something else was being done. Sections of steel rail were being laid flat, crisscrossed with huge timbers. All, he surmised, to be imbedded in poured concrete. Another Chicago innovation. He had read of a system used by that same John Wellborn Root—pyramids of rails, imbedded in concrete, each holding the footing for the steel uprights of the newest high buildings. But so close to the lake, such footings might settle unevenly in the mud. Best would be this solid flatbed, resting on the mud like an enormous raft, a kind of floating foundation. An idea someone had had, a solution, and he felt quickened, just as when he had an idea himself. This firm of Adler and Sullivan was another of Chicago's greats. Maybe even the best.

Andrew made his way back to the station. From the office buildings merging westward into warehouses and factories a new stream of people poured out, hurried men, each as though on some isolated pursuit, and girls mostly in pairs or clusters, with an odd way of holding their heads as though they did not see you, or would not acknowledge being looked at.

The station entrance was already illuminated, a bank of electric arc lights giving off an insectlike buzz and turning faces chalk white in the dusk. Andrew got his bag and portfolio; near the station were several hotels that looked businesslike and clean, not too expensive. He picked one. "Double or single?" the clerk asked. A single cost a dollar, and proved narrow but speckless.

He roamed again, this side of the river, coming to an open market square lined with farm wagons. Around were saloons, hay, grain and feed signs, stables, small cheaplooking hotels maybe for farmers. Already in the gaslight a few girls lingered by doorways, painted whores, the real thing, you did not see them in Madison, though there were a few houses where the college boys were known to go; sometimes on an evening stroll Andrew had walked past them. But in Madison there were no girls standing like this in doorways. He even heard a murmur from one, the word "handsome," and flushed. No, even here alone and free he would not do it, in ugliness and danger of disease. And even worse, unthinkable: to spoil the purity of love, when it came, by doing it this way the first time. He would come to his chosen one the way she would come to him. Andrew hurried on, into a larger street, store windows lighted, work clothes, a few cheap restaurants, three saloons in one block, he counted, men idling, drifting, some of them in overalls, others with a cleaned-up look. At one corner was a cluster around a man on a box, an evangelist. Men listened awhile, drifting on. There was another cluster around a speaker standing on the tail end of a small wagon. Alongside on the curb, under the gaslight, sat a woman behind an unfolded table, on which there was a sign, AMNESTY ASSOCIATION. A foolscap petition lay before her, for signatures.

The speaker was tall, with a large head hunched over toward the listeners, his coat open, his thumbs hitched under his suspenders. His easy, reasonable voice had a touch of a rural drawl, like a cracker-barrel philosopher in a country store; one might imagine a youngish Abraham Lincoln something like this, except this man wasn't so thin and angular.

"Only a stone's throw from this spot, at the Haymarket," he was saying, brushing back a forelock that slipped over one eye, "just a year ago come May, at a labor rally, a bomb was thrown by someone unknown, unknown to this day. Tragically, seven policemen were killed. And today seven innocent men wait in prison to be hung, their last-chance appeals before the higher court. And the whole civilized world," the speaker was saying, "is watching to see whether Chicago will hang seven innocent men, just because of their ideas and beliefs." Why, in England, Bernard Shaw was among those who cried out for amnesty. Here in

Chicago, there were signatures from tens of thousands of citizens, including university professors, lawyers and noted preachers.

Andrew heard his own uncle mentioned, the famous Reverend Bruce Daniels. In spite of being at this moment in defiance of Uncle Bruce, he felt a touch of pride at his fame, and listened more attentively. Wasn't he himself a kind of rebel, a kind of anarchist!

Even in Madison, the papers had carried cartoons of long-haired revolutionaries, wild-eyed, holding smoking bombs. One of these Haymarket anarchists had hidden out in Wisconsin, but on the day the trial opened he had walked into the Chicago court, giving himself up, to share the fate of his comrades. "Anarchist or not, I call that a man," the speaker said.

Now he was explaining why those people had been gathered in the Haymarket. There had been a big strike going on, some blocks west, at the McCormick Harvesting Machine works. What were the working people striking for? Why, for the eight-hour day. Nothing more revolutionary than to work eight hours instead of ten or more, so a man might have time to see his children in daylight, when he got home from work, time perhaps to read a bit, and improve his mind. But vanloads of strikebreakers were brought, with policemen helping them to force their way through the picket line. Fights broke out. A policeman fired his pistol and shot a striker dead. Next day, a meeting was called; in the late afternoon several hundred people gathered; one speaker was the same man who was later to walk into the courtroom of his own free will, his name was Albert Parsons. He had come to the meeting with his wife and two little daughters. Now, would a man about to throw a bomb have brought his wife and children along to stand in the crowd? Who was this Albert Parsons? Why, a writer, an editor of a daily newspaper, in German, the *Arbeiter Zeitung*, the Workingman's Times, for immigrants. Another of those now in prison waiting to be hung was a young printer on that paper. Not much of a crowd had come out, as there was a drizzle. But the worthy Mayor Harrison himself, of this city, who liked to keep a personal eye on things, had mounted his horse and ridden over to Haymarket Square, and listened awhile to those speakers, and decided all was orderly and peaceful, told this to the captain of the nearby police station and gone home. But once the mayor was gone, with night falling, the police captain had marched out his company, to the meeting.

Though Andrew had read bits about it all in the papers, he now found himself held by the speaker's intense sincerity. And, as he had come to stay in Chicago, maybe he ought to hear what was going on.

A bomb had been hurled into the ranks of the police. To this day the thrower had not been found. Why, then, was there such a fever to hang these seven men? Seven policemen had died, seven "wild anarchists" had been hastily tried and sentenced to death. What sort of trial had it been when the judge, even before it opened, declared that all the accused ought to be hung?

Hang them! Hang them! Never had he heard, never had this country witnessed such a bloodthirsty lynching frenzy!

Kill the anarchists! What was an anarchist, anyway?

Andrew found himself checking his own knowledge. Hadn't they started in Russia, trying to assassinate the Czar?

Anarchists wanted individual freedom, the speaker said. Wasn't that the American ideal? A maximum of individual freedom?

He was a bit of an agnostic, the speaker confessed, but, as this was the eve of Easter, the holiday of those who believed in Christ risen, he felt he should evoke that spirit of Christianity, in which he did believe, the spirit of great human commiseration. And, come to think of it, was not Jesus Christ in his way an anarchist, an advocate of the poor, of the lowest, a gentle anarchist . . .

A gentle anarchist: the term resounded in Andrew, as though he had found a name for his own feelings. Like what he was doing right now. Going off against even the orders of his uncle, the wishes of his mother—breaking out, to follow his own idea.

"Most of you men standing here," the speaker was ending, "are workingmen. Or men out of work." He himself was a kind of out-of-work small-town lawyer, looking for a start in Chicago. Oh, how he wished he could have been on the Haymarket defense! Now the last chance was the court of public opinion . . .

It was to sign the petition. The small crowd was dissolving, drifting away, but a few men waited their turn to lean over the table, and sign. It crossed Andrew's mind that he was underage—would it count, would anyone check up on the signatures? The woman smiled to him, the last fellow handed him the pen, and he wrote his name, half lettered, half scribbled, Andrew Lane, Architect.

He handed back the pen, the lady gave him another smile, and he walked off with a little snort of satisfaction at himself, at this first action, come to think of it, really on his own.

Sunday, Andrew roamed the city; not until he had a job would he make his presence known to Uncle Bruce. Only by walking could you get the feel of a place, and just as he had walked the downtown all yesterday afternoon, he now set out to see where people lived, turning west. The street was soon a clutter of frame shanties that must have been hastily put up after the great fire, indeed hadn't it started somewhere around here, when a cow kicked over a lantern? Among the shanties were occasional brick houses, even, on a street called Jackson Boulevard, a few opulent ones with yard space still around them, yet engulfed in a crowded area that, even on this Easter Sunday, with people dressed up, and children cleaned up, had an air of pullulation and poverty. Washing strung from windows. Alleys with heaped-up garbage.

On a car-line street, Halstead Street, there were cafés with Greek lettering on the windows. All around him he heard Italian. Farther on, there were bearded Jews, the street solidly lined with pushcarts. Sunday, with Christian shops closed, must be their best business day. Jumbled heaps of clothing, shoes, dishware, even women's bloomers hung on display, cartloads of fish, hawkers crying out in their Jewish language, kerchiefed women with huge baskets of seeded rolls. At every pushcart, people asking prices, offering less, throwing things back. Here in a doorway a slaughterer was slitting the necks of chickens that he pulled out of a coop, while his broad-aproned wife sat on a stool plucking their feathers. Cats, flies, children, refuse, smells, vendors plucking at your sleeve, bickering and even good humor, old furniture, cheap, new furniture in narrow shops, signs in Hebrew letters, then suddenly he was out of the Jewish street and farther on there seemed to be a street of Poles, judging by the reversed letters, OPTEKA, on a pharmacy window, and the families with flocks of children, everyone shined up, girls in bright colors. From a corner church Andrew heard singing. A thought came to him: suppose he should find his way to Uncle Bruce's church and slip inside for the service? Perhaps he'd by chance be recognized and at worst, after a scolding, get himself a good Sunday dinner. But no, he was going to stick it out and tomorrow on his own make the rounds of architects' offices and find himself a job.

On Michigan Avenue, the real Easter parade, carriages with pairs of splendid matched steeds in glittering harness, docked tails, plumed heads, top-hatted husbands, with wives and grown daughters wearing enormous hats with feathers and fluttering ribbons. The society folk, as their carriages crossed, dipped their chins to each other, the men raising their high silk hats.

On the sidewalk the parade was of younger women in pairs or droves, shopgirls in their finery, stopping to gawk at the society carriages and making remarks to each other, rising to high-pitched laughter. One pair, Andrew was sure, gave him the eye, then whispered to each other, with giggles. He knew he was considered handsome; at least un-

46

usual-looking; his thick hair, cut long, had a curl to it, and he wore his Windsor tie; an artist should look like an artist.

Crossing the river northward, he was among mansions. This must be what they called Chicago's Gold Coast, where lived the millionaires. In a hushed Sunday elegance, the broad structures stood behind their sweeping driveways, granite, and brick, with high-pillared verandas, high peaked roofs, conical dunce-cap spires, and flocks of tall, slender, slightly swelling chimneys such as he had seen in engravings of French châteaus. Mansard roofs, sitting like large hats over structures with opulent bay windows like blown-out cheeks. In the center of all this was an open square in which rose a hexagonal stone tower, crenelated, out of a triple series of crenelated bases, each with corner bastions. Silly but somehow quite impressive. This was the famous Water Tower that had withstood the great fire. Oddly, from the actual water-pumping station across the way rose a smokestack just as high, that he found more exciting to look at.

Farther on, among the mansions, came the culmination. In reddish granite, a Rhineland castle, famed as the emblem of Chicago opulence, the residence of the owner of the Palmer House hotel. Itself large enough for a hotel, the Potter Palmer mansion angled back from a ponderous porte cochere to a palace with medieval ramparts, crenelated like the Water Tower. Could he, Andrew speculated, get to do commissions of such grandeur? Did he want to?

Presently, the avenue opened up into a large park, with families laden with picnic baskets descending from the horsecars. Young men in vests played baseball on the grass, and there was a lagoon with young couples in rowboats.

Right after breakfast, Andrew got hold of the hotel's city directory, found "Architects," and made his list—the best at the top. A rule from his mother, always start with the best. He put Burnham and Root even ahead of Adler and Sullivan, but perhaps only because he feared he wouldn't have a chance there. Then came a dozen others picked somewhat at random, and at the end Mr. Olmstead. Even if he had to go there, he was determined not to mention Uncle Bruce.

Putting aside money for the hotel, he had three dollars left, before he would have to cry uncle.

Directly on opening the door, Andrew could count over two dozen drafting tables in the architectural sea before him, the draftsmen mature-looking, nobody as young as himself. From behind the railing, a bulky, large-headed man, passing, holding a rolled tracing, glanced questioningly at him. "Want to see someone?"

"Yes, if I could see Mr. Root . . ."

"Hmm. I've just got a minute." Luck! John Wellborn Root himself! With the rolled tracing, the architect motioned for him to come through the wicket.

Only now Andrew noticed a lady secretary to a side, giving him a look. Never mind, he had his man. Rapidly, he recited: worked three years with Professor Gamsey at Madison while attending university engineering courses but really aimed for architecture, wanted to get started, admired particularly their new insurance building—

"Yes? What did you admire about it?" Mr. Root was not unfriendly, but giving him a really keen look.

Well, the way the central section came forward a bit, to show the verticality.

He'd hit it right, Andrew saw. Mr. Wellborn Root, cocking his head, asked his name. Then Root motioned at his portfolio. Just a few renderings, Andrew said; here was a magazine copy of a drawing of a church near his home. Even as Mr. Root glanced at it, Andrew felt he had made a mistake.

"Olmstead," Root said, in a neutral way. "Do you know Mr. Olmstead?"

"Not exactly," Andrew explained. "My uncle, Reverend Bruce Daniels . . ." There, he had already leaned on the name.

"It's well drawn, you have a touch for delineation."

—Was there a hint of a smile in his repeating that word which Andrew had put over his signature? "Just now, Mr. Lane, we're full. Why don't you go to Olmstead? He has a considerable staff, an excellent office . . ."

"Well—I thought I'd try here first."

"I do appreciate that." The big architect looked at him with a good kind of smile. You even felt that Mr. Root meant to remember you.

He made a try at Adler and Sullivan. Another sea of drafting boards, fully as many, on the top floor of a building the firm had done, broad windows looking out to the lake. A long-nosed fellow, Jewish-looking, head draftsman, wearing black sleeve protectors, came to the railing and told him both Mr. Adler and Mr. Sullivan were away in St. Louis.

"I thought perhaps with a big job like the Auditorium they might be taking on . . ."

"As you saw, that's already under construction."

By lunchtime Andrew had been to half a dozen offices. Over a slice of meatloaf in an inexpensive, clean-looking bakery-restaurant, he checked his list. Except for that fellow at Adler and Sullivan's, who had made him feel a fool, most at least had looked at his renderings. Whenever he showed the chapel drawing the response was, "Why don't you see Mr. Olmstead?"

Not yet.

The second day was worse. At the last place he didn't get past the railing. A haughty lady said, "Only experienced men." He had sixty cents left. Olmstead, then.

The office was on Michigan Avenue itself, with an elegant wainscotted waiting room, English hunting scenes on the wall, surely impressive for clients for Queen Anne residences.

The telephone lady, middle-aged, wore a black blouse adorned with a gold watch such as his mother had pawned.

"My name is Andrew Lane," he said. "I'm an architect

. . ." She kept looking at him, in the way of a teacher who had received an incomplete answer. He was almost about to add the name of Uncle Bruce Daniels, when a thought came to him: "Mr. John Wellborn Root suggested I apply to Mr. Olmstead." She nodded—the teacher at a good reply.

The youngish-looking draftsman who came into the reception room wore a smock; he had a bright, easy glance, a neatly cut yellow mustache. Looked too young to be a chief draftsman, but it soon appeared he was. There passed between them a kind of instant cognition; Andrew felt this fellow would be on his side. Leafing through the portfolio, the interviewer commented, "Nice light touch," and then from the middle of the sheaf he pulled out the chapel rendering. "Well, say! For Reverend Daniels! Well, why didn't you just send this in to Mr. Olmstead?" Whereupon Andrew confided that he didn't want to come in on his uncle's connection.

His whole story came out as between friends. Indeed, when he had introduced himself, Andrew Lane, the draftsman had introduced himself back, Willis Moorehead, and as Andrew explained about not wanting to be hired simply because of his uncle, especially as his uncle was opposed to his leaving college, Willis was at once understanding, even slightly conspiratorial, "Well, I won't have to show him this one," and without thinking of it Andrew was explaining his whole situation, since his father, a minister, was no longer at home—

A minister? Willis chuckled. His too! And did Andrew know that Mr. Olmstead's father—

Also?

"Sure thing!" And not only the boss but two more of the fellows on the staff were preachers' sons.

So that was why Mr. Olmstead got so many church commissions!

Willis pulled down his mouth corners. Then, selecting a random sketch from the portfolio, a residence among trees, he went into the private office. Soon he was back. "Caught him just as he was leaving." For a start—tracings.

Only eight dollars a week, but it was sure to go up soon enough. "Soon as he finds you out!" "You didn't—!" "Not at all! You came here recommended by the eminent John Wellborn Root. Isn't that what you said?" The pulled-down mouth. They chuckled.

Guiding Andrew into the atelier, as it was called here, Willis introduced him all around. A board by the window, with a view of the lake was free. "Hang up your hat!" Where was he staying? "No point in wasting your money on a hotel." Willis knew a good rooming house only a block from his home. "But won't your uncle want you staying with him?"

At least, Andrew declared, he intended to relish his independence as long as he could.

He must get his things, come have dinner. Willis lived with his mother and older sister. Schoolteacher, naturally.

How was he fixed for money? With an "Oh, pshaw," Willis advanced Andrew his first week's salary.

Leaving the hotel, Andrew sent Mother a triumphant letter enclosing a five-dollar bill. He'd manage the week on the rest.

Willis' home had a piano, books, the mother and sister were nice ladies, the dinner was excellent. Afterward Willis showed Andrew his own books, he read fluently in French, the *Histoire des Habitations humaines*, Voltaire, and in English Oscar Wilde. They strolled over to the rooming house; it was mostly for university students. Andrew took a dormer, tiny but only a dollar fifty a week.

Settled. He'd done it! On his own. Though perhaps when Willis mentioned his name Mr. Olmstead had indeed made the connection? From the magazine with the delineation of his church, signed "Andrew Lane." Could Willis have been a bit sly? Well, never mind. If so, it was out of friendliness.

He had been introduced and had shaken hands all around, opened his Keuffel and Esser, started tracing a side elevation of a residence, when the architect came mak-

51

ing his morning rounds, a handsome, substantial man, with a wide English-colonel mustache, clothes finely tailored, a scarab stickpin. "Well, young man! You know, yesterday I was just leaving and didn't connect up your name until I was downstairs. Good thing we didn't turn you away! Andrew Lane: I remember that little—" he smiled as he chose the same word—"delineation. . . . Have you seen your uncle?"

Among the squat three-story brick apartment buildings going up along Drexel Boulevard shone the ample new Queen Anne church, just completed by Architect Allan Olmstead.

The parsonage was upstairs, reached by a side entrance. About time he appeared! His mother had already sent a telegram! Uncle Bruce surveyed Andrew, led the miscreant into his study. He really deserved a scolding! Headstrong, impetuous . . . That done, Uncle Bruce even granted that it was in a way natural, a young man wanting to stand on his own two feet. But why run off helter-skelter, with only a few more months of college? Once he had his college degree . . .

But he was years from it, didn't they understand! And at home—and he told how Mother had pawned her gold watch.

"No need of it! No need of it! She had only to let us know! Pride! Pride!"

How much was Olmstead paying him? Uncle Bruce asked. Why, how could he expect to help his mother out of that, while paying his expenses in Chicago!

It was only for a starter. He'd soon be earning a full draftsman's salary, at least double.

"Perhaps I'd better have a word with Allan Olmstead," Uncle Bruce began.

"No!"

Uncle Bruce assumed his air of patience with the impetuous. Still, why should Andrew waste his money on a dreary little furnished room? He should live here—

No, please, Andrew wanted to stay on his own.

At least he must come for his dinners!

Then they both managed a laugh, at the way Andrew had stuck to his guns.

On Sundays, there was no way out: just as in summers in River Valley he had to go to hear Grandfather Enoch or Uncle Matt in the family chapel, so now in Chicago he had to sit with Aunt Genevieve in the brand-new Temple of Unity, to hear Uncle Bruce.

In Madison, after Father had left, Mother had become liberal on church attendance; Andrew and Tess could come along if they wished; Marta spoke more and more of worship within yourself. Keeping the Christian virtues, truth, concern for all humanity—formal worship was but a reminder. Some people needed regular reminding more than others.

But here, Andrew felt obliged. Aunt Genevieve sat pigeon-proud when her husband preached, and indeed in a pigeony way she kept turning her cocked head, her bright eyes as though recording every face in the congregation: who had come and who had stayed away. And not only the faces present, but their degree of attentiveness, and even the clothes they wore. This Andrew also noticed, the silks, the brocades, the imported Italian scarves. Every costume seemed stamped Marshall Field's.

Within two weeks Andrew knew every detail on each draftsman's board and was sure he could take on designing. It was a friendly shop, youngish men, for as soon as a fellow found himself a client, Willis said, he started out on his own. Though two wheelhorses had been with Olmstead since the building rush after the Chicago fire. A diligently serious atmosphere prevailed as long as the boss was in the office, and particularly when he led in a client couple to view their house plans on the board. But as soon as they were safely gone, and Olmstead with them, to the site, there would come an outburst of mimicry, horseplay, flying erasers; Willis would break into "O Sole Mio"; then came a barbershop quartet.

Or, if something had been botched, as when a thoughtless draftsman put in a stairway with normal risers for a client who had a club foot, Willis had a way of mounting a stool and sermonizing: "You shall burn! First your sideburns, with the flames reaching your eyelashes, then your eyelashes, and thine eyes, until thy cornea pops, verily like unto a popcorn exploding!" and down to the sizzling testicles, halted only by having the stool pulled from under him. Or else there were sudden serious moments as when someone would bring in the *Architectural Record*, with news of some competition—a library in Kankakee. Which of them should go in for it? They didn't want to compete with each other.

Though the camaraderie was nice enough, Andrew wasn't sure how he felt about that last idea. Why shouldn't a man go in for whatever he wanted to? Besides, there was hardly a spark among the lot of them. Architecture was a good clean profession. Only with Willis he felt a kind of affinity—outside the office more than in. The first week, they went to a concert together.

Already—whether Uncle Bruce had had a word with Mr. Olmstead, Andrew didn't know—he now was up to twelve dollars. And Olmstead had, from those first few sample drawings, remembered that there was a special touch to Andrew Lane's rendering; when it came to foliage, trees, shrubbery, Andrew did not confine himself to the stiff mechanical lines of architectural drawing, but sometimes even let the trees and bushes obscure part of the house itself, with a touch like a Whistlerian etching. Certain clients reacted to an artistic effect, and already in the second week Olmstead had taken Andrew along to sketch a wooded site on the North Shore, where he wanted to present the client with an impressive rendition.

5

THERE WAS going to be a lecture by Louis Sullivan at the Architects Club, in the upstairs hall of the Art Institute. Rows of folding chairs had been placed, and, among those gathering, Andrew recognized John Wellborn Root, who, after an instant, smiled in recollection, and even introduced Andrew to his partner, Mr. Daniel Burnham, as an ambitious young newcomer.

It was Mr. Burnham who introduced the speaker— "Who needs no introduction, since you know Louis Sullivan as well as you know me. We don't always agree in our ideas, but there is no one with whom I would consider it a greater honor to have some differences, for I would know that he is deeply informed, and an ornament to our profession." Over that word "ornament," Andrew glanced to Willis, to show he caught the allusion to Louis Sullivan's specialty.

The man who stepped forward looked younger than Mr. Burnham, younger than John Wellborn Root, and instantly Andrew was measuring himself, would he in a dozen years—fifteen years at most between him and this leading architect—be up there addressing the profession?

The designer of what was to be Chicago's largest building, the world's greatest opera house! Mr. Sullivan was meticulously dressed, not as though for the occasion but as by habit, a finely barbered short round beard emphasizing a tight, round head that looked packed with knowledge and ideas—as though it had heavier specific gravity than other heads.

What he was going to say might already have become familiar to his colleagues, Mr. Sullivan began, for, like them, he was concerned with what was being built in this city. A new architecture, according to observers from abroad, was being born, American architecture at last was appearing, and it was even being called Chicago architecture. Yet aside from a few excellent and brave attempts, what did one see, in walking through this city? Every hodgepodge since creation. Turrets, onion-shaped domes, Italian balconies, Greek columns and columns sliced in two, columns that started up on the third floor of a facade and bore no weight, Gothic mansions . . .

Why, Mr. Sullivan was expressing Andrew's very thoughts, from his first-day walks!

"And should our self-made American businessmen sally forth out of their Gold Coast castles and châteaus, each morning, on caparisoned steeds, dressed in armor, spear in hand?" One might understand the need for swords and spears, indeed rifles and cannon, in the cutthroat competition of certain industrialists, but still, was not this country a democracy, and should not its architecture express the spirit of democracy?

Andrew wondered, how could these tall work-hives express democracy?

Yet, there was the great structure that Louis Sullivan was now engaged in building, opera for all. Well, hadn't the Romans too built their Colosseum for the masses? Who lived in hovels?

What Mr. Sullivan wanted now were questions, ideas from his colleagues and hearers, he was saying, with his head slightly cocked. Before Andrew could raise his hand, Mr. Burnham began.

He and Louis Sullivan were old friends with old disagreements, he said, with a warm smile at the speaker. As to American architecture, he was more for eclecticism. Andrew was on the point of asking Willis the meaning of the word, but it became clear. There was nothing wrong with a Greek or Roman pillar, a Gothic arch, or a Renaissance motif per se, so long as the historic motif was harmoniously used, Mr. Burnham declared. But this was a never-ending argument between himself and Louis Sullivan, so now let others ask their questions.

Andrew's hand was up, suddenly he was recognized. Name? Andrew Lane, sir. He was deeply impressed with Mr. Sullivan's ideas on the emergence of a true American architecture, but then how was it that the most important American architect, Henry Richardson, made constant and even dominant use of the Roman arch, and that the Romanesque style, used on the facade of this very building and the building next to it, dominated the design for the one right after that, under construction, the work of Mr. Sullivan himself, the great new Auditorium?

Excitedly he heard a kind of undermurmur—a clever question. "Excellent observation!" Mr. Sullivan began, looking directly at Andrew. —Now at least he'll know me, was the thought that came.

The arch, called Romanesque, the master architect said, was one of nature's own forms of structure. It harked back to the cave entrance. It carried man's very basic, instinctive feeling for shelter, protection. It signified man's first home. The way Richardson used the entry arch, often as a half circle directly on the ground, rather than raised up, was to be found more in Byzantine rather than in Roman structures, but no matter. It had not been his intention here, said Louis Sullivan, to declare that all previous ideas and experience in architecture should be thrown overboard! No, when he himself used the Richardson arch, he felt not only that it was a continuity to a great architect who had been virtually the first to think in terms of American structure, but that the pure arch was also a continuity to the natural forms that went back to the very birth of man's use of shelter. He smiled down like a teacher, and added, "Good question."

Andrew found himself saying, "If I may say so, sir— excellent answer. Thank you." He was surprised at his own audacity. Willis gave him a startled look.

Mr. Burnham chuckled. Sullivan cocked his head and said, "Thank you, young man. What was the name?"

Andrew was flushing. He'd been cheeky. But maybe these big ones would remember him.

"Lane," Willis spoke up for him. "Andrew Lane."

When the meeting broke up, he half expected some ragging, but nothing came.

They stopped for a coffee. "Well, now everybody knows you!" Willis said, twinkling a bit, as though having caught Andrew's own thought, but he went on, "No, no, it was all right! You did have a point. You saw something. I'd never have connected it."

The ladies sat upright in their stays, their fine Sunday brocade gowns with lace inserts. The sun rays brought gleams of brooches, earrings, bracelets, and, on the men, gold cufflinks, a ruby tiepin. From the entire congregation rose an amalgam of scents, colognes, wafting up good thoughts to the heavenly accountant.

And just then Andrew's gaze caught another pair of eyes from across the aisle, clear gray, fully open, meeting his. The encounter held, the girl's eyes adding in a touch of impudence, as though she had found him out.

In Andrew there was another reaction. He had found the One.

The face, like the eyes, was open and clear—beautiful, of course, framed in two clusters of auburn curls.

He had been awaiting this. Expecting to come upon the girl with whom he would fall in love. There she sat, next to her mother and father, and her eyes did not swerve away.

For her to look at him meant that she was definitely, willfully turning her head away from the pulpit. Oh, it might have been a quite natural and innocent survey of the congregation, taking notice of who was there and who was not. But once she met his glance, Andrew was sure that she had felt him looking at her and had deliberately turned to see. Then she turned her head back; indeed, there was a movement of her body, a kind of settling back as though some question were settled, and she looked up attentively to his uncle, as though, having satisfied herself about some personal matter, she could return her attention to the sermon.

This little, satisfied wriggle of hers already seemed as familiar to him as his mother's way of conclusively pressing together her lips.

Aunt Genevieve was noticing, so he turned his attention back to Uncle Bruce. His uncle was scolding them, stirring them up about corruption. There was corruption among the city's aldermen. A buccaneer had come from the East, and they all knew that Charles Yerkes was paying out enormous bribes so that the aldermen would vote him tramway franchises for Chicago's streets! Indeed it was an improvement to have these cable cars, but the franchise money should be paid, not to bribe aldermen, but in fees to the city, and used to alleviate the needs of the poor, to finance improved sanitation and garbage collection, for health measures, and to fight crime. In this city of Chicago, because of rapid growth, there were unspeakable slums, there was rampant open vice and gambling . . .

Heads nodded in sorrowful agreement.

Andrew now gazed deliberately, steadily at her, willing her once more to turn her head. She didn't, except—if it could be counted—at the very end, as the congregation rose. It could simply have been a natural movement in the act of rising, except that a little gleam came toward him, again with a hint of impudence.

That sealed it.

Though he usually slipped out while his uncle and aunt greeted parishioners, Andrew today timed himself to be just behind the girl's family in the crowded aisle, his mind nevertheless making the professional notation that even in this newly built church the aisle was too narrow. Her father was extending his hand to a personage with an impressive gold watch chain over a broad belly, and her mother, with a church smile, was accepting a compliment about her dress and her daughter's too. Andrew could hear everything almost as though he were part of their family. What, already! he joked to himself. But as they reached his uncle, the father making the "Excellent! I agree thoroughly!" remark, Andrew came level with them, so close that he could breathe the fresh warm scent of her neck. The summery dress, still girlish, left her arms half bare; they were nicely rounded. And as his uncle caught sight of Andrew and embraced his shoulder, the introduction became inevitable. His aunt made it, smiling—"Our nephew, Andrew Lane, from Madison, Wisconsin." Their name was Hewlett. "Our daughter, Helena." The girl gave him her hand but did not let it linger. "Our young architect, just come to build Chicago," Aunt Genevieve was saying. And the mother said, "Andrew must meet some of our young people." And in the chatter Andrew heard the girl say quite naturally, "Mother, why don't you ask Mr. Lane to come along with us to dinner?" Of course! A few young people, friends of Helena's, would be dropping in during the afternoon.

A quick glance among the older folk; his aunt's "Why, certainly we'll let him off! Andrew hasn't met many young people as yet!" And so he was strolling down Drexel Boulevard with the Hewlett family. In the sun her hair was coppery. She was finishing her junior year in high school, and some of her classmates were coming over—lovely girls, Helena teased.

She was lithe and natural, the gown was light green with yellow sprigs, and she wore a tiny heart locket at her throat; he could see her one day putting his picture in it. Or did she already have—? No, he felt sure not.

Her voice was low and her way of speaking almost confidential, even about such ordinary matters as her favorite subjects in school. They walked together behind her mother, father and little brother. The day was so perfect, early summer, just enough breeze to stir her curls. She liked math, which was unusual for a girl, she said, and history not so much. And she loved music. He too? Then, one by one: Mozart? A favorite. And Beethoven? Again! Of course Bach. She played, but just for home use, she laughed, and continued, as though a full account of herself was naturally due him. And presently without her seeming to ask questions Andrew was telling how he had decided to leave college and get started in architecture. Then they were in front of her house, a well-kept gray-painted frame of the earlier Kenwood, with a wide scrollwork porch and a mock turret, the kind of house put up by master carpenters. The living room had a mixture of upholstered armchairs, a French-style settee with a gilded frame, even a new Morris chair facing a shallow fireplace with a marble mantel. An upright piano. Past two braided columns, a mahogany dining table was laid out.

Only when her father stood to carve did Andrew notice: Mr. Hewlett had two fingers missing from his right hand. He managed, long used to it. And found a moment to explain—just to Andrew, so mother and daughter wouldn't have to hear the old story, though each uttered a shuddery gasp at the right moment, when he told how the stamping machine he tended as a child laborer at the age of eleven had come down and crushed his fingers; he had turned his head at another boy's joke. But every disaster in life has its compensation; wasn't that even a law of physics? Though he had not had much schooling, he knew this one: every action has its equal and opposite reaction. In any case . . .

Her father loves to talk, Andrew noted to himself.

. . . the accident got him interested in the whole problem of workmen's compensation, yes, even as a child—because he received none. And in a way this had determined his activity in life because he was in industrial insurance, yes, one quick way to sign up a company was to let the manager happen to see. As, the way you held a pen. Big companies like U.S. Steel, where there was constant serious risk of injury, oh, they now had it all worked out on a scale, did Andrew know what a finger was worth? Well, there was now a standard scale of value for each part of the body, a hundred dollars for an index, and so forth, it was a shame to have it so cut and dried, but this was the law. The laws were still lagging behind in this field, and one thing that Mr. Hewlett liked about Andrew's uncle, a great progressive preacher—Reverend Bruce Daniels kept emphasizing it was the citizen's vote, the law, and not anarchist bombs that would remedy social injustice.

Just after dinner came the young people, a florid, large girl cousin with her hair piled up, accompanied by "her young man," who was in the real-estate game, full of talk about amazing jumps in the price of building lots, and quite interested that Andrew was in the architect game.

Then three of Helena's schoolmates appeared, two girls and a boy; Andrew was beginning to feel out of place, when Helena got everyone to go for a walk in the beautiful day, and she walked with him, slipping her arm in his, right away.

All week Andrew found himself at random moments inwardly chanting her name, Helena, Helena, exactly as in sentimental love stories. Several times he wanted to say to Willis, "I met a girl . . ." but didn't, wanting more to cherish the feeling, as yet, to himself.

The next Sunday his aunt, as she saw the Hewletts arriving, smiled an invitation to sit with her, and, as though by natural process, there was Helena beside him. Again and again during the sermon—it was once more about those Haymarket anarchists, their only chance now was with the State Supreme Court—she turned her head to him as though to share some point. Her eyes dizzied him.

It seemed taken for granted that he was to have Sunday dinner with them again, and this time there were no young people afterward. It was such a lovely day, the kind of summer before summer that sometimes appeared in windy Chicago as though some howling lunatic had suddenly become quiet and smiling. They turned by unspoken accord toward the lake. On the bridge crossing over the I.C. tracks, Andrew remarked again how the railway spoiled the lakefront, there were demands to sink the roadbeds, and Helena began, "But my father thinks . . ." and they chorused, ". . . there are some things to be said for either side." Then in their joined laughter Helena took his hand. As they clambered now over the large rocks, he helped her, she was just the right combination of a girl who kept up with you but yet at certain moments waited for a man's extended hand.

Perhaps growing up by the lakeside in the house in Madison, he said, was why he hated to have the tracks spoil the view. She too loved a view over water, Helena said. Was their house right on the lake? Soon she was making him talk about his boyhood, and presently Andrew was even telling how his father had left home.

Helena said she wanted one day to see where he had grown up.

And there they had their first kiss. It had come of itself, much sooner than he would have thought, though she was certainly not a forward girl. Nor would he yet even have tried to bring it about, a real love kiss. He had never done it. Oh, a hasty peck, at sweet-sixteen parties he had had to take Tess to. But as they turned to each other with unspoken understanding, the kiss was softly applied, and with their lips slowly drawing away from each other it was as though something had been imprinted, an imprint that would remain in each.

And Helena of herself answered with what he was sure of, yet feared. Smoothing her dress over her hunched-up knees, she said, "You know, Andrew, I never kissed anyone that way—for real, I mean. Oh, at a junior prom or sweet sixteen. But for real, I never did." And she held back a moment before they did it again, and then said, "Oh, Andrew, if anything really happens between us, I want us to tell each other everything, good or bad, even things we're ashamed of."

Her eyes were so clear.

He wanted her to know, about himself, but a man shouldn't so readily declare his own innocence to a woman. Except that she must have guessed. "I know you're really shy. You're terribly shy with girls." Adding, "And I hope you always will be, except with me."

Another Sunday they strolled below Kenwood, to look at the grand residences on Prairie Avenue. Arm in arm they strolled down the wide sidewalk along the broad street of the rich, with its evenly spaced elms, the line of trees interrupted only by carriage driveways to the great mansions. The smartest victorias, broughams with shining brass side lamps, drawn by magnificent pairs of sleek horses, passed along the avenue. Here rose a château, like those, Andrew explained to her, seen along the French Valley of the Loire. And he pointed out each characteristic. Helena listened intelligently, and surprised him by at once picking out similar elements in other mansions along the street of the plutocrats. Here was a new one. —At least it was all in one style, a unity, he said, and not a hodge-podge of Renaissance, false classic, medieval turrets, and Gothic spires—like that one across the street. —And look, next to it, conical dunce caps sticking up from each corner! "That must be Merlin's house," she laughed. Oh, how quickly she saw as he saw!

This newest one must be the Yerkes house, she said, and from her father she knew all about that schemer's financial tricks, and from the girls at school she knew all the scandal, about his shameless affairs with women! He had got rid of his wife in Philadelphia and then had married a much younger woman who had been his fancy lady, a red-head, a real beauty, she was the daughter of a policeman or something, they had come to Chicago, and now this financier with his mistress wife was trying to break into the high society of Prairie Avenue! All the real society people were giving her the cold shoulder. But what did the rest of these society people have, to be so snobbish about? Helena wanted to know. One or two generations ago they were all nobodies! Butchers! So now they owned the stockyards! She wrinkled her nose.

Behind a really splendid wrought-iron fence, using arabesque motifs, was a huge residence fronted by a great curved window area—that must be where the grand ballroom was, Helena figured out. This was the house of the Prince of Merchants, Marshall Field, and Mrs. Field gave the most fashionable society balls in Chicago, more exclusive than the Potter Palmers on the North Side Gold Coast. The great annual charity ball, the Bal Masque, was given right here! "That's one place you'll never see me!" Andrew snorted. Oh, she'd love to go, just out of curiosity, wasn't he curious about the way such people lived? Fabulous Oriental carpets, and French chandeliers of a hundred candles!

Just a few steps onward was the largest palace of all, with a broad series of arches and—"Isn't that what you call a mansard roof?" she said, already an expert! A sweep of wide outer stairs, a stone balustrade—the entrance was supposed to resemble the Paris Grand Opera. This belonged to George Pullman of the Pullman cars. The interior was entirely paneled with all mahogany, Helena had read. "Just like a Pullman car!" Andrew scoffed.

"Well, then, how would you have built it?" she said earnestly. —First, he would cut off all the spires, turrets, towers—" "And dunce caps!" she joined. —No Greek and Roman columns, he declared. —But then what would he have instead?

She gazed at him so eagerly. And he had no answer. Suddenly Andrew felt something of an impostor. He could scoff, he could tear down all these gaudy frauds, but what would he build? Allan Olmstead's Queen Anne?

Helena had made him see himself! Though he felt

himself thrusting with energy, to design, to build—yet, as she had perceived, if given the chance, tomorrow, just exactly what would he design? Now he hesitated. "That's what I have to find out," he said, and she really understood, pressing his hand.

There was one house he wanted to look at, nearby, the last house built by Henry Richardson, Andrew told her, really American instead of a hodgepodge from Europe. And he explained to her about Richardson, who had died just after completing this house, just about the time Andrew himself had come to Chicago. "Oh," Helena said respectfully, and then gave him an odd look, as though to mean, was it a destiny?

There it stood, on the corner of Eighteenth Street, and honestly Helena couldn't help thinking it looked like a mausoleum. It certainly did look impressive and different from all the others, she said. The building was heavy and solid, of rough-hewn granite, with a few small upper windows, and actually slits below. It could almost be a prison. But Andrew was so engrossed, it was as though he had left her and were there alone. Presently he was explaining again—that half circle, the cavelike entrance, was called Richardson Romanesque. Everyone was copying it, even Louis Sullivan, the architect of the great new Auditorium on Michigan Avenue. Now, there was a man with whom he wanted to work! She grasped his hand. Her eyes told him he would! The successor to Richardson.

"Just look at Richardson's use of masonry," Andrew said. The perfectly fitted blocks of granite—the unity of it all, the simplicity. She was quiet, trying to appreciate it. Who owned it? Some millionaire, Andrew believed. "No! Really! " Helena laughed, and he joined; she squeezed his arm. Now Andrew recalled reading that this last Richardson house belonged to a partner in the McCormick Harvesting Machine Company. The Glessner house. Helena caught it as Glassner and joked, "Well, if you ever do a Glassner house put more glass in it! It must be very dark inside, with such slits for windows." Exactly! Andrew thought. Why not more glass space, yet keeping the simplicity and the rhythm? Helena even had architectural intuition! How right she was for him!

They went back up on the next street, Michigan Avenue. This, Helena said, was merely called Millionaire's Row. Prairie Avenue was the original Gold Coast, and now there was also a Gold Coast on the North Side, Chicago had so many millionaires! The North Side was where she wanted their house to be, Helena declared, because of the sandy beach there, and here on the South Side it was all rocks. And railroad tracks. —Just as soon as they were millionaires! Andrew promised.

Then it went full steam, ice-cream-soda dates, and a concert, and she wouldn't let him take her home in a hansom, he must save his money, she knew he was sending money home to his mother.

Andrew even wrote to his mother, "I've met a charming girl, her name is Helena, at Uncle's church, so you see how respectable it is. . . ." And by the middle of May they were inseparable, and Helena's mother wrote to Andrew's mother, because it seemed really quite serious between the children, and though Andrew was a fine young man and exceptionally talented in his work, Helena was just turned seventeen, and as she was of a passionate nature . . .

Even in the grandiose excitement after the all-Wagner concert, Helena firmly said they must not go to Gunther's it cost too much, and you could get the same ice-cream sundae for half as much at their usual place near home, when they got off the car. Naturally Gunther's was the place to be seen and to see all fashion inside, but "we'll go when you're famous and we're rich," she declared matter-of-factly as though it was settled they'd be together the rest of their lives. On the streetcar, Helena calculated what the evening had cost, it was a third of what Andrew earned all week even after his new raise! She knew he really couldn't keep track, he was too much of an artist and he could be thankful she was practical, not like the silly girls who would only brag about how much they got a fellow to spend when they went out. At her disgusted look over such an attitude, Andrew had to burst out laughing, she laughed, too, and the need to seize and kiss her was unendurable; she knew it, for she took his hand, and the warm throb was as though their entire bodies were joined.

In the ice-cream parlor, Helena again had a thought about money. Why didn't he make her his banker? They would decide how much he could spend and she would hold the rest of his salary for him, and that way he would always have enough to send to his mother. He wouldn't always be borrowing from Willis, especially now that he and Willis didn't see each other so much outside of work.

6

ROMEO AND Juliet were even talking of marriage! Though her brother Bruce could not, of course, in general approve of such an early marriage, he had to remind Marta, for Andrew's sake, he wrote, of the famous quotation, "It is better to marry than to burn." For poor Andrew was indeed deeply smitten. Bruce felt himself in a certain respect in place of the father that Andrew lacked at this crucial time, and he need hardly tell Marta that trying to guide someone as headstrong as Andrew was by no means simple. True, the girl was charming. Besides being very pretty, she had serious interests such as her music, and though but seventeen she knew her mind. As to her family, though they did not have the cultural and artistic proclivities that might be more appropriate and stimulating for Andrew, the Hewletts were well-to-do and well connected. Donald Hewlett was a self-made man, risen out of poverty —indeed a recommendation—and the mother's side was almost of Pilgrim stock; Albert Morton Doheny had been the founder of the Midwest Insurance Company. It was a case of Donald Hewlett having worked his way up and married the boss's daughter. He was now first vice-president.

The Hewletts and the Dohenys had connections that eventually might be of great help to Andrew in his architectural career, though doubtless this did not enter into Andrew's thoughts. Marta could consider herself lucky the lad had not, for example, fallen in love, well, indiscriminately. Of course Bruce recommended waiting, at the very least a year. It would meanwhile be advisable, indeed he thought it was time that Marta . . .

Undoubtedly she must go to Chicago and judge for herself. She could speak with the girl's mother. This could be an infatuation, caused by a young man's natural needs. Already Marta felt a tremor in the face of one day losing him, a woman always knew she must lose her son to another woman. Surely there should be at least another few years. Andrew must be firmly on his path.

Her thought was already half worked out: if by moving to Chicago now she could provide a home background . . . Oh, she did not blind herself to a man's physical needs, and her son was now a man; and in that vice-ridden Chicago. Yet Marta felt in her soul, even in a way in her body, that her son was keeping himself pure for his bride. Surely, living at home, this might be easier for him. And they would save.

At first Marta had thought of meeting Mrs. Hewlett on neutral grounds, so to speak—in a downtown place—but it was important to see the girl's home background. Nor, Marta felt, should she yet meet the girl herself, that would be too much of a step, though she was dying to get a glimpse of her. So it was to be an early tea, while Helena was not yet home from school.

Naturally, Lorna Hewlett had made inquiries; indeed, her husband through his company's having an agent in Madison, Wisconsin, had discreetly found out a few things. Of the family on the mother's side what need be asked—her brother was their own eminent Preacher Bruce Daniels. A prominent pioneering Welsh family, several older brothers owned a whole valley in Wisconsin—rich dairy farms. A sister conducted a private school that attracted pupils even from Chicago. The mother too had taught school and now conducted a kindergarten, using the latest educational methods. Intelligent, proud, idealistic people, yet down-to-earth.

As for the father, there Lorna had an uneasiness. Basically, as to stock, nothing was wrong. Indeed, the contrary. The son of a minister near Boston, a prodigy, entering Harvard at fourteen. Then he had had a varied career, held several pulpits in the East, practiced law, taught music. He had had a first marriage and suffered the death of his wife. Mr. Lane had come west, to Wisconsin, as county superintendent of schools in River Valley, the valley of the Daniels clan. Marta Daniels, then a schoolteacher, had fallen in love with the new superintendent, though Mr. Lane was nearly twenty years older than she. Even before Andrew's birth, the restless Mr. Lane had taken a post in Ohio, gone back to the ministry, moving every few years from one congregation to another, always well liked, it seemed, but ill paid. They had returned to Wisconsin. This time, in Madison, Mr. Lane had started a music school. His wife conducted a kindergarten. Suddenly, over three years ago, Sanford Lane had picked up and left the family. Gone west, leaving Mrs. Lane to manage for herself with two growing youngsters.

It was the father's strange, sudden leaving that troubled Lorna Hewlett. The son was artistic, like his father's bent, not so much in music, at least architecture was more practical, but young Andrew Lane went about long-haired and wearing that artist's flowing tie, and even Helena couldn't get him to have a proper haircut like everyone else. No doubt it was youthful defiance of conventions, and the boy—well, young man—certainly looked romantic. Even if they waited at least a year, her Helena might be marrying the son of a wanderer who had deserted his wife and children. Though one thing at least could be said: there had been no talk in Madison of Mr. Lane and other women.

At the tinkle, Lorna Hewlett went herself to the door; the maid helped the visitor with her things.

Marta wore a light cloak, capelike, that she had woven herself, of warm umber, with a dark-red border. As she drew out her hatpins she had her own moment to form an impression: the girl's mother was buxom, her eyes were woman-to-woman.

It was not a rich, rich house, but substantial, as befitted Drexel Boulevard. There was the usual reproduction of the *Mona Lisa,* and the *Angelus.* The furniture in the same taste.

The mothers smiled to each other, and Mrs. Hewlett took up a gilt-framed photograph, a posed picture against a painted balustrade, the girl in a white linen dress, with a girlish sash, looking seriously yet winningly directly at you. Well, Andrew could scarcely be blamed—a beauty. Full-formed like her mother, a strong chin, a resemblance around the eyes. "There she is. On her sixteenth birthday."

"Already a young lady."

"She's a bit taller now. My own height."

"She certainly does resemble you."

And so they led up to the situation. Each had no wish but what would be best for the children. This could be puppy love, but who knew—it could be a true early love. Romeo and Juliet, Mrs. Hewlett pointed out, had been even younger.

"I'm sure we're not the Capulets and the Montagues," Marta smiled, and noticed it took Mrs. Hewlett a half second to realize the reference to a tragic outcome.

"No, I should hope not!" Lorna Hewlett smiled in her shudder.

As to Andrew, Mrs. Hewlett had been quite perceptive: how shy he was with girls, though quite at ease with grown people.

Utterly shy, Marta confirmed; in high school, if virtually forced to attend a class affair, once or twice a dance,

Andrew would be off in a corner with one or two other boys.

Now, Helena, Lorna Hewlett said, was highly sociable. She was not, thank heaven, the kind that, as soon as she discovered boys, had fewer close friends among the girls. Indeed, her parents encouraged her to have young people over all the time. But now since Andrew, well . . .

An exchange of understanding smiles.

Came the tea. An expensive silver service.

Now Lorna Hewlett ventured to ask: As she had understood, Andrew's father was very musical, and perhaps it was from him that Andrew had his artistic bent? Somehow she had hoped that this would get Andrew's mother to talking of her marriage, even of what had gone wrong; perhaps indeed it had been mainly the difference in age. But at once Mrs. Hewlett felt that the barrier was up, the woman shied from any reference to her husband, saying that she had from her son's infancy dreamed of his becoming a great architect, she had hung pictures of beautiful buildings, cathedrals and Greek temples, on the nursery walls.

This woman was stronger than herself, Lorna Hewlett felt; perhaps her troubles had given her determination. And to her son also. "Your son certainly seems to know his mind," she said, and "Our Helena too is so headstrong! And nowadays— Well, they've even discussed how many children they want to have! Helena wants six, and without waiting! One right after another, she told me she told him. Naturally I made a joke of it and said perhaps she'd like to have them all at one time! But, modern girls! I never would have dared mention the subject to a beau."

Presently they agreed that to avoid anything impetuous, the best strategy would be, as summer was near, that for these months Helena and Andrew should see much less of each other. The Hewlett family usually went to Charlevoix. "Although Helena has already invited him for his vacation!"

"Well—" here Marta was helpful—"I'm pretty sure Andrew will be very busy elsewhere." For, she said, her sister wanted to go ahead with the building of her Home School; Andrew had already drawn the sketches, and had asked his employer for an extended vacation so that he could come home and supervise the construction. Even though he was head over heels in love, she was sure Andrew couldn't resist putting up his first building. And as Mrs. Hewlett's eyes welcomed her stratagem, she added, "Just make sure Helena doesn't take it into her head to come and visit him!"

Ah, and yet each woman sighed in her heart. If this, of their children, was true, true love? But then, in that case, a few months of separation would only make it stronger.

It was already nearly three, and though Marta was eager to see the girl, even only to glimpse her, she didn't want an encounter, that would give the affair too much importance. Indeed, in parting, the two women agreed that neither would mention this visit.

As she emerged, there again came over Marta the worry that all her hopes and plans could now go awry. Doubtless she had, unadmittedly to herself, been dreaming of a brilliant match, a famous architect's daughter, a young poetess—every mother's dream of a princess for her son.

Just after crossing the street she saw a little group, of high-school age, walking and laughing together, boys and girls. Marta saw them well. One had bright coppery hair—surely the one. Fresh, lively, a beauty. For that, trust Andrew! The group lingered a moment in front of the Hewlett house, as the girl detached herself from her friends and ran up the few stairs, calling back from the porch some last remark that made them all laugh.

So she had seen her.

Now the other reason, the half-plan, that had brought her to Chicago seemed even more urgent to Andrew's mother. She could rent out or even sell the house in Madison, and find a place here. Already, after the thought had first occurred, Marta had written an exploratory letter to a good friend from Madison to whom she had taught looming; Althea Bauer, recently widowed, was alone in her house in a Chicago suburb, a lovely area, Althea wrote, of tree-shaded streets, and less than half an hour from downtown Chicago. It was called Oak Park.

But for Althea's being in mourning, Marta, arriving at the station, would have had to look again to recognize her friend, so much had she aged, with the shrunken frailty and the wrinkles, the whole aspect, of being an old woman. Only for an instant could Marta wonder, for they were within a year of each other, whether she herself could possibly give the same impression. But already Althea was declaring, "Marta, you haven't changed, and look at me!" Marta reassured her, it was the shock, surely. Yet a thought passed, perhaps a woman was less solitary in losing a man through his leaving than through his death. For despite everything there were times when an imagining came of her husband's returning, altered, more appreciative of a home, a wife, and, even if aging, still . . . a man in the house.

Althea was describing everything. All the shops were right here along the way; a lovely town, very friendly—no saloons; in Chicago there was one on every corner, so, the saying was, at Oak Park the saloons stopped and the churches began. Oh, yes, there was a Unitarian congregation too, a small one, up to now meeting in an upstairs hall, but it was growing. "We ourselves are still—" she caught herself—"I'm still a Congregationalist." And added, "Oh, Marta, it's hard to get the habit of I instead of we." Her daughter insisted she come and live with them in Evanston, and of course—with Althea's old shrewd little smile—"Grandma would be most welcome to take care of the new baby. Well, I know it would be good for me." As they passed ample white frame homes, among trees, she identified the townsfolk, here a wholesale furniture merchant, there a downtown lawyer, a bank manager . . .

Marta noticed several new-looking homes, and others abuilding, surely a good place for a young architect. Oh, Oak Park was growing, her friend declared, but the residents were determined to keep the quiet character of the place—no Jews she laughed. As yet. They were passing a whole block, still wooded, untouched; she turned into a lane, unpaved, though a sidewalk was laid.

The house was a two-story frame; on the front lawn, an apple tree. At once on entering, Marta saw Althea's loom—and it was already as though she were settled here. In Madison, Althea had been one of her first pupils and they had continued to loom together for several years, while Tess played with Althea's little girl, Jennifer. And Jennifer now already a mother. Though she was a year older than Tess. Still, she had married at nineteen, wasn't it?

"Not quite," Althea said. "She was just out of high school, still eighteen." An Oak Park boy, they were high-school sweethearts.

The perfect advantage was that with a friend like Marta, Althea could let the house as it stood; just, she would like to keep a room for herself, to come to occasionally. "Of course! It's your home!"—There she would keep her personal mementos and things. Although, sometimes, people said, it was best to give up an attachment, to break off clean . . . Her eyes peeped for assurance, for advice, from a friend who had, even if in a very different way, gone through the experience.

With new families settling here, most of them because it was a perfect place to raise children, why shouldn't Marta start her Froebel kindergarten? And she began to enumerate: a four-year-old, only a block away, and two little girls . . .

But Marta had her own thoughts. If Andrew were to live here, coming home from his office would take him no longer than going to Chicago's South Side. Naturally, if he entertained his young lady, after seeing her home he would have to come back downtown in time for the last Oak Park train.

She would give him the large front bedroom, as Althea had already indicated she would rather have the rear one onto the garden. And in their exchanged look, the reason was understood—indeed, Marta too, at home, had moved out of the conjugal bedroom, giving it to Tess.

Now, for Andrew, she would make this large bedroom into a kind of studio, bringing his own drafting table from Madison—for if she knew her Andrew he had projects in his mind. Why, if she moved immediately after Tess's high-school graduation, hardly a month off, Andrew could at once start on his detail plans for Nora's boarding school. And Tess, indeed, wanted to come to Chicago to study fashion design.

Once back in Madison, as though fate were showing Marta that her plan was right, it turned out that Professor Gamsey had engaged an assistant engineer, a man with a young family, who would take Marta's house right away. And Tess, for some mysterious reason that young girls could have, was eager to leave even before graduation, the principal would let her off, in the last few weeks nobody did anything anyway and she could come back just for the graduating exercises; meanwhile she intended to find a summer job in Chicago before the big rush.

They were installed. Until the Hewletts would be off to Charlevoix, Andrew could still see his young lady, but it needn't be every day!

Yet with only that glimpse from across the street, Marta was not at rest. She had to know more. She could have him invite the girl for Sunday dinner. But wouldn't that be taking the situation too seriously? On Saturday he was taking his inamorata to the afternoon concert, as Helena had a class farewell party that night. Marta and Althea went downtown shopping, and attended the concert.

Coming down from the balcony at the intermission,

Marta spotted Andrew, with Helena on his arm, and her instant feeling was a doubled one of relief and dismay. The dismay she knew: that of a mother losing her son. Yet also relief—now that she saw the girl from close. "Oh, I have so wanted to meet you," his Helena said, and was blushing but poised. Andrew asked how the acoustics were up above, as the same architects, Adler and Sullivan, were building the Auditorium. —They could distinguish each instrument, Althea declared, each note! "You play the piano," Marta remarked to the girl, who modestly replied, "I'm not really very good, but it helps me to appreciate and understand." And then added, "Andrew says you play the harp, I'd so love to learn it, he says it is the most beautiful sight, a woman playing the harp—so you see I want to please him!" This was uttered with just the right degree of humor as the girl looked at him. "I've been watching the lady harpist, she does have graceful arms—" "Not a harp on the stage," Andrew interjected. "At home, before a fire." —From his boyhood, from herself, Marta thought, Andrew must have preserved this vision. How nice! Why, for years now she had not touched the harp.

Perhaps it was the meeting with the girl's mother that had put her off a bit, so ordinary a personality, though altogether decent, and their home,without personal taste. But the living girl, really lovely, was surely a person. Only . . . Only what?

Then was it already so? Already? Mated? Fated?

The crowd was dividing. "I really wanted seats upstairs," the girl said, and to Andrew, "You see, the sound is just as good." And again to Marta, "But you know your son! Nothing but the best!"

"You've nothing to worry about," Althea assured her, as soon as they had left the young couple—how else could one think of them: a couple. "She's lovely. They're so in love."

And the girl not even the age of Tess. Just finishing her junior high-school year.

As Chicago's furnace days came, men arrived home limp and cross; at least a good thing Marta had chosen this leafy suburb. Andrew would snatch up his letter from Charlevoix—they wrote to each other every day.

After supper he'd go back up to his drawing board, never an evening out, never another girl though Tess always had a bevy gathering in her room; Andrew was intent only on his working drawings for the Home School.

Nora had insisted he must accept the full architect's fee. It was a nice sum, and Marta even speculated whether the two children might be writing each other about getting married and setting up house on it; she was even tempted, some day before Andrew came home, to take a peek at the girl's letter; never before in her life had she been capable of a thought of that kind!

But apparently Mrs. Hewlett had indeed done something of the sort, for suddenly there came a letter from Charlevoix to Marta herself: the children were secretly planning to get married at summer's end! Lorna Hewlett had discovered the plan, in a letter from Andrew that she had "chanced to see" in Helena's room. Mrs. Hewlett believed the only thing to do now would be to send her daughter away to a finishing school. She and Mr. Hewlett were thinking of the Buxley School in Massachusetts.

It would do Marta good to see, Nora wrote, how in the fewest days Andrew had got all those grown men to respect him and to do things the way he wanted—Andrew's way. The town builder, Anton Siebert, knew Andrew from childhood, and here was Andrew the architect, giving him instructions! Between Andrew and Nora it was a little joke that Siebert didn't properly know how to read a blueprint; he was hardly more advanced than Carpenter Hagedorn.

It was a joy, Nora said, to see Andrew at work, what amazing understanding, what inventiveness! Clambering over the scaffolding, without seeming to interfere, he would show how to simplify the construction—and save Nora money. The cozy style also fitted Aunt Nora's idea, a *home* school, so that children who were for the first time away would not feel too homesick.

ALL SORTS of touches Andrew had thought out. A real parlor, with small-size sofas, with a fireplace for toasting marshmallows. For the schoolrooms he had designed special desks that Siebert was making—and at quite a saving. The desks could be moved around. In Mother's Froebel school, the children sometimes arranged themselves in little groups, or formed a circle; why should a good idea stop in kindergarten? In the dormitories too, different arrangements of the cots could be made, instead of their being in rows like in a hospital—or jail.

Sometimes Andrew felt easier with Nora than with his mother. When Helena's letters began coming to River Valley, he even read Nora parts of them. For herself, Helena said, the summer separation had only made her more sure, and if she was sent away to school, she would become still more sure!

The whole structure stood solid at the foot of the hill, the scaffolding still around it, the sheathing going on.

His! From the first sketch! It was the professional look of it that most satisfied him. Good clean job. Excellent proportions. Good taste, too. No frills, no furbelows, Andrew told himself.

Still, there echoed the question that Helena once had asked, "Then how would *you* do it?" This was not yet himself. Inside, he had got some good ideas. But something was still to come to him that would be his own.

"It's just beautiful!" Aunt Nora glowed.

Part Two

The
Master

7

ADLER AND Sullivan, Willis mentioned on Andrew's return to Chicago, were taking on designers for the interior details of the Auditorium. Now, with his touch, was his chance. Better money, too.

Andrew said he'd go if Willis went, but Willis said he didn't think he had the touch those people were looking for.

Rightly, Andrew supposed he ought to speak to Mr. Olmstead before trying elsewhere, but if he waited for Olmstead's return he might miss his opportunity. And what would he tell Olmstead? There was nothing more he could learn here. Houses, churches, stables, even apartment houses, were Queen Anne—as though the American Revolution had never taken place.

If he asked Uncle Bruce the dictum would be, "You must wait for Mr. Olmstead's return." And Mother would say the same.

At lunchtime Andrew gathered a few renderings—his newly built Home School, and a kind of "dream house" peeping from among shade trees. He walked over. The chiefs usually went out to eat a bit later than the staff.

The enormous, open floor was even more crowded with drafting tables. Mr. Sullivan recognized him at once, "Ah, the young man with the good question!" "Who got a good answer!" Andrew shot back, and the old partner, Mr. Dankmar Adler, turned on his swivel chair for a look at him.

With a quick, all-absorbing glance at his rendering, Mr. Sullivan nodded. Good touch. "What I'm interested in right now . . ." He gestured to his own board. Ornament. The Louis Sullivan specialty. Plant motifs, involuted with pure geometric design. "Think you could work up some of these?" He indicating the plant stem. "Know this?"

Andrew studied the stalk, with seed heads almost like tumbleweed. From the farm, a half-recognition came. "Onion?" "Wild onion!" Sullivan had a short laugh. "Grows all around this area. Indians called it Chi-ca-gou. Means Bitter Stink."

Working into the night, his drawing pen speeding as though of itself, Andrew sketched samples, first in Mr. Sullivan's own manner, using the same foliage motifs, then a few drawings that were more of his own, with little color dots and triangles instead of leaf forms. Just something to show.

"All right," Mr. Sullivan said, on those that duplicated his style. "Good." And over Andrew's own he gave a kind of knowing smile. The ways of youth. "Not bad." And turning to his partner, "Take him on. Fix it up."

Twenty-five dollars a week!

Enough even to get married on!

His great step forward, Mother called it. Though did she fully realize how important Mr. Sullivan was? Particularly now, for since the death of Henry Richardson the mantle had fallen on Louis Sullivan. Of course she realized! Mother eyed him; to her this simply meant that her son was moving closer to where the mantle would fall on Andrew Lane!

And what had Mr. Olmstead said? Ah, Andrew hadn't yet had a chance to speak to Mr. Olmstead, as Mr. Olmstead was away in Omaha. Then Andrew hadn't spoken to his employer before going to see Mr. Sullivan? Why, no . . . Why should Olmstead care, he could go right back and start somebody at eight dollars a week! Marta had that look as though trying to give his behavior the benefit of the doubt. Had he waited for the boss's return, Andrew said, he might have missed the chance. She raised her shoulders a trifle as though withholding judgment on his behavior.

And Mr. Olmstead, returning from Omaha while Andrew was finishing out the week, did make a remark. "Hm. I don't recall your having mentioned to me that you wanted to look for a change." Rather icily, he wished Andrew success.

As they started for Friday-evening dinner at Uncle Bruce's, his mother asked whether Andrew had asked his uncle about leaving Olmstead's. After all, it was really because of Uncle Bruce that he had got his start there. —Not exactly. He had got it on his own, before Uncle Bruce even knew he was in Chicago. —Well, still . . .

Why all this doubt of his behavior? He would be earning a lot more money—twenty-five! And working with a great architect! His real life could now be starting. He'd done nothing unethical—only been a bit impatient.

Andrew followed his uncle into the study. "You know, Andrew, I do congratulate you on your advanced opportunities." But it was not just once, it was twice now, that Andrew had—so to speak—walked out on a benefactor. For hadn't he done that in leaving Professor Gamsey in Madison?

By this, Andrew was taken aback. He hadn't connected his two actions. His mind jumped to the defense. It was Professor Gamsey who had brought in someone, over *his* head! But—true, he had departed without warning. As now. He had slipped away, like someone who might be doing something wrong.

Perhaps bad manners, but it certainly had not hurt anyone. His righteous family. A family of preachers. Yet Andrew couldn't raise his eyes to his Uncle Bruce.

With this new affluence, his uncle divined his thoughts, he hoped Andrew would not try to cut short the understanding regarding marriage. For surely Andrew realized how serious marriage was. It was not just a matter of going together to plays and concerts, but of entire life. In marriage, one could not, on impulse, go over elsewhere—

"But I love her," the words had come out of themselves. "It's like I know I'll be an architect all my life."

His uncle gave him that quick keen glance, as at a too-good answer. Then stood and placed a hand on Andrew's shoulder. Fatherly. And there leaped back into Andrew's mind: his father had walked out. No, Father had been sent away. Hadn't his mother and father, too, been in love when they married?

His uncle seemed finished with the session. They went in to dinner.

The next morning, Andrew did something unplanned, but that must have been forming in his mind. The entire forested block opposite the house had been bought by a new realtor, who was advertising lots for sale. That Saturday morning, without saying a word to Marta, Andrew went over and bought the facing plot, using his fee from Aunt Nora's Home School.

The realtor, a burly, enthusiastic man named Philip Whaley, congratulated him for his acumen. These lots were bound to go up. . . . What, an architect? Say, that would be great for both of them, an architect on the spot! Fact was, Whaley was thinking of building here, for himself! Say, Andrew ought to take the adjoining lot too, a corner, right on Chicago Avenue, great place for an office! And indeed Andrew added a deposit, to hold the lot. A warm handshake. Mr. Whaley was sure they were going to do big things together!

Marta, though startled that he had made his decision without even talking it over with her, did not really seem displeased, for hadn't she from the first seen that Oak Park would be a good place for an architect? And also, Andrew had shown he meant to remain right here, close to her.

The letter spoke of a big surprise when he would see her! At first, Andrew thought in alarm, could she be cutting her hair short, as some of those rabid suffragettes were doing?

The very first evening, he hurried over, and beheld his Helena just as she had always been, only more beautiful. More—what was it—womanlike, one had to say, and yet more girlishly bewitching. And her parents, after only brief greetings and inquiries, left them alone in the parlor. "Well, where's the surprise?" he asked. She sparkled. "Where's yours?"

"I bought a building lot, with the money from Aunt Nora. For our house."

There were tears in her eyes. They kissed a quick soul kiss.

Now where was her surprise?

"Not yet!"

Women had no idea of fair play.

Perhaps Sunday, Helena teased. He was to fetch her home to dinner. At last his mother had said, "Why don't you bring your sweetheart."

They had hardly more than a week before she would be shipped off to that fancy school for young ladies. Oh, the parents were not playing fair and would be served right by an elopement! But no, Helena didn't really dare. And after all, she *was* very young. And she ought to finish school. They had stood the test of their separation all summer, and they would stand this test too!

Sunday morning was glorious, a bright sun no longer with August heat. Andrew got up early to get to Uncle Bruce's services, slipping into the seat Helena had kept beside her, as in the first days of their romance.

Still, even as they started for Oak Park, she would not reveal her secret, and the whole time on the train she teased anew. Every guess he made was wrong, and her laughter was so joyous, heads turned.

As they strolled hand in hand from the station, they

came to the thinned space in the dense stand of trees. "Here?" Helena cried. Mr. Whaley had partly cleared the plot, leaving standing a lane of elms. just as though inviting you to walk down to the entrance of the house-to-be. "Here!" Andrew said.

Then and there, and luckily no one was inspecting lots, Helena took his head between her hands and kissed him, the most passionate of kisses, no longer girlish.

They walked down their lane to where the house would stand. She could tell he was already forming it in his mind, "I bet it won't be a Norman castle or even a French château!" Would it be brick? Would it be wood?

"The first person to please is the client's wife," Andrew quoted Architect Olmstead.

"Wood!" she chose. It cost less than brick, and was so natural. Oh, she had listened well to his discourses. Brick seemed more—well, more substantial, but wood was more romantic, even like young pioneers building a house out of logs; here, with much of the forest around still standing, you could imagine those pioneer times, two young people, a man and his woman, starting their life together . . . Helena looked so thoughtful and serious that Andrew in his turn took her face in his hands, and even though his mother could probably see them if she was at the front window, he kissed, in their new way. Then they presented themselves at the door.

Throughout the dinner, Marta and Tess had to join in guessing about Helena's surprise; though Tess tried to act superior to such girlish games, she got caught by curiosity. But in the end they all gave up, to Helena's peals of triumphant laughter, as she promised, right after dinner, to show them. Show them what? She hadn't brought any parcels.

Then, after helping Tess clear the table, not like a guest but already like one of the family, she offered to wash the dishes, but Marta said, "Why don't you go back and entertain your beau." Helena returned to the parlor, where Andrew sat sketching, their house she was sure, but instead of peeking, she slipped into the chair by the harp. Until the first plucked notes, Andrew didn't even suspect. Then suddenly his head turned. Helena, with her most enchanting, self-pleased smile, played on, "The Song of the Lorelei."

Oh, what a girl he had found! The sun shone on her half-bared arms, for she had thought to draw up her puffed sleeves, remembering Andrew's remarks about the loveliness of a woman's arm movements as she played the harp.

Andrew could have seized, devoured her with a passion kiss, but Mother, beaming, and Tess, with her knowing smile, had appeared in the doorway.

But where, how, in Charlevoix?

The summer orchestra there had included a lady harpist, and, knowing it would please Andrew, Helena had taken lessons.

Her eyes turned to his mother. If ever there had remained any doubt, the girl had won!

Now Marta must play. Oh, she hadn't touched the harp for so long! But she did, and as the two of them took turns, happiness reigned.

8

WITH THE Auditorium walls up, the Master was hurrying his ornamental design. The draftsmen, already on other projects, were supervised by Mr. Adler, so that the Master only walked through, when he arrived, for a glance at their progress. But with Andrew, placed next to the office, Louis Sullivan was in constant communication. Ornament was his love, but there must be nothing superfluous, as in over-dressing a beautiful woman. Ornament must never alter the truth of the structure's form—the way modern clothing could altogether distort the female form, with enormous bumps behind, and sleeves the shape of hams. As a boy he had hardly known that women had lower limbs.

Look to nature. Everything had its necessary shape and no exaggeration. Look at the perfect form of that pigeon come to roost on the sill. Fish, birds, animals, man, woman, all were perfect examples of natural form. The form came from the functional need—fins, legs, wings, head. All elements beautifully incorporated into a unified natural design. Decoration never interfered with form. And decoration too was functional, as in mating. Take the peacock. The spectacular tail feathers were folded onto the body form except when spread for attracting the female. Thus, in architecture, decoration should not extrude for its own sake. That was why statuary was almost always out of place on buildings—especially when high up. Look how the Greeks had recognized this, in making statuary functional—the caryatides. Egyptians too had realized this. Even the overdressed Gothic had kept sculpture within the form, as integral ornament to the structure, up to the last rainspout gargoyle. And Renaissance. But that concoction in Paris, the Opéra! Like some bedizened old lady with enormous rocks of jewelry on every finger. And everybody climbing great flights of stairs—as though that was going to make the music any better. No, what was wanted here was a native architecture, and architecture of democracy . . .

These impromptu discourses, often pronounced over Andrew's board, were scarcely listened to by the draftsmen. Yet within the repetition there came new glimmers, and always the sense of having been chosen, to carry these truths onward.

In those hours when he stayed on late to finish a drawing the Master wanted, or perhaps to fill in an hour before he met Willis—for, with Helena forcedly away, they were again two young men about town, and there was a whole season of Gilbert and Sullivan—in those after-twilight hours in the Master's office, with the gaslight forming a sphere around them, Sullivan would discourse. True American architecture must spring from the American earth, the farmlands and farm buildings. Like the great simple barns with their haylofts, perfectly formed to house the work animals, with their feed supply above . . . Ever work on a farm?

Sure, all summer every summer from when he was ten. Andrew described the valley, the adjoining farms of his uncles, his grandfather's farm . . .

Sullivan too. Every summer on his grandfather's farm. And it turned out that Mr. Sullivan's father too had been a musician. He too had wandered from one city to another, East to West. Operated a dancing school, here in Chicago. Andrew told of his father's music school in Madison.

They matched tales of predawn risings on the farm, and each told his age when he first swung a full-size scythe in the harvest. Then Mr. Sullivan would be off on a side lecture, perhaps Thoreau, Whitman, his favorite, "Song of Myself," he would recite, and once just after swallowing a nip he confided that he was in correspondence with old Walt Whitman, and even that he sometimes sent the poet some of his own effusions—yes, he occasionally wrote poems—and the great old man had been very kind about them. But Mr. Sullivan didn't offer any to be read.

One thing, still in the back of his mind, Andrew tried to find out about. The École des Beaux-Arts. The training that the profession set so much store by. Mr. Sullivan had gone through it. Even if you didn't want to follow in those classic styles, Andrew asked, wasn't the training itself useful?

Useful for what? Sullivan growled. He'd got more out of his one year in M.I.T. than from two years at the Beaux-Arts. First he had had to hole up for months in his tiny hotel room, perfecting their damn language so he could pass the entrance exam, oh no, not on architecture, they quizzed you about everything from the Old Testament to Napoleon's battle formations. Once you passed, you spent your time taking lecture notes on dead styles. Then they put you in the atelier system. That part wasn't bad if you had the luck to fall in with a good master on an interesting project. What he had got was an insane asylum!

But still, afterward, wasn't it a key to—to—what Andrew meant, but couldn't outright say, was whether the Beaux-Arts was the way to the top. Here in only ten years Mr. Sullivan was at the top of Chicago architects. And Richardson too had gone through the Paris École des Beaux-Arts. And that fashionable New York man, Stanford White . . . The Master snorted. Hell, a man who had the makings didn't need that Paris diploma. He himself had never finished. Fed up with their Renaissance, Baroque and Rococo. Why, look at Burnham—sure, he came from a fine Chicago family, traced themselves to John Alden, family of preachers, yes, his too! Some in business, rich, but Dan Burnham had flunked the Harvard entrance, kicked around mining, out West. Know how he got into architecture? Came back to Chicago, right after the Big Fire, selling plate glass. Got into construction. Look at Dankmar Adler. Civil engineer in the Civil War—same as Major Jenney.

Then, before leaving for home—Sullivan too lived with his mother—the Master took a last look at the iron-work design on Andrew's board, elaborated from his own sketch, thumbtacked above. Sullivan nodded, nodded. Suggested a technical simplification, for casting. —Here was another example, all these know-it-all young Harvard critics who had been to Paris and taken a subway ride were writing about the Art Nouveau ironwork designs on the Métro stations, saying that was where Louis Sullivan got his ideas! Why, Andrew knew just where this idea come from, no acanthus, no fleur de lis, but that good old Chi-ca-gou wild onion! And fixing his bowler carefully, Mr. Sullivan said his good night, leaving Andrew to lock up.

There wasn't, in the huge drafting room, the camara-derie, the horseplay and eraser-throwing when the boss was out, or the sudden serious discussion from board to board, among the ministers' sons, about the horrors of vice and crime that the *Daily News* was exposing. Here at Adler and Sullivan's, a number of the men were somewhat older—family men. A half dozen of the draftsmen, including the head draftsman, Stolz, were Jewish. After all, Mr. Adler was the son of a rabbi. To them, Andrew felt, he must be a kind of teacher's pet with his board moved next to the office. But after all, none of them really could draw.

At noon, a number of the men unpacked lunches brought from home. Andrew usually found himself back at the Bakery with Willis and the Olmstead crowd, or just having a quick sandwich somewhere so he could saunter the streets, taking a look at the progress of Burnham and Root's Monadnock; though tall, it was, like the Auditorium, solid masonry instead of the new steel construction; the Monadnock walls were twelve feet thick at the base. Narrow windows even up high. With steel structure, Major Jenney was introducing an especially broad aperture that was getting to be known as the Chicago window. Indeed, in a steel-frame structure, what were walls altogether except weather screens? They could even be entirely of glass!

Maybe the Monadnock and the Auditorium would be the last two great monoliths, examples of high-structure masonry, standing here in Chicago to be admired in the future like the Pyramids of Egypt!

Before returning to the office, he'd go over to the Auditorium site, riding up on the open construction elevator, to see how the tower was coming along, he'd spot the round bearded face of Mr. Adler peering down, his eye better than a plumb bob.

Dankmar Adler had a special worry about the tower. Would its added weight over the center front area cause the building to settle unevenly? To prevent this, Mr. Adler had used a clever engineering idea, spreading pig iron, like ballast, beneath where the tower would be, and removing this added weight as the tower was constructed.

But still, why had the decision been made for masonry? One factor, the Chief replied—safety. The great theater in the heart of the building would be holding over four thousand people. Imagine if a fire started. Ah, developments with steel framework were not quite far enough for taking a chance like that. In the great Chicago fire, iron columns had buckled in the intense heat. Mr. Sullivan, as a young man, had seen the same in the Philadelphia fire. Tile sheathing, now being used to fireproof structural iron, was too new. So he and Sullivan had decided, with the Commodore, on masonry. "But still, you're using steel trusses for the span of the theater ceiling," Andrew reminded him. The engineer had his warm chuckle. "New steel alloy. A salesman came and convinced me." Steel mills were making enormous progress. John Root was using the new steel in the Masonic Temple he was designing, going to top even this tower. There would be no limit— Andrew would be working on buildings that scraped the sky itself! These downtown streets would be thick forests of skyscrapers.

"Dark as a forest," Andrew remarked.

Adler nodded. Yet he had his benign look, as though progress could never be wrong. "The answer will come, in the problem itself the answer is always there, Andrew," he repeated.

The lunch crowd filled the sidewalks. Where a woman was bent over at a shop-window shoe display, Andrew had to sidle around her rear protrusion. Then he had to step off the curb to let pass a pair of women walking together, in their enormous skirts. He stepped into horse manure.

Why make people live like this? Wasn't there a better way than this whole upward concentration? What everyone was hailing as the triumphant American spirit—could it be wrong?

He had to take into account that his own impulse was often simply contradictory. Again and again in her letters, Helena teased that he would take the opposite side of everyone's opinion, just to be different. To attract attention! Ah, he wrote back, he didn't really do it to be noticed. He liked to think for himself.

Mr. Sullivan was working on a high office building for St. Louis, now using the steel frame. Most of the architects doing high buildings would design a set of three floors in one way, topped by a two-floor segment in another mode, then perhaps four with a common window alignment, so that the structure looked like a series of add-ons topped by a wide-brimmed roof like a cowboy hat.

Then one day the Master showed Andrew his completed design. It was a unity, one complete form. In a sense, it appeared to Andrew, the entire structure might be analogous to the form of a column: the first two floors, shops and commercial areas, served as a column's base; Then came the shaft—the office floors; and at the top a variation, the space being used for heating and ventilation systems, elevator machinery, so that, with its cornice, the top corresponded to a column's capital. The Master had found a form for the tall building, and before his pride of achievement Andrew didn't quite bring himself to raise the whole question that troubled him: whether this was really the right direction. Vertical?

What was so important about going up, up, a chase to build another floor higher? Just an American craze.

After work, staying downtown, he talked of it with Willis. Well, Willis put his mind to it, was it really so American? What about Gothic cathedrals? Even with the new skyscrapers, the spires of Notre-Dame were higher. And look at their latest, in France, the record-breaking Eiffel Tower, going up now, for their International Exposition. They too had the verticality craze. Indeed, wasn't the skyscraper impulse already there in the Tower of Babel?

No, Andrew persisted, it wasn't the impulse to reach God, nor the stunts like the empty Eiffel Tower, that he meant. What he saw was the ant-heap danger. After these ant-heap offices there would come beehive dwellings, tiny boxes piled one atop the other, and what sort of life, what sort of civilization, could that be? Was this the future for them to devote their thoughts and skills to? Wasn't an architect a designer of life, didn't what was built guide the way people lived? The whole idea, this verticality, away from contact with the earth, somehow made him shudder. A dwelling, he just naturally felt, was on the ground, you walked into it. Wasn't there room to live in, to spread out, in America?

"Yes. But think also," Willis said, "of the vistas, the sense of space, up there." "For the high and mighty." "Well, aren't Adler and Sullivan going to move the offices up to the top of the Auditorium tower?" Andrew too would be among the highest! No wonder he had illusions about architects ruling the world! But did Andrew really think it was architects who determined how people lived? It was the money men who decided to put up these high buildings, causing the crowding, the jammed streets. If there was any hope for democracy it was not in this architecture of democracy that Louis Sullivan liked to talk about, great builder and idealist though he might be. But there was an architecture of society itself, of government, and maybe that was where democracy still had a chance. Willis was all fired up about the ideas of Henry George, the Single Tax, based on land, on rents. "You ought to read him."

Then, though Willis rarely mentioned Helena, he asked, what did Andrew hear from his inamorata? Still intending to get married?

A swarm of things to say, and yet that he couldn't say to Willis, came to Andrew. Her today's letter telling him she was reading his favorite poet and in which she had copied out that quotation:

> When the materials are all prepared and
> ready, the architect shall appear.
> I swear to you the architect shall appear
> without fail . . .

If he mentioned this to Willis, his friend would have his wisp of a smile, at her sending the poem to Andrew. Feminine wiles. Yet to Andrew it was overwhelmingly endearing, her wanting to touch him in his very thoughts and ambitions. So, about marriage intentions—why, just as soon as Helena graduated and came home, he told Willis. What he really wanted was to build their house and have it ready.

Now Willis looked at him with an almost painful wish for understanding. Yes, Helena was a fine girl, lovely. "But you know, with all the girls you've met . . ." what always came to Willis was, why just this one, exactly? Why one pretty girl rather than another?

His friend was not being flippant, Andrew felt, but was

deeply asking. Perhaps puzzling about his own self. For, a number of times, Helena had even tried to think of someone for Willis, but finally said she had a woman's feeling— a woman!—that Willis, though very nice, and certainly not a woman-hater, did not really care for the opposite sex. Of course she and Andrew at once had agreed that it was nothing like those stories about Oscar Wilde. It was as though something was absent. Art, music, and the theater: such things seemed to be enough for him.

Peculiarly, Andrew felt that they had changed places; Willis had always been the one who knew the world, who took him along, who explained. How could one tell a friend who was the older, the more experienced in the world, about such a clear, natural thing? Andrew let the question slide as though Willis were joking him.

9

THE COLD blasting wind was already felt on Michigan
Avenue. Winter would not be long to pass, then—just a
few more months of waiting, they wrote to each other. In
the spring he would already begin to build the house, and
have it ready for them to walk into, right after the wedding!
Hadn't Susan and Gus during all that season before they
were married been planning their house down to every
corner, and even a baby crib? And Gus had built it.

At Olmstead's he had designed many a house, starting
with the "requirements" of a client and wife, usually first
came the ostentatious part, the size of the parlor, or, even
before that, the "impression" from outside.

One impression that Andrew agreed with, that was
natural, was the steep gabled roof, the sheltering element.
The way, it suddenly occurred to Andrew, the same way
one drew a house as a child. In Mother's kindergarten.
Then, alas, according to cliental whims, came the dormers,
turrets, spires, towers and, below, the bay windows,
porches, and other protuberances.

Idly, he continued his high-pitched lines down to the

ground; why, it was a tent. The primary shelter to keep out rain, hail, snow, and the howling winds. The next need was warmth, but this meant not only warmth of body but warmth of life, of family and friends gathered, most naturally, around an open fire. Now, with central heating coming into use, there were iron radiators plunked here and there against the walls of a room. Where was the sight of blazing logs?

Richardson had restored the great open fireplace, but now fireplaces were merely decorative marble frames around a shallow hole in the wall, the mantelpieces wide enough for a few geegaws and photographs in gilt frames.

And so Andrew began his home interior with a real, ample hearth, and seats extending outward like open arms. The inglenook.

He played with the half-curve of a stair going around a great freestanding stone chimney. He could see Helena in her lace morning robe coming down to have coffee with him before he left for his train. Or, even nicer, at night as, reading with him before the open fire, she yawned and, with a look at him, started up to their bedroom.

It would at most be a small, simple house. For where would he get money to build?

The Master had come in; Andrew slipped his house sketch under some papers, and bent to his drawing board, detailing the ceiling-beam ornaments for the great restaurant on the top floor of the Auditorium. The running motif was of Sullivan's favorite wild prairie plants; Andrew continued the seed pods into a spray of dots, and the Master smiled over Andrew's slipping in a touch of his own; he let it stay.

But in Andrew's mind, thoughts of his own house continued; he drew out his sketch, added a cross-gable for an upstairs bedroom on each side, bath to the rear. In front, full width, his studio, for work at home; a wide window. Above it, a New England touch, he drew a fanlight.

Mr. Sullivan, passing, glanced over, but let the crime go. "It's for my own house," Andrew explained, and decided that this was his moment. "I want to start building, have it ready when we get married."

The Master nodded. He had heard. "Quite modest," he said of the sketch.

"I don't know where I'll get the money, even for this."

"I see." The Master gazed at him. In Andrew there was an odd sense, of the man's puzzlement, as there had been with Willis. Sometimes, when Mr. Sullivan was going out of an evening, he would stay downtown. He even kept a set of tails in his closet, and more than once Andrew had espied him in a theater lobby, with a stunningly dressed woman, never the same one. Actually, Mr. Sullivan had quite a reputation for conquests; he was supposed to be almost on a par with that notorious magnate Charles Yerkes.

Now the Master's gaze turned a little whimsical, an older man toward romantic youth. "Well, Andrew, you know your mind." And with one of his odd moments of humor he repeated the line of a popular song, "I want what I want when I want it."

Andrew decided to plunge. "Mr. Sullivan, could the firm loan me the money to build? On a mortgage?"

For reply, Sullivan half turned back, toward Adler, in their office. "Andrew here wants to build himself a house —getting married."

The Chief stepped out, smiling broadly. Well! Congratulations! And in a trice, Mr. Adler had it arranged. With five thousand dollars, Andrew figured, he could put up the little house. Very well, said Mr. Adler, they would take the mortgage payments out of his salary. Give him a little raise as a wedding present. Make it a five-year contract, all his work only for the firm. And he'd have his house paid off! He was all set.

Arriving with Mother for one of those Friday dinners to which Uncle Bruce invited interesting people—Tess had begged off, she was going to the theater with a beau—Andrew recognized a face, from his very first night in Chicago. The lank lock of hair falling over the eye—that orator he had heard by chance, on a street corner, pleading to save the Haymarket anarchists from hanging. Mr. Darrow was his name, and at the introduction Andrew told about that first night in the city. "I even signed an appeal. Did the campaign do any good?"

Well, hadn't Andrew seen the papers? The United States Supreme Court had just refused to hear the case. "I guess that's the end of the rope," the lawyer said, the word play more bitter than humorous.

"Why don't they show contrition? If they would, I'm sure the governor would pardon them," said Aunt Genevieve, and Mrs. Darrow, a small, unimpressive woman who didn't seem to belong with her husband, eagerly agreed. The governor had practically declared that if there was contrition, clemency would be considered.

"Give up your principles, or your life!" This came from a youngish woman, nice-faced, with luminous yet all-seeing eyes. There was something a trifle askew in her posture, perhaps something wrong about her back. Miss Addams talked right on, turning now to the lawyer, now to Uncle Bruce. "I'm sure you agree, Clarence," and "I'm sure you know more than I do, Bruce"—except that she seemed to know about everything, just exactly who was influencing the governor to hold back a pardon, and what great personalities in England and France were sending cables for clemency. And all through dinner it was this Miss Addams, Jane, they called her, who seemed even to have taken over from Uncle Bruce, like a chairman at a meeting, but softly, deftly, and not failing to call on Andrew too, so that the younger generation might be heard.

Indeed, "being heard" was her credo. It was time for women to be heard. It was time for the working people to make themselves heard.

She even turned to a middle-aged wealthy-looking couple, the kind Uncle Bruce always had at these dinners, parishioners, who, Andrew had seen, might be tapped for a donation to a worthy cause. "The people must make themselves heard!"

From Uncle Bruce it came out that Miss Addams led a circle of active young women, college graduates—one of them, Mr. Darrow said, was Chicago's first woman lawyer. And Miss Addams had a worthy project. She and her friends had decided to "go to the people." They meant to establish what they called a settlement house, to live right in the crowded slums, and try to better the conditions around them. "What an original idea," Aunt Genevieve said, echoed by Mrs. Darrow. "The idea isn't really original," said Miss Addams. She and a friend had just returned from London where they had visited such a settlement right in the worst slums of the East End; there it was a group of young men who were combatting problems of alcoholism, disease, degeneration, but also bringing, right into their settlement house, culture of the highest type, the plays of Bernard Shaw, and lectures by members of the Fabian Society. Here in Chicago there were certain added problems. In London's underside the needy at least were in their own country, using their native language. But in Chicago, with the waves of immigration from Greece, from Italy, and the poorest of the Jews, most of these people hardly could speak English! Classes in English and citizenship were among the first programs on the agenda. And those immigrants who by some hook or crook, mostly crook, had got their citizenship papers must be taught not to sell their vote for a beer, to Alderman Bathhouse John Coughlin and his like. These immigrants must not only come into contact with American culture but also be taught to preserve their own native culture and customs. She and her friends planned to have studios for artists, also for handicrafts. But even before the arts came the most desperate needs: sanitation, health, child care, a kindergarten where working mothers could leave their little ones instead of locking them up in their airless flats. A child had been discovered, a two-year-old child, only a month ago, dead, still tied with a rope to a bedpost!

It was the Halstead Street area they were thinking of, people lived in shanties and back houses. A saloon on every corner! Young girls on the streets, driven into prostitution. Suddenly Miss Addams turned to Marta. "You must come and help us, Bruce tells me you have long conducted a kindergarten using the Froebel method . . ."

Mother promised to come as soon as they had their house.

Could she perhaps give two days a week to the work? Miss Addams was pinning her down.

Now Uncle Bruce turned to his perpetually smiling parishioner, who had not spoken except to compliment Aunt Genevieve on each dish, especially her candied sweet potatoes. In his real-estate operations, might he not be able to help Miss Addams locate a suitable building? —He would certainly try!

Miss Addams was appreciative. She had a wonderful soft smile, the smile, Andrew decided, of an invalid who had conquered. For his mother had whispered to him that Miss Addams had spent a year in bed, with a bad spine. Then, as though she in no way intended to monopolize the conversation, Miss Addams bent to her food.

Now that he was with Adler and Sullivan, Andrew heard Uncle Bruce asking him, how was the construction of the Auditorium progressing?

So it was his turn. The tower section was going up, Andrew said, and he had got a fascinating answer to something that had puzzled him. Then he gave an explanation of Mr. Adler's pig-iron weights, to even up the load on the foundation.

Well, how ingenious! Miss Addams remarked. His mother smiled as though it was Andrew himself who had thought of the idea. Turning to Mrs. Darrow, Miss Addams commented, indeed it was a fine thing to build such a great opera hall for Chicago. But also, some of these millionaires might think of building decent homes for the working people.

In fact one of them had, Andrew put in. There was the entire town of Pullman, out south, with model homes in walking distance of the factory. The architect, Solon

Beeman, had done an excellent job. What an opportunity —to design an entire community! It seemed there were no saloons—just like Oak Park.

"But, unlike Oak Park—no churches either!" Uncle Bruce was well informed. "The Catholics have to go outside the town limits—like the drinkers." Everyone laughed.

Still, Andrew said—the latest conveniences. Every house had running water.

"For which Mr. Pullman charges them by the gallon," said Miss Addams.

"Mr. Pullman makes a nice profit on the whole place," Mr. Darrow said. Besides, one attempt to talk union in his kitchen and the workman was out on the street with his whole family.

"And you can be sure he charges them for the eviction," said Miss Addams. "That's what makes revolutionists!" And they were back on anarchism. Would there still be a last-minute reprieve?

No! Now, this was too much!

Marta handed him the morning paper, pointing to a boxed notice: Public schools would be closed at noon tomorrow, to mark the hanging of the Haymarket anarchists. —Why not as well hold the hangings in front of that monstrous City Hall, and assemble all the city's schoolchildren to watch!

Not all would be hung, the *Tribune* said. Three had written letters of contrition, and it was believed the governor would in the last hours spare their lives.

It tore Marta's heart that the man she somehow admired despite all his wild revolutionary ideas, the one who of his own free will walked into the court to give himself up —Mr. Parsons—had refused to show contrition. He had not thrown the bomb, he had never knowingly harmed anyone, and to be required to write such a letter to save his skin was a last injustice, as medieval as the death sentence itself.

In the middle of the day an echo reverberated up from

the street, another Extra! A few men even left their boards and poked their heads out of an open window. A jail break? Dynamite? Rumors had been heard, "They'll never hang."

The office boy ran down for a paper.

CHEATS GALLOWS.

One of them, the youngest, named Ling, had tried to blow himself up!

Stolz read it out. Ling was the one in whose room the police had found dynamite, but they couldn't prove he was the bomb-thrower. Now he must have kept a firing cap hidden on him, for this morning he had put the explosive cap between his teeth and bitten into it, blowing off a whole side of his face. He was still alive in a hospital, but expected to expire before the day was out.

" 'If not, his hanging will be carried out, too,' " Stolz read.

Andrew had time before going to his uncle's; he stayed on. Sullivan put down his pencil and poured himself his end-of-the-day drink from the bottle he kept in the cabinet of rolled-up blueprints.

"Not that I don't sympathize with them. And not that I don't consider that egging on the bomb-throwers can be the same as throwing the bomb. But let me tell you something, Andrew. Each man has the thing he has to do first, above anything else. It can kill him, but he'll do it. He fights his fight. We fight ours. They fight theirs. They're men."

And he was off about construction, not destruction. Democracy, not anarchy. Anarch. Each man his own law. The idea of the highest freedom. But was man capable of such? Kropotkin—the Master had taken the trouble to read him. And Bakunin also. Their ideas came from a land of extreme oppression; the czars. Here in Chicago too there were czars, business czars, Marshall Field, Potter Palmer, George Pullman. A man like Charles Yerkes could buy the streets. Though he put in cable cars for the public, his bribing of aldermen so as to get the franchise vitiated democracy itself!

Who was building the Auditorium? A big capitalist. It ought to be the people. Henry George might have the right idea, the single tax, according to wealth. But always by common consent, not by dynamite.

No! Mr. Sullivan declared. He was against this hanging spree. But the people were crying out for it! That too was democracy, he growled, and drank.

Andrew did not know how to respond. These men were going to their destruction because they would not deny their beliefs. If he in his life should come to such a confrontation—and he had a dark premonition that he would, just as this seemed in some way to happen to every man who had an honest belief—then how would he decide? If there was something he believed in, against everyone around him, could he go through with his belief? "Truth Against the World," the ancient family motto proclaimed, over the chapel portico in River Valley. Need truth be always against?

In this mood he left for his uncle's.

With nightfall the weather had turned, and a fierce Chicago wind flapped Andrew's overcoat almost to a sail. The streets were deserted except for some carriages and on the sidewalk a few stray shivering panhandlers. A blotch of light at Henrici's. Willis was waiting at the I.C. station. They were almost silent on the short ride.

Uncle Bruce, Mother, and a few others were already in the study, where chairs had been arranged in a circle that made Andrew somehow think of a Quaker meeting, for there would be silences and then someone would have something to say. There was the lawyer, Clarence Darrow, and with him a Judge Altgeld, a small-headed man with intense eyes. Mrs. Darrow kept offering around plates of Aunt Genevieve's cookies. There was a Rabbi Hirsch, whose congregation were Reformed Jews, something like Protestants.

Professor Kaltenbrunner from the university hurried in with the latest extra: the anarchist who had blown himself up had just died in the prison hospital. Andrew saw his mother wipe away a tear.

His act, said the philosophy professor, had been the last effort of a human being asserting his free will. But Clarence Darrow declared Ling had been driven to it by an inevitable chain of circumstance. Uncle Bruce said, "God rest his soul." The rabbi said, "Amen," as did Mother and several others.

Silence endured for a moment, and then Darrow's friend, Judge Altgeld, declared that the conduct of the court in the case had been grossly at fault, even a travesty. A governor who could abet such legal lawlessness in the court, must be defeated in the next election. The labor movement must become a political movement. Only in this way could this horror serve some purpose.

Others spoke, decrying the yellow press that was making a children's holiday out of tomorrow's massacre.

It was then that the telephone rang. Uncle Bruce cried out, "Two are saved!" The governor had at the last moment accepted the letters of contrition of Fielden and Schwab. Commuted to life imprisonment! The telephone call was from the vigil at Amnesty headquarters. The French Chamber of Deputies had voted an appeal for clemency. In London, William Morris, Peter Kropotkin, George Bernard Shaw, Annie Besant were addressing an Amnesty meeting.

At the Bakery, Andrew and Willis read the final extra. The remaining four had gone to the scaffold. White muslin shrouds. Hooded, but heads high. Three hundred police with fixed bayonets surrounded the jail. All four, the paper reported, had been members of the International Workingmen's Association, started by Karl Marx.

Somehow, together with his human sympathy, Andrew felt as though this was outside his life. He had his own area of struggle, to get where he wanted. —This was a historic case, Willis declared.

10

ANDREW HAD insisted on having the wedding just as soon as Helena came home, even if it would still be two weeks before his birthday. Didn't he deserve the two weeks "for good behavior," he jollied his mother, and Marta gave in. Even Uncle Bruce. Mr. Hewlett—how could he withstand his daughter? Helena's mother gasped, there would be so little time to prepare! But what could be done against youthful passion?

How Andrew hated fuss and show, Helena knew, but for her wedding, *their* wedding, their marriage, her only wedding as a girl thought of it, Andrew was being an angel of patience. Even Marta marveled, and sister Tess made no snippy remarks! So Helena and her mother planned it small but perfect. The intimate family and friends. Her cousin and her dearest high-school chum and Tess even agreed, for bridesmaids, and her little brother in an Eton suit and collar. Uncle Bruce had three weddings to perform that morning and put theirs last so it wouldn't be hurried. And it went off to perfection, ah what an actor, how polite and gracious Andrew could be!

Marta, still a bit uncertain, still dreaming perhaps of

the famous architect's daughter that might have come along, kept repeating to Lorna Hewlett, "Just so they are happy! Let them be happy!"

So, arriving in Madison at late dusk, and shown their room, with the smirking bellboy handed a whole dollar, Helena started to change from her traveling costume and didn't say turn around, and she stood there in the lovely eyelet petticoat, so virginal, her arms and neck so pure, Andrew seized her, and the consummation took place, both impetuous, fearful, impassioned, confused. An amazing sudden feeling swept through him of possession, his, his, while her fingers pressed into his back and simultaneously each cried, "Mine!" "Mine!" And at this, both couldn't stop laughing.

It had perhaps been too impetuous, for, from off-color stories, Andrew had gathered it could go on for hours, even all night long. Indeed there was a blot of blood on the sheet. "Did it hurt?" "I didn't notice! It must have!" And they laughed. "We have to hang it out the window!"—an old medieval custom, he declared. And the thought crossed his mind: no more sheets soiled in torment.

And dressed and went down and ate ravenously; heads turned—honeymooners. What a beauty, he knew they must be saying. Then a walk by the shore, moonlit as though especially for them; she wanted to see the house where he had lived. It was lighted, he didn't know who was living there now, and didn't want to knock and ask if they could go in. But Helena espied the treehouse. Part of the branches were cleared away so that it stood out in the moonlight. Perhaps another boy was living here now, using Andrew's treehouse.

They went up early to their room. The second time it was much better, they were catching on! they laughed.

In the morning stroll, Helena looked so summery, muslin with lacy half-sleeves that she herself had crocheted. He liked the image of her sitting with her head bent over needlework.

Andrew showed her the university, the state buildings,

the Capitol. He wanted to see if Gamsey's new courthouse was done, see how it had come out. And there it stood, not yet open to use, but substantially completed, the dome already almost built.

As the sun lay across the curve of it, there suddenly returned to Andrew this morning's moment of awakening, the sun, and her nightgown still undone from last night; the morning sun on the round young breast had brought to him that same wild sense of mine! mine! Yet a reverence at the artistic perfection of the curve, the full form—no wonder, he recalled, he had suddenly comprehended, in the heightened perception of that first day in Chicago, no wonder men placed this form atop their houses of worship, even to the erect nipple! And just now as he walked with her, the sun's caress on the courthouse dome again confirmed what builders from time immemorial must have meant. How was it that it had taken him so long to see the meaning? What innocence! To have seen-and-not-seen! "You know why they put domes on buildings and churches?" Andrew asked Helena.

"To make them important?" She was hesitant; was this some architectural knowledge, or a kind of tease-riddle?

He chuckled. "What is the shape of a dome?"

"Why, like a globe. A half—" The she caught the look in his eye. Like last night, when they had sometimes been embarrassed, sometimes laughed at their discoveries. They had been both so ignorant! From girls, she had known even more than he! And now, as though by a mental message, she caught on. "Why, it's a breast!" Helena said, with such surprise at her never having seen it before that they both were convulsed. Then images appeared to Helena, pictures of the great St. Peter's dome by Michelangelo, of the great Capitol dome in Washington, and she had a flush of feminine pleasure as the thought came to her that men in their finest works gave this compliment to women. That was beautiful.

Then, right nearby—a steeple. He didn't have to say it. Helena blushed, and her laugh blurted out—and the two of them were laughing right there in the street, like silly children who had whispered a grown-up secret to each other.

But, as though fatedly, there had come a ghastly other-sight, oh no, not an evil omen, oh why did that thought at once rise in her, no! There could be no connection. A dreadful accident.

"Stay here!" Andrew cried and ran forward even an instant before Helena heard the slowly forming rumble. It was from inside the new court building, and now came a great rending sound, iron or the sky ripping. Crying out Andrew's name, no! God! he must not be hurt in there, she ran inside to be destroyed with him if that was to be. He was there safe just within the entrance, making backhand motions for her to get out. Men were stumbling out of whirls, clouds of plaster dust, cement, the dome up there was half tilted, was it an earthquake, screams came from up there, a man's hoarse screams. Andrew seized her and pulled her away, stay out here, don't worry for me, the worst is over. He rushed back inside. She could see he was careful and knew what he was doing, yet could not stifle the words, Oh be careful.

Now Andrew saw. One of those fake columns was sticking out askew like a broken bone, and the dome had tilted, and a worker up there was pinned in the iron structure screaming, then silent, dead. Helena must not see.

Andrew edged close enough: the base of the cracked column was awry where it had been imbedded, oh yes that brilliant architect Craig Kogan who had come into Gamsey's office had specified a broad circular pier for each base, so broad that the cheap contractor had filled in around the pillar with chunks of rubble instead of using solid concrete! Why hadn't the damn-fool architect inspected, discovered that fault during construction! Or had he seen, and let it pass! Andrew was in an elemental fury. A crime, the murder of a workman, a crime against the art itself, a fakery, the whole damn structure was a fakery, the false pillars, the needless showy dome, and they'd stick some damn statue on top, blindfolded Justice holding the scales.

Bells were clanging, an ambulance, police, he saw the partly wrapped body being clumsily lowered down the scaffolding. A growing crowd. "Stand back!" He made his way out and found her, drew her away. No, he began to say, he didn't know whether the workman was still alive, but over this came a peculiar thought: it was enough that this horror marred the first day of their honeymoon, he should not begin also with a lie, hadn't they vowed always the truth, so he said, "He's dead. His back was crushed." Guiding Helena away, he explained the cause of the catastrophe. Some contractor trying to save a little money. And behind it, fakery, grandeur.

There was an old wooden pier he knew where you could rent a rowboat, and rowing on the quiet lake, facing her, brought back calm, even a strange sense of a certain necessity, even on a honeymoon, not to forget the totality of existence, including evil.

When they had rowed back and he was helping Helena up onto the rickety pier, his mind was already distractedly busy, as though seizing any thought, to evade the scene of horror. A new pier here, on deep pylons, extending far out, for sailboat anchorages, and broadening to a circle at the end, where there could be a pleasant little refreshment stand, with sun umbrellas, ice cream and cakes.

"What are you thinking?"

He told her, and Helena softly smiled, as though she saw his effort to put that horror out of their minds.

That night their lovemaking was all in tenderness. They lay quietly for a time, in a solemn mood, for, much as Andrew had talked about what was behind the accident, with all his indignation over bad work, she had seen in her Andrew—more than ever before—the way he, like his family, had of turning every event, even an accident, to a moral meaning. Even though her own mother and father were conscientious and good churchgoers, with Andrew's family it seemed as though they were born with the Commandments engraved in their souls. It was the sorrow for the man and his family that haunted her, while Andrew kept talking of plain murder. Though Helena had not seen the body—Andrew had hurried her away and she had yielded—the death had been with her all day, in another way than his anger over it. As death. As it seemed to be for him also, now in his silence. And when they clasped each other, she thought: death, marriage, birth. A solemnity above joy was in the act of making love, as though now they were really taking their place in the order of the universe, now they were finally a grown man and woman, part of humanity, this was an act of replacement. And this intimate thought Helena felt as perhaps belonging to her as a woman; somehow she hesitated to communicate this to Andrew, her dear husband now, for she did not want his thoughts to turn in this moment to the death, if perchance it was indeed a life they were now creating. Yet in their almost solemn joining she sensed there came a new power from Andrew, as though asserting life by love, in defiance of the death he had witnessed. And perhaps he too was touched this night by the knowledge of procreation. She would count from this date, she assured herself, with again a flow of girlish-womanish secretiveness, even in the deepest doing with a man—she would count for herself, and know if it was so. (As in stories vaguely remembered from an Irish nursemaid, of a soul released by death, hovering, seeking to be born anew.) No, not actually the soul of the workman who had died there, but by some mysterious calculation of nature a soul of their combined souls. Only how? And here in their intense almost feverish clasping, her thoughts, she told herself, became almost without sense. A thought came of someone, she herself?, waiting to get into a crowded place—a theater? a crowded streetcar? —and "Have you got your ticket? Tickets first! Those with tickets please . . ." and her panic, I don't have a ticket, and Andrew saying, "I'll take you in," and his hand pulled her and she was with him, one with him . . . then a wild pulsing obliteration came within her, and she was astonished, as though she had for an instant seen a soul floating out of heaven, but already she couldn't recapture that bliss, yet in a way was still within it, and she clasped her young new husband to her while all within her resounded, "Mine! Mine!" and she felt at peace.

On the morning train, when the tracks entered the valley, even before Andrew could say this was his valley Helena already knew; the sun lay along the farmlands exactly as Andrew had described, with the river gleaming through long green fields, and on one side were round hills the shape of pillows. And within that first recognition Helena knew this was something her Andrew possessed where in her own life she had only Chicago.

At the small red station they were awaited. Aunt Nora, his second mother, sparse, with iron-rimmed specs, Andrew her adored one. And thank heaven in the instant of holding her off for inspection after the embrace, the pronouncement "Andrew, you chose well!" And all of them laughed, and Helena was no longer the least bit anxious. As they climbed up on the surrey, Aunt Nora handed Andrew the reins.

The village was a street of stores, hay-grain-and-feed, two groceries, a blacksmith, with farm wagons hitched to a railing like pictures in a school reader.

As they rolled beyond, on the broad dirt road, he would call off the names of each uncle, pointing with the buggy whip to some house down a side lane, Uncle James, and back a distance behind it she could see the house and barns of the pioneer grandfather, yes the real thing, pioneers in a covered wagon, and here down the river, a hundred acres, Uncle Peter's, after he divided up giving a hundred each to his two sons, and beyond on the other bank, up that hillside, other cousins of Andrew had bought land, oh it was a domain.

Now the horse clopped over a wooden bridge, to the hill that was Aunt Nora's, Helena could already glimpse, between the trees, Aunt Nora's white frame house, where they would stay; but, more important, exciting, there now came into view, slightly up the slope of the hill, much larger than she had imagined, the Home School that Andrew had built last summer, that large, broad house with arches on the porch, as expert as anything a full-fledged architect—she caught herself—a much older architect could have built. Last summer while they were separated, and he was being treated like only a boy, too young to know his mind, he had done this whole big house! His boss, Mr. Olmstead, the finest architect of half Kenwood, couldn't have done anything finer. She squeezed Andrew's arm.

"I know you want first of all to look at what Andrew built," his Aunt Nora read her thoughts. Oh, Helena loved her already, even feeling easier with her somehow than with Andrew's mother. So, hurrying up the green slope, they toured the inside, his aunt extolling all his clever ideas, the thoughtfulness, the chairs and desks to the right height for each grade, and, in the sleeping rooms, the way each cot had little shelves and cubbyholes built half around so each child had a place of its own, yet couldn't feel lonely.

Everything was the latest; even way out here in the countryside Andrew had put in the latest inside plumbing with bathrooms and water closets. And the kitchen was a model of practicality, he had thought out the problem of feeding forty children and teachers and housekeepers and all, so that the sink and the stoves and the dishracks and a broad central worktable were all placed so you didn't have to run back and forth and get in each other's way.

Now, behind the house, the playgrounds.

They climbed farther up the slope, to the rounded top, from which they saw the entire domain, both sides of the valley, cut through, no, more like held together, by the gently winding luminous river. Right up here on this open hilltop, Aunt Nora said, her eyes alight with an idea all prepared for her wonderful nephew, right here she wanted to put up a windmill, but not one of those iron-legged things that every farmer was buying, instead she wanted Andrew to design something beautiful. It would stand like a tower over the entire valley.

Already, Helena felt she could almost see Andrew's thoughts, ideas forming. He looked so intent, and Aunt Nora, in a further gush of love, cried out that she wanted them to know, right now she wanted them to know, one day this would all be Andrew's, this entire hill and all, she had put it in her will.

Their bedroom was large and filled with flowers. Large vases of gladioli, and bronze-gold carnations, and pink roses. Here in this same room, Helena could feel how Andrew had longed for her last summer, he had described the room to her, the Chinese screen, the brass bedstead. It was delicious now, a triumph, being with him where he had been so lonesome for her. "I know you'll change it around, the minute I'm out, Andrew!" his aunt laughed gaily, for it seemed a joke about Andrew that he rearranged furniture. Even in the hotel room, Helena had been surprised when just for the few nights he had pushed the bed so they could see the morning sun and, he jested, the sun could see them. Now immediately Nora was gone he was at it. The flowers, on a little low table against the Chinese screen— but no! they killed the pattern of the screen. He moved the flower stand against the wall, Helena holding the vase. And the screen itself—Aunt Nora had unfolded it around a dressing table installed for his bride. Andrew pulled one section open. —But why? —The better to watch her half dressed, he said, and Helena flushed with joy.

The great family dinner was across the bridge at the big house, as they called it, the house of the eldest brother, his Uncle Matthew, and on the broad porch Helena met them all, trying to keep them by their names, and who was married to whom, and which of his cousins were the children of which uncles and aunts, and which of the young boys and girls were the children of which cousins. And everyone was so good-natured. Oh, you'll sort us out, you've got a lifetime!

The uncles, broad-bearded, stood tall and sturdy, with large powerful hands, and had dressed for her in Sunday clothes. The women were strong-looking, too; a few seemed bursting in their corsets, their gowns with fine lace inserts, even close to the latest fashions. People of substance, they looked, all, they were like country squires. Then, when they went to the double-long tables, extending from the dining room into the parlor, there appeared, in a black preacher coat, the father of them all, Grandfather Enoch, surely into his eighties, a snow-white beard, triumphant small stone-blue eyes, apple-red cheeks, a small frame in the midst of those enormous sons and tall daughters and large-boned grandchildren. All the grown-ups seemed larger than Andrew. And this great abundance of life had issued—this gathering was so Biblical, she could not help, as she looked at the patriarch, saying to herself the words "issued from his loins," and feeling like blushing.

The patriarch's wife had passed away, so that a curious idea came to Helena: his aloneness made him more like God. And as he blessed her, her knees felt watery. All bowed their heads while, in a slow firm tone, as though for them to realize the meaning of each word, he pronounced the grace.

They visited the farms of the uncles, the cousins, they walked out in the fields and Andrew even lent a hand in the labor, now and again. They visited his cousin Susan and her husband, Gus, and admired the barn, already extended where Gus now had forty head of cattle, all beauties, and his whitewashed cheesemaking room, hung with ribbons from the County Fair, and Susan called Helena's attention to Andrew's covered walk from the house to the barn, that Gus appreciated in every blistering winter storm.

Helena helped Susan bathe her two darling babies, real rambunctious boys. And later in a woman-to-woman moment Sue told her, "You know, Andrew was the most *innocent . . .*" Yes, right up to when he left for Chicago. And Susan would bet that even after he got to that wicked city—she'd bet that even until Helena, he had never really kissed a girl.

With only a touch of wonder whether she should be jealous—for surely Andrew had been sweet on this somewhat older cousin—but with a stronger sense of feminine kinship because of this, Helena imagined that Susan might have taught him a few things had he been ready. Just as well he hadn't been!

Susan was asking, "Did he take you to our cave?"

Why "our"? And Susan perhaps sensed her feeling, for she remarked it was the cave of all the Daniels kids, their place for secret powwows.

And so Andrew showed her the place, on the next hill to Aunt Nora's, not secret at all! From the cave ledge, there was even a broader view of the entire river valley. Then, as they slipped through the rounded entrance, he informed her that caves were where the rounded-arch entrance of Mr. Sullivan, and Richardson before him, came from, and all the way back to the Roman architects, and even Byzantium. Impressed by that last word, and by Andrew's knowledge, Helena was surprised that she hadn't noticed the cave connection before, and glad that again she understood something that was important to her Andrew. "Now I see! But of course!" she told him.

Gazing outward, Andrew recalled that moment a few years ago, just after his father had left home, when he was standing here with Susan: the feeling of a woman beside you. Now he had his own wife. And crazily, real newlyweds, and no one could come up here without being heard, they made cave-love.

Arranging her clothing, Helena found her impetuous husband squatting outside, sketching something; an idea had come to him. Partly she felt piqued that in the midst of their passion he must have been planning—but, looking closer, she was proud, even excited, that this beautiful idea had been born in their love.

He had thought, for Aunt Nora's hilltop, first of Dutch windmills, round towers, the wheel a counter-roundness, and began with that idea. But such a tower, sixty feet high as he saw it, would have to withstand tremendous wind force when the real wintry blasts came along. Even though round, the wind-blasted surface, with the down-pulling weight of the wheel . . . ? To keep it from toppling, perhaps use a very deep concrete foundation? Something else was coming in to his mind, a counterform, supporting the round tower—sharing the weight of the wheel. More like two forms leaning against each other, supporting each other. Even more than leaning together—clasped. A vertical element, cleaving right into the round tower. Imbedded. If the wind hit the exposed part of the vertical, the tower held the forepart clasped. Or, if the wind struck the tower, the vertical shaft gave it support, by cleaving right into it, married. The wheel like a flower out of the union, a huge gay Fourth of July whirligig.

Helena had come behind him and was leaning over his shoulder. "Oh, Andrew, it's beautiful!" He wrote atop the sketch, "Tower of Love."

Bolted down into concrete, it would withstand a typhoon. Andrew explained: each form supported the other. Married. "Oh." She concentrated. —Support? Did they lean against each other? —More than that. He drew a cross section. One element—the upright—goes right inside the round . . . Her "Oh!" was the other kind, she was blushing, afire. Oh, you devil! Then her laughter, still a bit girlish. "I suppose it's all right if they're married!"

Moving the drafting table to the window, like last summer for the Home School, Andrew designed the windmill atop the hill. Aunt Nora was enchanted. Old Neil Hagedorn the carpenter was called. "Never stand up against a real gale," he declared. Andrew explained the bolting system into the cement foundation. Hagedorn shrugged.

His uncles sat in consultation. It would cost twice as much as one of those iron tripod contraptions, which were good and practical, Uncle Peter had one on his own farm. If Nora really wanted this, said Uncle Matthew, the cost could be managed. His wife, Tabitha, declared this would be the crowning glory of the valley. In the end, looking at the young couple, Uncle Peter grinned and gave in. Let it be built. "I'll build 'er but I won't be responsible," said Hagedorn.

"But I will," Andrew retorted.

In Oak Park, now that their house was nearly ready for them to move in, the tract owner, Mr. Philip Whaley, had taken to dropping by for a look. He might bring along a potential client, for Whaley was now advertising his residential plots, ideal for young couples. And here was the example, a most admirable young couple, the young husband an architect employed by the finest firm in Chicago, Adler and Sullivan, who were building the great Auditorium going up on Michigan Avenue. Have a look at the house young Andrew Lane had designed for himself. Very inexpensive, too!

Naturally it was not a big house, but inside it had plenty of room, and—with a wink at the young couple—it was expandable!

Or, for an elderly couple thinking of retiring to this lovely quiet exclusive suburb, Whaley would say, What bigger was needed? Less work to take care of.

Perhaps his constantly dragging in prospective lot-buyers to see the house was a nuisance, but Phil reminded Helena: every buyer of a lot here was a potential client for the architect on the spot.

The first client turned out to be Whaley himself. What his tract really needed was something more of a showplace; he should be attracting people of real substance, businessmen, even bankers. And so he decided to put up a large, impressive residence, and sell it ready built. He'd make out better than on selling the building plot alone, and besides, that kind of sample would raise the value of the rest of his plots. Andrew had worked for Allan Olmstead—and that was exactly the type of house he'd like to see out here, Whaley said. Substantial-looking. Only of course he couldn't risk too much cash until he saw how things would go.

"Like, a large house with a small cost?" Andrew repeated, and Whaley laughed along. Exactly! Expensive-looking but not costing too much! There were always ways to save, as he saw on Andrew's own house. For instance, that first floor layout—no corridors. Just turn from the entrance into the parlor, then turn around the fireplace to the dining room. Practically no doors. You needn't point it out as a way to save money, but just take Andrew's own argument: made the whole place look larger, friendlier too.

Now, for this sample residence, as to the architect's fee—now was the time for Andrew to pick up that adjoining corner lot on which he had put a deposit. An excellent deal, a fair deal for both of them. Whaley gave his lopsided grin, and stuck out his hand.

Of course, strictly speaking, Andrew pointed out to Helena, all of his services were due to Adler and Sullivan. Especially now in the crush of finishing the Auditorium. But he would be doing the Whaley job just as he was doing their own house, on his own time, nights and Sundays. Why, she said, wasn't it enough that he was always bringing work home, and besides, staying on at the office after all the men had gone home, gabbing with Mr. Sullivan . . .

Now, he stayed because he wanted to, just to hear the Master talk. —Oh yes, but who else in the office took work home? —Never mind. He was interested in what he was doing, maybe the others were not.

The realtor's proposition had already set his mind going. He was seeing houses, shapes—a touch of the Olmstead ampleness, the Queen Anne cozy richness, but still, one could do something with a large residence; the great corner bay window that Whaley had sketched with his hands—it needn't stick out like a fat stomach, but could be part of an integral shape. As in that famous Dutch painting

—Holbein?—the swelling curve of a pregnant woman. Soon enough he'd have the perfect model!

And then—money. Surely Whaley would get him other commissions, and those would be for cash. Though he was now earning the highest salary at the office, there was never enough. Extras, on the house. Electricity. If a huge theater like the Auditorium was going to be illuminated by Thomas Edison's new incandescent bulbs, every home would be, in the future. So, in addition to gas piping, the house had to have electric wiring, even though there was as yet no power supply in Oak Park. He could install a generator operated on benzine. Their house would be the first in Oak Park to have electricity!

While they still stayed at his mother's, the first article to be moved into their own house was Andrew's drawing table. This way he wouldn't keep Helena up, working in their room to all hours.

Sometimes now he remained downtown so late she was already in bed before he got home, and rather than wake her Andrew would go across straight to his study to work on the Whaley house. If Helena waked, and saw the lamplight across the way, she would slip on something and make coffee and go over and sit with him for a bit. He would tell her of his day.

The Master and the Chief were being driven to distraction by the Commodore, who was already planning the grand gala opening. Adelina Patti, whom he absolutely must present for the great occasion, had to be booked a year in advance. And once the date was set, the Auditorium had better be ready!

Even steady old Adler was at the end of his nerves. It was killing him, he said. The Auditorium stage was the largest grand-opera stage ever, and the machinery for raising the huge curtain was coming specially built from England. There were storms at sea. The ship was overdue.

Commodore Peck himself would suddenly appear in the unfinished hall, clambering up ladders with surprising agility for his years, and giving impossible suggestions, even orders to the workmen. As soon as Peck was gone, Adler would have to straighten things out again. For instance, today— But Andrew saw that Helena didn't really follow his explanations, his darling had no sense of construction —why should she? She must go back to bed, he wouldn't be long.

No MATTER how he tried to tear himself away from his contractor each morning so as to catch his train, there was always one more detail to explain. The first few times, late, there was only a winking jibe from a draftsman, about new-lyweds in the morning. But another time, the Chief noticed. "Andrew, till your house is done, you can come in an hour later, so you can go over the job before leaving." "I'll stay an hour later to make it up," Andrew said. Adler shook his head, no need, no need. "You're always working late anyway."

So it was that one morning as he was explaining once more to Lonergan that it was no oversight in the plan, but that he really wanted no wall between parlor and dining room, his extra hour slipped away. As he was hurrying off, he was blocked by an awkward young fellow who had stopped a buggy where the gate would be if Andrew had a fence and gate, which he didn't intend to have. This fellow half stumbled off his trap, probably wanted to ask a direction, but the fellow was asking when he could see the house owner.

"You're seeing him," Andrew said, "and he's in a hurry to catch a train to get to work."

"Oh—then let me drive you to the station." The fellow was quicker-minded than he looked. "Save you time."

"Save me time, but if you're selling something you're wasting yours."

"S'all right." They were off. "Noticed you're building a house, and I sell furniture." Well, give him credit, scouting around unfinished houses was one way to find prospects.

"Sorry, but you hit the wrong party. I'm building my house all right, but I'm also building the furniture."

"What? How's that?" Not with disappointment but with curiosity.

"Furniture should be part of the whole scheme," Andrew began, he could never resist a chance to expound. "Don't want to put you out of business, but as I'm an architect, that's the idea. Makes it harmonious."

"Oh yes. Oh yes." Saw the idea. "Say, that's interesting. But some items like—" he stabbed—"stoves? Kitchen stove? You're not going to build *that* yourself?" They both laughed.

"I'm out of cash. Have to cook in the fireplace, I guess, like my grandparents did."

The fellow chuckled, but said, "No you don't. We sell on credit. Fifty cents a week. I come around and collect. That's really the main part of my job—collecting installments. That's why they give me this horse and buggy, my territory is Austin, but I thought I'd see what's out a bit farther. I try to sell things, too, on the side."

The station was in sight. Still a few minutes.

"Say, if you don't mind, I'd like to see some of that fit-in furniture when you do it. I won't try to sell you anything," the salesman said in all seriousness. Odd kind of a bird, Andrew thought, wearing a real high collar to look businesslike. Just about his own age, maybe even a year or two younger.

"Stop any time. We're going at the furniture in a few weeks. Found a German cabinetmaker on Van Buren Street."

The fellow actually pulled out a business card. "Name's Dreiser, Theodore Dreiser. Anything you need. Get you a reduction."

"Mine's Andrew Lane. All right, come around. I may even buy a kitchen stove."

"Might save your house from burning down, in case you try to cook on the floor." He burbled a laugh at his own joke. Big buck teeth. "Say," Andrew heard over the train whistle as he hurried to the platform, "say, I sell fire insurance too!" And the burbling laugh. "But what I really want to be is a writer. I'm trying to get a job on a newspaper. Know anybody?"

For chairs, Andrew hit on a back design of long thin slats at close intervals, from the top down to the floor, like harp strings, harmonizing with the instrument that stood by the inglenook. That old carpenter on Van Buren Street was doing a beautiful job.

And as for his pagoda-shaped lampshade designs, even Lonergan's workmen exclaimed, "Say! Real original!" For the wrought iron, there was Jack Slater, the ironworks fellow with whom he had been carrying out the Auditorium designs; Jack got every touch, to perfection.

A kitchen stove arrived, gift of the Hewletts, a monster with nickel-plated frills and flounces that you'd need a slave to polish. Ah! If he'd only bought his own from that what's-his-name! Never did come around. Maybe he'd got his newspaper job.

Helena was carrying high, which his mother said meant a boy. The two of them were busy with all the womanish things now, and in a way this left Andrew free. Helena was strong, fine, busy around the house to the very last —good thing he hadn't hit on one of those delicate women who took to bed in wan helplessness. Once or twice Dr. Eagan had a look at her, the old Oak Park practitioner who had born everybody in the place, he claimed, didn't believe in interfering with nature, call him when the pains came.

It was a daytime birth, a bit ahead of schedule. Andrew got the news from his mother on the telephone: a boy, eight pounds, perfect, only an hour of labor, for a first child—lucky!

He took the next train home, Helena was amazing, wanted to get up! The room was flooded with embroideries, laces, baby things. He held the creature for an instant, feeling odd, with all the women, her mother, his mother, his sister, who was even being sweet to Helena—all this womankind . . . Well, at least there was one more male— the baby! But also, did a woman feel . . . like that moment in himself when a design was born? But shouldn't he also feel this? After all, he was part of it! And for some woman- ish reason they were laughing at him.

For a boy, they had already agreed on Wallace as the name, Wally, the name of Helena's mother's favorite brother, who had died young.

What he enjoyed was watching that little animal feed- ing. Andrew only hoped that afterward the glorious twin domes of her breasts wouldn't droop. He caught women- talk about it, now and again, rub camphor, or other such intimate knowledge. One sure way, he overheard from a high-school chum of Helena's, the best way for the breasts, was to get started on the next one!

THAT DETERMINED Miss Addams had found a building for her settlement, said Uncle Bruce. Certain alterations would have to be made for her purposes, and perhaps Andrew could go out there and have a look?

Uncle Bruce had been a wonderful help, Miss Addams said, his parishioner had traced the ownership of the house and persuaded the late Mr. Hull's daughter to lease it to them without rent! Bruce Daniels had even turned over his pulpit one Sunday to Jane Addams to explain her project, and substantial contributions had resulted!

With Willis, one lunchtime, Andrew went out to Halstead Street. The house, built when this had been a good neighborhood, now had a secondhand-furniture store in what must have been the parlor. Upstairs, Andrew and Willis found Miss Addams talking half-English, half-Italian to a lad named Emilio, from the downstairs store, who was painting her hallway. She and another of her band, Miss Lathorp, the first woman lawyer in Chicago, were already installed.

Miss Addams quickly filled them with facts about the

neighborhood; there were two hundred and fifty saloons and nine churches in the area. What must be set into motion first was a day nursery, here upstairs for the time being, but they were persuading the downstairs furniture man to move, and eventually the nursery should be there, downstairs, a nursery where working mothers could leave their bambinos during the day, and a lecture hall in the evenings. Now, to start with, this floor. A few partitions would have to be removed, and that was what she hoped to learn from them, they must tell her which walls were structural—she smiled, showing she understood the architectural term—and which could safely be torn down. A spark had already flown from her to Willis, Andrew noticed. Willis was making notations, he had come to life in a way Andrew had never seen. They toured the floor, tapping walls. Miss Addams planned to open an employment office up here, and next to that a penny bank. And of course a health clinic—that ought to be financed by the city, and Julia Lathorp was getting after the Nineteenth Ward alderman . . . Emilio followed from room to room; in his overalls he carried a thick folding carpenter's rule, taking pleasure in whipping it out and extending it on the plaster-cracked old walls wherever Willis pointed.

Downstairs, the parlor, once vacated, could hold over a hundred chairs. Enough for lectures, musicales, even theatricals! But how to combine the space, for a day nursery? Simple. One of those simple combinations that gave Andrew pleasure. Considering the high ceiling, put a stage platform at the far end, with sliding front panels to the understage, and there was the storage space. Stack the folding chairs in there during the day, pull them out for the evening and push in the kindergarten paraphernalia.

Even before Willis could draw up the details, those women had got the furniture dealer to move. Oh, to his own advantage! Florence Kelly had found him a shop on North Clark Street and suggested he letter ANTIQUES on his window instead of SECOND HAND FURNITURE. She and Jane would send him customers. Indeed, amidst his clutter were family items brought over by Italian and Greek immigrants that were veritable treasures.

A dramatic club had already been organized, and the Hull House Players were going to start off with *Ghosts*, the first Henrik Ibsen performance in Chicago! Exactly, Andrew remarked to Helena, exactly what the patrons of that neighborhood's 250 saloons thirsted for.

All Chicago's celebrities were at the opening. The sort of people, Helena half whispered, they really should get to know. There was even Eugene Field, she pointed out, her favorite poet in the *Evening Post*. There was also Mr. Darrow, suddenly a celebrity because of a front-page article in the *Tribune* about a big speech he had made at a Single Tax meeting, outdoing Henry George himself. Helena complimented him. Oh, that big fuss in the paper had got him a city job, he was now a prosecutor, Mr. Darrow said. All he had to do was send people to jail, but he feared he wouldn't be very good at it.

And in the intermission, Andrew found himself confronted by a familiar face, bucktoothed—why, yes, it was that loquacious fellow who had tried to sell him a kitchen stove! "Say, remember me? I never got to come back to see your furniture, I really wanted to, Mr. Lane—I was real curious about your ideas," but the fact was he had just at that time had a stroke of luck, his English teacher from his high school in Indiana where they had lived before his mother moved with the children to Chicago, well, his old high-school teacher had sent him a letter, she was going to pay out of her own savings for a year in college for him! She believed he was a literary genius—"You see, she knew that's what I always wanted to be, a writer"—and so by her generosity he had gone off to college. His older brother Paul had got a job singing in a show, that way the family got some help. Now that he was back he was determined to get into the writing game, he was hanging around the papers; a reporter had told him, "Just hang around, run errands, anything, one day the city editor will notice you and give you a chance." Say, he had a friend in the cast of the play, a very talented young actress, the one in the first act, he had met her here at the Hull House; in fact, as he wanted to write plays, they had let him stay around during rehearsals to get the hang of it. This play was very daring, the things people didn't dare talk about, but this neighborhood was filled with prostitutes who passed on the disease . . .

All the while as he talked, the gawky fellow seemed actually to be devouring Helena, she was indeed wonderfully blooming tonight, her young-mother flesh aglow, Andrew couldn't blame the fellow. But just then the young actress came out, the would-be playwright introduced her, charming, Helena told her she had been excellent, and the two went off. Just then a crowd movement left them facing John Wellborn Root, who recognized Andrew, smiling. He was with his wife and her sister, the poetess Harriet Monroe, a nice young woman who was, as Andrew knew, writing the ode for the opening of the Auditorium, it would be sung by a chorus of three hundred voices on the great stage. They too were whirled off in the crowd, and Helena remarked to Andrew, "Why didn't you introduce me to him?" "Who?" "That tall, skinny writer fellow you were talking to." "Oh, you mean *he* was talking. Trouble was, I couldn't remember his name."

The eighth of December. The eighth! It would be ready! In the last weeks, with the worried Commodore Peck darting into the office a dozen times a day, shaking his head, how could the seats, at last arrived, possibly be installed in time? And where were the gilt chairs for the special box on the side of the stage, did they expect the President of the United States to sit on a crate! And where was the dressing-room divan for Adelina Patti? And with the Master, when Peck left the office, taking out his temper on whoever was nearest, Andrew would slip off to the job.

The indestructible, solid Dankmar Adler was sometimes so fatigued he kept having to lean against the wall to regain his balance. Despite all of the Chief's carefully calculated schedules, another storm on the Atlantic had held back the hydraulic stage machinery. He had lost his humor, and no longer quoted his Eleventh Commandment, Thou Shalt Not leave things to the last minute.

But in spite of all, it was going to be perfect! It was going to be one great unified work of art. As the Master's final designs came, the decorative shields, the foliage impasto for the pillars and ceiling of the Long Bar—longest in the world—the pure excitement of achievement grew. The entire staff was feeling a kind of intoxication of boundless energy. And on the fifth, Andrew was in the hall supervising the final touches, the emblazonment above the proscenium of the motto the Master had chosen: "Oh soft melodious spring, first born of life and love."

That night Andrew stood with the Chief and the Master as the lights were tested, the golden and ivory ceiling arches in ever-expanding succession sending down their glow. Someone had cried out, "Let there be light," and as the bright incandescent bulbs began to reveal the harmony of side murals, the impasto foliage, the wrought iron, a delight of achievement spread, and no one felt the cry out of place.

A manmade brilliance as never before.

The great hall was the perfection of the Master's fully developed style. Yes, Andrew told himself, the richness was appropriate to grand opera. And yet far within, unacknowledged, even to himself, that unwanted questioning voice was there: how would he have done it? Wasn't it all overdressed, overcharged? Maybe appropriate enough for opera, but for a pure hall of music? Perhaps bare, a great, perfect form, unadorned? Doubtless he was jealous. Again came his feeling of being perhaps a dozen years too young, that if he had only been of the time of Root, and Sullivan, and Solon Beman, these giants whose buildings were filling the Chicago skies . . .

With the lights coming totally ablaze, the workers, who were scattered at a hundred tasks through the vast hall, on the stage, in the balcony fixing down seats, all broke out into a kind of hurrah—in an emotion that swept all of them together, a hurrah not only for the Master and the Chief and even the Commodore, but for themselves, for everyone who had had a hand in this.

Helena's father had been thoughtful enough to acquire a batch of seats for the opening, the moment they were placed on sale, for the entire family. And also for the next night's premiere of Adelina Patti in *Romeo and Juliet!* The women held endless discussions on colors, patterns; Mother had even got Tess to send her designs from New York, where she was drawing for a fashion magazine, of the latest in opera gowns. Tess, with her usual humor, had drawn in for Helena a huge tulle Windsor tie, *à la* Andrew! She really was incorrigible!

It was just the week when the downtown had begun to take on its Christmas atmosphere; the windows of the great stores were bordered in evergreen, at night all State Street blazed with electric arc lights, and before the Auditorium huge spotlight beams. In the afternoon, snow had fallen, but as by celestial benevolence the storm had stopped, across Michigan Avenue the open space was like a great white fleece.

Extra platoons of police held back the crowd of gawkers, and as Chicago's masters and their ladies stepped down hostlers hurried their carriages away, keeping the line moving.

By outcries from the crowd, the great names resounded; it was almost—Helena squeezed Andrew's arm —almost like in British plays when arriving lordships are announced. In the vast sparkling lobby the women began unwrapping their fur cloaks, mantles, coats; the lobby despite its size was soon glutted, for who would go to their seats without waiting for the arrival of Mrs. McCormick and her party. And Mrs. Potter Palmer, sure to be wearing her diamond tiara and her collar of pearls. And Mrs. Marshall Field might outdo her with one enormously valuable ruby worn quite naturally so that unless you knew, you didn't notice. But the fashion editors would. Oh, tomorrow's papers would be filled.

And now came George Pullman with his wife, upholstered, Andrew had to remark, as fancily as a Pullman sleeper. Helena hardly had a chance to utter an appreciative giggle, for again came that special crowd whoosh and a thrust toward the doors, almost preventing the entrance of the most stared-at couple of all, that car-line buccaneer, Mr. Charles Yerkes, appearing with his redhead mistress-into-wife, you had to admit she looked more regal, more society than Society, even if they had given her the freeze. And what a man of power—not ferocious at all but so sure of himself, a real American titan.

There—there! Where the peacock feathers bobbed above the crowd—that surely would be Mrs. Potter Palmer! The society queen's party swarmed around her so thickly it was impossible to get a view, and meanwhile Helena's father stood awed by the sight of the Long Bar—the longest in the world, Andrew assured him, calling Hewlett's attention to the great pillars with their decorative shields, like Old-World heraldic emblazonment except that these emblems were prairie grasses, the Master's favorite motif. With Helena breaking in, "Andrew did them all, just from a few scribbles!" Her mother took her eyes from the fashion display for an instant, and admired, but oh there was too much to see. And the new Edison lights, like beams of sunlight! It was Lorna Hewlett who found the word: the pinnacle—this was the pinnacle of civilization! Chicago had surely beaten Paris!

In the swirl of scents, like walking through a hothouse of mingled aromas, they were wafted along into the Auditorium itself, and here the blaze of splendor was beyond what had already been experienced. The high, ever-expanding arches, like an entry into heaven itself, like God's heavens opening into still loftier and greater heavens, thus were the arches with their banks of light. Overwhelmed, Andrew's father-in-law asked the number, and Andrew was able to tell him. Marta exclaimed at the form of the great hall, like a vast, vast eggshell, and yet like the firmament —a celestial eggshell!

Incongruously, for Helena, just then there came a thought, a kind of disloyal intrusion that she pushed back in her mind, for it was about something basic and important to Andrew and it troubled her like when in school she couldn't quite grasp what the geometry teacher declared was a clear, absolute rule. So many times she had heard him repeating the great architectural law that from the outside form of a building you should be able to tell what it was meant for inside. The same rule had been refined by the Master himself into the words "Form follows function" —so how did this building follow their basic law? From the outside it was a huge square block, with a tower rising like a top hat over part of the structure. And here, coming inside the opera auditorium, the ceiling was a rounded shell. This part you could see was for music, but how would you guess this shape from the outside?

In all this excitement and glory and triumph, there passed through Helena a slight uncertainty, whether she really understood something that was so important to Andrew, but the great hall was so beautiful, so overwhelming, this was sheer joy, and he was looking at her to see it in her face as she knew she had looked at him when he first held their baby. "Oh, Andrew it's perfect!" Helena cried out, while her mother handed her the ivory-inlaid opera glasses, for then the greatest awe-sound of all arose, as the royal party of the Infanta of Spain appeared, Helena's mother whispering—though with Mr. Adler's acoustics the whisper echoed all around them, but, after all, the news had been in the society columns how Mrs. Potter Palmer had snubbed the Infanta by not inviting her to the reception at the Gold Coast castle!

From the rows around them came firefly diamond-ray blazes as women arranged themselves in their seats but kept squirming around to stare. Andrew meanwhile was looking around for the others from the office. The Master sat in the front row, with his mother, brother and sister-in-law. Willis was a few rows behind, with his sister and mother; Andrew caught his eye, exchanged a grin. Now, in the side sections, and farther back, he began to make out draftsmen, engineers, all seeming a bit strange in their soup-and-fish, with their women beside them; some he had to look twice to recognize.

Now the orchestra struck up "Hail to the Chief," everybody rising, to behold the Presidential party arriving at the special box, the President of the United States and his spouse, followed by Commodore Peck and Mrs. Peck; the President was the Commodore's guest in his Prairie Avenue mansion, all knew; and the President bowed from the flag-garlanded box. Then, to the second box, came the Vice-President and his party. The forecurtain rose, revealing the assembled dignitaries, governor, mayor, civic leaders. "The Star Spangled Banner" burst forth, enveloping stage and hall, who could avoid tears at what Man, American Man, hath wrought! Now the second curtain rose, revealing, row on rising row, the choral singers. On the stage, a diminutive woman with just the right twinkle of golden sequins on her gown stepped forth; in a tone almost awed at itself Miss Harriet Monroe the poetess began to recite her dedication "Ode to the Auditorium."

> "Hail to thee, fair Chicago! On thy brow
> America, thy mother, lays a crown . . ."

At that moment Andrew saw Dankmar Adler slip into his seat next to his family while giving a reassuring nod to Mr. Sullivan. It was about the hydraulic workings of the curtain, Andrew knew, for it had been giving trouble to the last minute. As the Chief settled back, Andrew, relieved, also settled back, while the Augmented Apollo Choir sang:

> "Thine elder sisters from the peopled East,
> Thronged by the surging sea,

> *Lift foaming cups to pledge thy crownal feast,*
> *Calling, All hail to thee!"*

The row of luminaries in their special boxes, their gleaming white shirtfronts like some archaic symbolic armor, their all-beaming faces framed in finely barbered beards, for an instant brought to Andrew a vision of Assyrian monarchs, as on some ancient frieze. The mayor, the governor, the President! The Vice-President, the Commodore. Helena was torn between watching them and following the text as Miss Monroe intoned:

> *". . . robes impearled*
> *Mantles of purple, jewels for thy brow,*
> *Splendors new wrought to rouse the aging world.*
> *Thine shall they be. Here to thy hall of State,*
> *Thine Auditorium of liberty. . . .*
> *New thoughts are thine; new visions rise*
> *Before they clear prophetic eyes."*

And the great chorus joined:

> *"Out of the dark an eagle to the sun*
> *Speeds on. Awake! 'Tis day! The night is done."*

Amidst official and general applause, the poetess made a kind of half-bow, half-curtsy, and withdrew—and just then Andrew caught only a few rows before them the large Roman head of her brother-in-law, John Wellborn Root, and his wife sitting proud.

Now came speeches. The President of the United States! Praise, praise and glory, Chicago, risen from the ashes, symbol of human resilience, courage, energy, the spirit of *I Will!* Not only rebuilt, but built to a new destiny. Not only the city of industry, of commerce, the beating heart to which all railways, the nation's arteries, flowed, but also the center of American culture, expressed in this glorious edifice, the greatest in the world! Yet not in the spirit of grandeur but of beauty, of service to the entire populace.

Then spoke the Vice-President, the governor, the mayor, and finally the creator of all this, the Commodore, who had made possible this great civic monument to music.

The Commodore was modest. He praised all those who had helped him realize his dream, the public-spirited investors, the civic leaders; "all praise is due to the architects," Andrew heard before Commodore Peck went on to others, and only then Andrew realized that the architects had not even been named.

He saw Sullivan's head, held erect. Could the omission be an oversight? Andrew wondered: Or was it simply that to the entrepreneur it was not the architect of all this who really counted: not Michelangelo, but the Medici.

Yet, great praise flowed forth now for this great edifice, this house where the masterpieces of artistic genius, in that most composite of all the arts, the opera, were combined. All talents were blended to reach the combined human senses, eye and ear, the sensibilities, mind and heart, brought together in this hall, not for the royal and the rich alone, as in palaces in the past, but now and for the future —to the people of the most American of cities, the new world metropolis, Chicago!

In Andrew, through all these words, an impulse kept repeating itself: "I too, one day. I too."

Now there walked from the wings the possessor of America's, the world's, sweetest voice, Adelina Patti, amidst thunderous applause for herself, even for each person's being here and participating in the Pinnacle. Then utter quiet, as all settled to hear Adelina Patti sing "Home Sweet Home."

12

NOW THEY were set in the top of the tower. At the very top, the highest point in Chicago. The Master, from whose corner window one saw the endless expanse of the lake, like an ocean, window one saw the endless expanse of the lake, like an ocean, and the northward expanse of the city; the Chief, from whose windows the view swerved from the lake's edge in a semicircle over the city, north and west. Then came Andrew's own small office gazing over the downtown, with glimpses of the Chicago River, then westward onto the monotonous checkerboard blocks, thinning out to his own Oak Park, with a few lanes and railway lines seen on clear days reaching beyond to the farmlands, the prairie.

From the elevator corridor, a door led out to a narrow all-around balcony, to which noted visitors to Chicago were brought almost daily, bigwigs, and the world-famous singers and musicians for the Auditorium; Andrew soon took the attitude of not bothering to notice, except of course the day of Sarah Bernhardt, with the papers describing her deep ecstatic sigh, "Chicago is America!"

On the two floors below, lined board to board, were

the designers, the draftsmen. Only Andrew was with the chiefs. He was the pencil in the Master's hand.

But what about his own hand, his own eye, his own head? Working full steam all the time up till now on the Auditorium details, twice as fast as any other draftsman, he nevertheless had some unformed urgency inside him, a thing of himself. Get handed a sketch and fill it in, your mind in the track of another man's mind, while the whole time, maybe in rebellion, his own mind kept going another way. The Master and indeed all of them, John Root, Major Jenney, kept going up, up, up. He was thinking sidewise. Horizontal to their vertical. Down to earth, he said, to himself. Not merely to be contrary. Even on his first day in Chicago he had experienced an inner revolt to the vertical idea, the chase for going higher, the ensuing congestion, the unnatural life it would bring.

No, it was not as Helena said, that he was simply contrary. Even Helena, when she got a chance to get downtown—for she was a real suburban housewife, she now half complained, bound to her baby, and helping Marta in the kindergarten, even lucky if she could get to a luncheon of the Oak Park Women's Club—so when she could get downtown for a shopping spree, she too gawked at the latest, the tallest. Even while their new office in the Auditorium was at the highest point, you could look out and see the steel framework of the next record-breaker, that would top them all, the Masonic Temple, twenty-one floors, the work of Mr. Burnham and Mr. Root. Why did Andrew still argue against all this? Maybe it was only because *he* wasn't doing it, she teased.

Yet Andrew, at the bakery-lunch, would expound: What could you create, invent, in the vertical office building, except to go higher? And that was engineering, not architecture.

To SUMMON him the Master had usually only to glance toward Andrew's open door. Sometimes, a low "Andrew?"

Or occasionally Sullivan with a sketch in his hand would himself step to the door.

This time he appeared with a client. Andrew had already seen the man, involved in the prospective Stock Exchange Building. Solid, medium age, London-tailored-looking. Mr. Elgar Lattimer wanted a residence. "Andrew is the man for you," the Master told the client, "he does our residences." So? A new role! The pencil in his own hand!

Indeed, Andrew was aware that the Master, exhausted to the point of collapse by that last rush on the Auditorium, had been persuaded by the Chief to go off for a rest—though the Chief himself looked equally drawn and weary. Mr. Sullivan was going south, to New Orleans.

So here was freedom, without even a supervising eye. The stockbroker owned a corner lot on the North Side, just off the lake. When Andrew asked, "Did you or your wife have anything particular in mind?" Mr. Lattimer said, "You're the architect." Adding, with a short laugh, "Nothing showy. We're not competing with Mrs. Potter Palmer."

Only at the site did Andrew get the point of Mr. Lattimer's remark, for his lot, on Astor Street, was directly behind the Potter Palmer castle. Indeed, it would block their view of the lake. A solid wall, then, a back turned to the monstrosity.

Since the lot was on a corner, why not use the quiet street for open space, and build right up to the sidewalk? An honest city house.

Brick was his first thought, a citylike brick surface, flat roof, no peaks, no dormers, and, as a horizontal affirmation, edge the roof brim in white limestone all around. Beneath the top-floor windows, a narrow white-stone string-course, a reaffirmation. A white-faced entrance, overhung by an elegant second-floor loggia, with a row of slender columns, and recessed for a contrapuntal movement inward. Thus, an in-and-out flow of space.

For since he had built his own house something had

been coming to him, a sense of carving a structure in space itself. Wasn't that what he had tried, the flow from room to room, the modeling of the interior space? The art was where it had always been, in the balance of open and closed areas—the flow of space.

Exhilarated, hungry too, as always when ideas came pouring, Andrew was almost the first at the round table in the Bakery, but Willis was soon there, and Tony McArdle, from Burnham and Root's, and then, with his darting eyes, Bob Mann, who had recently left the Olmstead menagerie to strike out on his own. Andrew kept expounding his new notions. The idea of putting into the simple, horizontal house frame the technical advantages gained from the vertical skyscraper. Where could you go in the vertical design, one floor just like the other, except higher? "And higher fees accordingly!" said Tony, who worked for Holabird and Roche; instead of puttering with a single residence, and having the client's wife drive you out of your mind over every detail, you simply extended your steel frame a couple of floors higher, and the fee went up with the girders! As for Andrew's precious aesthetics, all that nonsense was over, there were no more fake columns, in fact everybody was now doing the Chicago style, unadorned walls, wide Chicago windows, all over the U.S.A. So what was so noble about the horizontal versus the vertical?

Why, read Emerson! Read Thoreau! Man's very nature. His contact with the earth. At least, when a man got home from his cubicle office, let him walk into his house, not into a crowded elevator. Space should enter into the home, not be walled out. Andrew couldn't stop expounding. Maybe Helena was right when she laughed that, with him, whatever he did had to be the most important thing anyone was doing. How long could you go on in architecture blowing one note? Andrew demanded of his friends. Up, up, up! Like a horn-blower who thought it was art to hold on to the same note the longest! Where was plasticity? In a residence, a home, he argued, you were free to shape, to use space. Why, only this morning . . .

He felt excited, his ideas flowing out of themselves, out of hearing himself talk. And they were listening, concentrated.

The food came. God, he was famished.

Hurrying into the Studio Building to have a look—for himself as well as for the Master—at new prints arrived at Sato's, Andrew found himself in the elevator with the girl of the piquant face, the young actress from that Ibsen play at Hull House, the friend of that fellow Dreiser.

"Oh, the actress!" he said to her smile; momentarily he couldn't think of her name. "Oh, the architect!" she echoed with light mockery. "Mr. Andrew Lane!" And her name now came to him, Estrella. Quite theatrical. —How was her friend Mr. Dreiser the newspaperman, he asked, and she uttered a trilly laugh, amused sorrow. "Gone." "Gone?" "Mmm-hm." Where to? Her little shrug said blown away.

She too got off on Sato's floor. Her place was next door, also with a view of the lake. Stop in for a moment and see it? Why not.

Oriental throw on the sofa bed, peacock feathers in a vase, India print on the wall; she was studying voice, diction, and in answer to his unspoken question declared, "Oh, I couldn't afford this place, I'm a West Side girl." Adding, with her sophisticated amusement, "I'm a kept woman."

And of her own, because the story was so funny, Estrella recited the tale of poor Teddy—that was Dreiser— who had got himself caught here, and kicked out of the little job he had finally clawed onto at the *Journal*. Indeed, got himself shipped right out of Chicago! Sucking her lower lip, the actress gazed out the window, bemused. Did he know, could he guess, who was keeping her, paying for this studio and her lessons and all? None other than the big woman-eater, Mr. Charles Yerkes! Oh, that devil was really overwhelming, fascinating, he had seen her in the play, he was going to make her into a Sarah Bernhardt, her laughter bubbled. But really she had wanted to know the feeling, what it was in him that conquered all the women! And her elfin look—was she flirting with him? Why, since she scarcely knew him, all this instant, intimate confession? Now her voice became warm, low. About poor dear Teddy. Really poor. He had been hanging around Hull House looking starved, it was before he even had the few dollars space rates at the *Journal*, and he was so earnest wanting to learn about plays, he really appealed to her, and when he got kicked out of his rooming house she had taken him in. Oh, the Big Man only dropped in once or twice a week, her turn! But—and her laughter rose in anticipation—Mr. Yerkes was *possessive!* And would Andrew imagine, he had got his wind up, and actually planted a detective in the room across the hall! She ran to the door, opened it to show him the opposite doorway. And this spy had called the Big Man, who came and burst in, catching poor Teddy stretched on the divan for a snooze! Gulping her laughter, the actress acted the scene, all parts. Poor Teddy! And, *sotto voce*, she really was *very* fond of him, she really thought he had talent, perhaps genius! Then *afterward*— the Big Man let it pass, still kept her, but the revenge he took on poor Teddy! With all his power, he got to the editor of the *Journal*. Wanted that Dreiser fellow out of Chicago! Well, the editor was decent enough to get Teddy a job in St. Louis, a real reporter, full-time! A high trill of laughter, abruptly halted as though for applause. —A glass of sherry? Courtesy of Charles Yerkes? "Tell me, has your lovely wife had the baby? A boy! How wonderful!"

It came over Andrew that nothing was meant, this girl was simply lonesome here. Loved to talk.

Then, with Chicago well over a million and a half, with more great railroads hauling in beef and pork to kill, with the Rockefellers donating millions for the university to be expanded farther south in pure fake Gothic, with a deadly scarlet-fever epidemic in the hovels around Hull House, so that Marta had to halt her volunteer work in the kindergarten there, for fear of bringing back the infection to little Wally, and indeed to her own kindergarten—in that same season came the call to celebrate four hundred years of America, for 1892 approached. And what city would be chosen for the quadricentennial?

Boston, Helena read, offered to restage the Tea Party every day! But the year to be celebrated was 1492, not 1776! Columbus, Ohio? New York, after all—the biggest! But Chicago's big men went down to Washington and outbid them all, five million dollars! Sold to Chicago!

Feverish architectural discussions for the "World's Columbian Exposition" were in progress. Something truly American! All the way from the wigwam theme, actually seriously proposed, to the idea of a single skyscraper, highest ever, the real Chicago idea. At last the Master was aroused from his exhaustion after the Auditorium. He saw all the exhibits and expositions placed in one immense building, with immense elevators hauling the crowds to the top floor, from which they would wander down through great displays of industry, science, inventions, art, commerce, American history.

Now came a new burst of argument: if there was to be only one structure, who should design it? —A competition! The American way! —No! A team of Chicago's greatest architects, cried the *Journal*. —But why let Chicago be accused of hogging the show? wrote a wag in the *Tribune*. Why not invite the five leading architects in America!

Once, after the staff had gone, while Andrew awaited Helena—they were to go to Hull House to hear Clarence Darrow and John Altgeld in their exciting debate, Which is more important, heredity or environment?—he suggested that the Master might like to join them. Indeed he might, Sullivan said, but tonight he wanted to work on an idea. And he pulled back the cover sheet on the "secret" board, the second drawing table that he kept for himself.

And there Andrew saw huge upstanding forms, massed in ascending blocks, stepped up at various levels to a central tower. It must be forty stories high! The Master's vision, his idea—Andrew at once understood—for the exposition.

In that one glance he knew: here was the vision, the art of the skyscraper form. Why, every child with building blocks—he himself in his mother's kindergarten—had done this instinctively! Why hadn't this inevitable conception come out of him? Andrew buried his moment of jealousy. It was the Master's.

And he, Andrew, had been the first to whom it was shown!

"What do you think?" the Master asked.

"You've done it!"

Outdone would be the 1889 Paris fair that had startled the world with the Eiffel Tower. For this was not simply a bravura outline, this was functional. From the Columbian Exposition onward would come vast setback structures in this style. Altitude, yes, but with open, dynamic space all around, with vistas, rather than chasms for streets. Thus the future American cities would be built!

Was he going to show it to Burnham?

Well, what for? They had their own ideas. This was a concept he had been playing with, possibly for a big insurance company that had approached him. The Master lowered back the cover sheet.

Not only had Andrew been given a look at the great plan, doubtless at the future of great American architecture, but even through the Master's proud reticence he had been given a glimpse of the other side, the backside of progress. The pulling backward. Sullivan had shown him this vision as a part of his education, his apprenticeship. For Mr. Burnham and his noted friends and advisers, such as the distinguished Stanford White, the New York marvel with his Madison Square Gardens, for circuses, indeed had their own conception. That word "eclecticism." Taste a bit from Athens, a morsel from Rome, make a big salad.

John Root had been preparing ideas, lagoons, canals for Venetian gondoliers, sketches for main buildings, the single-structure idea abandoned. Yet perhaps if they saw this sketch, they would still return to the concept? No; too late, too many ambitions involved. The Master had shown him his vision, Andrew felt, out of the need for someone to see. And also as a teaching. A surge of—yes, love came to Andrew, for this was the way of the Master, this teaching was not only of the form of the great structure, but of the pulling down to be expected from the pygmies. "Impossible to build, in the limited time." "Too costly." It would have to be a steel structure, instead of knock-downs.

The big decision could no longer be delayed, and to the great conclave Mr. Burnham, now officially in command, had invited Great Ones from all over America. To decide on Chicago's show.

The Master shrugged. From their high windows he gazed down on the January blizzard, and finally said, "All right. Come along." The meeting was at John Root's house.

The street had the quiet elegance you thought of as Londonish—distinguished small residences with shined brass door knockers—and there was something of a Dickensian jovial decency in John Root himself, greeting them in full evening dress as, he apologized, he had an early dinner engagement.

Root's sister-in-law, the distinguished poetess Harriet Monroe, was settling the distinguished guests in the circle of Chippendale chairs.

And presently the same old arguments were under way, pursued in tones of civilized moderation, everyone respectful to everyone. Yet underneath, Andrew felt hostilities, even war. While Chicago was honored as the host, Mr. Burnham proclaimed, the quadricentennial was of course a national celebration and therefore, he argued, a local character should be avoided. . . . Already, Andrew felt Sullivan stiffening. And while it was a national celebration, it was of international scope; each participating nation must be free to express its own genius. . . . Eclecticism.

Wasn't America itself composed of peoples from all cultures? America encompassed, and *harmonized*, the great cultures of the past.

Andrew had an impulse to leap up and answer, but restrained himself almost as though Helena were pinching his arm, whispering, "You're the youngest here, keep your mouth shut." Only now he heard some of the very things he would have said—and it was John Root speaking. Why should Europe, why should the world, come to Chicago to see what they saw at home? It was Chicago, America, they would want to see, the architecture that Chicago was bringing to the world, it was American genius! A single structure had given the Paris fair a world image—the Eiffel Tower. Why not exceed it, not with a tower that was an empty gesture, but the American way, a tower in *use?*

John Root was looking straight at the Master—had he been shown the sketch? Root was caught by a constricting cough. When he resumed, his eyes were watering, he really had a bad cold. "America, in four centuries, from the wigwam to the skyscraper . . ." But his argument trailed off.

The talk went in circles. Mrs. Root and the poetess served tea; all the while Andrew had a sinking feeling, that something great was slipping away. Oh, Mr. Sullivan had known even before. Now it was a unified motif that was to be agreed upon, a style that had never faded, Mr. Burnham said, because it was perhaps the perfection in architectural expression: the classical Greece of white marble columns . . .

"No!" Andrew wanted to cry out.

. . . easily simulated . . .

It was breaking up at last, with important men being helped on with their fur-collared coats, John Root hurrying out bareheaded in the blizzard to see them to their carriages, coughing as he came back, but with his fine smile aglow. Especially, as Root clasped the Master's hand, Andrew felt a promise that they would still somehow stand together—no Parthenon, but America, the new! Even if eclectic! And Andrew found his own hand grasped, too.

A few days later, John Root had developed pneumonia. Then John Root was dead.

When he told it at home to Helena, Andrew could not help saying, "There goes the last chance for the exposition." Even as he said the words, Andrew caught Helena's look, not so much reproachful as uncertain. What sort of person was he, really? Did architecture matter above life itself?

And so it was finally decided. What could be more beautiful than Classic Renaissance? A harmony of classic forms, a statement of world civilization. An America matured, in four hundred years, from a raw primitive land of log cabins, America caught up to absorb the culture of world history.

As a unifying element all structures were to have a cornice line not exceeding sixty feet. And all buildings were to be sprayed in a smooth white stucco, suggesting marble, a mush called "staff." "The icing on a wedding cake!" Andrew heard from the Master. The main buildings would be around a long lagoon, out of which would rise a forty-foot statue of Columbia. The official structures were being parceled out by the committee: industry, commerce, education, fine arts, a women's building too, to be designed by a female architect.

The spoils were apportioned. Not in vain had the architects journeyed from all over the land; few left without a commission. Four of the central structures were to be designed by Chicagoans, and to Adler and Sullivan came the Transportation Building.

The inner committee posed for photographs, with Gutzon Borglum the sculptor, close friend of Stanford White, remarking that never since the Renaissance in Italy had there been such a gathering of artists as here in Chicago.

With that little gleam in his eye—Andrew knew the portent—his Master set to work. No Parthenon columns. A vast Richardsonian arch for the entrance, a blaze of brilliant colors, telescoping inward—each concentric band so bold in ornament, the building would draw all eyes from the vistas of white staff.

Soon enough the committee decided that his Transportation Building could not be accommodated in the Court of Honor, and thus the unharmonious modern note was shunted to a side canal.

Once or twice they rode out together to the site; swarms of workingmen. At the Fine Arts Building, hundreds of mock columns going up, completely around the entire structure. Every visitor to the exposition who had a house to build would go home and build Greco-Roman columns, the Master growled. All over America! Architecture would take half a century to recover. In the press he declared, "American architecture has been halted just at the moment when it should have been proclaimed!"

At the Architects Club, Andrew noticed, Sullivan was more and more likely to remain standing by himself.

HURRYING FROM his North Side town house for the Lattimers to the South Side exposition grounds, Andrew found himself picking up still another task.

He had, in his whirling, stopped late one afternoon in Sato's shop, as Mr. Sullivan had left several prints to be framed. The bespectacled Japanese, ever in his alpaca duster, went to the back room to fetch the newest additions for the Master's collection, first as always slipping onto his viewing-table a few recently arrived works, for Andrew to enjoy. Returning with the package, Sato murmured that he had a favor to ask if he might. As Andrew was aware, one of Sato's daughters (there were three, American born, occasionally glimpsed in the shop, all beauties) was married to the Japanese Consul, of a most distinguished Tokyo family of imperial connection, and as Japan was participating in the Columbian Exposition with the construction of a traditional teahouse, there had arisen a certain problem

150

in which the distinguished architectural firm to which Mr. Lane belonged would perhaps kindly give advice.

In short, they were stuck with putting up the house. It had been taken apart and shipped; a construction master with a few helpers had indeed come with the *ho-o-dan*, but there were problems on the site.

It seemed that they didn't understand about a foundation. In Japan, each supporting post rested on a hollow-topped stone. Andrew supervised a shallow perimeter foundation. Sato's gratitude was boundless. The Consul would remember!

And as if he wasn't busy enough, Aunt Nora sent a notice from the *Madison Times* about an architectural contest for a municipal boathouse. Surely this was just for him! The site turned out to be just where, on his honeymoon, he had rented a rowboat and even remarked to Helena that a boathouse ought to replace the old pier. And an idea came. Just there, a small inlet cut through between hills to a lagoon where the boats could be kept; he visualized the refectory perched above, spanning the inlet, a roof with far-extended eaves. He'd do it!

The three Columbus caravels sat on Centennial Pond, perfectly reproduced, garishly painted, the white columns and domes of all the surrounding buildings reflected in the water, together with the enormous Columbia statue rising and outdoing, people said, the Statue of Liberty in New York Harbor. Andrew at moments even guiltily caught himself with a throb of excitement, as when watching a brass-band parade. Everyone would marvel. What use were the Master's lone fulminations? Indeed, against the very seduction of all this prettiness, the lovely magic bridges over the waterways, of Burnham's wonderland of transplanted trees and ordered-up nature, Andrew at times had to hold on to his conviction that the great opportunity had been killed, all this was wrong, wrong.

And so it was in a totally different mood than for the

opening of the Auditorium that he walked with Helena, with his special pass, leading their family group into the grounds. A hundred thousand were swarming to the event. And just as for the Auditorium, it was to open with a dedication ode by the official poetess, Harriet Monroe, whose family traced itself to the *Mayflower.*

It was said, Helena told him as she opened a copy of the special edition of the ode, that Miss Monroe had insisted on being paid three thousand dollars to write the poem! And a New York paper which had secured a copy and printed it in advance was having to pay damages of five thousand dollars! And Helena read, as they paused before the gargantuan statue:

> *Columbia, on thy brow are dewy flowers . . .*

(There they were, in stone.)

> *Plucked from the wide prairies, from mighty hills—*
> *Lo! toward this day have led the steadfast hours*
> *Now to thy hope the world its beaker fills!*
> *Lo! Clan on clan,*
> *The embattled nations gather to be one!. . .*

As he walked with Helena, arm in arm, Andrew felt her wonder, her excitement, and with that squeeze of hers she cried, "Oh Andrew, it *is* beautiful, it *is!*" Surely she well knew, from all the past months during the construction, what he thought of it, but Andrew told himself Helena didn't mean to contradict him, her taste was the taste of all. Hadn't he himself at times nearly been carried away by this prettiness?

Why need a man's wife, at this moment, think of the course of American architecture? Still, his wife could at least also say something that showed she realized this was all cheap popular taste, she could show she understood why he, and those few in the Master's camp, were disgusted. His moment of disappointment in Helena was not,

Andrew told himself, of any consequence. He liked her to be natural. Yet there was a physical impulse to take his arm away so as not to feel her clutching it to share with him all that was before them: the reflected rows of columns, the white swans, the gondolas.

In the vast hall of the Manufacturers Building, with five thousand voices swelling the orchestra and military bands, they heard Miss Monroe's elegy:

> *Clasp hands as brothers 'neath Columbia's shield*
> *Upraise her banner to the shining sun,*
> *Along her blessed shore*
> *One heart, one song, one dream*
> *Man shall be freed forevermore*
> *And love shall be supreme. . . .*

Helena followed the words in print—as with a hymn in church.

> *Then surging through the vastness, rise once more*
> *The aureoled heirs of light, who onward bore*
> *Through darksome times and trackless realms of truth*
> *The flag of beauty, the torch of truth . . .*

> *For lo!*
> *For now Democracy doth wake and rise*
> *From the sweet sloth of youth . . .*

Yet, in Helena, there came for an instant that odd sense one sometimes feels as of having dropped, lost something—but no, her parasol, purse, everything was there— and in the same confused instant she knew that this sense of something dropped, lost, had to do with her husband. Thus she identified him even in this fleeting moment, "my husband." Not just Andrew. She had known, from all his months-long fulminations, that there might be a difficulty today, and indeed as "my husband" she had long ago decided on a certain wifely rule: it was best when Andrew was in one of his architectural passions not to dispute his ideas.

Indeed, she kept in mind that Andrew of course knew and understood his beloved architecture better than she. Just as there were things about children she knew and understood better than he. He appreciated and loved the babies, of course, but he didn't seem to have the impulse on his own to fondle, pet, hug them; she had been told that many fathers were like this. A mother—something happened in her just by the baby-smell alone, but not always in a father. When the infant got a bit older, toddled, said funny muddled words, like Wally already, a man like Andrew began to tickle and play with him, but not for long at a time. Andrew did these things as though he knew that a young father should do them, rather than on a father's impulse. Well, he was a genius, his buildings were his babies, and she had made up her mind that even when a new building didn't excite her she would always show a pride, an excitement, at what her husband had made.

Now here—what was wrong with her feeling great beauty, an almost heavenly beauty, in the white buildings around the lagoon? And the hundreds of perfectly spaced Grecian pillars surrounding the Fine Arts Building? Hadn't Mr. Burnham himself declared in the papers that this was the most beautiful building ever built, even more perfect than the ancient, real Greek temples in Greece? As Mr. Burnham had said, the Greeks had reached architectural perfection, so why seek anything better! Oh, she wouldn't provoke her husband; to Andrew and his Master, this was a fight over principle. They wanted to produce American architecture. But did that mean you shouldn't enjoy any other kind? No, Helena would not let herself be intimidated. Indeed, having your own opinion was part of the new freedom of women. This lovely wonderland aroused in her the joy of beauty. Of course, that joy was highest when it was shared. So it had been between them when, as sweethearts, they first walked together along the lakeshore, not so far from this spot, once in a soft snowfall that was so beautiful it was like something holy, you held your breath.

And as though to get back to ordinary life they had pelted each other with snowballs.

Yet—as clusters of white-foamy fountain sprays shot up even to the height of the white columns all around, Helena this time held back her impulse to clutch Andrew's arm for joined delight; instead she had that sensation as of something dropped, perhaps lost. In the intimacy of husband and wife, where each sometimes feels what is in the other before it is known to the other, she felt in him a closing away from her.

To Andrew, all disagreements in taste had been unimportant until now, such as Helena's never really getting excited over Japanese prints except the easy ones like Hiroshige's rain on the bridge. But that his wife couldn't see, couldn't understand, with him, the basic importance of the argument here, couldn't *see* how this exposition like a white fog would spread and blind the public, the nation, blind it to all that was meant in new American architecture—this was a profound disappointment, a rift; his wife simply was not together with him in all that was deepest in him—a man's work.

He did love Helena, even more now as his "baby-maker." There had been that peak of joy when they saw their Tower of Love standing aloft on the hill, though to him it had been the structure, and to her the sentiment. But here now was a basic stand in his life activity in which Helena simply did not stand with him. Here now—couldn't she *see!*—here was the betrayal of his fundamental principle. And the Master's. Standing virtually alone, against all this easy popular glitter. Thus Andrew felt an added pang that even his own wife . . . Well, why should he expect more of her? Why should she resist what everyone delighted in? Why couldn't he dismiss all this as a big picnic, a white circus? Yet a premonition remained, that at some time, if things went wrong between them, it might reach back to this moment.

And Helena too, through Andrew, felt an apprehension. But perhaps no worse than when she noticed his roving eye halted on an unusually pretty woman. She would simply distract him. So now, "Oh, look!" The Christopher Columbus caravels sitting at the other end of the lagoon, brightly caparisoned with pennants and flags.

A band played "America the Beautiful."

There, as they approached the footbridge to the Wooded Island with its Japanese tearoom, a whole flock of young women passed before them, escorted, it seemed, by a single, tall young man in a straw hat. Helena recognized him: from Hull House a year or so ago, that fellow with the actress friend, what was his name—Dreiser.

A booming "Hello!" His face had filled out. His voice too, This charming flock—all schoolteachers from St. Louis. He, a reporter on the *St. Louis Post*, was escorting them, so as to write up their visit to the Columbian Exposition.

"Well! Say!" Together they entered the Japanese Temple teahouse, the *ho-o-dan*, the fellow talk-talking. Writing a novel. His brother was now a big success in a Broadway show, singing his own songs. Dresser, the brother called himself, instead of Dreiser.

With all his talking, the fellow didn't miss a single detail of the *ho-o-dan*. Looked very flimsy. Andrew gave him pointers on the structure. Having tea, squatting on a mat, Dreiser talked of his sister, here in Chicago, ran off to New York with a married man! Manager of a downtown bar. "Left his wife and two daughters!" Dreiser repeated. Turned up outside his sister's place one day, waited until she emerged, and swept her into a carriage. Just about kidnapped her! Some story, huh? Now, his other sister . . . There too was a story. Could make the great American novel, he only half jested. Ah, he hadn't accomplished anything yet. "While you," he admired Andrew, "already had a hand in all this." When he had gazed out over the lagoon of the Court of Honor, with that monumental sculpture and the all-white buildings, ah, what any over-

156

whelming feeling one had, of beauty, sheer beauty! "You're in the majority," Andrew couldn't help saying. Still, the would-be author was somehow a likable fellow. At least, the disagreement with Helena had passed.

13

TRAINS TO Chicago were crowded, there weren't enough Pullman cars, there weren't enough hotels, the exposition grounds swarmed, visitors from all over the world declared that Chicago soon would surpass New York and become the greatest city in the world.

With the new governor, John Altgeld, behind it, the eight-hour day for women became law in Illinois. Also, new laws to regulate child labor were passed. Uncle Bruce and Jane Addams were organizing the Universal Peace Congress; statesmen and leaders of the women's movement were coming from everywhere. The congress was a triumph, and even though it was the eighth month of her new pregnancy, Helena made the journey from Oak Park to meet Andrew at the vast assembly hall, and hear Uncle Bruce introduce Jane. At the storm of applause Helena remarked, in some surprise, "But she is a world-famous woman!" And they had known her right from the start.

The Madison boathouse prize Andrew took as though it had been inevitable. Just mentioned it to the Master by way of needing a few days to go up and get construction started. Sullivan snorted with pleasure, "That's the way to do it! Win the competitions!" While Adler beamed on him as though Andrew were his own son.

Helena gave a party. Phil Whaley was opening a new section, and every client would be introduced to his prizewinning architect! Whaley himself wanted a third house built, for a brother-in-law, of course it was to be the same design as the other two, so Whaley got Andrew to cut down the fee, but it was worth it as he brought more commissions. Indeed Andrew, on top of his work at his job, couldn't keep up with it all, he had to hire a draftsman, but where would he put him? Now, finally, he must put up a studio on that corner lot he had got from Whaley. And at the same time the house had to be enlarged, he had to borrow, Helena complained that she was always running out of household money and here he was, building!

In the middle of the fair, with everything going fine, Governor Altgeld had to go and pardon the remaining Haymarket anarchists. Three of them were still in prison, it seemed. Everyone said Clarence Darrow had put him up to it. Helena read out to Andrew the editorial in the *Tribune*, declaring that the governor's action was an encouragement to bombers and assassins.

Willis brought stories of tenants moving out of Altgeld's downtown Unity Building, into which he had sunk every penny. He had a half-million-dollar mortgage to pay, and now the only tenants Altgeld could get were labor unions and radical organizations that couldn't afford to pay their rent.

And as the summer waned, more and more troubles filled the papers. After her confinement—their first girl, and such a sweet, good baby—Helena less than ever got into the city, but Andrew brought back such ugly tales. The number of beggars downtown had grown so that from the office to the train he'd be panhandled a dozen times in every block.

The construction of the exposition had brought to

Chicago tens of thousands of workmen, swarms of Italians and Poles newly arrived from the old country, mostly pick-and-shovel men. Now they were all looking for work.

The mission houses were full, and homeless men were being allowed to sleep in the police stations. Even the corridors of the City Hall were filled at night with drifters stretched on the floor. The papers were full of awful tales. As they saw their children go hungry, fathers of families were caught stealing. And the trouble was not only in Chicago. There were big strikes in the coal mines, and an anarchist walked into the office of a mine owner and shot him. The anarchist was that Alexander Berkman who lived in free love with that revolutionist Emma Goldman, she had talked at Hull House. The mine owner survived, so Berkman only got sent to jail, instead of being hung.

Then one day just after the exposition closed, Mayor Harrison went himself to answer the door when the bell rang, and a young man shot him dead. At first everyone was sure it was an anarchist again, that was what came of Governor Altgeld letting them free, but the murderer turned out to be a crazy. He had gone straight to the police and handed in his pistol, saying, "I shot him," giving his name, Prendergast, and declaring that the mayor deserved to be shot because he had not given this Prendergast the job of building the elevated railway. He was crazy as a loon, but in the trial the jury sentenced him to be hung. Clarence Darrow proclaimed he couldn't stand to see a man hung for being insane, and he got Prendergast a second trial. Darrow's speeches were in all the papers, he had everybody in tears. Helena even thought he went too far, because he told the jury that if this poor deranged young man was going to be hung by the neck until dead, it was they, each of them, that had to do it. Anyway, they did it and the lunatic was hung.

One night Andrew came home quite late, he had stayed on at the office sitting with the Master, who was in a gloomy mood. That insurance company in Omaha had finally decided not to build. His greatest, his most revolutionary design, the one that might have been for the exposition. Business was bad. Several other commissions the firm had expected to get had gone to others.

"He drinking?" Helena asked.

Oh . . . Andrew shrugged that away. Certain things about the Master Helena didn't see the way he did, the whole thing together. That eclectic crowd the Master had blasted over the exposition now had it in for him. Nor did it help when articles came out in France and all over Europe declaring that Sullivan and Adler's Transportation Building was the only new, American structure at the whole Columbian Exposition. A French company was even putting out miniature replicas of his entrance arch, like replicas of the Eiffel Tower. Well, that was a vindication, but it didn't dispose the clique any more favorably toward him. He'd slap the cork into the bottle and put it away.

Then there was the toga story, by now all over town. Straight from the exposition, a banker had come to the office with a project for a downtown skyscraper, with the bank on the ground floor. Of course he wanted the entrance impressive. Broad stairs, to a porch with Roman columns. So Louis Sullivan had asked him, "Do you expect to go to work in a Roman toga?"

Another big commission gone elsewhere.

Yet here in Oak Park, with the buildings Andrew was doing on his own time, there seemed even to be an increase in demand, so perhaps things weren't so bad after all. True, one reason more people wanted Andrew Lane houses was that his structure was economical. By his bringing down the ceiling height, not only materials and labor costs came down, but in winter, heating costs. Now he was trying another idea. Raising up or even eliminating the basement.

What use was a basement anyway, Andrew argued at the round table—a basement was a damp hole that got cluttered up with broken chairs, bundles of old newspapers, and junk that people ought to throw away. As for the furnace, put it behind the kitchen and you could reach it without bumping your head or shins stumbling down a rickety basement stairway.

Then, on the South Side, for a doctor friend of Uncle Bruce, he designed a clean-cut brick residence, somewhat in the style of the Lattimer, but with a wrought-iron balcony, and set the house directly on a concrete slab. As soon as it was built, the client's brother wanted the same. He had a lot near the lake, on Dorchester.

The slab had just been poured, on Dorchester.

As it happened, the Master, after his mother's death, had turned over the family house to his married brother, and himself moved to the Windermere Hotel, by the lake. And on a Sunday-morning stroll, troubled over shrinking commissions, idled draftsmen, whom to let go next, Sullivan avoided Jackson Park, it would only remind him of their damned exposition. He was strolling down Dorchester when his eye was caught by a flat expanse of concrete —a foundation. Were others taking up Andrew Lane's idea? But on second glance, he could virtually read the open floor plan, and a certainty came, it was Andrew himself, sneaking another job here.

Naturally, he had been aware of those houses in Oak Park, built on Andrew's own street; well—Sunday work. But this was something else. And how much of this sort of thing was Andrew Lane doing all over Chicago?

No, he was not a tough employer. He was glad to have his men enter competitions and didn't mind if they kept busy by doing that work right in the office. There was that boathouse competition in Madison that Andrew had won.

What made him angry, Sullivan told himself, was the sneakiness. Had Andrew asked to take on a job on his own time, especially now that things were slack, he would not have refused. Though correctly the client should have been referred to the office. With the usual bonus. But this was plain sneaky. And when the fellow was receiving the highest pay on the staff. And when, only last week, the firm had had to let go two men who had been there since the start.

And so, first thing Monday morning, he called in his protégé.

"That your job on Dorchester?" Sullivan asked.

All the arguments, explanations, welled up and left Andrew mute, overwhelmed with a sense not so much of guilt as of loss. He had lost his Master. What use to protest that he had not used a moment of office time?

It was as though all was already said in the silence between them. From the Master: You well know that a man owes all of his professional effort to the firm. You signed a contract. From Andrew: I gladly did all you ever asked of me, giving extra time without a second thought. So Andrew continued, aloud, "As you feel the way you do, I'm resigning." When he had full control again he added, "I would like to ask you to send me the mortgage on my house. I believe it is about paid up. I'll pay the rest."

A tone so impersonal came—a tone he had never heard before in the Master. "No, I can't do that. The loan was made by the firm."

"I've said, I'll pay it out in full."

Sullivan was silent, even turning away, in that imperious manner he could assume: the matter was closed.

There was nothing but to go into his side office, collect his drawing implements, snap shut the Keuffel and Esser and slip it into his pocket. As he was doing so, Adler opened the door. "I didn't know about this, Andrew." He approached and even put a hand on Andrew's shoulder. "I'll see that the mortgage is sent to you. There's no need to worry about that. I'm sorry this happened, sorry to see you leave." Then he seemed to feel that something more was needed, for the parting. "You know my father was a rabbi; yours was a preacher. My father liked to tell stories about an old rabbi from Biblical times, named Gamzu. It was really a nickname. Because whatever disaster happened, he was in the habit of saying, *'Gam zu l'tovah.'* That means, this too is for the best. Andrew, you shouldn't have any difficulty. Things are slow for big jobs, but people are always building homes, that's your best field, and you already have a good start, a reputation. Even if it led to this unfortunate trouble! *Gam zu l'tovah!*" He chuckled reassuringly. It crossed Andrew's mind that he had hardly ever heard the Chief use Jewish sayings the way some Jews were always doing. "It could really be a good thing for you if you start now on your own. In times like these people look for something new and economical."

Adler put out his hand. "Those last few mortgage payments—since we deducted the payments from your salary, Andrew, never mind, forget about them, figure one thing ended with the other. Well, I'm sorry to lose you, and—I know he is, too. . . . Still—we solved some tough ones, didn't we!"

Should he go downstairs and say goodbye to the draftsmen?

On his board lay the drawings for the wrought-iron elevator doors of the Stock Exchange Building, the only big job the firm still had in construction here. As it happened, Jack Slater, the ironwork man, was due any minute to go over the casting points with him. The Master had left him virtually free on this design; it was far more open, light, geometrical than the work on the Auditorium; Andrew had combined rectangles with large, segmented circular elements, but used no encrustations of foliage. He was pleased with this piece of work. There was a rise in his spirits. It was time to go out and be completely on his own. Though he could go right over to Burnham.

Burnham was busy enough. And despite the big disagreement on the exposition, he had become quite friendly, as he had been living out there in a cabin in Jackson Park, hustling along construction, in the months Andrew had supervised the Transportation Building. And since John Root had died there would be a real opportunity with Burnham, to do major design. But suddenly Andrew felt as though his mother, his righteous uncles, had heard his thought. Wouldn't he be betraying his Master? Even though virtually fired?

Was there something opportunistic in him? Twice,

three times now, this had happened. All right, Professor Gamsey had understood and not minded. But Olmstead had definitely felt he had crossed the rules, behaved wrongly. And now the Master. What would Uncle Bruce say to this one? Even though that fateful South Side client had come through Uncle Bruce himself.

Besides—Andrew recovered his spunk—absurd that a man couldn't do his own work on his own time! Did an employer own every thought in your head? No, he wouldn't let all this affect his feelings toward the Master; it was a streak of temper that came out in Mr. Sullivan at times, more frequently lately—

Just then, Jack Slater walked in, glanced at the iron-work design, looked more closely. "Say, this one is a beauty!" And he understood where each detail came from. Now, here, all the geometric interplay—"That's yours."

Jack had been just about the best part of this job—aside from the Master and, indeed, the Chief. Hardly older than Andrew, with artistic leanings, Jack Slater had worked since sixteen for an ornamental-cast-iron outfit,then started on his own, getting in with several of the biggest architects, who took to him because of his sheer enthusiasm, his readiness to solve the most intricate piece of casting. Especially with Sullivan. "There's a fellow that appreciates design!"

Jack was doing well, had just built himself a new plant, had just got married, and to the daughter of a contractor, a Southerner who had come up to Chicago after the fire —carpetbagging in reverse, as he called it, and making a fortune. For Claffin's own new mansion on Prairie Avenue, Jack had done a spectacular wrought-iron fence, and carried off the daughter, Vicki.

Slater suddenly said, "What's up, Andrew?"

To Jack's candid blue eyes one could only reply without bluff, "I just got the sack."

The brow furrowed in surprise, bewilderment. "Things that bad here?" Jack knew what was going on in every architectural shop.

"Oh not that bad." Andrew still felt protective of the firm. "Sullivan found out I was doing that house on Dorchester on my own."

Jack chuckled. "Missed a few, didn't he!" Naturally Jack knew; he'd done the ironwork on all the Oak Park dwellings. "Hell, you did it on your own time. Who doesn't sneak in a few, if they only get the chance?" Jack lowered his voice. "Andrew, you can walk in anywhere, even if things are slow. Burnham would grab you." He cocked his eye. Naturally Jack knew of the Sullivan-Burnham feud. Andrew shook his head.

Then, more seriously, Jack said, "You know, Andrew, if you can swing it, this could be just the time to go out on your own. Have you thought about that? You've got lots of good ideas. Money-saving, too. People are beginning to hear about you. This may be the best thing ever happened to you. Listen—keep in touch. Let me know where you are. I may have an idea." Half jestingly he preached, "One thing, young man, never appear like someone who got the sack! Why, Andrew Lane walked out, to better himself! He's on the way up! *You* decided to leave, to build up your own career." He grinned. The American way.

Andrew stood at the window. This view he hated to lose. Anytime he'd felt the need to lift his eyes from his board—this vista outward over the expanse of the lake. The way he used to sit in the treehouse in boyhood, gazing out over the water to the infinite. Now, turning his eyes from Lake Michigan to the ever-growing city, its surging energy rising palpably, as in midsummer sometimes, emanations of heat, rising even to here. Gazing over the city, picking out the new towers going up. The Adler-and-Sullivan Schiller, practically his own design, carried out that year when the Master was worn out and mostly away.

To go down from here to some drawing board in a row of drawing boards? Nonsense! Or even to stick himself away in Oak Park.

All at once Andrew saw exactly what he would do. He'd go to the newest, the dandiest: the Schiller! He was almost certain that the tower floor, the walkup flight beyond the last elevator stop, was not yet fully rented.

He went over at once. He'd been right. There remained an excellent corner space, one view to the lake, the other over the city—his same two vistas! They'd been asking a high rent, but for him they'd bring it down. But even so, with the last wages handed him by Adler he could just about pay the first month. Then, a thought. This space was easily large enough for two—he'd get Willis to come in with him! In a surge, Andrew felt that everything could be as he planned. As in designing a house, once he had a basic idea, everything fell into place. He saw the space divided, the entrance, not the usual railed-off anteroom but a good-sized consultation room, with a broad table large enough for spread-out plans. Morris chairs, but his own design. A bookcase—not only with architectural works, but with books by authors like Bernard Shaw and H. G. Wells. On the other wall, his Hiroshige of the bridge. A handsome vase placed off center on the big table, which should have a glass top. And the entrance door itself—it must at once proclaim a different atmosphere, distinguished, but accessible. He had it! Instead of the usual door, why not a portal entirely out of plate glass? Not even a wooden frame. Thus, at once, the sense of the open, the fresh, the modern. Their names in modest-size lettering, gold leaf. Even the inner door to the drafting rooms should be full-length glass; thus you could see right through the entire suite and out the windows, the view of the city, the lake. He'd got it! Simply have to find a way to manage the hinges.

The decision buoyed him. Right off, Andrew called Willis to come out for a coffee, told his tale, he had been considering quitting to go on his own anyway, the outside jobs were getting to be more than he could handle on the side. This was the time for the jump. Did Willis want to share an office with him? Each on his own, split expenses, practice independently. He'd already found an excellent spot, top of the Schiller. Got an excellent price on the rent.

Willis' slow smile was beginning to bloom, the half-amused smile of the old days, at his younger friend's quick enthusiasms.

Still, it was true, as Andrew long knew, that he was in a rut at Olmstead's. On the other hand, people were being let go all around, things were slow, and Olmstead's weekly paycheck felt good. "Hell, Willis, you don't have a wife and three kids!"

"Already! When did it come?"

"Due any day now."

Willis' mother had an annuity, his sister earned her own way, and Willis himself had a pretty sizable nest egg, Andrew was sure—about all he ever spent was on books and concert tickets. Though with his shyness it might take him some time to develop a clientele.

"You know," Willis said, "I might do it, just to give architecture a last chance."

He should probe that remark, Andrew knew. You were friends with a fellow, shared opinions, poked fun at the same pretensions; suddenly came this remark. Why, a thought like that could never come to his own mind! The same instant there was that hovering uncertainty in Willis' eyes that Andrew had seen only once or twice before, wasn't it once when Helena spoke of a girl who would be just right for Willis? A kind of opening and simultaneous shutting off. Yet right now Andrew didn't want to probe the disturbing remark, he was intent on his plan. Perhaps Willis should have been a teacher, a professor—he was a really capable designer, that was true, he could do Olmstead's Queen Annes with his eyes shut. But his friend was not, Andrew realized, *plagued* with architecture. Willis could get more excited over certain outside things: the Single Tax; the Fabians, now he was talking about those lectures that were making such a stir—"If Christ Came to Chicago," by that British pastor who had come to Chicago for the exposition and gone around really exploring the city, even standing in long lines outside the missions for a bowl of soup. And the masses of prostitutes, the hordes of men out of work. Indeed, Andrew ought to hear that Englishman blasting away, it was an experience! Yes, Andrew quoted Uncle Bruce, "Takes a stranger to come into town and tell them the things you've been telling them for years." Now, about going on their own?

Willis finished his coffee. Could he have a look at the place?

They'd go right over.

Andrew described the full glass door, their names in modest gold letters. Willis gazed at the view. Then all at once he said, "Hell, Mother's been poking at me to get out of my rut. I'll do it." And they danced a crazy little Highland fling.

Andrew rushed over to Horder's big Wabash Avenue store and bought two drafting tables with the very newest tilting and swiveling devices. Then for that big table in the foyer. All he could find were for corporation boards of directors. He'd design it himself.

On the way home Andrew considered it would perhaps be best to tell Helena he had himself decided to make the jump, without mentioning the row with the Master. Indeed, his own bitterness had by now been submerged under plans and excitement. Perhaps Sullivan had not really meant to fire him, just to dress him down, and then had been upset by his sudden resignation. No, damn it— refusing to give back the mortgage! But he would never let all this diminish the greatness of the architect, nor would he ever belittle what he had learned from him. But that the Master . . . And the bitterness came back almost to tears so that he had to turn his face to the train window. Better stop this before he got home. Though Helena was a great healthy girl and had come through the other two births with no fuss at all, still why upset her needlessly?

So he cheerfully announced at once, "Well, my dear, I've taken the jump!"

Helena's face had that uncertain look, of trusting in him but wondering what new quirk of genius . . .

His mother was there, in the kitchen. "Andrew, what's happened!" Marta demanded. "You look as if you were the one having the baby."

"Maybe I am! I've taken my own office!" he proclaimed. "Top of the Schiller Building!"

Helena's eyes were uncertain. "You've left Adler and Sullivan?"

"This is the time. Those South Side commissions will carry us through."

Something had gone wrong, Marta sensed. But done is done. "He's right!" she said to Helena. "He's gone as far as anyone can go, with them. With the prize in Madison, and people hearing about him, Andrew shouldn't stay under Louis Sullivan's shadow." She approached, and kissed him. "Congratulations, son!" It was her old dream coming complete at last, her son the eminent architect.

Helena's smile grew steadier. "Oh, wonderful, Andrew. Success!"

But still, why just at this moment? Then she knew. "You had a row!" And laughed! She really could see right into him, and a surge of Andrew's earliest feelings took hold of him, oh that girl! There was even, in her outcry, Helena's girlhood teasing at catching him out. "Don't tell me that old drunkard fired you!"

"Now, just hold on. Yesterday he happened to pass that foundation on Dorchester, so he came in this morning pretty furious. He recognized it had to be mine."

Now she was all on his side, ablaze! "What business is that of his! You do it on your own time, nights and Sundays, God knows you haven't an hour for your children, not to mention your wife! And how many times a week have you stayed downtown hours overtime, finishing work for him and listening to his maundering while he was getting sozzled!"

"Helena. He's a great architect and taught me just about all I know. He caught me out."

"Andrew. Don't disparage yourself," his mother put in.

"Don't worry about Andrew disparaging himself!" Still taking it in good humor. But that house on Dorchester—how had Mr. Sullivan caught on it was Andrew's?

The slab. "Who else does it?"

His mother even looked rather proud. They all soon would.

Helena had another thought. Why need he take an office downtown? Oak Park was growing, so that even a new architect had come out, Malcolm Reese, and he seemed to have plenty to do—

"With his family connections," Marta put in. The father a lumber king.

"Here everybody knows you. Who's going to find you downtown?"

All at once, in Helena there was a feeling, surely a natural feeling in a woman, for having her husband never far off. Doing his man's work right upstairs. Coming down for lunch, the children having their papa around. No, but an office upstairs—imagine his clients tumbling over Ned, who was always crawling up and down. Andrew could rent something in the new Commercial Building, it surely wouldn't cost half as much as the Schiller downtown . . .

Only, his mother agreed with Andrew. Even the Oak Parkers would feel more impressed if they had to go downtown to the top of the new Schiller Building to consult Andrew Lane! And besides, situated there, he'd have the whole of Chicago for prospective clients. They weren't going to come out to Oak Park! He was already building on the South Side. And as he had to be downtown, he was right—the finest address! The newest and the best! For herself, Marta believed in simplicity, but this was the way people were. The Schiller Tower! The very top! No, the days were gone when you built the better mousetrap in a cabin in the woods and people beat a path to your door!

Andrew began to describe his ideas for the plate-glass door, the two names in gilt—

Two? Oh, he'd forgotten to mention—Willis was coming in with him. Share the rent. Practical. And he'd got a real low rate.

"Willis? Willis too?" Helena was puzzled. Were things so bad even at Olmstead's?

No, Willis hadn't been sacked, Andrew laughed. Willis had agreed it was time for him to make the jump, and was leaving Olmstead.

Suddenly, to Helena, all seemed brighter. Willis had real good sense. And the expenses shared. And, though neither she nor Marta would say it, Willis was no competition for Andrew Lane. With something like enthusiasm now, Andrew's women listened to his ideas for the great glass-topped table, the bookshelves, even a sofa, to give the place tone.

Now Helena began to have ideas, they'd send out hundreds of announcement cards, Andrew must design them, a distinctive emblem—it was quite ethical to send out cards with a new address, even doctors did it. "Andrew Lane, Architect, Schiller Tower." Uncle Bruce was sure to have an excellent list, and of course Phil Whaley. The Oak Park weekly would even put in an item, like a social-column notice—she'd seen things like that. And her father was acquainted with well-to-do people in the business world. And her high-school classmates—this was the year they were all getting married! And Helena even had a wild thought: that new doctor who had rented a house on Grove Avenue—he was a nephew of that Mr. Hemingway that had the oldest Oak Park real-estate office and did more business than Phil Whaley. Indeed, why wouldn't it be better for her this time to have a doctor who lived nearby, this Dr. Hemingway was said to have taken special courses, all the latest in obstetrics, as they called it. And by getting to know the Hemingways—the wife was said to be an opera singer and Helena could invite them—

"Whoa! Hold on!" Andrew burst out laughing, and Marta and Helena had to laugh, too.

Part Three

The
American
Home

14

HE HAD hardly got the drawing tables delivered, they were still unpacked, meanwhile there was trouble installing the plate-glass doors as no standard hinges would do the job, he'd have to design something, Jack Slater could make it —when lo! Jack appeared. How had he discovered where Andrew was? Everybody knew. The talk was that Adler and Sullivan were really slipping, to have to let go their top designer!

Andrew already knew the talk. From the lunch circle, no matter how much you denied it. So here was Jack, come up to wish them good luck.

He looked over the plate-glass door, real original. Had an idea for the hinges, and while on his knees, measuring, asked how was Helena, and with that humorous lip-thrust of his made the expected joke about Andrew in a rush here to deliver this baby, ahead of his wife. Then dropped his big news: they might soon be neighbors, as he'd got hold of a piece of ground out there, just past the end of Oak Park, right by the river. —Wasn't that the big Arthur Kaiser estate? A huge tract, Andrew knew, held by a wealthy real-estate speculator. So Kaiser was about to open it up? Not really, Slater said. Only, as a personal friend, Arthur had sold him a plot. "Thought I'd better hurry up and build, before you're too busy."

All that Andrew could manage was, "I appreciate it, Jack." Then, picking up the bantering tone, "I suppose you have the plans all drawn for me, in your pocket?"

Now it was Jack who dropped the banter. "Listen, Andrew, I talked this over with Vicki. We want you to have an absolutely free hand."

With this second surprise, Andrew felt more than moved—exultant. To have such a friend. Oh, he'd do something—something that would make them proud! If he had anything in him, this was the time!

Jack Slater went on. Naturally he knew the Lattimer house and the few others Andrew had built when his chiefs were too busy with the skyscrapers. Jack had done all the ironwork on them. And on Andrew's Oak Park houses too. He'd heard Andrew spouting some new ideas, and Vicki had real modern taste. They didn't want Queen Anne or whatever. They wanted a home that looked good and was real livable. No fixed ideas. Number of rooms and all that —well, they expected the family to expand, he grinned. And Vicki liked to entertain but not in the style of Mrs. Potter Palmer. So there it was. Hell, Andrew knew them.

Perfect! They talked of cost, and presently Andrew had spread out a sheet of drawing paper on the floor and they were crouched over it. Indeed, when Jack said his plot backed up to the Calumet River near the bend, Andrew recalled one Sunday when Helena had got him to go canoeing with the kids. There was a strip of forest preserve on Jack's side. He even recalled a red farmhouse across the river. Open prairie.

"Exactly! " Jack cried. "What a memory!"

"We tied up the boat, and got some milk at the farm for our picnic."

Once he was alone, the thing began to come to him. Andrew didn't even stop to set up the drafting table but spread another sheet on the floor. A house low to the ground, the horizontal line stroking the flatland, the far-stretching prairie. Even the chimney staying low, instead of flaunting itself in the sky. One side of the fireplace opening to the reception entrance, the other to a deep dining room ending in a full-width bay, a virtual half circle of glass, already within the garden. Dining room and kitchen the core, and a U around it, the living room on one leg, the entry hall the base, the library the other leg. Vicki liked big parties, Jack was gregarious, kind of ambitious, give them a lot of entertainment space, so, going back to the entry hall—make it deep, with its own fireplace, with an inglenook, so that in a large reception the entire U was an open flow. An idea: he raised the inglenook a half-step, and marked it off with an open row of light pillars, forming an oasis. Fireplace chatting.

The facade, against yellow-glazed brick, a white-face pattern something like what he had done in the Lattimer house. The golden-oak door with its art-glass panel, the two high square windows, a geometric pattern, bold, new. Green foliage all around. The bedroom floor upstairs beneath all-around extended eaves, sheltering the windows. Unlike the high-pitched roof of his own house, here he would put a low-sloping hip roof.

A box, they'd say. All right. But a form, without excrescences.

To stand before the entrance he sketched in a pair of flower urns, on pedestals. Dignified, almost formal. The rear of the house melding with the garden, open, free. And for the porte cochere, a huge open Romanesque arch, posed directly on the ground, balancing the volume of the house—a salute, in his own mind, to Henry Richardson. And Louis Sullivan.

Willis was finishing out the week at Olmstead's. He stopped over, looked, nodded and nodded: the balance, the bold simple facade, the quality of shelter from the overhang, the elegance! One thing was sure, no one had yet seen a house like this!

Willis too had something. The remodeling of an early South Side mansion into an extension for the girl's school where his sister taught. Not much to get excited about, but still, for bad times, a start.

Since establishing themselves at the Schiller, they had stopped lunching at the Bakery; a little circle of men on their own was forming, something with a touch more of class than the Bakery was indicated. They settled at Kinsey's, a place where well-known folk were sometimes seen, newspaper writers—Eugene Field was occasionally among them, Clarence Darrow sometimes came by, this time bringing a lanky young writer Jane Addams had sent him, the fellow was gathering material for a novel. All those out-of-work derelicts in the breadlines . . .

Had they seen the solution offered in the *Tribune*? Darrow remarked. It said that the simplest solution for unemployment was to put arsenic in the handouts to the bums.

After the sour laugh, the writer remarked that they weren't all bums, he had been hanging around the stockyards gathering material. Some of these derelicts came from there. These Polish immigrants had been brought over when they were needed, there were blocks of shanties sold to them as new—with a coat of paint slapped on—and when times got bad and they lost their jobs they got thrown out, losing every penny they had paid on the house. Their families broke up, some of the men became drunks and drifters . . .

This kind of gruesome talk about the panic made Andrew uncomfortable. It never led anywhere. Now he tried to pull the talk back to architecture.

"Architects!" said Darrow. "What can you fellows do about all these homeless wrecks? Why, anyone that uses an architect is already well off!" And, still with that way of calling Andrew "young man," he remarked, "Why don't you come down from that high tower of yours one day!"

"Well, aren't you the lawyer for a big railway?" Andrew shot back.

"You got me!"

Well, then, Andrew did have some ideas. Decent cheap houses could be built—let the city build them. Clean out all the shanty slums. Put a lot of these people to work on construction. Use sectional concrete, with doors and windows already set in—save money. Andrew felt himself carried away, like sometimes at a drawing board when the pencil seemed to take over. After all, wasn't architecture the design, the structure, of society, of the way men lived!

Darrow was softly chuckling. "When I run for mayor, Andrew, I'm going to get you out campaigning." It was no longer "young man." And his running for mayor was a half-joke.

But Andrew felt a little foolish. It was obviously all utopian.

River Foresters had so far reserved judgment on the Slater house; they would stroll by, but with an air of doubt and puzzlement. It certainly looked different. No porches? And one neighbor asked Vicki—about the entrance—"Is that how it's going to stay?"

Finally, done, Jack decided it was great! Original! They would move in and have a big housewarming.

And then came their furniture. The gilt Chippendale. Jack was good-natured as always, freely agreeing that the furniture didn't fit the house, but what was he to do? He was in no position to rush out and buy new furniture. And, after all, the guests had to have somewhere to sit.

"Let them stand!" Andrew snorted. Or he'd get some planks, nice clean pine, and slap together a few decent benches . . .

Then Vicki decided Andrew needn't worry, because probably no one would come anyway. Hadn't he read about that awful Pullman strike, in the papers? How were their guests going to come out to River Forest?

"Darling, they're not coming from Chicago in Pullmans!" Jack made his joke.

But Vicki said the situation was not funny. She was on the side of the workingmen, only why didn't they compromise?

Jack said, Had they read about that striker's wife, they lived in one of those Pullmantown company houses, and now when her husband died—

"That was really something!" Helena cried. He had worked thirteen years in the Pullman plant, the family was destitute and still the company was demanding sixty dollars in rent arrears!

"They're certainly getting into the papers!" Vicki said.

That was because they had Clarence Darrow for their lawyer, he knew a lot of people in the press, Jack said. And that was really a sensation, the way Mr. Darrow had quit as attorney for the railways, and gone over to represent the union!

"Maybe the unions are paying him more," Vicki joked.

"To work! To work!" Andrew proclaimed, finishing off his chicken leg. Helena had brought over a picnic lunch. They were trying to arrange the furniture, or rather, Andrew was trying to hide it all, using Marta's hand-woven fabrics as throws. Never again would he allow clients to murder a house.

Every day the situation looked worse. Strikers, unhooking Pullman sleepers on side tracks, set the cars on fire. Mob Rules! Army troops came to Chicago and camped on the lakefront. It seemed the whole world was about to explode—for now it was the President of France that was assassinated by an anarchist! Those anarchists had a secret world organization, Vicki told Helena, and any day there could be revolution in the streets. People were scared to go out. Maybe nobody would come to her party.

Nevertheless, beginning in the midafternoon, guests appeared. Philip Whaley brought along a coffee importer to whom he had recently sold a lot. Robert Mann had got there, his quick eyes taking in every detail, every fresh idea. Even a young lady society reporter from *Oak Leaves* was there jotting down names and remarks. Helena tried to catch what they said. "Unusual" meant they really didn't like it.

Everyone took the tour, Helena making sure they noticed the innovations. No dark closets and wasted hallways. —And with that curved glass wall of the dining room the outside came right in, she explained, while they remarked on the glorious day, a true glorious Fourth—only better not set off any firecrackers, people would think the anarchists were starting the revolution!

—How lovely, from upstairs, to watch the canoes paddling down the river.

Jack wheeled Andrew especially to meet a good friend, Alfred Eastman, first whispering, "Thinking of building out here." Eastman, a magazine publisher, was a handicraft amateur, a Roycroft enthusiast, and appreciated the natural way Mr. Lane had handled the wood in this house. He was thinking of a house with a home workshop where he and his two boys could do things together.

Another appreciator was Sato, who had brought along his American wife and the eldest of their beautiful daughters, with her husband, the Japanese Consul, who wore a frock coat, and who again thanked Andrew for the great assistance he had given in the construction of the teahouse at the Columbian Exposition. One day—he included Helena and Jack and Vicki in his salutations—they all must be honored guests in Japan. "I might just take you up on that!" Jack said, for Jack had started to do a little business selling Japan scrap iron from his plant.

On into the evening the housewarming continued, the long driveway crowded with carriages arriving, carriages leaving. More and more relays of women remarking to Vicki and Helena over the clever conveniences of the kitchen, the way the washing and stacking and all was planned—had Andrew himself planned all that? —Every detail! —Ah. There was a man who understood women.

Vicki had already been working on Mrs. Eastman, showing her all the original kitchen ideas. Now she was working on the big property owner, Mr. Kaiser, to agree to sell the Eastmans a building plot alongside this one. And to Helena she mentioned, about Arthur Kaiser, that Andrew ought to pay some attention to him, he was a man with big ideas. And plenty of money.

And when Kaiser and his wife stopped in the library entrance to admire Andrew's three-tiered gaslight sconces, Jack spoke about the importance of detail. Kaiser, a man who saw everything with half-hooded eyes, was laconic, each statement like a decision. Andrew felt something brewing there. With this man he could get on.

In the soft nightfall, little groups on the lawn were having the inevitable discussions about the railroad strike, imagine Clarence Darrow, throwing up his position as general counsel for the Chicago and Northwestern Railroad so as to switch over to the union!

Well, they would just see if he could keep that union boss Eugene Debs out of jail, because, one sure thing, that was where George Pullman meant to put him.

Until the fireworks, with Jack doing himself proud, great arching sparklers in the backyard and you could even hear some of them sizzling into the river.

Ah, if explosions could always be so harmless, just glorious and peaceful, Vicki sighed.

"Like our good old Revolutionary War," Jack jested.

And at last there were only the four of them, to draw the conclusions. Was the house a success? Vicki repeated what this one and that one had said. So original! So *different!* Helena kept silent about a few remarks she had overheard: "Apple crate." "A joke." She only hoped Andrew hadn't caught any of it. —She was sure the Eastmans were interested in building, she said. And Jack said he had had a talk with Arthur Kaiser. That fox had bought up not only this area along the river but half of Lake Street. He was planning some large apartment houses there. Andrew ought to get to know Kaiser better.

"He knows where to find me," Andrew said.

In the following days so much was happening in the

world, how could you worry about what people said about a house? Strikers, going through the back fences of Pullmantown, wrecked a car on the factory siding. An excited deputy sheriff shot off his gun, and an onlooker, a plain innocent citizen, fell dead. RIOTERS THIRSTY FOR BLOOD, the *Post* headlined. Was there going to be another Haymarket Massacre?

When Andrew got home from the Schiller, Helena read him her favorite, Finley Peter Dunne, in the *News*. He had made his own investiga-shun of the blood thurst of the Pullman strikers, he wrote in that Irish way of his, but after visiting a dozen saloons, all the thurst he had discovered among those bloodthursty strikers was a thurst for beer. Not one barman had had a call for blood.

She had clipped out for him an article in *Oak Leaves* about the newcomers Jack and Vicki Slater and their brilliant housewarming in River Forest, with elaborate descriptions of the new gowns worn by the ladies. Not a word about the architecture.

Then the Trib headlined DEBS STRIKE DEAD. Thirty people had been killed, thirteen in Chicago. The Federal troops decamped from the lakeshore. From their high window, Andrew and Willis could even watch the soldiers pulling up stakes. Willis quoted an article in *The Nation*, it had been "wealth against commonwealth." Now that the industrial war was over, business had more confidence and things were picking up.

Even in his own commissions, Andrew could see it. There had been a scary month, not because of the strikes, but because of a nasty joke going around out there in River Forest. The joke was about Jack Slater slipping down a back lane every morning to the station, so he wouldn't meet his neighbors laughing at his crate of a house. No more had been heard from that prospect the handicraft lover, Alfred Eastman, who had talked at Slater's party about building on a nearby lot. Helena wanted to invite the Eastmans when she invited the Slaters, but Andrew wasn't going in for that kind of thing.

Then that hustler who had sold him his lot, Phil Whaley, saved the financial situation at least. He had sold his Queen Anne, Andrew's first commission out here, and he wanted to put up another just like it! That would be the third!

Helena let the story be known, in her women's-club circles and teas. People who lived in Andrew's houses loved them. And Vicki Slater would rave about her amazing kitchen. And the absence of those old-fashioned dust-catching moldings. And the way the garden seemed to come right into your house!

And then came another surprise. Right down the street, a history professor had bought a lot, and Whaley said every architect in Oak Park had got in touch with him. Suddenly, the professor came around himself. Just because Andrew was the only one who hadn't pursued him, he said.

He had the little smile in his eyes of a man who considered himself knowing and shrewd. Now, he appreciated that Andrew was an innovator, a man with decided ideas. Some liked the Slater house, some did not. But he had made his inquiries and one thing people agreed, that Andrew Lane knew how to build, and to build economically. Now, the professor himself and his wife, like most people, had their own idea of what they wanted their house to look like, and their idea—their dream home, if you wanted—was a half-timbered, gabled house, maybe like Hawthorne's House of the Seven Gables, he chuckled, his wife's favorite book. So if Andrew had nothing against building a house in that style, why, this would be quite a large house . . .

To Helena's relief, Andrew, when he related the story, was even amused at the reputation he was getting as a stubborn fellow. Why, he had pointed out, he believed that a client had a perfect right to the kind of house he wanted, Georgian, New England, Revival, he had done them all. But when a client *didn't* know what he wanted, and even his wife didn't have a pet idea, "Ah, that's the architect's opportunity!"

The big house meant a big fee. They could pay all

their debts—the grocer had been carrying them for six months. But the moment he got the first payment on the fee, Andrew went right over to Kimball's and bought a grand piano. In debt again! And where would they put it? Why, in the big children's playroom he was about to build upstairs. Also, he was starting the studio on the adjoining lot. He needed a draftsman out here. Maybe two. For another commission had come through. Alfred Eastman had got over his scare and come into the downtown office to discuss a residence. Yes, something in the style of the Slater house!

Oh, Andrew with his teasing! Why hadn't he told her at once, before telling about buying the piano?

But even with two new commissions, how would he pay for all that construction?

Andrew's luck—he won another competition! Not just luck, his mother said, and Helena said it, too. This was some kind of invention for decorative glass prisms, with light coming through the design. It would pay for the playroom, and the studio too! So Andrew went out and bought an expensive, large canoe, to take the children boating on the Des Plaines on Sundays.

Directly in the path of the corridor that would connect the house with his studio, there grew a tall willow. The tree would have to come down. But the willow was Wally's first love, slender enough for the boy to embrace and climb. Now one morning there arose a great din in the yard as Wally with an Indian drum hung from his neck led a march of the tots around the willow, howling, "Daddy! Spare our tree!"

Maybe deflect the corridor? Then Andrew had a better idea. Simpler. One thing about his contractor, Lonergan: that fellow never balked at a crazy notion—"You want to do it? You figure out how, and I'll get it done." Then why not simply leave the tree in the middle of the passage, let it poke right through the roof? Easy enough to seal the roof with tar around the tree trunk.

Sometimes one simple and natural idea attracts more

attention than a big innovation. No sooner had that little corridor been built, with the tree left in the middle going right through the roof, than it became the talk of the town. Neighbors brought friends and apologetically asked Helena if they might show them the tree. Wally would rush forward as a guide, little Ned tagging after, and inevitably Wally would demonstrate, shinnying up so his head bumped the ceiling.

No longer were there sideways smiles at Andrew Lane's ideas. The residents of Oak Park were tree lovers, and he had with this one stroke won their hearts. A story spread that the tree grew right through the architect's living room!

Besides, just a few blocks away the large Seven Gables house with the half-timber walls was taking form; Andrew had even enjoyed treating it as an exercise in style, the way a composer might, with all respect, observe the rules of a gone-by period, and the history professor's manse was indeed nothing to be ashamed of, well-proportioned, dignified even while romantic, even opulent. So, coming after the "odd-looking" Slater residence, it was now pointed out that Andrew Lane could handle a conventional house quite beautifully, if that was what you wanted—he was no stubborn experimenter after all.

And the studio, with its statuaries over the entrance, its usual facade, was accepted, even admired. For an office, it was really impressive, high-class.

Commissions were coming in. Though the fees still got spent before they were paid, Andrew wasn't going to pinch. He bought a fine pair of horses, keeping them at the best stable in town, and as soon as Helena was up from the fourth confinement she had a stylish riding habit made and went riding with him—the best thing for a woman, to bring back her figure. And indeed she was amazing, firm, erect, her breasts so lusciously full again!

Mornings, he stayed at work in Oak Park, supervising his draftsmen—now three—in the studio, then cantering from one construction site to another. For this Andrew wore his riding boots, jodhpurs, Norfolk jacket, his flowing Windsor tie. In autumn, especially on days that looked like rain, Andrew added a short dark-blue cape of Marta's hand weaving. The costume was practical, not only for riding but for clambering about on the job, and when he went into town, why change?

On Mondays the round table was usually pretty full; there was some talk going on about an improved concrete mix, reinforced with steel rods. Just then Bob Mann came in with that knowing look in his eyes. Been talking with Frank Whitaker, the old hand at Sullivan and Adler's. And, looking directly at Andrew, "Seen the Master lately?" Like everyone, Bob knew that since the row they hadn't spoken.

"Well, Adler's left."

The effect around the table was as Bob had wanted. But Andrew heard the details in a kind of reverberation, through a heaviness of heart. —Yes, things had got slower and slower. Meanwhile Dankmar Adler wanted to bring in his son, freshly graduated in architecture. Sullivan objected, there just wasn't enough work. Here they'd been letting people out and were down to a skeleton crew. In fact there was hardly enough income for the two of them to draw on. So Adler had cleared out. Oh, no quarrel. All in friendliness. Fact was, Dankmar Adler had already been sounding things out. A big corporation, new hydraulic elevators, had made him a fat offer, supposedly engineering —but really, Bob had gathered, it was for selling their elevators through his acquaintance with every big architect in the country. So Louis Sullivan would now be carrying on on his own.

First there was a kind of awed reticence. Several of the men around the table had at one time or another worked for the great firm. Then came remarks. Damn shame. Just a streak of bad luck. And when things were picking up. In an undertone one heard, "Hitting the bottle." But also, "Made too many enemies over the exposition."

Mann, in a tone of respectful regret, was giving out more and more bits of information and conjecture. Yes, the firm would be coming down from the Tower. Sullivan would be taking a smaller office, on the Wabash Avenue side, he supposed.

Some damn fool had to say, "What a comedown."

Andrew wanted to burst out with the words reverberating in his mind, "The creator of American architecture!" But it would sound like an epitaph.

On the way home, Andrew felt uneasy about telling Helena. If only she wouldn't make some remark about the drinking. Suddenly he recalled the brilliant night of the opening of the Auditorium.

Helena saw on his face that something had happened. When he told her the news, she was quiet for a moment. Then she said, "Oh, Andrew, I keep seeing that night, the opening of the opera, remember." And added, "Oh, it doesn't pay to be too original."

Nor did they go so much to the Hull House, though Willis was more and more involved there. Helena, with four young children, was exhausted by evening. If they went out, let it at least be for relaxation. They attended concerts with the Slaters, sometimes the opera. Besides, the mood of things seemed to have changed. When suddenly the eight-hour labor law for women, which had so triumphantly got voted through the state legislature, was declared invalid by the State Supreme Court, it seemed as though that whole exciting time was over.

Yet, as the century completed itself, Andrew felt he was, in his work, on the verge of something of his own. The eaves, the overhangs, projected farther and farther. In two-story houses, with verandas, this began to have a certain look, a character. An underscored horizontality. He was getting at the answer to "How would *you* do it?" Just walking down his own street, in the number of houses he had built, he could see a progress, from the early ones, the Queen Annes, toward a form of his own.

TOWARD THE closing of the year, a few surprises came. Of all things, the Master got married! A woman, a writer it seemed, whom he had met as she was walking her dog. And he was doing a big nine-story department store on the busiest downtown corner, State and Madison, with huge wide windows, Andrew was interested to notice, in horizontal emphasis. Well! And the wrought-iron work over the entrance was the Master's masterpiece!

Then Clarence Darrow got divorced. All in amity, said Uncle Bruce, but the quiet Mrs. Darrow had never really fitted in with his growing celebrity. They had been married for just about twenty years—like his own father, crossed Andrew's mind. There was a son, too. Clarence was moving to bachelor quarters, near Hull House.

And Jane Addams went for a tour abroad. In Russia she visited Tolstoy, to come home with new inspiring ideas.

Joining Willis, and Uncle Bruce too, for the welcoming party, Andrew and Helena partook of the home-baked bread that Jane had learned to bake, from Tolstoy himself! Helena and Marta and a whole circle of women learned to bake the bread—good dark Russian bread, eaten warm.

15

NOT SIMPLY a new year but a new century! In all the press, in all the magazines, predictions and admonitions were appearing, from fortunetellers, scientists and preachers. In the new century there would be wonders beyond belief, man would learn to fly—and the papers showed those old Leonardo da Vinci drawings of a man with mechanical wings. Man would master every pestilence, the average life span would rise to the Biblical hundred and twenty . . . There were imaginary pictures of cities of the coming century, buildings fifty stories high, with enormous balloons floating around them.

The sense of man, at last master of his environment, and of his own limitless capacity, infected you. And as the new century approached, Andrew, with each successive design, felt himself working with a new ease, a kind of mastery. He was working at last with a sure sense of intention, a sense of exactly what he meant, a mastery over materials. Sometimes you did things by instinct and only afterward saw the principle of what you had done. At the lunch circle, he poured out ideas. Take steel. Because structural steel happened to come with the chase to go higher, there was a confusion, he said. Why, steel was a great new tool and could be used in any direction—horizontal, as it had begun, with rails, just as well as vertical. It could be used in cantilevers, projecting porticos, verandas, whatever you wanted. What was being done? Same old post-and-beam construction, same old building methods since man came out of the caves. And now that man had great new structural materials, the best he could think to do with them was to pile one cave on top of another. Not even as much imagination as the Aztecs, who at least had set back their multiple-story dwellings, for space, light, air. Now with steel you could support any shape you wanted, it had flexibility and tension. Excited, Andrew stuck out his arm—you could do that, with steel, cantilever straight out, no props, no supports. A whole new architecture could come. Steel, and concrete forms! The American idea! If you only were not afraid to use new ideas, new inventions in new ways—*there* was the impulse of America.

Some were smiling a bit at his being carried away.

There was a fellow named Randolph Stacey, who was connected with the *Architectural World*, and had taken to sitting in on the lunch circle, off and on, picking up information on building projects, that he used for notes in the magazine. In a way, Andrew had been talking at him. And indeed he came around as the group broke up, saying he intended to get out to Oak Park and have a look at what Andrew was doing.

At last Andrew felt he had his own elements of design, of construction, flowing into a style. Just as ten years ago he had known exactly what elements of design to use if one wanted a Queen Anne house, the bay windows, tall chimneys, porches, shingles, today he had virtually achieved an architectural language of his own. A style. People spoke of it, indeed, and though he knew it was his own, his own creation, already it was being used, in part, sometimes in whole, by half a dozen others—the first, of course, having been Bob Mann. But most of them used only an element or two, they adopted his hip roof just as they might use a mansard roof if the client desired. They adopted his extended, sheltering eaves. Windows in a continuous band of glass, forming an element of design, instead of just a series of holes punched in a wall.

Helena still got angry at the copiers, but his mother said it was the best compliment. And in the architectural world everyone really knew where the ideas came from. And now there appeared Randolph Stacey's article in the *Architectural World*, calling him the foremost of the young creative architects! And with photographs of the Lattimer house, the Slater and others. There were now exactly fifty, if he counted those under construction, and that was pretty good for having been out on his own for only six years, especially as the newest commissions were up in the twenty- and even thirty-thousand-dollar category.

Certainly Bob Mann was doing as well if not better, he insinuated himself everywhere, and Malcolm Reese was doing very well, but then, Reese had high family connections.

Now Andrew was thirty-three, and at about that age the Master was already designing the Auditorium! The very thought of the giant, like some Samson in chains, took down Andrew's ebullient mood. After that brilliant downtown corner store, Louis Sullivan was designing a linoleum plant, and a foundry, Andrew had heard. The marriage didn't seem to have changed things. He sometimes wondered if the Master kept an eye on what *he* was doing; surely Sullivan would see this article in the magazine, and perhaps, even, a sign would come from him. But no sign came.

In the coming new century Andrew meant to work strictly in his own way. He could afford to now. Young graduates were coming to him, to become apprentices, there came a blushing fellow named Stephen Gaylord, same upper-crust type as Malcolm Reese, indeed they had a vague family connection. And young Gaylord had blushingly mentioned that Malcolm Reese had assured him Andrew Lane would be the best for an apprenticeship.

Also clients were coming from outside the Chicago area. There was Stover in Buffalo. Ran a big warehousing operation. Visited his brother here in Oak Park, in what Andrew felt was his finest, a newly completed large residence. Got all excited over the place and wanted a big house in Buffalo that would make people sit up and take notice—all the latest ideas. For the new century.

Just as Andrew himself had felt it, others were now seeing it. A style. He thought of each house as a naturally grown organism, an organic structure, the way a body was organic. A being—a fish, bird, reptile, quadruped, human being, each was an organism grown to its use and form. Something of what the Master had talked about, but this kind of house, Andrew felt, was his own development. A structure too was an organism, even if made of stone, cement, steel.

With this thought came a principle that he had started to use by instinct perhaps, but now used knowingly: the flow. The Master had spoken of continuity, of how one form led into another, but with him it had seemed a theory rather than an active principle. How could it work in a high office building? Offices, strung along a corridor? Yet in a home, down on the ground, there was an active sense of flow, as the inhabitants, the family, moved about within the structure, coming together at meals, being together in the common living area, the "living room" instead of the parlor; there they could carry on their activities, separate or joined, children at their play, parents reading. Only in sleep quarters need there be separate arrangements. What he had first felt as elimination of needless separate boxes, of corridors, Andrew now felt as an elimination of separations. Rather than a mere spatial continuity he now found himself expatiating on a kind of plasticity, a molding of space, not only in horizontal flow but upward as well, sections of ceiling could be left open to the roof, as in his barrel-roofed playroom for the children. There now came a sense of mastery of the flow, of molding space into areas of greater and lesser privacy, using partial walls, turns, all within a single form, the wholeness.

The idea showed, even in an amusing way, or a nuisance, in that playroom, for he had left a small extension to the balcony over his drafting room. Well, a child could slip through and look down on the draftsmen at their work, including Papa when he wasn't in his private front office. And it hadn't been long before Wally was using a bean-blower up there.

It was a time to think things through, even, Willis said, to write out some of his ideas. The horizontal aspect, the earth-line of the prairie—Andrew, at least, had ideas, whereas for himself Willis was somewhat discouraged, doing mostly remodeling. After his sister's school, there were several old buildings around Hull House that had needed to be virtually rebuilt inside. The settlement kept expanding. True, there were new structures built, a theater, and studios for resident artists, but the architects seemed to be chosen by the donors, and Willis was not the kind to put himself forward, though Andrew would indeed have wanted to have a chance at the theater. In the old buildings, nearly a square block of them as time went on, Willis helped install carpentry and handicraft shops for neighborhood boys, sewing and cooking rooms for girls, a pottery shop, a gymnasium, small apartments for volunteer workers who kept joining Jane Addams—young college girls going out into the neighborhood to teach women how to take care of their babies, even if some of the women demanded, "Excuse, lady, you don't yourself have *bambino?*"

Then Willis' mother died. His sister would be moving in at her school, where Willis had provided living-in accommodations, and Willis decided to move to the men's residence at Hull House.

One morning he came into Andrew's section at the office and all at once declared, "I don't know what I'm doing in architecture, altogether." He had thought it out, and come to his conclusion. "You, Andrew—it excites you. For me, it was a nice, clean profession to learn." In a way, he had perhaps done it for his mother. But now what little he had to do he could do at Hull House. Two evenings a week he supervised a boys' club. There was always activity. It was a varied, useful life and suited him. Well, they'd remain friends. His first friend, Andrew realized, from virtually his first day in Chicago.

Alone up there, Andrew felt an emptiness. Somehow he couldn't bring himself to get someone else to share the place. Hours, between client visits, he even experienced a sense of isolation, of loneliness, that he would not have believed in his character.

A group from the round table at Kinsey's were taking a loft on Wabash Avenue, in the Kimball Building, dividing it up into drafting rooms, with a shared central office and secretary. Though he didn't feel as comradely with the others as he had with Willis, the arrangement would be advantageous. And so he came down from his high, lone tower.

16

HELENA WANTED her New Century party to be in the spirit. Not like a horn-tooting New Year's party that would leave a mess of confetti that kept turning up under the pillows for weeks afterward, but also not stuffy with the awesomeness of a new century. Cheerful and friendly, an open house, but still—an impressive event. They would use the studio as well as the house; push back the drawing boards, make a space for dancing. Move in the piano.

Getting into the spirit, Andrew decided this was the time he would design a new gown for her, his chatelaine moving about in a gown that harmonized with her domain, the fabric in tone with the room color, and the form with little vertical tucks to echo the harp lines of his chairs.

While Andrew liked to have parties at the house, he often let it seem as though, outside of their circle of old friends, Jack and Vicki, Alf Eastman and Georgia, he hardly knew whom Helena planned to invite. Just as in the days when he "didn't want to know" about her playing the young architect's wife who made social contacts with prospective clients. Those days were over. But Helena would laugh at him, why, half the neighbors along the street, with whom they had dinners back and forth, were people whose houses he had built.

And this was the time at last, she said, to invite Dr. Hemingway and his wife. Andrew made the expected groan; for years he had been avoiding having her invite that squalling Hemingway woman with her opera-singing airs. And well he knew what was in back of his Helena's inflexible mind: the Hemingways, still living in a rented house, were soon going to build, and indeed the opera singer's palatial ambitions were widely known, from her own descriptions. It was going to be not only a house but an opera house, with a vast, two-story music room with a platform, where her chosen pupils would give recitals. Not to mention recitals of her own. Doubtless Helena meant to remind that woman about his hand in building the Auditorium with its unrivaled acoustics!

Why, she just thought it was high time she invited them, only to be neighborly, as they were going to build so close by, Helena said; she hoped they weren't already tied up for New Century's Eve!

The Slaters too seemed never to give up on finding him clients, for Vicki had that meaningful look as she introduced their friends, recently married, named Garnett. "We're trying to convince them Oak Park is the place to live!" At least they didn't have the fresh-paint newlywed glow. And the wife, with nothing of merely polite flattery in her tone, spoke of her admiration for the Slater house. Andrew almost had to bend his head to listen, for the woman had one of those low, personal voices. And as they moved along, Andrew saw that she noticed each piece of his own-designed furniture.

Vicki was breathlessly regaling Helena with the history of the couple. A college romance. She was real brainy, even took a master's degree. Didn't want to get married, got herself a position in a library in Michigan. Poor Ralph had pursued her, all these five years, and finally Laura had given in though she had insisted on keeping "obey" out of the vows.

The husband, having caught the last part of the story, declared his wife had never had to insist, as he believed in equality! "Hear, hear!" cried Vicki, while Jack cried, "Traitor!" And in the merriment Andrew had a look at them. The husband with a decent face, athletic build. The ex-librarian—maybe library work was the explanation for her whispery voice—was tallish, with a wide, clear forehead, her hair upswept. Though too serious-looking for a Gibson girl. A long white neck with not a chain or bangle, fine arms, her periwinkle gown in good taste, no frills. Garnett had his own factory, manufactured something electrical, Andrew didn't quite catch what, as a whole new swarm was just entering, shaking off snow—yes, perfect for the new-century night, great soft snowflakes wafting down, you could see as the door opened. And just at that moment the kids, the whole caboodle of them, even tiny Cynthia, suddenly broke out with a concert of horn blasts from the top of the stairs, Wally conducting.

Into this came the Hemingway tribe, both generations, the real Oak Parkers from the time it was farmland, husband and wife one of those elderly couples that had grown to resemble each other, and their son the doctor with his operatic wife, a romance from Oak Park High School. Tonight Grace really looked a Brünnhilde. Statuesque with bold bare shoulders, in a French evening gown. The doctor husband was stalwart, an outdoorsman, who, once you established that you didn't hunt or fish, seemed to have little to say; but his wife made up for this, as she had opinions about everything.

Helena had hired not one but three servitors for the occasion, a white-hatted chef behind the buffet—which was laden with a huge roast turkey, a beef roast and a dozen other dishes, salads, condiments, desserts—while two maids, one in the house, one in the studio, kept circulating with trays of tidbits. Though they themselves and Oak Parkers in general weren't too much on alcohol, there were large bowls of a potent grog in studio and house, and a case of French champagne was ready for the midnight moment.

To the coming century! people kept toasting, in higher and higher pitch.

Had this been a good, great, bad, or indifferent century? It was America's Century, they generally agreed, the continent at last entirely opened up, one land! And the Civil War, all solemnly recalled, had sanctified the Union in blood, just as the Revolutionary War had sanctified the previous century. Others spoke of Progress—electricity, the telephone, railways, telegraph. A knot of architects spoke of the skyscraper—with no limit in sight.

But on the dark side, there were the anarchists, the assassinations; the new century would most probably see greater upheavals, even revolutions! Just as democracy had conquered monarchy, so, in the new century, might not anarchism, socialism and communism conquer democracy?

At one moment Andrew found himself in a circle where the women were holding forth. In the new century, women could no longer be denied the vote. That whispery-voiced librarian, with a smile, wondered if they'd use it better than men had, and her husband laughingly raised his grog glass and cried, "Hear hear!" Then someone—a male voice—started up the Lydia Pankhurst song. Then a circle was around the piano, singing "My Old Kentucky Home," and, with Vicki banging away, this merged into "Tipperary," and soon someone called out for Grace Hemingway to honor the company. She let herself be persuaded, and presently was standing beside the piano. Vicki declared, oh, she wasn't good enough to accompany. However, Grace's mother was ready to oblige.

An open circle was formed, so that suddenly it was like a recital, as Grace Hemingway announced she would sing what she had once sung at Madison Square Garden.

Andrew had to turn his face away, and accidentally caught the eye of that librarian, what was her name—

Laura—likewise suppressing a smile. They exchanged amused looks as the Brünnhilde boomed forth, indeed with enough power for Madison Square Garden. It was only her weak eyes, which could not endure powerful stage lights, that had, as everyone knew, prevented Grace from becoming an opera star.

Soon the hour would sound. For the magic moment, Helena had threaded her way to his side, and as they raised their champagne glasses Andrew felt the moment transmuted back into the unbounded sense of inherent power, of overflowing life, he had felt at their time of young love. Now here he was, master of his own house, father of five children, confident of his creative resources, and with a growing reputation. Why, he was going to be invited—Bob Mann had just a while ago tipped him off, for Bob had got himself onto the Architects Club committee—to address the coming convention, in Chicago, of the Architectural League of America!

Helena, mother of a whole brood, yet youthful and sparkling! That was why she had had all the children right off, one after the other, she liked to declare. Pressing close, she said, "Well, we haven't done so badly!" In spite of their bad times, their money troubles, an architect's occasional flirtations with clients' wives—and it was really the women who started it—here they were! A marriage in full bloom!

And as the lights were snapped off, with only candles glowing in Japanese lanterns—Andrew himself had placed each one for exactly the proper effect—and with the log fire ablaze in the great studio fireplace, he and Helena, other husbands and wives were kissing, and Grace Hemingway's Brünnhilde voice rose in the one song of all for the occasion, it was again their night of the Auditorium with Adelina Patti singing "Home Sweet Home."

Then everyone was singing "Auld Lang Syne." Happy New Century! Happy! Happy!

A remark of Willis' hovered for an instant in Andrew's mind, from one of their early, solemn, philosophical discussions: "Is happiness the greatest desideratum?"

17

IT WOULD be three years until Laura and Ralph Garnett decided to build their home in Oak Park, and naturally came to Andrew for the design, for in that time, living in a rented house on Kenilworth Avenue, they had become familiar with the Lanes. Laura Garnett had a year ago given birth to their first child, a little boy, and now was in her early pregnancy with the second; this Andrew knew from a remark of Helena's, for Helena, as though their brood of five weren't enough, had, after being careful during four years, slipped into the family way, reminding him that she had even before they were married told him they would have six children, and, as he knew, she was not one to . . . Oh, yes indeed, he knew! She was not one to give up an idea! And, the way women talk among themselves, Helena had brought back to him the news that Laura Garnett was also in the early stages. And since the Garnetts had not built their house for their first, they wanted to have their own home ready for the second.

It was not Helena's old architect's-wife habit that had brought the Garnetts, she had even given up on the Hemingways, who were now about to build their palatial mansion-with-concert-hall on their lot in the block behind. So many things were coming Andrew's way that Helena didn't even know half of what he was doing.

For indeed, from the start of the new century, his career had gone into full stride, but, even more important for him, the surge of ideas that he had felt in the few preceding years, ideas, forms, sometimes inchoate, had come into focus. He knew now exactly what he was doing. Though occasionally, for a big commission, he agreed to what was for him a mere exercise in style, he could now turn such work over, with a preliminary sketch, to one of his designers. Thus free of details, Andrew had found himself in a spurt of creativity, in one house after another, some of them quite large and lavish, he had perfected his style, and now there was even the name—the Prairie House. The low silhouette with pure horizontal lines extended in the projecting cantilevered overhangs; and inside he had played with floor levels and open ceiling areas, until a house seemed really to breathe. His style was becoming nationally known, the Andrew Lane house was a symbol of the modern, the new.

Thus it seemed appropriate that he should speak before the Architectural League meeting this year in Chicago. Andrew was sure it was his former chief, Dankmar Adler, who had arranged for his appearance, though Robert Mann let on that it was his doing, for, a few months before the assembly, Dankmar Adler had suddenly died of a heart attack. Surely it was the strain of the Auditorium that had killed him, even if a decade later. And the breakup with Louis Sullivan. But Adler had remained respected in the profession, a voice in the League, and thus, Andrew was sure, had done him a last kindness and arranged this recognition.

And almost as though the Chief were listening, Andrew talked earnestly before the professional assembly. What had happened, in the last generation, to architecture? Where was the architect's authority gone? Any silly housewife could tell an architect what and how to build!

Architects allowed themselves to be given orders by the ignorant and tasteless, they were put into the role of copiers, of caterers to the whims of the wealthy, the showier the better, more gilt, more Italian this and French that, while the native American impulse, the simplicity and craftsmanship of the Quakers, the surge toward an indigenous style by the Richardsons and the Sullivans, was shunted aside. Surely, new young architects must break through! Architectural firms no longer had personality, they were now corporations. Bailey, Quincy, Appleseed, Dinkerman, Abercrombie and Copyman, he parodied. Enough that corporate architecture choked the streets with office structures—human beings still needed homes. The family was America, let the young architects work close to the earth and the hearth—there a truly American architecture was growing!

In the crowding around, when he stepped from the platform—congratulations, objections, questions—Andrew caught sight, at the edge, of his mother and Aunt Nora, a teasing look in his aunt's eyes, oh she had got Marta to bring her and they had slipped in. They'd seen his exhibit and were all pride—why, Andrew had more space than almost any other architect! And certainly, though naturally they were prejudiced, his was the most original, the most exciting work. More people had been gathered around Andrew's part than anywhere else. (Watching from the back of the room, Andrew had noticed that himself.) Now Aunt Nora had something to ask. The school he had built over ten years ago was outgrown. She was ready for a large new edifice. An expanded Home School.

THIS TIME—what a difference! How he had learned, in these years!

From that staid, conventional structure he had so proudly put up, his first real building, at twenty, to what he was designing now! At each end of the new, wide-windowed classroom structure would be a cross-expansion, gymnasium, assembly. On the dormitory floor, over the classrooms, a continuous unbroken span of windows. How every element dovetailed, supported the other! What a sense of the whole. His best so far! Must be the effect on him of the old homesite, the valley.

And he was trying a brand-new invention. Instead of the usual ugly radiators for the heating, clumsy protrusions even when he designed openwork covers for them, why not get them out of sight altogether? Bury them! Under the floor! And even, radiant floor heat, pleasant to walk on, especially when the children got up in the morning. Yes!

Worked out fine! With the structure complete, and having lately taken up photography and built himself a darkroom in the studio—as if he didn't have enough, Helena said, to keep him from spending time as a father with his children—Andrew now locked himself in his closet. Nevertheless he lugged his huge camera and tripod all the way out to River Valley on the train, got excellent plates of the Home School, and hung a huge print in the entrance room of his downtown office.

Women's clubs had taken to asking him to speak. And that new label was spreading: the Prairie House. A decade ago Chicago style had meant the skyscraper. Now Chicago style was beginning to mean "Prairie architecture." The term kept appearing in the journals, with his name as originator, though more and more names were now added, Robert Mann's usually next to Andrew Lane. "The Prairie School."

Let them all hitch on, it was still he who led the talk at the round table, and he had another idea that was breaking through. Machine art. Now that the machine had taken over in American life, now that machine-made elements were used more and more in construction, why not design directly for the machine? Why should thousands of miles of bulbous newel posts be automatically turned out, and furniture with tortured legs, why should handicraft be imitated by templates, why not design directly, gracefully, honestly, for what the machine could do? Metals, ceramics, wood, in forms that were frankly machine made? Once, at Uncle Bruce's Sunday dinner, Andrew got onto the subject and Uncle's favorite guest, Jane Addams, was there. She had been bemoaning the way immigrants were losing their native handicraft skills, and declared that Andrew's idea fitted right in. He must come and lecture on this. Precisely *because* Jane was trying to preserve the skills of the immigrant craftsmen. Let hands do handwork—thus true craft-work would become sought after again, while the machine product had its own style. Indeed, Jane was planning to start an Arts and Crafts Society, and such a talk would be perfect.

Where didn't Jane have her connections! The *Tribune* printed an editorial about the brilliant young architect Andrew Lane and his important idea. The article was widely quoted, and there came a letter from New York, from the *American Woman*, signed by no other than that one-time installment collector, then erstwhile newspaper reporter, Theodore Dreiser. Here he was, now a magazine editor!

The letter, after just a few words of friendly regards, was quite businesslike. Would Andrew consider doing an article, including sample plans for a modern house—a house for young families of modest means? What so many young married people dreamed of, a small house with lots of room in it, and also the possibility of expansion as the family grew.

Well, that wasn't a bad idea at all. Andrew read the letter to Helena. "Remember—that fellow that wanted to be a writer."

Why, Helena had just lately read some scandal: This Theodore Dreiser had actually written a novel. A publisher had printed it, but then refused to put it into the bookstores because his wife considered it was dirty. And Dreiser was even suing the publisher.

"Well, now here he is a magazine editor."

"You know, his brother is that famous songwriter, Paul Dresser, you know, 'Banks of the Wabash.' "

Andrew's own thoughts went to that afternoon in the

Studio Building, with that strange inamorata of Dreiser's —and all her tales of the notorious Charles Yerkes, the car-line magnate, driving poor young Dreiser out of town. At times, since that encounter, Andrew had wondered in himself, was he meant to have tried, should he have tried —with her? Had all that eager talk, sometimes ethereal, sometimes daring, been an invitation?

. . . But this was a wonderful chance! Helena declared as she read Dreiser's letter. Andrew ought to do the article!

And so he did, and there even came several commissions. That novel of Dreiser's, Helena said, was finally on sale. *Sister Carrie* it was called. Helena got hold of it at Brentano's bookstore downtown, you had to ask for it, they had it under the counter! But she didn't find it so scandalous, certainly it wasn't dirty, Helena said; indeed, there wasn't even a single good love scene in it. Just a story of a working girl who took up with a traveling salesman, for the easy life, living with him as though they were married. It all happened in Chicago, and then this creature even double-crossed her traveling salesman, while he was away she took up with a friend of his, the manager of a fancy downtown bar where he had used to take her—you know, like the Palmer House, where respectable women could be taken. But this bar manager was a married man with a family. He was so crazy about Carrie, he carried her off to New York, even taking the day's receipts that he was supposed to put in the bank. Then that slut left him and became a famous singer. And the poor man just went to the dogs. Now, when they had met Dreiser at the exposition, hadn't he talked of a sister who sang on the stage? Imagine, writing a book like that, about his own sister!

Andrew started indeed to read *Sister Carrie*, but Dreiser was as long-winded when he wrote as when he talked to you, and, as Helena had said, the book really didn't contain even a single exciting love scene. Still, when Theo Dreiser asked for another article, Andrew wrote him that the book had realism and power. That was true. And even from their long-ago first encounter, the horse-and-buggy ride, the fellow had told him he wanted to write books, and Andrew, because of his own self, he guessed, felt strongly for a man who did what he set out to do.

Another who spoke about the book was Laura Garnett. The four of them had met at the all-Beethoven concert, and gone to Rector's for a bite, and there Helena and Laura got to talking about the scandalous book. Laura saw it in a different way. It was, she said, a story that showed the degrading position of women in American life. Of course Mr. Dreiser was influenced by Zola, but still, you saw a girl of poor family coming to the city to try to earn her own living, working long hours in a sweatshop, and just to buy a bonnet she had to accept gifts from a man she had met by chance on the train. And so she gradually let herself become his mistress. Mr. Dreiser was out to show that in our kind of society a poor young woman could find a comfortable life only by trading her body. Sister Carrie did not become a prostitute, but still, trading her body was the only way open to her. Of course the rest, her becoming a star in a show and all that, was romantic, and for how many was it a solution, one in a million, but at least in the early part Dreiser had faced the real problem.

Laura Garnett was not particularly indignant, she didn't become emphatic like Helena. She stated things in a clear but rather sorrowful way, not so much sorrow for the girl, or really the man in the story, but for this kind of failure all around, in American life. Ralph listened with his look of pride at his wife's intelligence.

Now she turned to another aspect. The essence of all art. Style: Really Dreiser's style was atrocious. You never found yourself raising your eyes from the page and saying, "How beautiful!" Andrew recognized the feeling. That same feeling he sometimes had had about a structure—the great hall of the Auditorium. And Laura Garnett looked at him, as though she were saying that he, surely, would understand.

18

AT THE Buffalo Pan-American Exposition, President McKinley was shot to death, this time it *was* an anarchist, and Helena said she only hoped Clarence Darrow wouldn't go and try to keep him from being hung. Anarchists were being arrested everywhere, Emma Goldman and all the rest of them, as for the Haymarket hangings, but this time at least the police had the real assassin and he was quickly tried and hung and that was the end of it.

Discussions turned to other topics. Andrew even found himself invited to Darrow's lively group at the Langley apartments, to give his talk "Art and the Machine." Clarence had a new lady friend, it seemed, a newspaper reporter, who openly stayed with him there, she was twenty years younger than Darrow, and Helena warned Andrew not to get any ideas!

Clarence wanted a place somewhere maybe in the woods where he could get away from all this and write, yes, he was going to write a novel that showed the helplessness of a man caught by fate, step by step until he is driven to murder. But how could he get to writing while he had to save a fourteen-year-old boy whom they wanted to hang because his mother had given him a pistol and told him to shoot anyone who came and tried to throw them out of their house, and when the bailiff came he had done it. No sooner had Clarence got that boy off than he had to go to Pennsylvania to represent the striking coal miners.

And no sooner had Andrew found a site for him, not only secluded but with a view of the lake, and begun to sketch an ideal cottage, then there occurred a disaster, Darrow's closest friend, ex-Governor Altgeld, died. On a lecture platform in Peoria, Helena read, and she recalled only a few months ago hearing them debating "Is Life Worth Living?" Clarence always "no," and Altgeld "yes." Even though after he had pardoned the anarchists he had been reviled and ruined. Until Darrow saved him by taking him in as his law partner. Yes.

ANDREW WAS so busy, with eight houses going, he could hardly find time for the dream of Uncle Bruce, a six-story community house with a church inside. Uncle Bruce was sure he could get his congregation to raise over a hundred thousand dollars, but he had to have a beautiful rendering to show them. No sooner had Andrew made a sketch than Uncle Bruce wrote an eight-page letter of details, he wanted the assembly on another floor, he wanted higher basement windows for the cooking room for girls and the woodworking room for boys, he wanted Andrew to submit the plans to an "expert" in New York. Who would have imagined all this from Uncle Bruce! Overloaded, with the big Stover job in Buffalo, Andrew got one of the other architects in the shared offices to join on the project and take over Uncle Bruce's specifications. More eight-page letters. From "Dear Boys," they were now addressed as "Dear Messrs. Phillips and Lane."

Over a year of argument with Uncle Bruce had gone by, Andrew had to spend weeks in Buffalo, where he was introducing all sorts of innovations, an enormous skylight over open space with rows of desks four stories down; and he was developing an idea of good old Dankmar Adler's, from the Auditorium, air blowers over huge blocks of ice, providing constant coolness in midsummer.

In the midst of all this, that big real-estate operator, Arthur Kaiser, came along and bought the Rookery! It needed redoing, he told Andrew, especially the entrance. Surely he wasn't going to touch that magnificent open double stairway in the lobby, the first sight Andrew had had of architectural daring in Chicago. No, not that, but Andrew ought to come over, in fact move in. Kaiser would fix him up with a suite of offices, they'd work something out. And so, leaving Phillips to finish with Uncle Bruce, there Andrew was at the Rookery, on his own again!

ONE SUNDAY he managed to get over with the Garnetts to look at their plot. It lay in the middle of a half-built-up block, but was wide enough so as not to present a squeezed-in aspect. There was a downward slope, perhaps fifteen feet. Much as he disliked basements, this decline might be useful. Already, Ralph had said something about a billiard room. Maybe below? Also, he intended to buy an automobile. So, at the lower end, wouldn't that be good for a garage?

Late one afternoon, the Garnetts came to the Rookery.

Andrew had kept the glass-topped consulting table, and saw that Ralph was impressed. Laura gazed at his large photograph of the Home School. "How beautiful," she said. "Where is it?" And he described his home valley in Wisconsin, and his Aunt Nora's school, even Governor La Follette's little girl was a pupil there.

In his first sketch for Ralph and Laura he had got away from his now "standard" Prairie House. This one was square, with a pyramidal roof. Instead of a front entrance, a simple door on the side; somehow he had felt that Laura would like this quality of privacy. The continuous band of windows came down as French doors on the veranda, which had a waist-high parapet, so calculated that the street was open to the householder while from the street the residence couldn't be seen into.

She appreciated this at once.

For the interior, behind the broad central fireplace was an open stairway down to Ralph's billiard room, fitted snugly under the rising front part of the plot. The main living area Andrew had left open to the slanted roof, so that several height levels came into play; he could break up the space without breaking the flow, indicating side alcoves, and a cozy area before the fireplace. Altogether, a variety of groupings, and yet, when they had a lot of people over, a continuous space. It pleased him. One of his best. And Laura saw it; she smiled.

Behind the low-shouldered fireplace, the flow continued along a half-open hall to the bedrooms, the nursery, a room for her sister to live with them. Another room for a nursemaid?

Laura seemed hesitant. She didn't like too many people in the house, she said, again falling into her whispery voice, almost as if this were a personal confidence. Well . . . he had a thought: as there was going to be a garage, why not put a servant's room above it? —But in the winter, she said, with the cutting wind, and snow . . . ?

What Laura Garnett really wanted didn't come out until a few weeks later when she stopped in, downtown, for the next look. Andrew had indicated a room over the garage.

Now, with that whisper, which could be either shyness or even a kind of confiding, Laura Garnett said, "You see, as my husband will have his own place, downstairs, I thought of perhaps using the . . . above the garage . . . for me."

Andrew couldn't help a chuckle. There was your equal rights for women! No mere "sewing room" and such. Her own private place. And what, he wondered, did she mean to do there? A man usually made his "den" into a place to hang his hunting and fishing trophies—and to tell off-color stories to his cronies. Then, as one might tell an intimate symptom to a doctor, Mrs. Garnett was explaining: she felt the need of a place of her own, for—well, she was trying to write. Indeed, she had received some encouragement, been accepted into Mr. Herrick's special class at the university. And so— She stopped, and gazed at him.

A pulse of personal feeling, a kind of tenderness, rose toward Laura. He had indeed, in their social contacts before, at the Slaters', or once or twice with all of them at the theater or a concert, noticed that she was an attractive woman. The long line of her throat, her easy movements, a body-flow rather than the sense of a dress form carried about. And an emanation, not so much a scent as a delicate freshness. As Helena sometimes not too jestingly repeated, he had an eye. In the goings-out of friendly couples there was always a touch of flirtation in the guise of gallantry. Andrew had kept it up for years with Vicki, just as Jack had with Helena.

But the whispery way in which Laura had told him about her "wanting to write" had touched him. "You see," she added, "just as a man sometimes needs to get away by himself, so does a woman."

This had never quite occurred to him. Not with Helena. Indeed, women never seemed to want solitude. Still, he was already visualizing Laura Garnett's retreat. Not "feminine," but yet a personal, a graceful room. And then, the point she had brought out earlier, the going back and forth across the yard in the cold winds. And also, going up through a dirty, cluttered garage. He began to sketch a little idea, perhaps from way back when his cousin Susan was getting married and he had suggested that covered walkway for Gus, linking house and barn. So here, spanning the lot's downslope, he could have a little enclosed corridor-bridge from their bedroom to the upper room of the garage. He would give the corridor a slightly pitched roof, matching the house and the garage; that way all became a single whole. And Laura could comfortably, privately, slip out to her refuge whenever she chose.

"Much better all around," Andrew said, looking up. "You see, it makes a continuity for the whole structure, and for a useful reason."

Her face lit up, like that of an earnest student in a class. She saw his art. Even in such a detail. "Well, thank you so much, Andrew. I'll bless you every time I walk into that corridor, with the wind howling outside!"

But the little design had also made something—like a secrecy, a connection—between them. What did she write, or want to write? And the thought of her, sitting there concentrated, her white neck bent over her writing, did not leave him after she was gone.

He had an additional idea. Light. The way a clarity emanated from the woman herself. Thus, he indicated a continuous strip of windows all around her studio; it harmonized with the fenestration of the house.

Laura Garnett swore by Dr. Hemingway, Helena said, and this time she was determined to make the change.

Even while Helena went on about old Dr. Eagan's breath getting more and more sour, and his puffing it into your face, Andrew was putting out of mind some peculiar reaction about Laura Garnett.

Later, when he took up the Garnett sketch in the studio, that same peculiar reaction returned. The gross talk had it that a woman in pregnancy was all the more tempting. Freer, more abandoned. Andrew stopped the whole train of thought, somewhat self-embarrassed over having slipped into it about Laura Garnett. The sight of pregnancy, in other women than Helena of course, the plain evidence of another man's entry, had always destroyed rather than heightened any masculine arousal in him. Yet, with his own wife, with Helena, the periods of pregnancy were the best, between them. Indeed, he suspected this was why she had chosen after a lapse of four years to have this little carelessness, a miscalculation she had said, but then added, why not? For she felt the womanly hunger once again to hold a baby in her arms. Oh! he knew his

Helena, and her system of accidentally always getting her way! He supposed he wasn't unpleased.

The Garnetts were to come on Sunday for dinner, to look at his completed rendering. Ralph Garnett drove up in a brand-new Duryea, the brass glowing, and the kids were all around it even before Ralph and Laura, in their goggles and dust coats, climbed out. Wally—at least he had asked permission—was already squeezing the horn.

Ralph must really be doing well, to afford a car even when he was building a house!

After the meal, before going to their lot, Andrew wanted them to have a look at the kind of house he was doing now, though theirs would be different; he was rather proud of the way this one was coming out. It was just at the end of the street. And so the three of them—Helena didn't come along—strolled down what was now jocularly called Andrew's Lane. As they passed the Phil Whaley houses, and other earlier efforts, he pointed out what was wrong with each one—there he'd let them talk him into an "excrescence," and in this next one he'd given way to a client's desire for Tudor half-timbering, and there, the worst, dormers! for servants to hang out of to get a bit of air—until Laura softly laughed, to her husband, "Can you imagine what he'll be saying about ours, in a few years!" She had a warm, throaty laugh.

The new house at the end of the street had his most daring projection until now—a cantilevered veranda, extending the building's line into space itself. "A real prairie schooner," Laura caught the feel of it. "But ours," she said, "will have the sheltering idea of a tent." She had caught that too.

PLUNKING DOWN the first Garnett money, Andrew bought himself a Stoddard. The automobile was low, and long—this was exactly what he had meant when he talked of the art of the machine, at last the automobile makers had got away from the horse buggy! Here was a motorcar to go with his kind of house. And the fine leather seats, the gleam and sheen of the whole, the throb of power! The boys were incessantly poking around the vehicle when it stood in the driveway, polishing it incessantly, Wally and Ned, those rascals neither of whom he could get to run a simple errand. And hosing. If he tried to chase them off, of a Sunday morning, Wally would turn the hose on him.

And perforce, now on Sunday afternoons he had to pile the whole caboodle into the back seat; Helena had got herself a voluminous motoring costume with a hat combining goggles and veil, and thus, the canoe neglected, came the family picnic, as in the valley of his uncles. Wally— Andrew had only suddenly realized the strength of the lad —insisted on doing the crank-up, and kept trying to put his hands on the steering wheel. Andrew kept the keys strictly to himself—one day that youth was liable to get hold of them, sneak out, and even try to drive. What an obstinacy! And yet inwardly Helena laughed at him when he complained, for she saw that Papa Andrew was pleased.

So they rode forth in great clamor, with heads turning and neighboring kids and their dogs chasing the monstrous vehicle, the dogs the last to give up.

On his construction rounds, though he continued to wear the riding pants and boots, Andrew now rarely used his mount. He even ventured in the Stoddard to the city itself, and to the North Shore, where he had a lakeside job nearing completion.

And in River Forest a very large residence on a veritable estate. It was amazing how the Prairie House idiom adapted itself to a three-story mansion. Six draftsmen were now crowded into the studio; he had even put up a balcony, hanging it from chains so as to keep the working area below clear of posts.

In the new automobile, he would convey his city clients from the station; naturally the women came more frequently, not only because the husbands were busy downtown, but because it was the wives who were concerned with details. They would arrive all accoutered for motoring, with foulards that streamed in the breeze. As Andrew drove right through the center of town, heads turned—there were still no more than five automobiles in Oak Park, and horses still shied and even reared. The ladies shrieked and clutched at him. About certain ones, particularly the young and vivacious, Helena took to repeating, in her amused and sarcastic manner, remarks that were being made. Andrew Lane was getting himself quite a reputation! Perhaps Helena felt it more than usually—in her final months she was blotched and formless, but that would soon be over with.

By contrast, Laura—perhaps because this was only her second, while for Helena it was the sixth, Laura, even in these late months, had an upright ease of bearing. He took her frequently to the site, for their house was now nearing completion; there was a quality almost classic about its simple form, pure geometry was really the best way. Indeed, when he found Bob Mann, one morning, come over from a job of his own to have a look, he knew it was damn good. Bob even shook his hand in congratulations and announced, "This is a great one, Andrew." Laura too understood it was coming out like an exhibition piece, and they were discussing the interior finishes, and furniture; she had herself noticed the terrible clash of the Slaters' Chippendale, and she was eager when Andrew offered to design the furniture—even to the bedroom. Though she flushed.

And for her own place above the garage—her studio, he had at first called it, but, seeing that she didn't herself use the word, he had gone back to saying her "place"— Andrew recalled a remark she had once made about her years as a librarian, how she had really liked her job, she would love to live surrounded by books. And so below the band of windows there was now a band of bookshelves around the entire room, interrupted only by the door. Everything was handily within reach, with no floor-level shelves to make you get down on your knees.

As each time when she entered to see the progress,

Laura gave her throaty sound of pleasure, for, flooded with all-around light, the room seemed afloat in the sky. Now, with the shelving, how thoughtful he had been with the details, even for books of different heights. In the center he had placed a large table, circular except for a bite where a chair fitted in. Laura uttered a little sound, between laughter and dismay. Clearly—for he had even thought out arrangements for ink, paper, an overhead light—this was the writing table. And indeed the chair was unusual, with armrests, and narrow vertical slats in the style of his own furniture at home.

"But Andrew . . . I . . ." He saw that something was wrong and that because Laura recognized how much thought he had given to the room, she was hesitant to voice any objection. "You see . . ." she began, and then explained in a whispery rush: she didn't even know whether she ever could become a writer, she was trying to find out, and . . . all this was so important-looking—like for a Balzac!—and what she really felt . . . she felt like hiding when she tried her writing; she always hid away what she wrote, she wasn't ready, all she wanted was a nook—and she scrunched herself together. Their eyes met, and they both laughed. This time Andrew found himself holding down a desire.

He did away with the circular table, and in the far corner extended a shelf outward to form a writing surface. From the other wall he angled a set of bookshelves into the room, making a secluded nook, with a pagoda lamp over the shelf-desk. There, in her private study, she'd be virtually hidden. Indeed, the corner desk fitted so nicely, with an open view into the trees, that it seemed detached from the work—the only obstruction being the corner post, and why not eliminate it? What a feeling that would give, just suiting that airy clarity about Laura. To take over the corner post's roof-bearing function, he could set a post several feet back, where the bookshelves angled together, and from it project a roof beam to the corner, using his favorite method, the cantilever. Thus the glass angle would be totally unobstructed, free, the panes mitered into a perfect joining. A new thing. It pleased him. And he could already see Laura's pleased smile.

When it was finished and he brought her in to look, Laura impulsively kissed his cheek.

Undoubtedly Helena had sensed what was happening. Then one day she chanced upon the chair design. She had been coming less and less into the studio, usually sending one of the children, most often little Cynthia, when she wanted something—almost always money to pay an importunate tradesman. But this day Helena had gone in, while Andrew was downtown, to ask the newest apprentice, Gene Tillit, to help her with some curtains in the house. On Andrew's board lay a sketch for a corner desk, with a special chair with thin upright slats. It was like her own chair that he had designed, the harp-string chair they had called it. This was of course for Laura.

When he got up from dinner, Helena followed to the studio entrance. "Who's the chair for?" she asked.

The Garnett house. Did she like it?

"That's my chair!" Helena was startled at the vehemence in her own voice, and so, she saw, was Andrew. Yet she continued, though quietly. "It's for Laura, isn't it? For her private room?"

Naturally he had mentioned the room, an idea of Laura's, even made mild jokes about it, equality for women, den for den.

Helena came out with it. "All right, Andrew. Are you in love with her?"

He had not even admitted anything that far to himself. "You're out to that house every day, with her," his wife persisted. —Not so, but no use trying to make a woman keep to facts. He must tell Helena that she was, in her condition, simply overwrought. "Helena—"

"The whole town is talking about you and your lady clients—especially this one. What do you think I feel like? And the way I look."

"Helena, she's just as pregnant as you are. Why should I—how could I—"

Then she was bawling. He tried taking her in his arms, but this was awkward and she pulled away. Even in the midst of this he was suddenly possessed by a longing for Laura, for the coolness and clarity around her, for her low voice.

They hadn't really touched. The little kiss on his cheek, a thank-you. True, they had sometimes lingered on, in the unfinished house, and talked a bit. She would discuss her ideas: someone should write about the woman of today. Oh, not a task for herself—she wasn't at all ready, writing was such a responsibility, and . . . And there was the whole question of whether writing should be for art's sake or for the sake of an idea, even a cause. Just now everyone was talking about that new book about the stockyards, the killing floors, with that poor Polish immigrant begging for work even when the job meant wading in blood and entrails. And his poor young wife dying because of their dreadful poverty. So *The Jungle* was really an exposure of social problems. Yet from a literary point of view, she meant the actual quality of writing, the style, this young Upton Sinclair's book was really not better than Theodore Dreiser's. And so it was difficult, in such writing, to measure the value . . .

Should he tell Helena they held literary discussions? After all, hadn't he used variations of that same chair design in several other houses?

Even though it might simply be the usual thing, while a house was in construction there was usually a kind of honeymoon between the architect and the mistress—at that word Helena had herself a bitter laugh. Usually the flirtation would break off when the job was over. But she could not dismiss her instinctive feeling—this with Laura was something more.

And that downtown office. Andrew was always staying late, alone. It would be a nice place to meet a paramour.

Oh, she was getting to be like a doctor's wife, jealous of all his female patients.

And then she had to laugh at herself. In the seventh month, big as an elephant, blotchy and feeling clumsy and ugly, no wonder she was having a jealous fit. Especially since Laura, taller, though showing quite fully now, carried so well, with her skin unblemished. And then Helena thought of an idea, a piece of wisdom she had once heard from Vicki. For Jack Slater was really awful that way, letting on about every woman they met, announcing he could really get interested in this one and that one, and imagining which ones were passionate and would really let themselves go. Then he would pass it all off as a joke. Still, Vicki had once confided to Helena that if she got suspicious about Jack and some other woman, a good idea was to make close friends with the woman. Being close friends with you, a woman would feel too conscience-stricken. Vicki was pleased at her strategy, yet to Helena it seemed scheming to be a friend for such a motive. Her own way in life was to feel absolutely open and honest with her friends. And besides, as to a rival being conscience-stricken, what was there to conscience when it came to real passion? Weren't you always reading about the great passion that swept all aside, husband, even children? Like in that book by Tolstoy, *Anna Karenina*.

She had, as through her earlier pregnancies, made it her way to keep up all her activities as usual, so at the Oak Park Women's Club when the book program leader, Georgia Eastman, looked over to her, as it was her turn for a discussion, Helena agreed. And as what they usually did was have two women read the same book, to start the discussion, so, next, Georgia asked Laura, and all the women laughed warmly, because the two of them being just even in their expecting.

It was to be the new book all Chicago was talking about, *The Jungle*, showing the horrors of the stockyards. Helena even remembered meeting the author a few years ago at Hull House, Jane Addams had invited him, he had been in Chicago gathering material, and here was the book, really a sensation. Of course the first thing everyone said was that after reading about those poor workmen shoveling blood and guts and diseased meat into the grinding vats, who would ever eat sausages again! And Helena herself had already stopped buying a certain brand that was supposed to be the company he wrote about, she certainly couldn't take any chances, not only because of the children but because of herself in her condition. But already it had come out in the papers that the company was going to sue this Upton Sinclair, and reporters had been invited out to the stockyards and everything had already been cleaned up, the workmen were even described as wearing big white aprons!

Laura had read the book, trust her. Now Laura suggested they should discuss not so much the sausage scandal as what happened to the woman in the story. How that poor young Polish wife also had to slave in the meat-packing factory, to pay the installments for their shanty, and when her husband was thrown out of work and they were starving and about to lose the house, she was forced by her foreman to go to one of those places on Twenty-second Street, and prostitute herself. That was what was done to women in an industrial society.

Laura recalled another example, from *Sister Carrie*, by Theodore Dreiser. "Oh—we know him!" Helena began to tell the story of the kitchen stove, but Laura said Oh yes, she knew it.

Had Andrew told her? Sometime when they were together?

"You and Andrew told us that story." Laura was so clever, she could read your thoughts.

But the important thing, Laura went on in her brainy way of analyzing books—after all, she had not only graduated from the university but had taken a master's degree—was to use both stories to show the place of the poor working girl. For Sister Carrie too had had, in a different way, to prostitute herself—

Oh? People were saying Sister Carrie was the story of Mr. Dreiser's own sister! Anyway, Helena said, in the stock-yards book the poor little Polish wife did what she did for the sake of her husband, they were starving—and then the poor woman died in childbirth, maybe that was divine retribution though cruel. But Carrie, Carrie was just a hussy wanting pretty clothes. And she ran off with that married man, the bar manager. He suddenly walked out on wife and family, in his passion for another woman, giving up everything, destroying his life.

The wave of fear, jealousy, had swept up again in Helena.

Yes, Laura said, really sorrowfully. Poor man. But she gave the example of *Anna Karenina*, by Tolstoy. In that book the man, Anna's paramour, did not suffer—he married a society girl, while Anna, the woman, was outcast. And for her love she had given up everything, even her child!

"That I really can't understand," Helena said, "I can't understand how any woman could leave her child."

And in that moment there was a bond between them, their eyes met in sorrow over the tragic happenings, the passions of men and women. In that moment, Helena felt they were really, before anything, women together, each could never hurt the other, and especially now—each with a new life throbbing within her.

Helena's child came first, a fine, nine-pound boy they named Richard, and Laura's was two weeks later, a little girl, almost eight pounds, whom they named Maida.

Everything subsided. Andrew was again in Buffalo, two residences there were almost done, and as the Stover office building neared completion he found himself in one of his streams of inventiveness, each idea brought forth another. From the idea of the closed structure, with its controlled temperature and ventilation, came a broader fireproof concept, particularly after all the horrors of that fire in New York City, when so many young women in a shirtwaist factory had died. If his structure was closed to air currents, a spreading flame was already prevented. Besides, he would avoid inflammable materials. Desks, cabinets—he would have them all made of metal. Came a fury of desk designing, recalling his ideas for a writing table for Laura. And another innovation, a seat with an adjustable back support, swinging out from the desk, so that the floor area was clear, making cleaning easier. Every new idea intrigued not only Stover but his staff.

The unique-looking building was already being discussed in the architectural magazines, almost always with high praise, and two of the Stover executives commissioned residences.

Each time Andrew came home to Oak Park, there was the old circle, with the Slaters, the Garnetts, the Eastmans, with the air that nothing had ever been. And if there had been a little something, it had amounted only to a kind of affinity with Laura, while building the house. Yet there persisted in Andrew a sense that Helena knew even better than himself. When they were all at the Slaters', or went in a group to the theater or the symphony, he was conscious of Laura's presence, had indeed to be careful not to let himself be drawn to little subterfuges for sitting next to her, or brushing against her. In everyone's opinions of a performance, an art exhibition, it was somehow theirs that were most likely to coincide. An affinity.

Nothing was said. Yet the thing was felt among them all in their little circle, unless perhaps Ralph blinded himself to it.

Then, at an intermission, Laura managed in her whispery voice to say that she must see him, that Ralph seemed upset. Andrew's office downtown would be best; she would telephone.

And so she came to the Rookery. Just at that time Andrew had only a boy around the place, a combination office-boy and apprentice, a lad sent up by Willis from Hull House—bright but a bit cheeky. So he sent the fellow out on an errand.

Laura arrived, coming directly through the reception

room to his drafting table, so that he felt her freshness before seeing her. She would not let her hand linger. Yet, in her whispery discussion, there was no disguising the feeling that was between them. Ralph had made some remarks; she could not have Ralph feeling that he was being talked about. They must not hurt Helena and Ralph.

The talk went on a little longer, in itself an admission as of something understood between them.

Andrew's impulse was to seize, embrace her, but Laura, anticipating, had already slipped out the door.

Gazing after her, Andrew saw that the large vase on the table was now filled with flowers.

Just then, that idiot of an apprentice returned; he was smirking. He looked at the flowers and winked. Andrew could not hold himself back, and cuffed him.

THE SLATERS, surely knowing, made a suggestion. They were traveling to Japan, and Helena and Andrew must come along, he was overworked and strained, and Helena could easily leave the children with Marta, even the baby. Jack was making a business trip, why not all go, the four of them, Andrew could gorge himself on Japanese prints!

"Yes, and spend every penny we don't have," Helena commented, for as usual, despite all his commissions, they were overdrawn at the bank. Jack insisted. He'd advance the cash for the trip. He was absolutely getting rich, and it all went back to Andrew's connection with the Japanese Consul. Jack had developed his scrap-iron business, the Japs absolutely had no iron there, no natural resources, and Jack was buying up carloads to sell them, cleaning out every junkyard in Chicago. He had been invited to Tokyo by his best customer, a baron related to the family of the Celestial Emperor, they would all be put up like royalty!

Well, why not go. Things were momentarily slack. Even that lakeside retreat he had taken pleasure in designing for Clarence Darrow was put by, as Darrow had just got married to his Ruby and they were off for a long stay in Italy, where he was going to write his book.

So it came about, after a few hesitations from Helena, about leaving the baby, and she could not imagine herself riding in rickshaws with humans like beasts of burden . . .

"Oh, let's get away from all this and just have a good time! A second honeymoon!" Vicki gave Helena a meaningful look, for after all it was she who had brought Laura and Ralph into their circle.

19

CROSSING THE Pacific in style, first class, was already a great relaxation, Helena in a better and better mood, the two couples taking romantic deck strolls in the moonlight.

And from the arrival in Yokohama, everything was to Andrew just like a Hokusai. In Tokyo, met by a bowing official in a frock coat, they were escorted to an exclusive-looking inn across from the walled Imperial Park. Would they prefer to sleep American or Japanese style! That, Jack laughed, meant on a bed or on a floormat, and, being in one of his plain vulgar boisterous moods, Jack declared he had always wanted to try it on the floor. The Japanese maid surely got his meaning, for she put the back of her hand over her mouth, swallowing a giggle, while Vicki mock-slapped Jack's wrist.

All four tried on kimonos, wobbled on wooden clogs. Laughter never ended. Their host returned to escort them to what was surely a very fancy restaurant, a private little compartment, and kneeling on cushions, with a geisha serving, oh yes, these were geishas, their host assured them, and he quite solemnly explained about the various ranks and grades of geishas, in the higher ranks these girls had the finest cultural education, and training in singing and ceremonial dance, and as for the tales of the geisha profession, of course there was misconception abroad, a high geisha was an entertainer, and as to bestowing her favors she was free to say yes or no. "Like your chorus girl, I believe?" he said, and Jack and Vicki were convulsed.

It didn't take long—they had strolled out, got lost in the tangled lanes, nevertheless Andrew espied the shop of a print dealer, and by the next afternoon every print merchant in Tokyo was bowing at their door; Andrew was spending like a sailor.

But Helena and Vicki were becoming disenchanted. At meals, they were always the only women present. No matter how often Jack's distinguished business contact in his correct English explained that in Japan it was not the custom for the lady to go out in public, and no matter how often the Baron's representative assured them that the influence of women was most powerful, as husbands bent to the wisdom of their wives, Helena and Vicki kept declaring to each other that the role of woman here was abominable, she was an inferior creature, living only to satisfy the male. And even in that department, the lords and masters were not sufficiently gratified, it seemed, and summoned their geishas. And worse, for, with much double-smiling and little male titters, there were pointed out to them the bathhouses; Vicki was the first to catch on and divulged the fact that men were massaged in the nude, by—not exactly geishas, but female attendants. Oh, nothing more, it was claimed, than the massage. After all, such was the custom in Sweden and Finland too—females massaging males. But Jack was full of gusty innuendos, and kept insisting he was going to try it. "Just you do, and I'm going straight home to Chicago!" Vicki threatened.

More serious matters were going on; aside from the visits to shrines and theaters, and the strange raucous music and the dance-acting with masks, just as in the most beautiful Hiroshige color prints, which, Andrew pointed out, were actually real portraits of celebrated actors.

Their host had been advised by the Consul in Chicago, a nephew of the Baron Okira, of the imperial family, that the American Mr. Lane was a most distinguished architect. They would be most gratefully indebted for his thoughts on a certain matter.

Thus, Andrew was led to a conference with the Baron, a strong-faced man sitting behind a desk in a Western-style office, though wearing the kimono. Such an office, Jack had informed Andrew, was specially for receiving Western visitors; the real office was behind the sliding doorscreen; the desk there, of course, would be a lacquered taboret on the mat.

One syllable from the Baron, and servant-assistants appeared, slipping in and out by the silent sliding doors, in, out, back with a document that was wanted.

What the Baron desired was the distinguished American architect's opinions regarding a grand hotel in the style of the Western world. More and more business was being conducted with the West; foreign businessmen were not always perhaps most comfortable with Japanese accommodations, thus the Emperor himself was interested in the construction of a fine hotel, with American plumbing— Ah, Andrew interjected, although he agreed about Western plumbing, he trusted they would keep to Japanese surroundings! Indeed, the Baron repeated—American installations, the finest, a Western-style bathtub in every room . . .

"Plus an Eastern-style massage girl," said Vicki, when the husbands got back.

But the prospect was serious. The Baron had in mind a central location just opposite the Imperial Palace—outside the walls, of course.

Only, the Baron mentioned at the end of the second conference, there was one great problem. A problem not unknown to America, particularly in the state of California. The great city of San Francisco had suffered from it . . .

Earthquakes.

Indeed, he did not speak of small tremors, which one could feel almost every day, though he hoped they would not be inconvenienced. Just as a person of firm body—he stretched his outspread hand before him—might at times suffer from a tremor of the hand. But in the great earthquakes, for example in 1855, fifty thousand houses had been destroyed, with devouring conflagrations in which thousands perished. That which one had oneself to suffer, one could not ask one's guests to risk. Therefore a lodging house for foreign guests must be built in such a way as to withstand the violence of an earthquake, should it come.

It was already known to the Baron, through the high praise of Consul Okira in Chicago, that Mr. Andrew Lane had constructed a building to withstand flames—how was the word: fireproof.

The Stover. There in Tokyo they already knew of it!

In an earthquake, as all knew, the Baron repeated, the fatalities were from conflagrations. Fires started and wind swept flames through the wooden city, just as in Mr. Lane's own city of Chicago a great fire had once destroyed an entire metropolis, now entirely rebuilt, mostly of brick and stone. "And steel," said Jack Slater. The Baron nodded. "But even a steel-frame structure can be swept by flames," Andrew said. "The problem is to so build it as to impede the currents of air."

"I see that you have given much thought to the subject," the Baron observed.

But precisely. A fireproof material, stone or concrete, wouldn't go up like a tinderbox, but if shaken to its foundations in an earthquake, with fissures opening, it could be swept by flames.

Then this hotel must be so built as to stand intact even against powerful tremors.

Both quakeproof and fireproof? Such a structure had never existed.

The Baron's direct gaze reminded Andrew of a print of

a samurai warrior. The face now moved into a formal smile, and, with formal expressions of appreciation, the Baron concluded the interview.

Had the samurai only been probing him for information?

For the safety of Japan's guests, the Baron repeated in parting, no effort would be spared in seeking a solution. This solution must be sought all over the world. —Was he saying this was open competition?

Andrew supposed that he should make a sort of bow. He wished them success, as a solution would mean a great advance for architecture—and humanity. Soundlessly, the panel had slid open.

"Don't expect anything," Jack said. "They're funny. Sometimes they're so quick they knock you over. Or, they'll sit on a proposition for years, then they'll pick it up as if you talked about it yesterday."

Jack too had had his conferences, the Japs would take all the scrap he could supply. As people at home were all now buying automobiles and wrecking them, he saw a great future!

And in exhilaration Jack insisted how about it? The two of them led by interpreter-san, could try a nice massage bath before going back to the inn. Jack just could not leave Tokyo without knowing exactly what went on in those places.

So each entered his cubicle with his smiling young woman who kept the same perfect smile, uttering a few Japanese words with titters, for turning over. Jack later insisted that there had been a special titter of praise over his equipment. And massaging there too. And then a hot towel. Delicious. Clean. Here was something the U.S. could learn from the Japanese! Andrew grinned along, without admitting to Jack that he had, throughout, left in place the covering his attendant had spread, down there.

Naturally Jack couldn't keep from relating the adventure with great laughter and gusto, plus gestures, to the wives, though omitting the final attention. Vicki laughed as she scolded, but Helena didn't think their exploration of such places at all funny. No matter how many times Andrew repeated about Sweden and Finland.

Worse, Jack absolutely could not refuse a strictly male farewell banquet in the Yoshiwara. Yes, there would be geishas, but you know, the highest level, famous for singing and their traditional dances. "Chorus girls but high-class," said Vicki.

As the wives had their own meal served in their quarters, Helena was still fuming. How Vicki could take all this so calmly! Oh, men! Vicki said. And as long as there was no serious affair, she didn't even care if Jack might occasionally have his spree, she looked on it as just animal spirits. Maybe because she was from the South and look what had gone on for centuries with nigger girls. Nor should Helena imagine that all that was finished after the Civil War! There was simply an animal part in the nature of man. As long as the beast at least was careful and didn't bring her a disease.

There was a faltering in her sophisticated tone; in her eyes Helena felt a sisterly appeal; in an instant Vicki might burst into tears.

They shared confidences. Vicki's Jack was the kind that openly bragged about his experiences before marriage, but with Andrew—Andrew had been just as ignorant and innocent as Helena herself. And this Helena didn't add, but she knew her Andrew, knew his puritanical upbringing, his preacher family, on both sides, and within her soul she had a confidence that even when out with Jack, her Andrew wouldn't, he couldn't, besmirch himself. That was her safety. If Andrew by now, after all their years, might have less than his early ideal love of her, nevertheless he would not demean himself to something only animal. No. He had too high an opinion of himself, thank heaven.

Then, yes, she must say it to herself, what of Laura? Had they really ended whatever it had or hadn't been? Wasn't this "second honeymoon" supposed to be Andrew's proof? "For me, and I really think for Andrew too," she said to Vicki, "even the physical part has always been—kind of sacred."

Oh, Vicki said, with her and Jack, deep down she knew even Jack believed in the one, sacred love. Otherwise she couldn't have stood it all these years. She knew that Jack really loved only her; that was something a woman knew. Those other things—it was being sporty. Boys getting drunk, on a toot. Of course she would like it better if he didn't but . . . High spirits. She laugh-sighed. And in a country like this, it was the custom.

The world wasn't perfect, Vicki said. It was far from perfect. It had to be admitted that even though women had their strong longings and needs—her eyes were intimate and Helena didn't deny—maybe men did have something terribly stronger pushing—she giggled at the word—pushing them, a terrible need. And Jack—a spree didn't really *mean* anything. The time to worry was if some certain woman *meant* something to a man.

For an instant Helena wondered whether Vicki was alluding to *that one?* It was better, Vicki said, to let a man have his spree once in a while, than have him get hankering after some certain woman.

But how . . . after she knew he had . . . and he came to her . . .

Vicki uttered her high giggle. She never let herself think of it. After all, she never really knew for sure what he had been up to. Except sometimes when he came home extra passionate, almost wild—then she kind of suspected. Then he was a demon. Couldn't have enough!

Now Vicki uttered a different kind of giggle—with an indrawing of breath. Helena felt that their talk had perhaps gone too far; though it made her feel tender and close to Vicki, yet though she was no prude she was a little afraid of revealing those intimate, those last personal things that were between a man and a woman, husband and wife. She had conceived six children with Andrew. Oh, she knew he made a show of himself with those clients' wives beside him in the open car, but she honestly felt he had been faithful to her. Unless . . . Now she looked Vicki calmly in the eye, for she was convinced that Vicki, if anyone, would know the whole truth about Laura, and Vicki couldn't lie to her face. Vicki flushed, yet she made it appear that the flush was about herself. She believed, she told Helena, in the voice of confiding to her closest woman friend, that Jack had maybe once had something with a certain secretary. She hadn't ever asked him, but that secretary was gone, Helena could be sure.

Now they were all undone to each other, in that womanly intimacy as after unlacing each other's corsets. And Helena wondered was this Vicki's way of finally telling her that it was best not to want to know such things for sure.

The men returned from the banquet early enough so that they could claim with endless laughing that nothing had happened. A very high-class respectable establishment. Just a few high-class famous geishas, doing elaborate fan dances in exquisite costumes. Those high-class geishas put the Japanese men into fits because each fan motion was supposed to have a certain meaning. Then the girls sat among them and did match tricks! Yes, match tricks! Making stars out of matchsticks, the way the kids did, and then snap!—and giggle as the matches flew apart. . . . Oh, lots of sake. Jack declared he hated the stuff, and Vicki knew just what he thought it tasted like! Vicki hooted; Helena too knew the word he meant, and that alone with Vicki he'd have said it. Andrew never would.

Probably indeed really nothing had happened, because Vicki reported in the morning to Helena that she could tell. Indeed, Jack had been especially sweet like in their young days. Vicki thought maybe there was something very wise, after all, about this Japanese civilization.

Helena said she had had enough of this place, enough of balancing on these damned clogs, of squatting on her knees, and was longing for her baby. She was ready to cut the trip short. Besides, Andrew had spent his last dollar on kakimonos—not kimonos, oh no, those wall hangings. And

Helena wanted Vicki to tell Jack not to advance Andrew another cent, and she meant it. Well, Jack had gone pretty wild himself collecting those lacquered Japanese boxes, and Vicki was also ready to leave.

The time away seemed both short and longer than it had been. There was the whole caboodle rushing out of the house, and Marta, with baby Richard clinging to the tips of her fingers, showing he could walk! The toddler pulled loose and ran and fell and Helena swooped him up with all her children smothering her and giving hugs and pats to Papa, and Helena plopped little Richard into his arms. Andrew had determined to be more of a daddy, but surely the youngsters didn't constantly have to be shown, surely they knew he loved them. Yet behind his mother's beaming he as always felt that uncertain worry, was he like his father in remoteness to his children? Andrew stooped to little Cynthia, felt her damp fresh little-girl kiss on his cheeks and kissed hers; he again roughed the hair of Jonathan, slapped the shoulders of the big boys, Ned and Wally, while gazing with awe and even a bit of embarrassment at daughter Ellen's suddenly ripe bust. In two months! At only twelve, or was she thirteen? Helena always had to remind him of their approaching birthdays. And with the flurry of carrying in baggage and unpacking gifts, the Oriental marvels, Ellen, to try on her kimono, started to slip off her dress and then darted behind a screen.

As they were all so busy, Marta took the moment to tell him—a letter would not have arrived before they sailed, and a cable would not have seemed right—that word had come from Claire, Claire Barr . . . It took him a moment to recall that Claire was the eldest daughter from his father's first marriage. Claire had written that Mr. Lane had passed away. In Pittsburgh, where he had apparently settled in his last few years.

Thus, his father was dead.

Marta had not yet told the children, somehow feeling it should come from him. How should he put it? "Your other grandfather, the one you never saw or heard from—that is, my father . . ."

Wally, Andrew mentioned it to first. "Oh, I didn't know he still existed." But quickly the boy swallowed his levity. Ellen had caught the news, for she was staring. So Helena made the announcement to them all. "You know Mr. Lane, Sanford Lane, your father's father, who separated from the family before you were born, he and Grandma were divorced, he lived out West somewhere, he was a preacher and a musician, a lawyer too—well, he has died. He was quite old. How old was he?" She turned, her question hovering between Marta and Andrew. Marta said, "Eighty-five."

Well, Andrew could not help thinking, his father had lived to a hearty old age. As they did on his mother's side too.

There was a puzzled moment among them all. As they knew, his mother added, Mr. Lane came from an excellent stock, the fourth generation in America from before the War of Independence. Preachers. He had graduated from Harvard at eighteen.

"Oh," they responded solemnly. This was the epitaph.

But his father's death remained on Andrew's mind. Twenty years without a sign, a Christmas card, a birthday card to his children. Had he known when his son got married, had he known of his grandchildren? Or when Tess went off to New York to become a designer, and married her boss? And also—this thought Andrew hardly allowed to come to the fore—wouldn't a man have wanted to know of his son's work? Of his fame?

One knew about divorces, of men and women who could no longer live with each other. But one always heard of the struggle of each parent not to lose the children. Had his father kept in touch with those other two, the daughters of his first marriage? Vaguely Andrew recalled two grown girls in the house when he had been very small, and then they had vanished. As his father later vanished. Had Marta been too strong for the man, Andrew now let himself speculate, knowing his mother's determined nature. For the aura of his father that remained to him from childhood was a gentleness.

Yes, he felt sorrow. And a current of inevitable speculation. A man cuts off from a whole area of his life. A clean break. Cancel what was an error. Then perhaps it had been out of pain, the silence. A sensitive, gifted man, for from what other source did he himself have his artistic gift? If indeed all was inherited.

Presently he could look into the studio. Gene Tillit hovered under a "welcome" sign, lettered in pseudo-Japanese ideographs; he had not wanted to break into the family's reunion.

The place looked deserted, drawing boards bare, and Gene explained that those two others had gone off on their own. Even, he suspected, with a commission intended for the office.

There was a pile of bills on the desk, and on his drawing board at first glance what looked like a sketch of his own . . . That Wally! Though he disliked for other hands, even his son's, to use his instruments, his board, Andrew had to smile. Not bad at all. A boy's clubhouse, with projecting eaves, Andrew Lane style. Indeed, the lad was now hovering right behind him, so Andrew proclaimed it was fine—professional! "Have to send you off to M.I.T.!"

Though perhaps he'd have been even more pleased if the boy had drawn something totally different from Papa's style. Even if bad. Odd, Wally was so rambunctious, and as a youngster always turning the water hose on Papa, and yet here the boy had wanted to do this in Papa's way.

Meanwhile more news from Tillit. About the bills: the sheriff had been to collect, and even threatened to sell at auction, but agreed to wait until his return. While Tillit spoke Andrew remembered that even before he left, Tillit himself hadn't been paid for a month or two. Gene flushed. —Oh, he could wait, and he finally accepted a Hokusai instead of cash.

But things didn't look too bad; several inquiries—one

big job in Wisconsin—and meanwhile Gene Tillit was pridefully describing the visit of a French professor with his group of architectural students on tour in America; they had come particularly to see the Andrew Lane Prairie Houses—already renowned in France! Even knew which ones! They had wanted to see the Slater, the Garnett— Laura Garnett herself had shown it . . .

Her name affected him like her presence.

Of course the French group had been disappointed that Mr. Lane wasn't here in person, but the next day Mr. Mann had taken them in charge.

And so all was the same.

One project here in Oak Park had been awaiting his return. His mother told him of it, at the big family dinner. With Marta wearing the bright silk embroidered jacket that Helena had picked for her, Ellen tottering on her inlaid clogs, they might as well be eating off a mat on the floor! Now Marta mentioned that her own congregation, the Oak Park Universalists, had grown and were at last ready to build their Temple. Naturally they were not too rich in funds, and wanted more than they could afford—a fairly large worship hall, plus space for community activities. Lord, was he again going to go through an agony as with Uncle Bruce's church? And this time with his mother!

Meanwhile, there was Arthur Kaiser with his Lake Street property become valuable, wanting a large apartment house at low cost. An untried idea suddenly came back to Andrew. Poured-concrete sections. Save on materials and labor. Then why not also use it for the church? An all-concrete monolith. What more perfect than the cube? A large worship room—the most inexpensive form: cubic. What better symbol of unity? And as for their social and cultural activities—a secondary cube. General entrance in a corridor connecting the two sections. The pastor's office above the corridor.

Soon he had converted Marta's committee to the idea of concrete. Even for a church. They saw the low-cost figure, he saw the innovation. Unity not only in the basic cube, but in the single material. He sketched in a high-up series of windows. Gave the cubic form variety by using impressive corner pylons, as in the Stover in Buffalo. And as in the Stover, a large skylight, opening the worship hall to the firmament.

No steeple, no spire, no finger pointing to God, no posturing in his church.

Within, three sides with benches, somewhat recalling the honesty of a Quaker meeting hall. And richly, above the pulpit, the organ pipes in a full golden arc.

There were as usual the doubters. The structure was original, daring, and the cost surprisingly low, but . . . was this a church? Others, however, considering themselves advanced, intelligent, soon were talking of the symbol of unity, the purity, the simplicity.

Design approved.

Soon Andrew had devised standard wooden forms, concrete was being poured.

Helena had the Whaleys, the Eastmans to the house, relating tales of Japan; Jack and Vicki came, adding their tales. Occasionally Vicki would drop some remark about Ralph and Laura Garnett, just barely glancing at Andrew for the effect.

It was not until the Unity dedication that he encountered her. Groups were strolling around the structure, and one could sense a withheld dubiety. A church? This block of cement? Opinions hovered; it would take only a bold voice to make ridicule the accepted reaction. Even in Helena, behind her loyally proclaimed approbation, and the broad smile of the architect's wife, Andrew sensed a puzzlement, if not actual dismay. She really didn't like the thing.

Harriet Monroe, the poetess, now the art critic on the *News*, had come, and in her polite faint praise Andrew felt that she too did not really like what he had done. And yet —what would her idolized John Root have said? And if John Root had been here to lead her, wouldn't she see?

What did people know, what did they really understand? Even "critics."

His mother was staunch. Mother's pride. Uncle Bruce could at best say, "Well, Andrew, it certainly is original." And he praised in a professional manner as a pastor the way in which Andrew had provided the two units, for worship and for community activities, linked by the minister's office. Not like his own church, he boomed for all to hear, where the halls became a clutter of folk dancers and Bible-study groups. Yes, this was excellent and practical. With a certain hesitancy he added, "Monumental!"

Rounding the corner, they met Jack and Vicki Slater, and with them the Garnetts. At one moment, while all the others were exchanging nothings, Laura touched his arm. In her low, private voice she said, "Andrew, it is beautiful." The singleness of the material, the form of the cube . . .

She saw.

Wally and Ned, he noticed, were backed off across the street. Wally was expostulating to his brother. Did his son feel the full spatial intention, in relationship to the street. Andrew wondered.

As the crowd moved inside, and now as the effect of the space, the colors, the art glass, the lighting fixtures came upon the viewers, a prolonged "Aah" arose. He had reached them. The high windows with their triangles, circles, oblongs of pure color, nothing pictorial. And as Marta responded to the loftiness of the great room, with its skylight to infinity, "Oh, Andrew! You've done it!" he could feel the same response in Helena. It was as with the Slater house. Outside, people had not got it, some had laughed. Inside, it had got them.

And yet there remained to him, from outside, that first disappointment. Even his wife had not felt what he had created. A pure structure. Only Laura had got it.

AND AS with the Slater house, the Temple was creating something of a hullabaloo. Harriet Monroe's review was for and against. Some truly original ideas, some handsome interior effects. But any reader could feel that the critic had not really liked the structure. The "squatness." Let it go. John Root should have been with her, to explain.

Then the *Architectural World* came out with a good article by Randolph Stacey. There was a man who really understood form. He explained the whole meaning, the play of volumes. And declared that Andrew Lane was America's most original architect!

And unexpectedly, there came an offer, a strange one, from Daniel Burnham. The old animosity over the Columbian Exposition, for Andrew, was buried—if not forgotten. What had been good about the exposition, the gracious layout of the park itself, mostly John Root's, was continuing in Burnham's growing park and boulevard planning for the city. He talked and wrote about "Chicago the Beautiful," and though there were jokes about it, the idea of a layout for the whole, growing city appealed to Andrew. Now came a dinner invitation from Alfred Eastman, and there was Daniel Burnham, and in his courtly way, in Eastman's library in a kind of British-style cigar interval without the ladies, he came out with a suggestion for Andrew. Seconded by Alf Eastman. Andrew, they said, was surely the most talented and original of America's younger architects. This was not flattery, but a plain fact, said Burnham. All Andrew needed, to surpass the New York crowd, even Stanford White, was to incorporate tradition with innovation . . .

Already, Andrew saw where it was going. The same old eclecticism. And indeed, Burnham's idea was for him to take a few years off and attend the Beaux-Arts, even with a finishing year in Italy. They would pay the expenses, including his family expenses. At the end, if he wished, a partnership. But above all it was truly for the enhancement of a great talent, it was for the growth of American architecture.

How could they see, and not see? And so it was, with

great regret, No, thank you. But he was deeply touched. Shall we join the ladies?

And withal, business was picking up. That old rule: no matter what was said about you, so long as people talked. For one, Clarence Darrow came back for his lakeside house, only this time not a lone retreat; now married, he wanted a real nice place out there, where he and Ruby could go sometimes to get away by themselves. The Darrow apartment was becoming too popular. Every visiting writer, celebrity, Wobbly, and the old chums from the Langley Apartments too, would pop in, anytime. Sure, he and Ruby liked people. But maybe not everybody, all the time. And he still wanted seclusion, to write.

A second-story study, then, projected right out over the lake, using Andrew's favorite structural method, the cantilever. And with continuous windows all around, as he had done for Laura. He got right at it.

THE DISTINGUISHED Goethe authority Professor Paulus Vogeleider, come from the University of Leipzig to hold a seminar at Harvard, had been persuaded to deliver a lecture at the University of Chicago, and then had been so kind as to sit in with the graduate students at Professor Kaltenbrunner's seminar on German literature, and there Laura had asked questions—in German—showing such a high understanding of Goethe's philosophy that the visiting authority had lingered on into informal talk. Learning that she had come all the way from a suburb called Oak Park, Professor Vogeleider exclaimed, "But I have been there!" Yes. He had journeyed out to Oak Park particularly to see a remarkable new structure, the Unity church. He was most interested in the new American architecture, having been inclined toward the profession in his youth.

Naturally, Laura mentioned that she knew the architect, Mr. Andrew Lane, who was also the creator of an American style called the Prairie House, of which Professor

Vogeleider had read? But of course! Could he perhaps meet Mr. Lane?

"*Prachtvoll, prachtvoll,*" the professor kept repeating as Andrew placed one design over another. "*Ausgezeichnet.*" His eye caught every detail. He asked technical questions; sometimes Laura had to translate. A pity that his visit to Chicago was at the end. Just now he must leave them for his farewell dinner with the university faculty. Carefully the professor noted down Andrew's address, for he intended to put him in touch with Germany's most influential architectural authority, Professor Gottweiler.

Thus they were left. Here they were as in the old days in his drafting room when her house was being planned. Her smile hovered. She started pulling on her gloves.

Andrew took her hands and sat her down. Laura made a slight effort to withdraw her hands but then let them stay.

Just this, and a restfulness was in him.

"Laura, it's no use. Come to me," he found himself saying.

She gazed at him steadily. He ought to take her in his arms, kiss her with this love, here and now. But without her shaking her head it was as though her eyes made such a motion: not this way, not this way. Because of the unuttered things they both knew. The ensuing, continuous deceptions, the lies, he to his wife, she to her husband. And the conniving, when, how, where to meet; no, neither of them was that kind of person.

They both had children. Even very little ones. For a man, perhaps . . .

Perhaps indeed for a man this was different, a man didn't know that constant awareness in his very organs, of the being of the child. It was true, Laura was not an all-mother like Helena. She kept a nursemaid, and her sister in the house was like a second mother.

As though each of his thoughts had coursed through her, Laura withdrew her hands, and rose.

"If we are even seen riding home on the train together

— Oh, Andrew, I don't want to be drawn into that sort of thing. I can't."

But then they were standing embraced, their mouths joined.

Not this way, not in wild passion here, a confusion of clothing . . . She had withdrawn her mouth.

"I suppose when it is like this, two people should have a right to find out," Laura said, yet drew out of their embrace. Then her voice dropped to a kind of torment. "Oh, I don't know, Andrew. I thought we were safe, by now. How many years?"

Then she softly laughed, with self-irony, even a touch of mischief. "Imagine us—becoming adulterers." She moved a step toward the door.

There were "discreet" meeting places; a whirl of half-information went through Andrew's mind. But no, not with Laura. How could he even ask her? And to a decent man like Ralph. And again, "Andrew, we can't do it to them."

Sometimes, at the concerts, or at a gathering in Oak Park, they encountered each other. An exchange of glances, while talk was going on around them. And yet the sense of something between them seemed to be in the air.

When Helena, was it meaningfully, showed him the headlines about the shooting of Sanford White—though he had already seen them—she kept reading the scandal part, about some jealous husband, some millionaire, who had shot "America's greatest architect" over that actress, Evelyn Nesbit. Yet even under the shock of the death Andrew felt that old bitterness about the exposition, and wasn't it true, as Sullivan had predicted, that they had set back American architecture for perhaps half a century? "America's greatest architect" indeed! Couldn't Helena ever understand!

Downtown, when Willis occasionally turned up, his talk was less and less about architecture. Willis talked about the big labor leader in the bombing case that Clarence

Darrow was defending out in Minnesota; it seemed the anarchist dynamite days were not over. An ex-governor, notoriously antilabor, had been killed, three mining-union officials were on trial and again everybody was screaming revolutionaries. Naturally Clarence Darrow had gone out there to defend them, Willis was convinced they were being framed because the leader, Big Bill Hayward, was a radical. But, with one of his great impassioned speeches to the jury, Darrow got them off.

Now it seemed that he had developed a mastoid and made that last great defense speech half out of his mind with pain, and then collapsed. Ruby was nursing him out there, as he was too sick to be moved back to Chicago. Of course for the time being there was no question, Ruby wrote Andrew, of going ahead with their lakeshore dream house.

Everyone was saying that Clarence Darrow might be dying.

20

FOR ANDREW'S fortieth birthday, Helena and Marta, weeks ahead, had their heads together planning. He wasn't supposed to know the details; the favors were going to be little cooky cutouts of various of his buildings, Wally and Gene Tillit were secretly cutting out the molds, in the studio, when Andrew was downtown. The Tower of Love, of course, the Lattimer, the Slater, the Unity—all in white icing.

And whether for his fortieth year or not, the Art Institute was this year giving his work a separate show, all to himself. He had an idea Willis had been pushing it.

There were plans to dig out, renderings to redo. Tillit was a marvel at copying, and for his own part Andrew shut himself up in his darkroom, making prints of some of the early photographs he had taken. As he went over all his old work, a sense of growth and achievement grew in him, he could not deny himself the pleasure of it, yes, he had done something, started, if he had to declare it himself, a new area in architecture. And with the Art Institute exhibition, this would become manifest. A style, an idiom, an entire school. By forty, that wasn't bad.

The whole of Chicago's architectural world, and some of the art and literary world, was circling around, and of course there were a good many Oak Parkers, especially clients whose homes were being shown. But there was Phil Whaley, loudly proclaiming that he had given Andrew Lane his first commission, and then approaching with a half-grin to admonish him, "Guess you're not proud of our place!" for Andrew had omitted all but a minimal sampling of the Queen Annes. Eastman's young son, Wally's chum, stood together with him for quite a while in front of a rendering of Andrew's latest, a residence on the South Side's Woodlawn Avenue that was the perfection, the close, of the whole Prairie House period. An energetic young manufacturer had gone to a dozen architects with ideas for his ideal home before being told, "The man you want is Andrew Lane." The client had proven so sympathetic that Andrew had taken over a year to perfect details. A long, three-tiered corner house, with projecting overhangs so far extended that Andrew had not been sure the steel beams would hold, until the owner himself had told of a new ship-unloading derrick he had seen, extending so far that the steel was welded together. Welding! Why, they could run their channel beams the entire length of the ceiling, extending into twenty-foot overhangs on each end! This would be the first use of welding in house construction. And maybe the last of his Prairie designs. The culmination. Andrew felt he was done, as with an entire epoch in his life; he had evolved a new, a total architectural style, and could be proud of it, it was the American house that he had set out to build, and this last example was its complete expression. He felt the word justly due: a masterpiece. Then perhaps the place to stop.

Yet, at the earlier designs, Helena and his mother—how they were preening. Mostly, Helena hovered close to his old photograph of the Tower of Love, next to that of Aunt Nora's Home School. It was the school, of course, that was the important work, the first fully developed structure in his own style, but people only glanced at that, and gawked at the sentimental Love Tower.

Even the appearance of Laura did not raise his spirits. She and Ralph came with the Slaters, who hovered around the display of their house, somewhat like owners at a horse show.

His eye was caught by the little Monroe woman giving each item her attention with the scrutiny of her responsibility as a critic. Well, despite her not having liked the Unity, now that everything was together here maybe she would see the progression, even see the way the Unity emerged out of the forms of the Lattimer. Andrew began imagining to himself the kind of review that could be written: twenty years of a man's progress, the invention, the development of a style, his growing understanding of the flow of space, the harmony of interior furnishings as part of the architect's design . . . The way her beloved John Root would have seen it.

When the reviews appeared, in spite of Helena's cheerfully reading him words of praise, the emptiness deepened in him. Oh, on the whole the reaction was "excellent." An important exhibition, a successful career, surely with much still to come. Even Miss Monroe's review. Some outstanding works. And why he did it Andrew couldn't explain to himself, but he sat down that night and wrote Miss Harriet Monroe a long letter. Perhaps because she herself was a poet and because every artist longed for that needed understanding and recognition of what he was really after, even if critical, some sign that there were those who saw the whole, rather than the pieces. . . .

Andrew found himself covering several pages, even speaking of John Wellborn Root, of his continuing respect for Root's artistry. Should he send it? He sent it.

The reply was friendly enough, she appreciated his serious approach to his work, and his remembering her talented brother-in-law, John Root. She had written her honest reactions, and he must remember the limitations of a newspaper review. Perhaps in the future . . .

Perhaps as a result of the noise about the exhibition, of the "eminent architect" label, an important prospect came. Ah, he had reached the peak—the inquiry was from none less than the king of the meat packers, Lionel Sloan. Mr. Sloan had acquired on the North Shore a site for an estate. A most beautiful site along the waterfront, with a small promontory. Would Mr. Lane be interested in inspecting the site, and preparing preliminary sketches?

Andrew inspected. What a site! Sea and land brought together, the promontory a natural focal point. He'd do something new, fresh! Away from the Prairie House!

It was Tillit who sorted the mail; noticing "The Chicago School" as the leading title on the cover of the *American Architectural Review*, and glancing through the article, receiving the shock, he thought at first to keep the issue out of sight, even to throw it away. But Mr. Lane would be sure soon enough to hear about it, so he fetched the magazine, open at the article, and laid it before Andrew.

A large reproduction of Bob Mann's latest was the centerpiece. Except for its gracelessness, it could almost have been mistaken for an Andrew Lane. On following pages came renderings and photographs of several more houses, a mansion by Reese and Gaylord. Well! So the *Review* was at last getting on the bandwagon: ten, twelve years late they were discovering the Prairie House, now presented as "the new Chicago School." Andrew leafed the pages. He hadn't before seen anything written by this Angus McBride. Growth and spread of the Chicago School's innovations—the horizontal style, related to the prairie, the overhang, the continuous band of windows, the open-plan interior. The talented Robert Mann. The successful team of Stephen Gaylord and Malcolm Reese, who had received a record of thirty-five commissions in the past year . . . the Chicago style had spread to Texas, California, Minnesota, and was attracting international attention. American home architecture had arrived at last.

Once, in the middle of a list of over a dozen "practitioners," he saw the name of Andrew Lane.

All right, he could shrug it off as someone's spite. Like talking about the electric light without saying that the inventor was Thomas Edison.

Yet when he went downtown, though it was noon, he didn't stop in at the round table. In any case he hadn't been going there regularly, lately. Let Bob Mann hold forth in his glory.

In midafternoon, Mann called him. Looked for him at lunch, as he wanted to say that that thing in the *Review* was a damn shame. "Why?" Andrew asked blithely. "They gave you an excellent write-up! Congratulations!" And who was this Mr. Angus McBride, the author of the article? Oh, yes, the fellow had spent several days in town, seen most everybody, but Bob was sure it must have been when Andrew was away on one of his out-of-town jobs and that would explain— The fellow was really quite decent, rather young but a graduate of Harvard who had specialized in the history of architecture. . . .

Andrew kept it all on a level of professional persiflage. Maybe Mr. McBride had been led around Oak Park with special blinkers on his eyes?

After that great exposition at the Art Institute, Bob Mann said, what did an oversight like this really matter.

And he was all eagerness to hear what ideas Andrew had for the lakeshore mansion of meat-packer Sloan. Seemed he knew all about it. Oh, Andrew said, he was considering a structure the shape of a ham—

Bob roared in appreciation. But Andrew meanwhile checked himself. Bob would have it all over town in an hour. Could cost him the damn commission.

The day was soured. The sense that someone hated him enough to have done this petty thing in the *Review*. Probably not Bob Mann—he was too smart for anything so crass. Then Andrew told himself that every artist worth remembering had made enemies. Look at the Master, lucky to get a small-town bank to design, in Iowa. Yet even so, making them into small masterpieces. Then another shuddery feeling. Those malicious stories, spread all over Oak Park, that his roofs leaked. Next, the Big Butcher turns down your design, and word is spread that you failed.

Then, disgust at himself. What was he after? To build a still bigger mansion for a still bigger multi-millionaire? Was that the challenge to architecture?

And yet—not one of those fellows touted in the article had ever had an idea of his own. "All, all of it came out of me!" Five, six of them had worked as his apprentices.

And he didn't want to get home and hear Helena, "They're beneath your contempt! If they have to resort to such filthy tricks . . ."

Then came an odd realization. That he didn't want to talk to his own wife about something that could make him so sick of rotten humanity. And his mother. It would hurt poor proud Marta more than it hurt him! Then whom did he want to talk to? Willis, good friend. See it philosophically, in perspective, he'd say. Do what's yours to do, and don't let their pettiness get to you.

Then Andrew made himself work on sketches for the lakeshore Sloan house. Not an idea in his head. What he did, he told himself, looked like an imitation of an Andrew Lane by Robert Mann. Or any of the rest of the "Chicago School." Maybe he was really emptied out. Finished.

The next time the telephone rang, the voice startled and changed him. Until now, Laura had kept to their unspoken pact.

She had seen the magazine at the Slaters' when she went over for coffee with Vicki; Jack subscribed. She thought he might want to pour out his wrath . . .

Anywhere—for tea?

Laura wore a dove-colored hat, with a sliver of veil, raised so that her fine forehead was clear. She repeated, "I thought you must be seething, with no one to say it to, because you have to act as though you ignore it."

He reached for her hand; it pressed his, and withdrew.

"You don't mind that I . . . broke the understanding?"

"I suppose the only satisfactory thing to do," he said, "would be to horsewhip whoever worked up this petty little scheme." As they laughed together over the imagined horsewhipping scene, the whole thing, at least for now, was gone.

And then, a silence between them. The silence of something important to say, held back, but yet nothing else can be said. With a small determined movement of her head, Laura at last began. She was troubled because she was unable now to be a wife to her husband. To Ralph. She did not mean to use the word simply for the physical act. It was not only that but the total that Laura meant, the wife in heart. For even though Ralph knew that she and Andrew were not seeing each other, he knew her feeling and this stood between them.

She had thought of going away. Even spoken to Ralph of this, as a final attempt to find out . . .

Find out what?

She raised her eyes, looking into his, directly. "If what's between us is love. If love is love."

Then how could she find out by going away? "Come to me."

She shook her head. That part, they had been through.

What she had thought of was to go with the children for perhaps six months to Colorado, to a woman friend, from her college years, who lived in Boulder. As soon as the school year was over, her sister Christina would come there and join her.

But how would that help? Being away from everyone?

There was her wistful smile. She hoped, in a kind of vacuum, to reach clarity. For herself. Whether she could remain as Ralph's wife, or must leave him. It need not involve Andrew. What she wanted to know, to decide, was for her own self.

Laura took his hand.

AND THEN, when she had gone away, and there was no thought of encountering her by chance at the symphony or on the train or here or there in Oak Park, there came a morning when his old brain was working again: an idea for the Sloan house. It had appeared in his head full-formed, and he had an impulse to write it to Laura, but didn't.

On the promontory, a central stairway tower, with cantilevered outreaches at varying levels, all around, like a tree with a chamber on each branch. Extending over the sea, the way he had intended for that studio room for Clarence Darrow. Only, here several such rooms, in all directions.

His thoughts tumbled on. Not only for this house; the possibilities of the form were limitless. The cantilever principle, breaking away altogether from the post-and-beam.

He felt free. Free, too, of the Prairie House, discovered, developed, completed in that last, perfect University Street residence. Done. Let all his imitators keep building Prairie Houses. Who of them could go on to new ideas, like this one! He was free of their pettiness, of professional conniving, his mind was soaring again.

The letter was phrased in those polite business circumlocutions that even pretended to take account of your feelings: Though his design was of great vision and merit, the problem was that what Mr. Sloan, and Mrs. Sloan too, had envisioned for their home was not . . .

"Envisioned!" What goddam vision did they have except for hog pens!

First crumpling the letter, Andrew then smoothed it to put it into his personal file. For history.

The design grown out of the very nature of the site! The opening of a whole new method of construction!

Never to be built! For who else but a hog butcher could afford such a mansion? No, they'd probably put up another crenelated castle, to outdo the Potter Palmer.

Instead of shouting his rage his first impulse had been to hide that letter. Though from a lowered glance from

Tillit, who had seen the embossed envelope and even put it on top of the other mail, Andrew supposed Tillit divined that the project had gone wrong. Anyway, he couldn't break out with it to a Tillit.

After a blow like this. To speak to the one being—to your woman.

She, the real one, was away in the Rocky Mountains. Helena—if things had been well between them he could walk through the tree-corridor and speak to his wife. Oh, he knew what she would say after expressing scorn and sympathy: Did they pay? Yes, paid. Here's the draft for the rendering.

He ought to publish the cantilever plan. With a bold heading: "The Hog Butcher Says No." But this would be just what his backbiting detractors needed. Andrew Lane losing his touch. Plans turned down.

No, he couldn't talk to anyone. Surely not Marta, of defeat. Maybe to someone like Willis he could say, "I'm sending Sloan Hams another plan, gratis. Based on pig-pens, with a central ramp."

Turn to your work. A brewer in Milwaukee had "greatly admired" a house he had done in St. Louis and wanted . . . Andrew found himself pulling out one of the Buffalo plans and handing it to Tillit, with a sketch for an adaptation. The entrance more like the Marcus house in Urbana. —Fix up something . . .

He had never done that before.

Part Four

The Hegira

21

THEN CAME the other letter, indeed as though there were some deity of justice, providing a counterbalance. Had he somehow expected it? Expected that just as evil news had come, so the opposite must appear? Perhaps a beautifully stamped letter from Japan about the project of several years ago. But instead—German stamps. The letter was in English, typewritten on heavy watermarked paper, an intricate Gothic letterhead. The Kunst Verlag, Berlin, publishers. Herr Dr. Hermann Reiner, the director, had the honor . . . As the work of Mr. Andrew Lane had become known to him through Herr Professor Paulus Vogelleider of the University of Leipzig, recently returned from America . . . , he would welcome the possibility to publish a portfolio containing drawings and plans of Mr. Lane's completed structures—*ausgeführte werke*—which he considered of great originality and importance. Could it be possible for the distinguished architect to come to Berlin?

Away! To prepare a whole book, *Completed Works*, a summation thus far. Already, renditions, layouts succeeded each other like lantern slides before Andrew's eyes. The growth of an idea. The realization.

Again the upswelling impulse to tell, to share! Good news was easier, he could even turn to the draftsmen bent over their boards: "Well, it seems that although we are not known to the *American Architectural Review*, we have been heard of in Europe . . ." Tillit was glowing. His newest apprentice, a young woman named Gladys Beam, put down her drawing pen and clapped her hands. "That's very important, Mr. Lane." He'd be away for how long? . . . About the work on hand—no need to worry! Indeed, she did remarkable renditions, and, and being unattractive, was reliable.

Then, the magical thought—Laura with him! Hadn't this, in reality, come through her? A year to test, not in separation, but in being together, if love was love. They had the moral, the human right to ask this.

And he was perhaps, as only she understood, at a turning point in his work as in his life. What must open for him now was a new freedom of creation, a breakaway from the very form he had created and completed, a finality by setting it down in this folio.

She must join him. He would book passage and she must come with him to Berlin. All must be done at once. But not in subterfuge. He would explain to Helena. And Laura must tell Ralph. They would speak of this reciprocal year, after the separation, their right to find out, together.

Only, when Andrew spoke to Helena, he could not bring himself to say Laura would be with him. A year abroad, to restore himself. Somehow, for some time now, it was as though the joy had gone out of his life, of his work. This publication of his work was a perfect opportunity—

—Would he be alone?

Andrew hesitated.

"She's going with you." Helena said it without drama, but with fatalism, as of a blow long expected. Almost with relief.

"I don't know." That was true. He had not yet heard from Laura.

Helena kept knitting, knitting. At times Andrew wished a man could do that. She didn't even increase her speed or stab the needles.

"Things have not been right between us for a long time. Years," she said. "Sometimes I even believed, better nothing than this. But I don't want, I never wanted, anyone else." She looked at him and even declared, as one who has examined beyond grief, "I only ask, don't put me to shame. Don't put the family to shame. Ellen is coming into womanhood. What is she to believe about men if her own father . . ."

Her voice was so soft, and even without reproach. She could look into his eyes more steadily than he could keep his own facing hers. Helena said, "Andrew, I know something has happened to you that you cannot help. But I believe it will pass. I am ready to wait, in the hope that the children, the family . . . You say you need a year. Go. I believe this will pass. I believe it. Your home will be waiting for you."

Could they ever be man and wife again? Lie down together? Since forever between men and women this kind of changing had been happening, the tragedy was when it happened in one and not the other. This harmony he had sought for, a house, a woman moving about, even her dress in harmony, a charade he had made for himself.

"Go on, Andrew." She'd stood up, and as he did not move from his chair, Helena, in the right of a long-shared life touched his shoulder, and even, with a tiny gasp like a contained sob, hovered for an instant as though to kiss the top of his head.

EVEN SO small, the children must already sense something. Johnny followed Laura around from room to room, poor child, as though she might disappear. Tiny Maida, too, sulked at lunch, with no appetite. Could she have the same intuition as Johnny, that their mother was going away? Yet Christina was closer to them than she; Laura had long ago concluded that she had no gift for small children, even her own. Nature was perverse: her sister the old maid was more of a mother than she herself. That thought was indeed her main support, her excuse in contemplating her year's hegira, as Andrew had curiously called it. With Christina, the children need hardly miss her. And she, them?

Oh, with all her fearful self-questioning and guilt, Laura had in fairness to herself to believe that she was not unnatural. Perhaps she could not, like Christina, spend hours at child's play, join hands in endless ringarounda-rosey, or sit and cut out paper dolls—No, be fair, for Christina this was her work and she enjoyed it, not like a child but in her love of children. Helena too, Andrew's Helena had such a gift, devoting hours to Marta Lane's kindergarten as though her own children weren't enough for her; it was perhaps a natural function of the female, attenuated in herself. Then how explain, how understand, her own sister who possessed that natural female child-rearing absorption and yet never had seemed to be possessed by the first call, the engendering? For wasn't it that part, a certain hollow sense of unfullfillment in her very organism, Laura considered, that had at last lured her into the marriage with Ralph? She had long puzzled about her sister Christina, and for that matter other women who were quite able to live their lives without males, without the sex part. True, she had lived it herself, beyond the usual years. And in all these last months out here. She supposed Christina must do in secret things that girls did, that she herself had done in bed in shame, until, perhaps mostly to ease her body's demand, she had married. In those arid library years she had endlessly felt the need of a man. Christina didn't seem really to feel that need. Or perhaps her calm was pretended? It was just about too late now, with her bad teeth, and she'd let herself get so shapeless, the same desire for sweets that rotted her teeth had made her obese, she had just let herself go despite Laura's scolding, and she was so good-natured, how could you let yourself hurt her feelings? Nor was she like Jane Addams and several of the women at

Hull House who were so active. And if there was a feminine love between them, Laura did not judge. In herself, this could never have been a substitute, nor, she felt, was Christina made that way. The Sappho part. No. One had to understand all forms of human behavior. Especially as she still hoped one day to write. Laura intensely felt this need to understand, yet did she comprehend her own sister? Maybe there was simply a demand of the organism, diminished or absent in some women—you might even consider them lucky!

For what was this need in women, Laura told herself, but a function imposed on the female, her body made to bear and suckle children? Yet her brain, her mind, need not be limited, constrained, because of this. And in a dreadful conflict such as she found herself in now, which way was the more unnatural—to suppress her womanly need to be together with the man she so longed for, who called to her, and to be that monster, as all would say, a mother who deserted her little children, or to remain enclosed in a desperately unsatisfactory life, an unhappy woman, but a dutiful mother? And what of the man, who would be going away from *his* children? Though people joked about Andrew and his brood—he too lacked the gift, as he had once rather shyly admitted to her, for spending hours with infants—he loved his youngsters, he loved to horse around, as he called it, with the growing boys, and he had made a whole orchestra of them with their different instruments; and she knew Andrew's pride in Wally, picking up Papa's T square and his triangles and always, even though Andrew had bought him his own set of drawing instruments, trying to use the old man's. Just as she herself loved the moments when Maida naughtily used her powder puff. Oh, her heart would be lonely. Yet, perhaps at last that locked-up part in her that pressed to write, perhaps in some strange way connected with the constant self-constraint in her life with Ralph, would in this flight be released.

And the children would be all right. Christina had

promised. Should Laura need to go away for some months, as she put it still somewhat vaguely, the children would be all right. But would Ralph not resent the presence of the sister in the house, the presence constantly reminding him of his departed wife?

He would understand that for the children Christina was needed. He was a man who believed he did not allow himself any prejudice. Of his qualities, Laura gave Ralph his full due. Was it not for those qualities that she had, even with no compelling love, come to marry him?

Then should she not be utterly honest with him and write to him now? Explaining: a year. A year of hiatus.

But if—suppose even in physical consummation . . . ? Though surely one's instinctive—or was instinct truly a certainty? And if it proved wrong?

The coming back. It was impossible that her husband, that Ralph, would accept her back, as Helena would take back Andrew. A wife could accept back an errant husband, father of her children. A husband—to take back an adulterous wife . . . There too was your double standard.

She would have lost her children.

How long could it be, a week, at best a few weeks, before the secret was out that she and Andrew were together in Europe? She must not delude herself. Her own marriage was dead, and Ralph also must feel it, for he had not objected to this long summer separation, so far away, telling her, "Stay as long as you want." Even without her going to Andrew, could the marriage continue?

She had carried up the mountain with her a few books. Nietzsche in German. An odd thought: Zarathustra came down from the mountain, but she, Laura, had carried him back up, as though to verify his original source, his truth. Yes, a certain solitude was necessary to come to a decision within one's self rather than from within the crowd, the multitude the philosopher scorned. Even his outcry was becoming a catch phrase to the multitude, already spread in the first circle of the knowing, those who listened to lectures on Nietzsche by Clarence Darrow. Follow your own drumbeat. Could this also mean heartbeat? "Live dangerously." Yet, as she read again, the scorn came upon her, how the poet-philosopher scorned the little people who did not dare think an unconventional thought! Much less to utter it! Worst, to live by it. Still, Laura could not automatically agree that a thought, a way of life, simply because accepted by the mass was necessarily wrong. The average person might also perceive and accept a truth. A natural truth.

What this poet, this original philosopher, perhaps the truest since Goethe, asked was for man in search of truth to *exceed* everyday human limits, to grow to his highest capacity. What Nietzsche called the superman. And to make judgment on that level, rather than the mundane. Wasn't this demanded of her now? Or could this become an excuse for simple selfishness?

A phrase came: Womanhood or motherhood.

The second book she had carried with her was in Swedish. The phrase was there, in Ellen May's book about women.

From her mother, Laura had learned Swedish. She still had at home the shelf of Swedish books, the whole of Selma Lagerlöf, that her father had wanted her to take, at her mother's death.

In childhood she had partly caught onto Swedish; it was the special language used by Mother and Father when she, the child, was not supposed to understand. The secret grown-up language; but certain words were also pet words that her mama used for her. And food words. Some special things to eat. Her mother was from Sweden and her father from north Germany, and they had met on the ship to America, that was their romance, Father adventuring with three or four young cronies from a city called Rostock, they believed in new ideas, freedom, equality. Swedish immigrant families were on the vessel, and thus the romance was a proper one.

Father and his friends had come as far as Chicago; a good mechanic, young Bendersohn had gone to work in a locomotive maintenance roundhouse and in less than a year gone to Minnesota to claim his Inge. The railroad had moved him down to its workshops in Georgia, and there Laura had been born.

English her parents determinedly spoke, but they often slipped into German, and, for secret things, to Swedish. By the time she went to school, Laura knew all three languages, but Christina, a baby then, never learned more than a smattering of Swedish.

Then Youngstown; her mother never at home in the South, and her father not liking it, he had got himself transferred. A small house near the steel mills, where her mother fought ceaselessly against soot. She had died of tuberculosis.

Through high school, Laura had kept house for her father; then he had remarried, a German woman. He had been strong for her going to college, not so much because of equality for women, though her mother had had such views, as because perhaps of his powerful aversion to waste. You had a brain—man or woman, it must be developed, used.

With a sigh-shrug, Laura returned to her book. Womanhood or motherhood? Oh, how could such an absolute equation contain an answer? A title for a discussion. But the inner argument went on:

To remain in a false marriage because of the children, because of motherhood. Would it be fair to *them?* Wouldn't her inevitable resentment injure her relationship with them, indeed injure them, as they grew? Even bring them a fear of marriage for themselves, one day?

To seek full expression of her womanhood with the man of her mature desire? Again, the powerful feeling of a call to Andrew; his isolation, his gift. Even to help him reach his greatness. No, not for those reasons. Her constant wanting to be alongside him.

Somewhat to her surprise, and great relief, her sister, who had not known the torment of involvement with a man, understood all her thoughts, without discussion. Then, finally:

"Christina, the best would be if you take the children back with you to Chicago. Tell him I've decided to stay on here for a time, by myself. I'll write to him."

"You're going, then?"

She gave Christina the name of the ship, in case of some emergency. In her sister's look there was a kind of pity for the lot of women, not like herself, who were enslaved by their inability to remain free of men.

And strangely, it was Christina, not herself, from whose eyes there came a spurt of tears.

She was coming, she was coming!

Despite the unexpected letter from Mr. Henry Ford, Andrew decided he would not change his plan, delay. His passage was booked, Laura would join him, nor would he delay the *Ausgeführte Werke*, even for this. Rather, the inquiry from Mr. Ford was more like a confirmation that he must erase the self-accusation of a failure because of that preposterous rejection by the hog butcher. It seemed his name still remained in fashion with the big millionaires. An Andrew Lane label on the mansion. Mr. Ford and his wife would like to include an indoor swimming pool! Well, why not? And this looming big commission was even like some providential signal that the course he planned was the right one, for here was promise of large funds to come; he hadn't been sure how he would carry through for the entire year, the double expenses, keeping the family here, themselves abroad.

Nor would he simply, as had been his first temptation, rapidly adapt the cantilevered-treehouse idea. It would not fit the site, nor did it combine with their indoor pool, the latest requirement for the ostentatious. During an entire night, no brilliant thought came to him. That hardheaded Detroit mechanic . . . Maybe the house in a hexagonal pattern around the pool? Tillit could detail the floor plan,

Gladys could work up a rendering. Send it to them from Berlin. The more inaccessible you were, the more they wanted you.

In those few days before leaving Chicago, Andrew Lane was like a hurdler in his fixed narrow lane, his eyes unswerving. Weeks later when all became known everyone said they should have guessed. Such a frenzy could not have been due simply to his going abroad even though to produce a book to be published about his work. True, Randolph Stacey of the *Architectural World* said the Kunst Verlag had the highest prestige in Europe. And to what other American architect had such an offer come!

There were a few cynical remarks: Andrew Lane had always known how to grab attention. There were even hints that Andrew might be paying for the publication—after all, why had he rushed around selling everything but his T square? Mann had bumped into Andrew in the Studio Building, Andrew was lugging a thick bundle of Japanese prints, going up to Sato's to sell them. That great collection he had brought back from Tokyo a few years ago. He was so crazy on Japanese prints, you'd think he'd rather sell his eyes than part with them. One story was that he had first tried to put them up as collateral for a bank loan, but the bankers were slow, so he was dumping masterpieces at Sato's for any cash he could get. But why should he be pressed for cash? Andrew had a dozen jobs in the works, and it was said—yes, Stephen Gaylord had it straight from Tillit—that he had just got a huge commission from Henry Ford, no less! An enormous residence with an indoor swimming pool. Even after that fiasco with the Sloan lakeshore estate! You'd think, for a deal like Henry Ford, a man would postpone his trip, but Lane was leaving a sketch for his downtown office to carry out. He had closed the Oak Park shop altogether, moved everything downtown.

Well, who could understand a genius?

First, Andrew had thought that Tillit could manage, but no, Gene was an excellent draftsman but not the man to deal with clients. Not his fault. Andrew even thought of making some arrangement with Stephen Gaylord, some sort of sharing. But a resentment lingered, the way the fellow, once he had absorbed every element, every detail of the Andrew Lane style, had cleared out.

Ask Willis? Willis was now in his other world, working as an inspector of factory conditions, ventilation, toilets for women; Jane Addams had got one of her aides appointed chief factory inspector for Chicago, and so Willis was telling horrendous tales, even being quoted in the press, about sweatshops and firetraps, airlessness and filth. No, Willis could no longer put his mind on a drafting board.

So Andrew had come to the round table, for the last time it would be, maybe there he would decide on someone. From the doorway he saw Frank Whitaker, from Sullivan's, sitting there. Frank didn't often show up. And as Andrew neared, he felt an unusual quiet. Was it to do with him? His departure? Across this uncertain impression came an added idea: Why not turn everything over to the Master? Through Frank? Fifteen years had gone by. Yet just as the idea had come, the possibility canceled itself out. Though Louis Sullivan, as everyone knew, was barely managing, still he was Louis Sullivan, and to ask him to fill in for some other man—someone he had kicked out of his office . . . Even that was not the true reason, Andrew knew. For beneath lay a truly horrible professional doubt.

What all knew. The drinking. Andrew's inculcated puritanism held strong—a shrinking from the drinker. But before his thought was clear, before he took a chair, the entire situation had become known to him. Even Frank Whitaker, the last, the faithful, had been let out. Sullivan was all alone in that small office down by the roaring elevated. And in this moment, this wrench, Andrew simply could not bring himself to follow that first impulse and make peace. Instead, the news came as some fearsome, tragic prophecy of himself. Himself brought down, one day, in some such failing. Like a sign of a fate awaiting him. And if he made an offer to Whitaker, now out of work, it would seem like some vengeful slap at the Master. He couldn't.

The moment wrung and numbed his mind; he barely spoke. Agreed with the others—a shame, a pity.

Just before the last day, going down the hall Andrew ran into his office neighbor McArdle, also headed for the elevator. A solid, somewhat older man, McArdle always made him think of Allen Olmstead. So, why not McArdle? Knew the game. None of those imitators blowing about themselves in the architectural magazines.

And right there in the elevator, Andrew proposed an arrangement. Simply on the business side. See to the completion of the several jobs under construction. And split any new commissions coming in during the year. His own office could handle the actual work, but contractual arrangements, that sort of thing . . . McArdle was understanding and agreeable.

There, he was practically set to go.

The farewell to the family. Helena made it all festive. The youngsters were used to his vanishing on trips, to job locations, and this would simply be a longer absence. And to Europe! A book about Daddy's work!

And so backslaps from the boys and kisses from the girls. Avoiding the questioning look in Ellen's eyes that moved from himself to Helena and back.

And that part was done.

Jack Slater had insisted on seeing him off at the station. Made the expected joke as Andrew came along lugging a golf bag, but it was just right for rolled-up blueprints. Small talk until the walk alongside the train. "Keep an eye on Helena and the family." "Don't worry, Andrew." And then Jack came flat out with it: "She coming to Europe?"

It was a moment when you couldn't let a friend, maybe your last friend, feel he was being put off. The answer was in Andrew's look, half troubled, yet lit by that glimmer he had when he went ahead and did something all his own way.

Jack asked, "Ralph know anything?"

"No. Not yet. You don't know anything, either."

Jack said, "Well," with a kind of sigh, and put out his hand. "Bon voyage." And the laugh "Good luck, you'll need it!"

Andrew mounted early on the liner. He had taken separate staterooms, and had a look at hers as well, then hurried back down the gangplank to a flower cart, returning with a mass of yellow roses. He called a steward to her cabin for a vase; the table was badly placed but fastened down. So be it.

There remained nearly two hours before sailing. In his own cabin Andrew sat down finally to write the letter to Ralph Garnett. He had been forming words in his mind. A man and a woman, mature in their years, affected by a powerful affinity that was not impetuous but had remained undiminished after years of trial, surely that man and woman had a natural right to follow their feelings, to the ultimate test of being together.

That was his moral position. He would not demean this action through deception.

With Helena, Andrew was convinced he had made himself understood. "Then go, Andrew, if you cannot conquer it, I'd rather you did it this way. Better than these last years. Everybody looking at me." Let him take his year. Find out. Though a woman's going off with a man to a holiday—she had, he could tell, bitten back the word "honeymoon"—would still not be the same test as living day to day with a man like him, and taking care of his children. No, going off to Europe, it could not be the real test. "Still, if you have to do this—oh Andrew, oh Andrew, with what we've been through, I can go through this too." And then sorrowfully, as though only to herself she had added, "Maybe my woman's life is over." He let that pass, not so much as though unheard as though uncalled for.

Laura had telegraphed, she would come directly to the ship. Andrew understood. Not to have him meet her at the train, but to come to the ship by herself, would be more an act of equality, each deciding on this, independently.

Never before on an ocean liner, he roved the vessel, keeping his mind busy, to displace any impatience or even lingering uncertainty of her coming.

The deck chairs in rows—a rogue's gallery. So easily, a variety of enclaves could be arranged for friendships or for privacy. Still, first class, an agreeable atmosphere of ease.

A taxi ride's time after her train was due, Andrew saw her arriving. A dark-blue traveling dress, a rather small, flat hat, her head carried in that way of hers, her smile upward to him while the ship's officer glanced at her ticket and passport, the porter went off with her luggage, her nod at the steward's directions as though, well traveled, she knew her way, and her approach to him as he came toward her —so beautifully controlled, her eyes so clear. "Andrew."

They clasped with both hands. "I'll settle my things, then come to visit you." He repeated the number of his cabin.

In a few moments, her light rap. She had changed to the soft blue-gray duvetyn gown, the one she had worn that day to his office, when she had left him the yellow roses.

During their embrace the ship's siren sounded, all visitors ashore.

They must go up so as to watch New York, America, fading from them.

Why had he not at once, with the urge that thudded within him, why did he not now, as though it had had to wait for the open sea, seal their—not their adventure, not flight, but their long and at last unhampered drawing toward each other? But exactly because of their years of waiting, their joining must not have any mark of a bedroom adventure. Their union must come with grace.

Thus it was only after the dinner at the captain's table, and the stroll under the stars around the deck, her arm tucked under his, and the length of their thighs moving in unison, that they went within. For it must be from her that he took the mood. Last night in his Pullman berth he had, like a youngster indulging in fantasy, let himself imagine a rushing together of passionate lovers. But all afternoon and evening they had behaved like a long affectionate couple, certain of each other, constantly smiling into each other's eyes. Let the rhythm come of itself, let it come as a pattern they would live in for a long time, and not in a tempestuous joining as though that were all. Yet there remained the unavowed anxiety: suppose after these several years of strained denial, of each one's barriers and now these up-heavals, the breaking off with their spouses, their children, suppose as in some punishing farce this long-withheld union did not work? Like virgins on their marriage night who discover that all the heart's certainties could be, in the flesh, mistaken? Even this apprehension might have been part of the day's protraction, as though the enlarging ex-panse of ocean, distancing all past connections, would leave them utterly themselves, facing each other.

But the time had come; farther along the rail, in the soft bluish glow, other couples, indeed young honeymoon-ers, embraced and then as by sudden joined impulse hur-ried away, disappearing within.

Should he then turn with her at her corridor? In her small voice, her way not of whispering but of speaking small, to you alone, Laura said, "I'll come to you."

Thus, he left her and entered his stateroom. The champagne bucket and glasses had been brought. He placed them less conspicuously. Surely they should not do this so commonly.

He would be in his dressing gown.

At her tap, Andrew opened, and saw her in a fluid sea-blue robe, with, below, a wave-froth edge of nightgown.

In his mind there intruded the thought that one might design a nightgown for its true purposes. Let it fall at a touch-pull on a ribbon, doing away with the awkward movement of the garment pulled over the head. But as, still with this thought, he slipped the door lock behind her, Andrew turned to see Laura with her hands at her shoulders, two little bowknots undone, and the nightgown slipping, after her robe, a silken glow on the carpet.

One long-submerged and unpermitted worry in him. Laura's breasts were perfect. At last the final uncertainty in each, that secret fear of perhaps nature's misleading, was gone; their persisting desire had been the truth.

Not drained, but slaked; now rocked in the long rhythmic movement of the vessel. Not driven to fierce possession, but fused in the long vibration. He had determined, hoped, not to think of Helena, surely not to make comparisons, as though by this same talisman Laura would not think of Ralph, and in the afterglow they smiled to each other, an unspoken reassurance, all was theirselves only. Yet in some recess of his mind was the negative comparison, Helena, full-bodied, meaty, clutching, her head reaching up from below his own, instead of this total unity, full length, toes entwined, mouth to mouth, eyes to eyes.

And for Laura the relief from obliteration, from her never overcome sense of Ralph's overpowering body, despite all his tenderness, using hers.

No, of a certainty now, they had not been misled by their long persisting longing; love was love.

22

AS HELENA served, all were subdued. Many times Father had been away, supervising commissions as far as Montana, absent for several days, even a few weeks, but in those times the table had not been subdued—even more mischief would break out than when he was present. The girls especially were virtually silent tonight. Did they know? Were there already rumors? Among the young? Helena did not turn down her eyes, but faced them all with spirit, speaking of their father's great opportunity—this German publication would make their father world famous. Only, at one point little Cynthia said, "Mother, why didn't you go along, a second honeymoon!"

Ellen must have kicked her under the table, for an ouch! half escaped from Cyn, and Ellen flushed at her mother's gaze. Ned spluttered his soup. How much did Ned understand? At seventeen? And even Jonathan? At least Wally was away at college. —Father would be so busy there, all the time, Helena answered Cynthia.

Besides, who would have taken care of them? Helena said. And who would have helped Marta in the kindergarten?

"But grandmother can manage her kindergarten, and would have kept an eye on us," Cynthia persisted. "And I could help Ellen in the house."

"There are reasons we're not supposed to know," Ellen silenced her little sister, but with an arch look at their mother.

"In this house your father and I have always been open and truthful with our children," Helena made a declaration, adding, "there are times when a man and a woman need a vacation from each other, particularly a man like your father who is not an ordinary person."

"The genius." Ned risked a touch of sarcasm.

"He *is* a genius," Helena said, "and he needs this time for himself, and we decided this together. It is . . . a kind of hegira."

A what?

"Hegira is . . . like a pilgrimage." Jonathan showed he knew more than his older brother, and Ned half hooted, while Ellen's eyes remained intently fixed on her mother. This time Helena felt, coming from her daughter, a growing understanding, even a kind of awe at what could face a woman. The children began to dispute smarty Jonathan's knowingness about that word "heja—." To prove he knew, Jonathan spelled it, and was half off his chair to get the dictionary. Ellen backed him up, declaring it was Mohammed who started hegiras. Jonathan further declared, to be exact, "not only Mohammed, but Mohammedans, his followers. They make a pilgrimage to their holy city of Mecca." That was a hegira. Richie piped up, "Is Papa a Mohammedan?" and they all exploded in mirth.

That lightened the atmosphere. After the girls helped clear the table, Helena said she would do the dishes herself, she really felt like it. And alone in the kitchen she had the urge to go across to his mother. Not that Marta would know more. He had always shielded his mother from anything that would spoil her picture of him.

After she had wiped the last plate and set it on the rack that he had designed in perfect harmony with the chair backs, a thought that had before been unformed showed itself. Andrew's father leaving. When Andrew was the same age that Wally was now. Was this perhaps why Marta hadn't come over tonight? But it hadn't been the same. There had been no other woman. And Marta had even wanted him to leave. And between Marta and her husband there had been such a difference in age. Yet, could some kind of inherited fatedness, as Clarence Darrow would argue . . . ? And he too had left his wife. Despairingly, Helena felt she could not quite grasp a pulsating, head-straining feeling of a truth that lay there to be drawn from her brain. Oh, it was too hard. All this was too hard. She did not yet have the wisdom. Perhaps older people . . . Then why didn't she want to talk of all this to her own mother? Even less, her father. He would only rage.

But now her mother-in-law's little tap-before-entering came at the kitchen door. Helena said, "I was just thinking of coming over to you for a cup of tea."

"Well, my dear, I thought you might be feeling—"

The word popped out from Helena—"Deserted?" and she heard her own bitter laugh on top of it. Then she plunged. "The moment before you knocked I was thinking about when your Mr. Lane left you."

Her mother-in-law held in abeyance the kettle she was about to put on the stove. "But Andrew hasn't left you. He went for his work . . ." It was between a question and a denial. An anxiety. They faced each other, and Marta came out with it. "Did he go away alone?"

"I believe she's with him."

"You haven't heard from Mr. Garnett? Anything?"

They were two distressed women, it came to Helena, trying to put together what little knowledge they had, of that slippery world of men. She had never, indeed, felt Marta as a "mother-in-law." More than her own mother, Marta had taught her so much—children's ways, and keeping house. And Andrew's ways. Yet always there had been one exception, the sense that his mother would tolerate, would find excuses for, *anything* Andrew did. Now the question came to Helena: If Andrew really and finally went over to that witch? It could even be that his mother would accept her.

Within the shock of this perception, and a guardedness it created, there was still her first feeling, of needing wisdom from the older woman. Marta had gone through it. Even if it had not been the same, even if Marta had *wanted* her husband to leave.

Then the unformed question became clear to Helena —the fearful question that had turned her thought to Marta: Was this the end of her womanly life? If he didn't come back? For so it had been for Marta Lane, whether she had caused her husband to leave or not. It had been the end of her womanly life. She had never again had a man. Marta must, Helena told herself, have been just a few years past the same age that I am now.

All Helena's fears, questions, were jumbled together so that she could not find exactly how to ask this of Marta. Not as a mother-in-law, but as a woman whose womanly life had ended in her early forties. This was the fullest grief, even terror, Helena recognized, that now lay within her.

From now on, only to be a mother to her brood?

Examples came to her. Divorced women. It did not necessarily end for them, oh no, the jokes were the opposite. And even widows. Both those kinds would remarry. Even, bitterly, Helena thought of that witch, her own age —*that* one's life as a woman wasn't ending! Oh no!

And this was what brought her burst of tears.

Never would she . . . With another man. She couldn't. It would demean all that had been. Andrew's children, all around her, grown inside her. The whole of herself and him and them, like one being, a family. Andrew —how could he do without this? Without the boys, Wally and Ned already imitating him. And, sniffling, she saw the horseplay on Sunday mornings, the water fight when they were little rogues. And, oh unbearable, the huge tall Christmas tree every year, its tip touching the high arched

276

ceiling of the children's room he had built for them. And Christmas coming, not so far away—oh, she would not become maudlin.

His mother now said, "He'll come home, I know it. It's not the same as it was in my life, don't imagine it, Helena dear. He'll get tired of her, get lonesome and come home. If you'll have him." She even smiled at that needless question, and poured the tea.

Helena couldn't reply, still sniffling, wanting to cry Mama, Mama, like a tormented, befuddled little girl. And this brought another trouble. When must she tell her girls —tell the children the truth?

His mother stayed for a long while, and after the children were all in bed they talked again, said the same things, circling always back to *that one*—giving up her two little children, for giving up it was, Ralph would never take her back, never let her have her children, how could a woman be so unnatural? Was it, then, really a passion, an overwhelming passion as with Anna Karenina? Helena could not utterly banish the vision that came and was gone in a flash before she could erase it: Laura falling on the rails under the locomotive at the Oak Park station! Oh, how could she have such murderous vindictive thoughts! But then came almost an inner giggle. Of course she didn't really mean it. Why, she and Laura had even given a discussion together on that book at the women's book circle!

And when Marta had gone, the terror returned: Why should she believe he would tire of that other? It was of herself he had tired. Laura with all her lofty ideas, and her college education, even a master's degree, while she herself . . . Well, Andrew wasn't so highly educated, either. He always bluffed about having nearly graduated college. He had gone hardly more than a year. He was nearer to her own amount of education than to *that one's*. But what was she herself now, after six children, with her fallen breasts, her lumpy body? And that witch—she didn't even need a corset.

A violent, animal surge of hatred toward that false, high-minded witch, that—. She overcame it, it was unworthy.

But for a woman to leave her own children! And she would surely lose them forever! How could a mother— No, it was unnatural. Laura, all the time, had been an impostor. She was unnatural, evil, a witch.

But it couldn't be an overwhelming passion. Laura was so cool, so cold. And yet at this moment they must be in bed together. . . . What was this new, nasty feeling? Shame for herself as a woman, that her man had gone elsewhere? But in twenty years, despite his declarations that it never happened, surely Andrew might have. He had had opportunity enough. Even if he had always been careful here in Chicago, even if it was true that never before with that witch, there had been all those times away from Chicago. And with those women he was building a house for, who got romantic about "their" architect. With his staying in hotels and such. Yet, finally, no. Helena somehow did feel that out of some Thou Shalt Not in Andrew, out of those preachers on both sides, it could well be that until now, yes right now . . . And again tears choked her. For herself, for herself with him, because all these years until now, just like herself, he . . . Just the way the very first night they had been the same, virgins. And she could even let herself believe that until now, unlike Jack Slater and most every married man . . . And now right this minute! Oh!

She looked across the night toward his mother's window. Marta's window was dark. Then Helena commanded herself to be controlled. He had spoken of a year. He himself was not sure, did not know. If a man came back, that did not mean shame for his wife, but a triumph. No, the other woman would have to be the one to feel shame.

Which nightgown she wore had always been a signal; the time near the beginning when, after designing her dress, Andrew had started a half-silly discussion about nightgowns, designing nighties that fell open at the right places, he was even going to put them on the market!

Naughty nightgowns! She had actually gone and sewn one of them for their anniversary, a surprise . . . And how he hated the ones you had to pull up over your head. Wearing one of those was a kind of signal for her period. Or even after a half-quarrel—meaning, If you want to make up, you'll have to go to the trouble . . .

She couldn't get to sleep and, with near-tears of anger at herself, found her hand in that place, as when a schoolgirl. Oh how bitter sad she was for herself, she was still a young woman. And she could not stop, and yet blubbered, and choked everything down because perhaps Ellen must be lying awake worried for her and might hear.

Not a few nights over the years, particularly the last few years when Andrew was building as far off as Texas and would be gone for weeks at a time, Helena had slept alone in their bed. And even when he was at home he would often work late in the studio and then she would only half sense him slipping under the covers, but even in her sleep it was a sense of all in place. Something similar but of course not the same would come in the afternoon after school when all the children had come home. All in place. Let them run out again, but they had, as boys might say, touched base.

There had over the years been many times of anger, even close to estrangement, between Andrew and herself, somehow assuaged, as all wives and husbands knew, with the coming to bed. Not that it always had to mean intercourse, but it was the circle of your life.

But in the morning Helena felt a determination. She began to think, to seek. First, despite what he had done she decided not to let the thread be broken. She would write to him. No, not in anger. Perhaps simply this or that about their children.

She took one of the Unity Temple postcards. Wishing his voyage was successful? It came out, "I hope you are finding joy in life, as you so longed for." She addressed it in care of the Kunst Verlag, the address in Berlin.

An afterthought came, about using that postcard of

the Unity. He had known she was unenthusiastic over the church.

A letter had arrived, Ralph Garnett said on the telephone. "This concerns us both, Helena." So it was certain. —They had best have a discussion, Ralph said, but in the circumstances, as she would understand, he didn't care to set foot in Mr. Lane's house. Could they meet somewhere, perhaps for coffee?

She suggested the little restaurant near the station, but he hesitated. —He would perhaps best pass by, Ralph said.

At once he brought out the letter. It was from Andrew. "If you will excuse me . . ." Ralph did not hand it to her, but read what she ought to hear.

"A man and a woman when they persistently feel an affinity to each other, have a natural right . . ." —Ah, it came to Helena—she had already heard it. ". . . even, for all concerned, an obligation to determine the truth of this affinity . . ."

"That's a new word for it!" Ralph interposed, with anger rather than humor.

So, no more possible doubt; they had taken the ship together.

"Our marriage is of course finished," he said.

Ralph had his letter from Laura too, which—as she could understand—he did not produce. Laura asked, he told Helena, that despite all, so as not to deprive the children, he keep her sister Christina in the house.

There was nothing to be understood from his tone.

What could she say to him? Perhaps because of her own hatred last night, Helena even experienced a wave of pity for Laura. For a mother to give up her children, at their most lovable age . . . Yet again came the sense of something hideous, unnatural; Laura was not truly a woman, but a cold-blooded witch of some kind. Andrew would find out, and that would be the end. —Surely, she said to Ralph, he wanted the least suffering for the children. Wasn't Christina even more of a mother to them?

Though it would be somewhat painful, Ralph said, he would keep Christina at least for the time being. Indeed, he felt Laura had used her sister, as she used everyone else — But he stopped. And, letting down for a moment, he blurted, "What came over her? Does she think she is some kind of Anna Karenina?" Perhaps that was what had got into her, her constant novel-reading, her absorption in literature so that it was more than life itself.

The main thing now, his reason for having had to see Helena at once, was: as people would quickly begin to put two and two together . . .

One and one, Helena's mind said to her, in that kind of wild spurt of the ridiculous that came in the midst of tragedy. She didn't repeat the joke to him.

On his part, Ralph intended to say that all he knew was that Laura had stayed on in Boulder, Colorado, to work on her writing. Thus perhaps the scandal could still be avoided, at least for a time; he did not want it to affect the children; even though they were very young and would not understand, gossip still could hurt them.

He was asking, what did she intend to say?

She didn't yet know. She would not of herself bring up the subject, but if the children started hearing tales—after all, hers were older. She and Andrew had made it a rule always to tell the children the truth. Within the ability of a child to understand, but the truth. Already they knew their father would be away for some time.

"You didn't say with—"

"On a hegira, as he called it. A spiritual search."

"Spiritual!" Ralph let out his fury. "Affinity! Soul-mates!"

He recovered his self-control. "You're an amazing woman, Helena. I suppose you would even take him back."

"I would," she said. And, on impulse, touched the back of his hand.

He slowly shook his head, a man being manly, strong.

It came to Helena that for all the ideas of equality, in a thing like this, a taking back, a man might be worse off than a woman, for he could not permit himself, as a woman could.

Suddenly Ralph said, "I suppose she was always way above my head and got tired of being with me."

Poor man, it had made him see the truth. Then, within Helena, the same chasm opened. Was this also true of Andrew, the brilliant genius, and herself?

The morning hours Laura passed on deck, snugly tucked into her blanket, reading; it was Goethe in the original, and Andrew would spend an hour in the adjoining deck chair with *Faust* in English, Laura had thought to bring this along, and sometimes she read the German aloud, while he followed in the translation. It was her idea to get him familiar with the best sound of German, surely better than those idiotic phrase books that could make people laugh at you.

Later, Andrew would go to his cabin and work over his portfolio. Laura might put aside the Goethe, and read for a time in the essays of Ellen May. She had not mentioned the idea to Andrew, but surely Ellen May must be translated into English, and Laura was trying to decide which work would be the best for a start: the women's movement or the peace movement? The writing was so calm, so lucid.

For the folio, there must be a progression, showing the development in his conceptions. But . . . the Tower of Love, for instance. Well, perhaps on this he would consult the publisher. After all, it was not a dwelling. Yet . . . as an early work? He placed the drawing and photographs among the doubtfuls. It had not led to anything architecturally. He remembered a saying of his father's, when teaching him to play the piano, "Watch out for sentiment."

All was unified in the long slow breathing of the ocean. An idyl. And each admitted now to having had the same misgivings—that perhaps once they were totally together they might soon come to weary each other. "Just give me twenty years," she said, pressing his arm.

At the Adlon—a Berliner aboard ship having advised this as the best, Andrew had cabled for a suite—the desk clerk, in a high wing collar, repeated in British English, "Ah, yes. Mr. and Mrs. Andrew Lane of Chicago." Andrew signed that way in the register.

Laura felt a touch uncertain. Perhaps, as on the boat, for form's sake, she should have her own room. But Andrew had already signed.

Directly to the publisher. What a broad, handsome avenue, their renowned Unter den Linden. But the buildings—uninteresting. This was what was meant by Middle European.

They were bowed into the innermost office, Herr Dr. Reiner greeted them, light on his feet, a brush mustache, quick eyes. To Laura, after her first words, his compliments: What an excellent German! Much better than his English! . . . Coffee? With or without *Schlag*' ? And meanwhile, like a prepared speech, thanking Mr. Lane for having made the journey, which he trusted had been comfortable? The crossing not too rough?

An excellent ship, Andrew began, but he had a few simple ideas for staterooms . . .

Ah! the publisher twinkled. Ocean liners could bear some modern ideas! And doubtless Mr. Lane would redesign the Hotel Adlon, as well?

"He's already moved around all the furniture," Laura said, and Herr Dr. Reiner was delighted. Then he continued his speech. He regarded this project as most important and felt certain that the publication of the Andrew Lane portfolio would have great influence on architecture in Germany, indeed in all Europe, which was just beginning to stir in the wave of modernism. In his view, though the skyscraper was generally seen as the distinct contribution of American architecture, the symbol of the New World, he agreed most fundamentally with his friend Herr Professor Emil Gottweiler, who, he hoped, would write the preface to this important work, that equally important if not eventually even more important as an American contribution was the work of Andrew Lane.

Andrew caught the meaning but listened also to Laura's translation. The words were gratifying but also, he deemed, correct. Here, from the vantage point of distance, the value of his ideas could be measured.

For while the skyscraper was dramatic and flamboyant, what Andrew had discovered and developed was the basic modern dwelling itself, Laura translated with satisfaction.

At this, Andrew expanded on some of his concepts: the open plan, so that people, even in a family, were not shut away from each other. And as Laura interpreted, each man looked eagerly at the other, they were in accord, perfect accord.

Andrew opened the portfolio of his selections. Get right down to it. With noddings and noddings, the publisher agreed. But also, in his view, the book should have a unified aspect, the plans, the renderings, should be drawn again, oh not in any way altered, but in a unified format. He saw here an unusual artistic touch, delicate as etching, and trusted that Mr. Lane would agree, for the plates, to redraw, in the same style . . . Several months of work would be required. A studio.

Here in Berlin?

Why, wherever they chose. Daily consultations were surely not necessary! Perhaps rather than the Berlin winter they would prefer the south. The publisher smiled to the *gnädige Frau*. Should they decide to remain in Berlin he would be most pleased, and should they wish to meet any particular personalities . . .

Laura had a little request of her own. As she was deeply interested in the writings of the Swedish author Ellen May—. She believed the books were widely read in German?

284

Ah, indeed, Herr Reiner said. Were Ellen May's books also well known in America?

They were untranslated, Laura said, and so—

Ah, Herr Reiner was, as it happened, acquainted with the German publisher of Ellen May. It would be a pleasure and an honor . . .

It was not only the absence of Andrew himself, but already, in hardly a few weeks, Helena felt, like some constant discomfort, the absence of the man around the house. When he was there in the studio next door, attached by the corridor, or even when he was downtown, his work place here was a presence. And now the studio closed, an emptiness. Not only the times when some stupid little thing went wrong with the heating or with the electricity that was now antiquated. Of course the boys could do it; though Wally was away at college, Ned and even Jonathan could handle such things.

But there were things of a different nature, times when she thought, If only a man . . . There was the situation with the Hemingway boy. Little Richard had formed an adulation for him, as children will with someone just a bit older and stronger; they were two years apart, and though a boy of nine would not usually let a boy of hardly seven tag along, Ernest accepted Dickie, using him as a kind of scout or even slave, or maybe an admiring audience in his excursions and adventures. Partly Helena didn't mind because, on one side, Ernest was a very reliable boy, she could feel safe if Dickie was with Ernie, that lad knew the woods like an Indian, as he proudly stated, he knew every poison leaf and was an expert on snakes, even if around here there was only the garden variety. The main trouble just now was that the Hemingway boy loved to hunt birds, was deadly with his slingshot, and now was teaching Dickie to hunt and kill. This had begun while Andrew was still home, and she had meant him to talk to Ernest's father, Dr. Hemingway, about it, but in that last week it was one of the things Andrew had neglected. Now the boys had even invaded the copse at the back of the lot, and Ernest had taught his dog to retrieve. Dead robins and even poor little sparrows. Helena was not going to have her little Richard loving to kill, sportsman or no. Indeed, Andrew had felt the same way. None of the older boys had such proclivities. And killing in their own back yard! And the child now begging for an airgun for his birthday. Again and again she remonstrated with that Hemingway scamp. He was, to make it more difficult, what people would call well-behaved; Ernest would listen seriously and yes-ma'am you, and have that look in back of his eyes that plainly said, What did a woman know about such things, then he would promise not to do it in your yard if you objected, ma'am, and run off, with Dickie trotting after him.

Next thing, that damned fawning mongrel dog had scampered back wagging his tail and deposited a dead bird on her kitchen stoop. Ernest appeared at the edge of the copse, calling his dog back, yet even from that distance she could tell he was laughing.

A man in the house would have taken care of such vexations. She could, of course, herself administer a slap, but she was sure he'd only go off, laugh at her, and do as he pleased. It needed a man to show that boy, or at least little Richard, that there were men also who abhorred needless killing—as Andrew did. Besides, Dickie was getting from his idol Ernest the attitude that women didn't count; of course a child of two or even three years old had to take orders from his mother, but afterward a boy didn't always have to listen, you just said yessum.

No use talking to Grace Hemingway; you had practically to make an appointment with the grand-opera star even if she was your backyard neighbor, and besides, everyone knew she had not the slightest control over that boy. He even mocked her opera airs and arias to the other children. Finally when Dickie taught their own little terrier to retrieve and follow him home with dead birds, Helena decided to talk to Dr. Hemingway. Not simply because he was Ernest's father, but because to a man Ernest would listen. When Andrew was still here, in the studio, Ernest would sometimes slip in and stand quietly watching—just as their own boys had done at his age; Andrew would give him a T square and a triangle and some spoiled tracing paper and let him fool around with a lettering pen. He was pretty neat and careful and right away learned to letter his name in thick strokes; that seemed to be all he wanted, and he'd go off. "No architect there," Andrew had laughed. Still, if Andrew were here and forbade the shooting, Dickie would obey him, and that Ernest would at least keep it off the premises.

The last exasperation was after she gave the two of them a talk about fine, grown-up men who were against any kind of killing, against wars, and even killing animals and birds, when not needed for food. The boys marched off together and Helena just knew that as soon as they got out of hearing, Ernest would break into a big laugh about women, and Dickie would feel he had to join, even if the laugh was over his own mother.

Dr. Hemingway was most friendly, as ever, and called her at once into his office, which had a combination of medical specimens in jars and hunting and fishing trophies on the walls—a stuffed hawk and a huge swordfish. So what use would this be? Everyone knew Dr. Hemingway was a great sportsman and proud of the boy, having let him fire a rifle when he was no more than Dickie's age. On Ernie's very first shot, his father exulted, the boy had killed a rabbit. When the Hemingways went off to the Michigan wilds, every summer, Ernest was already allowed to go hunting on his own, with a real gun.

So Helena said her piece. Their two families had different ideas on upbringing, and she respected his and expected he would respect hers. Almost, she had added "and my husband's." The men in her family, she said, happened not to be sportsmen and hunters. They didn't believe in needless killing just for the sport of it, and she didn't want her children to be taught that idea.

Oh, but he assured her, he indeed taught his boy the

basic idea that hunting was only for sustenance. And of course there were certain animals of prey . . .

He was very serious, a kind man, after all a healer, a doctor who saved life, Helena recognized. And there was also on the wall a photograph of him in boots and full accouterment standing smiling beside a dead bear. All this was not going to change her views; she would not have her boys thrilling at a kill, and said she would appreciate it if Dr. Hemingway would exercise some discipline over his son on this subject, regarding *her* own son.

His lips all at once trembled a bit; Helena sensed that, perhaps because of his overbearing wife, this man didn't feel sure of himself in dealing with women. Then he gave her a broad reassuring doctorly smile. Perhaps it would also help, he began, if Mr. Lane were to explain to their son— But he caught himself up. The Hemingways had already surely heard the gossip.

There came a letter from Andrew. As Helena saw the foreign stamps and the Berlin postmark she stilled her heart.

He hoped all was well. And with the children. He had had a fine meeting with the publisher and was setting to work.

Now came his purpose, oh, Andrew was sure to have a purpose, to want something, oh, how she could see through him. Though in this, his wanting something, she had never minded, it was in her to do things for him, and indeed, that he still felt such a need brought her, even with bitter feelings, a kind of inner flush.

What he wanted was for Wally to come over there!

It seemed the drawings would require far more work than he had counted on or could manage by himself in time for the planned publication. Wally's touch was almost impossible to tell from his own, the boy had grown up with it, though later, Andrew was sure, Wally would find his own individual style. But just now Wally could benefit from doing some of the plates, professionally, and Europe would be a great experience for him at his age. He could take the coming semester off, arriving the first of the year. . . .

Not a word about anything else. Hoped all was well at home.

Yet she fell in with the idea. It was true that the work, the experience in Europe would be highly useful for Wally. And also—a young man free in Europe. What every young man dreamed of! Only, of course, going there, Wally would now have to know the whole story. Even though here in Oak Park there were whispers, Ralph still kept the pretense that Laura had stayed on, for her writing, in Boulder, Colorado.

But before Helena had to decide what to write to Wally, at college, the scandal was in the *Tribune*.

As a matter of routine, Heinrich Müller, of the *Berliner Zeitung*, stopped in every morning at the Adlon and a few other leading hotels to glance at the register, not only for names that might be of interest to the German public; he had built up a neat source of additional income through sending special notices to newspapers in American cities, when he found their citizens present in Berlin. Usually a mere listing was all that was wanted, but sometimes this also led to requests for special interviews. His English was adequate.

Here was a bold signature, "Andrew Lane, Architect, and wife, Chicago, Illinois."

And thus the *Chicago Tribune*, in its Sunday society-page listing of Chicagoans abroad, included "Andrew Lane, Architect, and Wife, at the Adlon Hotel in Berlin."

Who did not read the Sunday *Tribune?* What should Helena say to Ellen, to the other children? Even if Ellen herself did not notice, surely some of her friends would read the society page.

Oh, in that instant for the first time she hated him. But also with a gush of bitter humor, that Andrew had been so inexperienced and awkward at this sort of thing as to make such a blunder.

And who of their Oak Park "friends" would be the first to telephone the *Tribune*, saying, "Andrew Lane the noted architect may be in Berlin, but his wife is right here in Oak Park. Why don't you inquire the whereabouts of Mrs. Laura Garnett, also of Oak Park, wife of the prominent manufacturer Mr. Ralph Garnett?"

The telephone, already. Helena's mother, with her father breaking in, "Divorce him!" Nothing but scum, without the slightest decency. Not even to think of his children, a young daughter at the most delicate age—imagine the shame! And to think that their own pastor, his uncle the noted Bruce Daniels, had introduced them. And that woman, to leave her own babies—she ought to be stoned! They were coming right out. Divorce him immediately! Enough she had endured! And now this dastardly humiliation. . . .

Then Ralph Garnett. "The hounds of the press will be on us at any moment. I am closing the house and taking the children and their governess. I am sending a cable to that publisher address in Berlin regarding the divorce. But for your sake and the sake of your children, Helena, I intend not to name him in the action. I don't want any filth in court, nor for you either. There can be no question about her and the children. She's burned her bridges. She knew what she was doing."

Ned had marched in, looking solemn. "Mother, I swear if he came up the walk I'd knock his block off."

Ellen, though her eyes were duly downcast, had an irrepressible giggle. "Oh, Mother, I'm sorry I—but imagine, Laura Garnett a vampire!" And Ellen took, for an instant, a Theda Bara pose. Then ran to Helena with a sob and buried her head.

Already a reporter, a woman, telephoning from the *Chicago Tribune*, and as the reporter gave her name, Helena in the midst of all her distress, anger, bitterness, almost felt a satisfaction, for Genevieve Wynn was their star woman reporter, even starring above the men. Perversely a memory intruded to Helena, of Laura's pointing out that Genevieve Wynn wrote with a style that was, for newspapers, superior. And with such understanding. Besides, though married to another star reporter, Craig Hartley, Genevieve Wynn used her own name.

Helena said yes, she would be glad to speak to her. For she wanted the truth told, not gossip and scandal.

In a few hours, then.

Waiting, Helena went across to Marta.

"The thing that I don't understand," said his mother, "Andrew doesn't lie." Why had he signed "Mr. and Mrs."?

Almost, Helena had a scolding impulse, as though to keep him from more stupid mistakes. His career could be ruined by this scandal. And all of them ruined and poor. Perhaps that German publisher would now refuse to bring out the book. The only chance perhaps to save him, save the situation, was to make people understand. Even she, his wife would declare—when Genevieve Wynn arrived— that this was no vulgar affair of a man running off with another man's wife. She had known of his—of this infatuation. They had discussed it. Such gifted artists as Andrew Lane could not always behave according to conventional rules. Artists, great composers of music, poets—was the course of life ever smooth for them? Andrew was a good father, he loved his children, his home, but in some way in the middle of life this infatuation had come upon him. . . .

The reporter arrived, a tall stick of a woman, long-faced and rather plainly dressed, but her warm brown eyes at once gave you confidence, and she and Helena settled to each other.

Helena showed articles about him in the architecture magazines. Partly, she believed, Andrew had reached an exhaustion. He had come to a point in his work, his creative life, when he felt he must think things through. A kind of year of hegira, he had said.

"Oh yes!" Genevieve Wynn repeated the word with understanding. "A kind of spiritual hegira." But yet . . . And the reporter delicately brought up the subject of his companion. A woman, she understood, of their own circle —a friend?

And Helena tried to explain without anger, though at moments she had to pause, and conquer tears. Old friends. Often going out two couples together, downtown to the theater and concerts, and visiting in each other's homes, with other couples in their circle.

Then they had all known each other for some years? Did it begin when Mr. Lane designed the Garnett house?

They had known each other even before that. And Helena told of the book reports she and Laura Garnett had given together, and of their even marching on Michigan Avenue together in last year's suffragette parade.

"Oh yes." Genevieve Wynn too had marched, while also covering the event for the *Tribune*.

Indeed, Helena recalled her article. It had been magnificent. Miss Wynn thanked her. Now—this other woman's special friendship with Mr. Lane, had it been going on for a long time, or was it sudden?

Oh, for a long time it had been noticeable that there was a kind of affinity between them, Helena said. And at first—as friendly couples do—all four of them had sometimes made little jokes about it.

Mr. Garnett too took it lightly?

Mr. Garnett was a fine, intelligent man, very advanced in his views, as were all of them in their little circle, but of course that did not mean . . . And Helena was thinking of the time it got so bad, the Slaters had got her and Andrew away on the trip to Japan, and she had even persuaded herself when they got back that it was over.

Under the sympathetic gaze of the famous woman reporter, a cry came out of her, "Oh, I don't know how this happened! And Laura Garnett, to desert her own children! She's a witch, she bewitched him!"

Genevieve Wynn waited understandingly until Helena

had regained her control, and then gently asked more about the "affinity," could they perhaps have thought of themselves as soulmates?

And had Mr. Lane, in speaking to his wife of his need for this year of . . . hegira—had he told her that Mrs. Garnett would be his companion?

"Oh no!" Though, to be fully honest, Helena might have had her own thoughts.

Then would she take him back at the end of this year of . . . hegira?

"Yes," Helena said. He was her husband and the father of her six children, and he was a genius. If he returned home she would be his wife, she would feel that the year of the hegira was like a fever that had passed.

Genevieve Wynn told her she was a remarkable woman.

Now Helena asked, had Miss Wynn spoken to Mr. Garnett?

She had called, but Mr. Garnett could not be reached.

"A strange affinity tangle," Miss Wynn wrote, "a spiritual hegira, in which the abandoned wife understands and loves her husband and would take him back." Ellen read it with unchecked tears, threw her arms around Helena and said, "Mother, I am so proud of you. Now I can go to school with my head up! I don't care what they say."

Marta came over and declared she was a remarkable woman! Oh, Andrew would realize.

Vicki Slater came over and declared Helena sounded like a modern saint. She, she would have cursed them to hell and perdition, she was ashamed she had ever introduced Helena and Andrew to the Garnetts. Though you couldn't blame Ralph.

The long cable to the Adlon was from Jack Slater. Their story was on the front page of the *Tribune*, plus an interview with Helena, Ralph unreachable. Jack advised them, best disappear until the scandal blew over.

Laura's first worry was for Andrew's book, would the publisher be offended by all this.

Andrew snorted. Since when would a publisher be put off by notoriety!

No—not the notoriety, but when Herr Reiner discovered they had deliberately deceived him. She had been presented to him as Mrs. Lane and he had already invited them to dinner with his wife, and to meet personalities.

Andrew shrugged. Europe was not that provincial. Probably the press here wouldn't even be interested.

But during breakfast there came a note from a journalist, a Herr Dr. something, even yellow journalists were Herr Doktors here, a request for an interview. Andrew crunched it up. He had meant anyway to go south to start work, why stay in this cold wintry city? They would go to Italy, he even had a contact in Florence already given him by Herr Reiner, someone to help him find a studio, they need only stop at the Kunst Verlag to pick up their mail.

A postcard had arrived for Andrew from Helena. The Unity Temple picture card. On the back she had written her hope that he would again find joy in life.

The clerk said hesitantly, there was a cablegram from Chicago for a Mrs. Garnett? Yes, that was for herself, Laura said. He handed it over, expressionless. The cable was from Ralph, demanding avoidance of further notoriety.

Herr Reiner received them smilingly; there was no sign that he could have heard anything.

They had decided to go at once to Florence, as he wanted to get to work, Andrew said. The publisher deepened his smile. To work! Good! Laura added, in German, excuses for their not remaining for the hospitality he had so kindly offered.

No, No! Herr Reiner fully understood a man who wanted to get to work! And he hoped on their return to Berlin to have the honor . . .

On the way out of the Kunst Verlag, Andrew left instructions with the clerk to forward mail for himself, and also for Mrs. Garnett, to Thomas Cook's in Florence.

And so they packed and he checked out of the Adlon.

"If anyone should inquire for Herr Lane?"

"Why, just say he left—for Japan!"

23

BAGGAGE STOWED, settling back, Andrew laughed. Look at him! A middle-aged Casanova, in flight.

"Find joy," Helena had written. And oddly, in this instant, a sense of joy came over him. A youthfulness. An escapade! He kept laughing, and then Laura softly laughed, too.

They had scarcely seen Berlin. A stodgy city, with the Brandenburg Gate impressive for monumentality perhaps. Now Florence. Andrew re-avowed his scorn of the Renaissance, though Laura caught him lingering, absorbing, before the cathedral. In a flagstoned courtyard. Arturo Fassanelli, designer of flamboyant posters called Art Nouveau, whose address Herr Reiner had given him, puffy, with a single tuft of hair that Laura whispered made him look like a Tibetan monk, announced that he himself was going away for three months or perhaps even longer and could let the American architect friend of his friend Herr Reiner rent the studio. It could even be lived in, although —he glanced at the American lady, and Laura well knew that the signor did not make the mistake of seeing her as the spouse—the living arrangements, for a lady . . .

Ah, but he was thinking of it for his son, Andrew said, who was coming to assist him with his architectural drawings.

Ah, for a young man! His face now a smiling Buddha, Arturo showed the arrangements, a curtained-off kitchen space and a closet with a squat toilet. For a young artist, and a beautiful model?

A thick envelope arrived from Jack Slater, with the front-page scandal story of a "prominent architect's" suburban love tangle, "a strange affinity hegira." And Helena's noble interview, even praising his "habitual honesty" in registering in Berlin in his own name. But as for Laura—a witch!

And his young daughter remarking with mirth, "Who would ever have imagined Laura Garnett a vampire!" They laughed, but Laura handed Andrew her letter from Ralph's lawyer: her husband would not name her consort, but would divorce her on technical grounds of desertion; of course he would retain custody of the children.

The children were well.

Yet Andrew felt a renewed life, a humming. Signor Fassanelli even ran about with him to procure the most modern drafting tables, on display in a crumbling once-palazzo with a slanting floor still covered with beautiful ancient tiles.

Once he had his first rendering under way, an even lighter mood set in with Andrew. Arturo Fassanelli brought an enormous charwoman, who moved about with incredible delicacy and left the studio shining clean. And now Arturo was departing on his own voyage with a signora; yes, Venice was the destination of his own hegira, he confided, beaming and winking as he spoke the word. He was to produce a splendid book for Herr Reiner on Venetian art. Ah! Arturo knew Venice as no other, and they must come and he would show them. Venice in midwinter. They would see, this was the fabulous Venice, muted, wrapped in a pearly haze, empty of tourists, ah, they would see.

Why not, for a few days? From Venice, Laura would continue to Berlin; the Swedish authoress Ellen May had responded, she was coming to lecture, and they could meet. Meanwhile, Wally would arrive, Andrew could install him in Florence and rejoin her, bringing first drawings for Herr Reiner.

AT THE top of the gondola station stairs the huge Fassanelli awaited them, with the companion of his "piccolo hegira," young, slender, one of those Florentine girls that made you feel that human art was a needless striving.

They even let silliness come. Andrew made awful jests about gondolas sinking under Fassanelli's weight; he bought a jaunty felt hat with a green feather and trotted behind Arturo into palazzos opened especially for their inspection, he uttered no more diatribes over the horrors of the Renaissance that had been the ruin of American architecture at the Columbian Exposition. On the narrowest canal he would have the gondola halt, and half close his eyes as he gazed up at a palazzo—"Ah, here, it belongs!"

And once, walking with Laura in the early morning when the city was a suspended cloud, Andrew stopped and made a rapid sketch in those codelike notations of his. Well, next time a pork butcher wanted Venice, he'd be ready for him! Venice on Lake Michigan. And Laura looked at what had taken his eye—an ancient facade with a fragile balcony; in the wintry fog the structure seemed not to rise from the water but to float in the mist.

She had not fully realized his sense of failure, there in Chicago.

"Dad," Wally had written, "I don't pretend to understand what happened between you and Mother, I'm not taking sides, you want me to come and work, you say that only I have your touch, and for the work, I'll come. Also

I'm doing you no favors, as I am sure this will be excellent for me."

As Wally came down the gangplank in Genoa, there was a kind of man-to-man pat. But then they looked at each other, openly, and Wally grinned; it was all right. Andrew asked of the family. Oh, fine, fine; Wally brought love from Grandma, yes Mother too, and from all the kids. Except, Ellen had said to tell Pop he was a rat, but nevertheless she still loved and even kind of respected him. That was the sole reference to the affair. While the porter took Wally's bags, Andrew noticed his son keeping hold of his case of drawing instruments, wouldn't let that out of his own hands. Good.

Meanwhile Wally had a message from the office, from Gene Tillit. There probably was going to be trouble with the Ford commission. Mrs. Ford was having second thoughts. In a kind of disgust Wally added, maybe it was because of all that newspaper stuff. The Fords were supposed to be pretty straitlaced, kind of hicks.

Then they were considerably together, father and son. Perhaps he had really brought Wally over, as Laura had remarked, so as to show at least one of his children—the eldest—that he wasn't altogether inhuman in what he had done. Laura was acute, she ought really to become a writer. Was he missing her already, Andrew mused, and why didn't he at all miss being with Helena?

FOR A test Andrew placed Wally's first rendering side by side with his own, unsigned of course, and showed them to a few artist friends of Fassanelli's in the same studio courtyard. None could tell the drawings had been made by different hands.

When he explained, they cried out, What joy this must be to a father! But Andrew wondered, must it not trouble Wally, simply to copy his old man? Still, there had been Bach after Bach. Wally was what anyone would call a fine young man, easy-tempered, already having a good time.

But there did not come from him that even unspoken touch of understanding that a man might hope for from a grown son. A few times, it was true, Wally made little jokes about Mother's ways of running your life. As though to show he wasn't altogether blaming Andrew. He didn't touch on Laura.

The lad's response to the task itself was simply workmanlike. Probably knew these designs too well; all his life he had seen these houses growing. Though Wally did remark—"Hey, Dad"—did Andrew know they were teaching the Prairie School in Tech?

"No doubt as developed by twenty other people!" Andrew hadn't wanted it to snap out with acerbity. Wally reacted only with a collegiate grin. "Oh, they mention Andrew Lane first. At least when I'm in class!"

At least he had a bit of the old man's humor. Sometimes a needed protection.

Andrew went with his son to the opera, to concerts. They sought out an old Romanesque chapel. Here was Wally just about the age of his own self when he came to Chicago. The poor lad must be going through all those damn torments of the young male, but Andrew couldn't bring himself to father-and-son advice. Though he made a few remarks about the prevalence of syphilis and gonorrhea in Italy.

Wally had quickly got friendly with a few young blades and already knew that in Italy sisters were watched as in medieval times. You'd quickly find yourself hogtied and married, with your dear friend her brother (who wanted to get to America) holding a stiletto against your back. "Dad, don't worry." —But these girls here sure were luscious.

The lad seemed cheerful, happy. Andrew gathered together the first sheaf to take to Berlin.

THESE FEW weeks away from him, though lonely, had been needed, Laura told herself. Equal-standing persons must be able, if so life fell out, also to stand alone. The test was longing. She longed for the children. Now for Andrew. Her consort, yes. Not a woman possessing a man, or a man a woman. Had she not come away, also, for the equality of woman?

Take the Italian women. In Venice, they seemed not even outraged at the constant ogling, the brushing against them, the hand-touches. They even took it gaily. "I'd be worried if they didn't." A whole people perpetually in rut. Andrew had laughed at it. "No, honestly," Laura had demanded, "do you feel the urge to brush against every passing female?" Men even whispered as they passed, "Come with me," or words far worse. Surely they could not really expect a result, except from prostitutes, so what was it for? Could Andrew as a male explain this to her?

"Why don't you say '*Sì,sì!*' and see what happens!"

His humor.

Only, Andrew must never be allowed to feel obligated just because she had burned her bridges. Oh, if they could remain free and so dear to each other. She was not a Lydia Pankhurst to throw bricks at the windows of Parliament. She was not an Isadora Duncan with wild adventures in free love.

It was not true, as even her own sister sometimes seemed to believe, and of course Ralph, that she lacked that primitive—no, not primitive, but natural physical motherly attachment. The children's absence came over her a thousand times a day. The mere sight of children of their age walking with their mothers to school, or buying cakes in a bakeshop, or of flocks of them all muffled up running at recess into a schoolyard, was enough to arouse a physical void, not too unlike, Laura observed in herself, the void, the ache, in the absence of your man, your consort.

But just as she could not permit the children to be the chain that held her in a wrong marriage, so now it seemed to her that for Andrew her loss of her children might be like a chain on him, a binding—and never must she allow such an equation: in coming to you, this woman lost her children.

Morbid ideas. Because she was by herself just now. Ironically, though they had left everything together, here she was alone. What self-pity! Andrew was soon coming.

Laura had kept herself fully occupied, reading in German intensively, studying the new authors, especially an amazing poet named Rilke, attending a lecture course on Nietzsche, studying Kierkegaard.

And tonight was the lecture by Ellen May. This way, before approaching her, Laura could form an impression. Ellen May was speaking about the peace movement. Indeed, since coming to Europe, one felt very strongly the growing threat of a clash of the great powers, something that in America you only read about.

In the hall were a few hundred people, more women in twos and threes than women with men. Onto the platform behind the chairlady there came the speaker; her face was familiar to Laura from photographs, but the entire person was something of a surprise. Though not tall, this was a monumental being, and from her solidity came a sense of great calm. When Ellen May spoke, the effect was as of inevitable truth, of your own ideas and convictions stated with lucidity. As with Jane Addams at home.

The way to peace began with teaching children a spirit of cooperation, rather than teaching competition, stimulating rivalry. How Laura agreed! And teaching was mostly in the hands of women. Further—when women universally had the vote they would be able as a great social and political force to work for peace. . . . Pacifists, if they stood alone, were easily made to feel outcasts. "Unpatriotic," in time of national danger. Such had happened in Spain, and Sweden too, when pacifists refused conscription. Everyone wanted to "belong," yet there was a great danger in merely "belonging" without sustaining one's inner truth.

"Belonging," Ellen May quoted Kierkegaard, "belonging" contained the danger of avoiding responsibility. The individual left everything to the group, and became devoid of moral decision.

Wasn't that, Laura asked herself, precisely why she had had to come away? As well as for love?

On the edge of the little circle of question askers, Laura waited until the woman herself turned to her. Ah indeed, the letter about translation. "You are the friend of Miss Jane Addams of Chicago!" Then came an invitation to tea, at her friend's home.

In the small sitting room, the furniture unexpectedly decorated with doilies, Ellen May soon had learned whether Laura had translation experience? A publisher? Still, as she could work directly from Swedish . . .

Presently Laura found herself telling her situation, Ellen May nodding sagely at each step. Yes, a woman's children. As Laura had already understood for herself: there could arise this conflict, the conflict that she called "between womanhood and motherhood." But if a woman, to fulfill her natural role as a mother, remained bound to a man she no longer wanted, would she not even destroy her womanhood? They must discuss more. Laura could indeed inform her, as she herself had never had children. Nor been married. She had been a schoolteacher, and begun to write . . .

THEN ANDREW arrived in Berlin. Laura had taken the flat of a professor who was absent for six months in Oxford; in the apartment was a large study with plenty of room, should Andrew wish, to install a drafting table.

But didn't she want it for her own work? For her translating? —Ah, there was an old-fashioned little boudoir, she could set a writing desk in the corner there. And they began moving about the furniture.

Now even a sort of social life began. Invitations for the American architect and his friend, from advanced Berliners, feminists, socialists. While during the day doing his share of the drawings. Herr Reiner was most satisfied with what Andrew had brought, and he also could not tell one hand from another. Thus, with Wally at work in Italy, they would have time to travel a bit, too.

Oh, it was a relief, Laura said, not to have to go everywhere alone, and, she laughed, not to sleep alone. And when she described that remarkable woman Ellen May, her ideas against war, and also showed Andrew her first translation efforts—for with translation she did not mind showing her work—he became quite engrossed. Perhaps he could even interest his friend Alfred Eastman, who did fine editions, to bring out the English version. Now, here and there Andrew had a question about an expression, a turn of phrase—perhaps she was translating too literally? And his suggestions almost always helped. That was a good feeling, going over her work together, their heads bent under the lamp.

Laura had come to dread the legal envelopes in the mail. —Put it all in the hands of Clarence Darrow, Andrew said. —But how could she trouble a man so busy with big struggles, defending labor? —Never mind, Andrew laughed, always go to the best! Besides, Clarence had never paid him for that house design!

And indeed Mr. Darrow sent back a long ruminative letter: he might try to mediate, he hated divorce actions in the courts; in any case, this must wait until Laura returned to America, and he went into all the Solomonic possibilities —as he called them—to divide the children, the boy to the father, the girl to the mother, or to divide the year. . . . And he must warn her, sympathy in Chicago, because of her flight, was entirely with her husband.

Then, the letter from Christina. She had moved out and was now living with a teacher friend, nearby, but Laura need not worry, she was seeing the children every day, after school. As Laura could imagine, it had been difficult for her to remain in Ralph's house. He had not asked her to leave, nor been in any way unpleasant, but each time she sat down to dinner . . . And then, he had brought in a new governess. . . .

The large business envelopes to Andrew, too, were disturbing. The Ford commission on which he had largely counted for this year's living, for them here in Europe, and for his family in Chicago, was definitely off. Never mind, he said. New work was bound to come in. Perhaps he would even pick up things in Europe when the big Reiner folio appeared. Andrew was not going to be ruled by money.

From his mother came homey letters, mostly about the children. Here was a funny story, he told Laura: That Hemingway boy, Ernest, little Richard's idol, when Richard asked him what was a hegira, Ernie had gone and looked it up in the dictionary, and replied it meant his father was a Mohammedan! The Hemingway boy had even shown Richard a picture in the dictionary, of a bearded Mohammedan wearing a white turban. That, Marta wrote, was how the child expected his papa to look when he came home! The last words Andrew had not meant to read, but nevertheless Laura smiled.

Having done her sample chapters, Laura was fearful. Would he go for a few days with her to Sweden?

24

THE CURVED snow vistas on the low hills, and the stark straight trees, could have been Wisconsin.

The house by the frozen-over lake was ample, honest, and the household of middle-aged women did not feel to Andrew as strange as he might have thought. The others were not as strong-faced as Ellen May; one had soft cheeks like his mother's, and the other was subdued but with a devoted light in her eyes, constantly toward Ellen May, who had taken her in, they soon learned, a woman beaten by a brute husband. She was always baking.

Ellen quickly relieved Laura's anxiety: the chapters were excellent. Only here and there, if she might suggest . . .

They went on long, booted wintry walks, where ideas that had been discussed attained a new clarity. A thought even came to Andrew, for his own situation.

Here was this woman in this isolated house by a small lake, two hours' train ride from the city, and yet here she carried on a vigorous career, her writings, her ideas widely known not only in Sweden but on the Continent and soon in America. Why did one have to live in the center of things? Thoughts of Thoreau returned to him.

In another of his mother's letters, Marta had remarked almost casually, by way of a family matter, that her hill next to Aunt Nora's was now his. Marta had at last sold the house in Madison, and used part of the money for the hill. Thus Andrew would always have land of his own, at home.

And so his idea came. Why not? Instead of returning to compete with all those rapacious idea-stealers, commission grabbers?

To live away somewhere, do only what he chose to do, new things that brought challenges to him . . . Not that adage of a better mousetrap. He would keep the downtown office in Chicago. But also, why not live within the natural world he knew? And Laura too had grown up in such a natural world. A dignified, decent life, doing their own work in their own place, as this woman managed to do here, by this remote lake in Sweden.

But only, so far, a notion.

With the folio drawings completed, approved, and Wally gone home, they decided to find a retreat in Italy, where Andrew would write out his presentation.

Just above Florence, in Fiesole, they found it: the *casa* as though grown out of a single cell multiplying itself in every direction, rooms into rooms, garden walls and vines merging into house walls, windows peering out of trellises, the little estate a tangle of paths, of zigzagging grass-tufted stone stairways, haphazard flower beds, grape arbors, olive trees, a fusion of scents.

They rolled carpets off flagstone floors, pushed towering armoires from one wall to another, decided where the bed should be. In the mornings, each worked, door closed.

Andrew even found himself sketching out a small house, nestled in this hill. Perhaps remain in Italy?

They lunched on a terrace, or under a pergola, or in

the grape arbor, changing at whim. The housekeeper, a few black hair strands usually stuck to her cheeks, taught Laura her lasagna.

They sat close over a table as Laura translated into German what Andrew had written for his preface. In the late afternoons they strolled arm in arm, usually into the village.

A number of English stayed hereabouts; it was not unusual, strolling, to encounter painters working at their portable easels, some quite good. A few eccentric elderly women.

Yet over this idyllic retreat, the money disease. One could live on very little here, a few commissions a year would suffice, but at home the debts increased. Then came a cool letter from Helena. With the summer problems she would not trouble him, both Ellen and Ned had found jobs to help out, and Wally, until his return to college, would be working as a draftsman with Malcolm Reese and Stephen Gaylord. He was, she had to say, disappointed at the small sum his father had paid him for his winter's employment (Doubtless the firm of Reese and Gaylord would be more generous to his son, Andrew read between the lines.) Only, now college money had to be found for Ned as well as Wally, and as for Ellen—Andrew knew the way all the girls dressed at Oak Park High School. Little Richard was running around in torn shoes, virtually barefoot. . . .

Good old Phil Whaley the realtor wrote in his blunt way, frankly Andrew's name was still mud, the scandal was still a big stink around Oak Park, yet, even so, Phil might be able to scare up a house or two. One prospect Phil had in mind was a client who had bought a double lot on Kenilworth, the man was himself remarried after a nasty divorce. He knew and admired Andrew's work, but he would want Andrew on the spot in person, no substitutes. Then came another ray in the sky, a letter from Alf Eastman— must have heard from Jack Slater that Andrew was hard up. Alf wanted another building on his place, nothing big

—a gardener's house, still he wanted it in keeping with the main house, of which he and Georgia were so proud, one of Andrew's greatest.

Another letter from home. Wally had run the car into a ditch. He was all right, but the car needed extensive repairs.

Finally, from his mother. It was of course not of any need of her own that Marta wrote. But of his "pledge." Hadn't he spoken of a year? A year away, as he had declared it, and the year would soon be over. His wife had shown the world a remarkable example, with her tolerance and faith in him.

His mother was not judging him; she devoutly hoped the year had given him the refreshed vision he sought in his work. Surely now Andrew would keep his word and return. Whatever he thought of for the future, surely, just as his family had given him the freedom to try another life, he owed it to them perhaps to try a resumption . . .

Things had to be clear, Laura said. Clarence Darrow had written: he had approached Helena, who categorically refused, even with full control of the children, and full financial guarantees, to consider divorcing Andrew.

But even if he could get a divorce, Laura told Andrew, she didn't want him to feel obliged to marry her. She didn't know whether she herself wanted again to enter into a marriage. Or whether it was really a life suited for Andrew. Even if Andrew should want to return and try his domestic life again, she would understand.

Now they must truly say: did either feel that this being together, of theirs, had failed? Not for him, Andrew said.

Laura slowly shook her head, and took his hand.

Then it was a question of practical problems. He had to go back to recover, rebuild his practice. Perhaps, at first, they need not live together, it would only revive all the hostilities.

She thought it best that she even remain here for a while, that they did not return together. She had her courses to finish. And as the year would soon be over, Andrew ought to keep his word and return.

This day, on their walk, the silences were lengthy; the physical link, their linked arms, helped. She would stay on at least a month, Laura thought. She might go again to visit Ellen May in Sweden, and work on another translation. She might go to Leipzig for a few special lectures, on the new poetry. If Andrew returned alone to Oak Park— she made herself say it—perhaps he should even try going back to his family.

He smiled as at some idea that had no bearing on real things. They walked on in silence.

Then Andrew realized he was thinking of another plan entirely. Of truly going home. The hill land his mother had given him.

He saw the entire structure in unity, striated walls of stone from the nearby quarry, placed like rough outcroppings, molded to the hill's contour—a natural house, his basic conception of the house as an organism. Perhaps living here in this hillside cottage had given him the thought—the structure was haphazard, a room added here, a wall there, but with a certain cohesiveness through the use of the natural materials of the place, stone and wood.

"I have it," he said.

"Have what?" she asked.

"I was thinking of a house—"

"Here?" For he had been toying with the idea of trying to establish himself in Europe.

"Not here. There."

Now Laura could not follow. Did he mean Oak Park?

There was an impish impulse to make it a mystery, or rather to keep it in himself until he would sketch it out and show it to her, whole.

"On my land at home," he said. "In Wisconsin."

A hill house, rounding with the form of the hill. A water flow, from a hilltop reservoir, the stream guided down to gardened pools in the recesses of the dwelling . . . Andrew knew the precise site, he told her, just above a stand of elms, the house to be level with the treetops.

He had surmounted. He was creating again. Oh, Andrew was so dear to her.

Now that the house was forming in his mind, in greater and more perfect detail, Andrew's spirits revived. This would be the renewal, and his best work, a whole new conception and yet born of all he had done until now.

He'd have to go back to Oak Park first. Once there, as Phil Whaley, as Jack Slater and his remaining loyal friends were writing, his business within a few months would revive. He'd have money to build his River Valley home. Yes, he'd have to seem a good boy, his fling over and done with. He'd reopen the Oak Park studio. Even though it wasn't his way, to dissimulate, but for a few months—one thought he couldn't yet bring himself to explain to Laura—it would have to appear that he was living as before, at home with the family. In a few months he could start construction on the hill site. A house in Wisconsin for his mother, he'd say. For Marta to live near her sister and brothers in old age. Or whatever. Nobody's affair. A house on his own hill. With this project to sustain his spirit, he could do all the rest. And when the house was done, he and Laura would go there and live there. He could keep his office in Chicago, but have his drafting room on the farm. He would manage with fewer commissions, but they must have a whole life, a natural life, and his vision expanded: barns, cattle, their own milk and butter, sheep and goats on the hill, he'd have farm help, grow corn and wheat—a total life, natural, independent, free.

Would she want that? To live with him, far away from the city? After all, they wouldn't be far from Madison, a great university, and Wisconsin the most progressive of states, La Follette practically a Socialist. Strong for women's rights, Andrew teased her. People there were more open-minded. They could live without sham.

He was suddenly in high spirits.

"Only one thing," Laura said. "Andrew, if when you return there you find— I want you to know you are free."

But their hands remained clasped.

As though on a last spree, they went touring, all the new art they had neglected to see—in Italy itself, a new spirit, Futurism, a painter named Marinetti with angular, machine-inspired compositions, much, Andrew said, as his own work had predicted ten years ago, though he did not take to the style in painting. And in Vienna, the new music of Schönberg. Yes, he took to it. And an architecture of flat surfaces, Andrew's cube in Oak Park had surely influenced this. And flat-designed paintings by Gustav Klimt, strong colors on the murals, faces of the new women, this he liked better than Italy's Futurism.

In Munich, in a secondhand bookshop, Andrew discovered an entire album of Japanese prints, including a Hiroshige! Hardly managing to keep his face from showing the find, he got the album for a song. And the next day came Laura's turn, from an outdoor stand she pulled a brochure, hardly a dozen pages, elaborately printed—"A Hymn to Nature," by Wolfgang Goethe. But in all her Goethe studies she had never encountered this poem! Hours of searching failed to show it in the university bibliography.

Together, they bent over her translation. Certain passages were like a credo to Andrew.

Nature!
With the simplest materials she arrives at the
 most sublime Contrasts
Without Appearance of Effort she attains utmost Per-
 fection—the most exact
Precision veiled always in exquisite Delicacy
Each of her Works has its own individual Being—
 each of her Phenomena
the most isolated Conception, yet all is Unity.

She must show it to Professor Vogeleider, the Goethe authority, in Leipzig. But not yet. That meant after Andrew sailed. Meanwhile, in Holland, they must see a Prairie House, built by a young architect with all homage to Andrew Lane. And back in Berlin, they found Hermann Reiner's office redone with gleaming metal furniture by a young architect named Gropius; the publisher showed Andrew plans for a factory all of steel and glass, with mitered corner windows, "You see, your influence grows!"

And so, his proofs read, the paper chosen, Laura, not wanting to burden him with an image of leaving her deserted in Europe, went off for her visit to Sweden. Andrew took ship.

Almost a year to the day of his departure on the hegira, he arrived in Chicago.

25

HELENA HAD given thought, and the best attitude seemed to treat the whole affair as an episode, now done with, the fling of a man past forty. An artist. Just ignore it. Poor Laura, she would be the one who had lost out. For Helena, despite her bitterness, could not but admire the chance Laura had taken as a woman. Only, what a decent, fine husband Laura had lost. And her children! Though Ralph, the Slaters said, would be quite generous in the divorce, about the children's visits with their mother.

Andrew's letters had been mostly about the state of his money affairs. Inquiries about the children. Wally, on his return, had not seen Laura Garnett; she had remained in Berlin. Well, at least they had shown that much embarrassment.

Should she have the children stay home from school? But he had not written an arrival hour, and she still felt uncertain as to how it would be.

In her worrying, the night before, Helena had a dream, or more like a memory. It was of that terrible horrible accident they had seen in Madison on their honeymoon, thank God not the first night but the next morning. They stood in the unfinished building of the courthouse, only it was also the Court of Honor of the Columbian Exposition, by the great colonnade that he had so disliked, and that she had hardly dared to say she, like everyone, found beautiful. They stood and saw a huge pillar crumbling, as they had really seen in Madison, and it crumbled onto a man, and that man was Andrew—oh, the horror! —but still it wasn't he, because Andrew still stood there alongside her . . . She awakened, sat up to drive out the dream.

In the morning after a bit of uncertainty Helena decided yes, and got herself into the dress he had designed for her, to match the house. After so many years her waist had not spread all that much, though she pulled the corset awfully tight. When she heard the taxi coming into the driveway, Helena opened the door, and stood there smiling as he paid the cabby. Old Elmer kept repeating welcome back and helped carry the bags into the house. The welcome-home kiss; nothing could be told from it. Andrew did notice the dress, said, "Well! Still fits!" and she had to laugh because he wore a comical Alpine hat with a feather. Once the bags were inside, Helena stood awaiting the real reunion, and he embraced her. Oh, she did have the same weakness for him, her man, after this dreadful starved year, and she let her mouth press, did not hold back her hunger. But the same did not come from him.

She could not yet know, she told herself. Perhaps there was even a kind of shame in him, holding him back.

One bag he opened, gifts, a beautiful hand-crocheted Italian shawl for his mother, Helena forbade the thought that *that one* had gone shopping with him and chosen it. Now for herself, a lovely glittery opera net for her hair, then at least he had remembered her beautiful hair, and, putting it on, she again in her kiss of thanks tried—but he was already unfolding things for the children. For the girls, each a lovely Italian silk blouse, oh again she hoped that witch hadn't picked them, and just at that moment Marta came in, for so they had agreed between them, Marta should wait a few minutes after the cab.

Andrew kept telling Marta she should not have spent her money to buy him that land, yet there was nothing he could have wanted more!

Then he had to telephone Tillit; yes, there was mail, there was an important inquiry, just recently, too late to forward, about an office building in San Francisco, yes, a tall one, thirty stories! . . .

A wonderful omen, Helena told herself.

Little Richard was the first to come rushing in for lunch, he began punching at his father, and in a moment they were rolling on the floor, Andrew letting himself be overcome, Richard sitting on top of him, then came Cynthia with huggings, at once trying on her lace blouse, then Jonathan and Ellen hurrying during their lunch period. For Jonathan he had an Alpine hat just like his own, with a feather. And Helena saw Andrew's surprised eyes at Ellen, breasts like her mother's at her age, though he did not say it. He even twitted Ellen about her saucy remarks in the *Tribune*, but that was the only allusion, and quickly passed by, Ellen too hurrying to try on her beautiful blouse. The lunch was noisy, with sudden silent spots, in one of them Richard burst out, to great laughter, that Ernie Hemingway was a liar, as Dad had no Mohammedan beard! "Oh, not really a liar," said Marta, "Ernie just likes to make things up."

The family table made Helena feel it would all be the same, it would be as it had been, but after the children hurried off there was again an uncertainty. He had to go downtown. Things were urgent.

Gene Tillit was actually red-faced with his welcomings and apologies for not having cabled about San Francisco but at least he had at once written to them—he showed the letter—that Mr. Lane was on the way back from Europe and would be in touch with them on arrival. Good. Andrew got off a telegram, most interested, send details. With such a commission, he'd have the money to build his house in River Valley.

The rest: Gladys Beam still kept trying to explain about the Henry Ford fiasco. His office neighbor, Holst, had taken over the Memphis house, as they insisted on having the architect on the site. There had ensued, it now appeared, two additional commissions in Memphis, which Holst declared were legitimately his own.

On the better side, Alf Eastman wanted not only a gardener's house; his wife was planning a children's school, and she wanted a children's theater included. Fine! Fine! Things were picking up.

Willis appeared, to say, "Welcome home." This time Willis was all involved in a strike—the garment girls, hadn't Andrew looked at the papers since coming back? Fifty thousand strong! The girls had walked out of the biggest factory, Hart, Schaffner and Marx. Police were trying to pull them off the picket lines, by the hair. Clarence Darrow, naturally, was their lawyer—only, right now Clarence was going off to Los Angeles. Hadn't Andrew read about the dynamiting of the *Los Angeles Times?* Twenty men killed. As usual, labor organizers were being accused. Like with Big Bill Haywood. Who else but Clarence Darrow could defend them? Why on earth should union leaders plant dynamite where it would kill men at work!

Then Jack Slater. And as between old friends, How was Laura?

She was translating a book, Andrew told him.

Coming back soon?

For the present, best nothing said. Jack nodded. Not finished, then? Andrew slowly shook his head, finding himself in a curious way relieved that at least someone, a real friend, knew.

All at once, on the Oak Park train, the skyscraper stood clear in his mind. A central core, with giant radials. That rejected lakeside tower, only not four stories, but thirty! Elevators shooting up in the central core. And all the paraphernalia, heating, electric cables, garbage, centralized there. And reaching out on each radial, the office suites, high above the Pacific!

An architectural revolution! Oh, they could not refuse. Why had they come to Andrew Lane if not for something original! He hugged the image in his soul.

All through dinner, with his secret, he was in great spirits.

And then, along the tree-corridor to the studio.

Well, that was as always, Helena told herself, even if on the first day. It gave her more of a feeling, in a way, of having him home.

In a great spurt, he sketched it. Good, good, great! At last, his turn at the tall building, the vertical. Every radial free in space. Vistas. No crammed pigeonholes. His pencil flew.

With the children gone to bed, Helena still didn't know. At last she went up. She had intended to wear the nightgown that was a signal, yet she was filled with misgivings. She used a little scent. Brushed her hair; it still had such sparkle.

His light was still on, in the drafting room. What could be so urgent? Yes, he had to catch up.

She had a strong impulse to go to him. Even prepared the words. "Andrew, we have at least always been honest with each other . . . At least don't shame me before our children." From the first moment of his arrival, she had shown him how she felt. But she would not demean herself.

The lighted upstairs window. He was not without feeling for her. The passion they had had, the sight of her, enough to set him off. Helena had, all considered, preserved herself well. A still presentable woman.

What sort of animal was he? The other time, going to Laura, he hadn't felt it adulterous. This time he would.

Andrew drove himself in his work. After a time he saw that the bedroom light was out.

There was a cot in the studio.

While she was giving the children their breakfast, Andrew slipped up to the bedroom—she had put out his dressing gown. Thus he appeared.

Home routine resumed. Except that Ellen's bold eyes, with the overknowing look of a young girl who knew too much but yet didn't know, swerved from him to Helena, and back.

Helena poured his coffee, put his bacon and eggs before him. There was chatter. The youngsters went off, Ellen adjusting her tam so that a cowlick fetchingly protruded, then kissing the top of his head, offering her cheek, while her eyes still glittered with curiosity.

Helena sat down with her second cup of coffee. She wanted clarity, clear explanations between them. For her part she had learned in this year that she could live this way; it was not a real woman's life, but if his mother had done it, she could do it. (She need not have brought in Marta, but he made no remark.) However, the children. If he meant to stay, then for the sake of the children let it appear normal. If he meant to sleep in the studio, very well, at least the children were used to his going there and working until long after they were in bed, so it would seem normal enough. For their friends in Oak Park, and surely to rebuild his practice—all she asked was to keep up appearances.

It was Helena the strong-minded girl of twenty years ago; he had to admire her. If only his emotions had remained.

"I suppose she'll be coming back for their divorce," Helena said. There was a rise in her voice. "What do you intend to do?"

"I intend to do my work."

She started to say something angry, tightly closed her

lips, went to the sink with her cup. He went through the corridor, back to the studio.

An item appeared in the *Oak Leaves*. The noted architect Andrew Lane had returned home after his year-long hegira in Europe, where he had completed the album of his designs to be published by a distinguished Berlin firm. Mr. Lane was the first American architect so honored in Europe.

How he took care in his letter, that she should know he was sleeping in the studio. She must come now, things were going well, an enormous commission in San Francisco, and he had a tremendous plan! "Remember that idea for the little tower by the lake, with cantilevered radials over the water?" Now he saw it ten times higher, extending over the Pacific Ocean! It would revolutionize structure! And with this fee, he could build their house in River Valley! She must come.

And Jane Addams wrote, luckily the head of Chicago's public library was a good friend and, with Laura's qualifications, could indeed place her at the Hull House branch. Of course there would be room for her at the residence! Jane would be delighted, as would everyone!

THERE WERE laws of life, of beauty, that existed in themselves, like laws of physics; they existed independently of a human perception of them, just as moral laws must exist. This was what came to Andrew, late one evening, as he gazed for a long time at the perfect print of Hiroshige's formalized waves that he and Laura had found in Munich.

And the way they had responded to it together—the unity, not a word needed.

What he thought was, to take a small apartment in town, though still remaining officially at home, at least through the Christmas holiday.

Their letters crossed. Ellen May's household, she

wrote, had a fascinating newcomer, a gentle half-balmy murderess who had killed a brutal husband, served fourteen years in prison, and been given refuge here on emerging. But, Laura confessed, she could live solely in female company for only a short while, and then began to feel unreal. Besides, she must face her situation in Chicago. At least at first, Laura thought of staying at Hull House; she would be working there as librarian, and Jane was keeping a small apartment for her, and there Christina could bring the children to visit her. . . .

True, she deeply missed him . . .

He must find a place. The Studio Building on Michigan Avenue—no, it was too notorious for that sort of thing. The near North Side. On Elm Street he found a building already divided into small apartments, the second floor with a front bay window. There he would place his drafting table. The bedroom had only a small window on an airshaft. But if things went right, he might buy and remodel the building, something charming could be done here, a sort of town house. If he ever got clear of Oak Park.

A week before the holiday, on the Swedish steamer threading between ice floes, Laura made her crossing, arriving in Chicago wrapped in bright hand-knit woolens, hood, scarf and gloves, with her portmanteau filled with more such colorful knitted things for the children. There at the station was Christina, puffy as ever, but Laura's prevision of Maida and Johnny advancing at first shyly and then running the last few steps to a hug, especially Maida, this didn't materialize, Christina quickly explaining that Ralph had decided against such excitement; the children would be brought after Laura had settled in.

On the way to Hull House, Christina told of Andrew, he was living at home but people said it was just a show, he slept in the studio. The Eastmans were giving Andrew some work, and a few other friends stuck by him. As to Ralph, he went to concerts sometimes still with the Slaters. If he . . . did anything . . . had anyone—Christina blushed a little—it must be downtown. Though of course it was some months now since she herself had been living in the house.

Jane was eager to hear about the prospect of women's suffrage in Europe; it might very well come in Sweden first, Laura said. A war? Yes, there were fears. They'd talk more later. Here they had been busy with a scarlet-fever epidemic, worst in this area.

First thing, alone, Laura found herself pushing the furniture around in the tiny apartment, placing the sofa with its back to the window—then she laughed at herself; the Andrew influence.

The children didn't rush melting into her arms, but she hugged Maida while helping take off her wine-red coat, and the child even carried a fur muff to match her little hat, expensive, from Field's obviously, and red fur-topped snow boots, and John even let himself be hugged—had she seen the North Pole from the ship? Or polar bears on icebergs? He crunched the Swedish flatbread. —Wasn't she even coming home for the Christmas tree?

No, but of course there would be an enormous tree here at Hull House; she would see them a lot, and they would go to all sorts of places during the holiday. But as she and their father were separated . . .

Maida sat very close on the sofa, with certain quick little glances at her mother as though secret understandings existed between them. She knew, she said. Her best friend in school was also divorced. "You mean her mother and father are divorced," John corrected.

Even though the scarlet fever had now subsided, Ralph had severely instructed that they were not to mingle with the mob of children at Hull House, so Laura kept them in the room. They'd look too different from the children here, anyway. Like being taken slumming. She showed them the library where she worked.

Was she poor, was that why she lived here? John

asked. —Oh, no. Miss Addams and her friends wanted to help the poor people in the neighborhood, and in Hull House there were doctors for them, and mothers could learn how to take care of their babies, and laborers could have union meetings, also have good times, dances, and there were things for the children—music lessons, and plays, woodworking shops, and cooking for the girls. "Just like we have at school," Maida said.

On Elm Street, Laura found herself glancing both ways as she entered the house. During the embrace they were like young lunatics, unbuttoning, and only after the shudder of total appeasement could they really talk. Never before had the longing, the need, so overwhelmed her. As you read about drug addicts, as in Thomas de Quincey, of the indescribable sense of relief, of peace, when the long-needed drug flowed into the body after the deprivement.

Would it ensue now, the kind of skulking about they had chosen to avoid in their year-long escape to Europe? An hour snatched now and again, oh what was this to be?

Until her divorce—until her affairs were in order. But even afterward—as Helena would never agree to a divorce?

It had its small charms, this love nest, as the press would call it should it be discovered. Laura could imagine the headlines: ARCHITECT AND SOULMATE IN NORTH SIDE LOVE NEST AFTER EUROPEAN HEGIRA . . . Yet Andrew was ebullient. It was here, on his board, that the new free-form structure grew. Not in the office, not in his River Valley drafting room, but here, their place. Only, she could come so rarely; they had to be so careful.

Though Darrow was warm and easy as always, even starting with a greeting in Swedish, as his Ruby too was of Swedish extraction and that ought to make them all re-lated, Laura could feel the burden, on him, of that looming Los Angeles trial. Perhaps it was best—as he must soon go there, he said—for his partner, Edgar Masters, just now in court, to take care of her situation. "He's a real lawyer. You know what they say of me, I'm just a courtroom preacher." But was that Edgar Lee Masters the poet? She had even read something of his, quite classical, with thees and thous. "Don't worry, to him the law is poetry," Clarence declared. Besides, the divorce agreement, as he had written her, was practically arranged.

He pulled his hand over his face, sighed. He really didn't want to go and get into that battle in Los Angeles. There had been a second dynamiting, of an ironworks, and some stoolpigeon had brought all sorts of accusations against a union official—it was going to be the Hayward case all over again, and that had nearly killed him. And the Los Angeles crowd were relentless reactionaries, they'd stop at nothing. Ruby was already packing and storing the furniture and closing the apartment, because this was going to be a long one. Well, as Laura knew, Ralph had all the legal right on his side. He could forbid her even to see the children, claiming she would be a bad influence. Again Clarence rumpled his face. "I don't believe you could be a bad mother. Hell, there probably is no such thing as a bad mother." But until the papers were signed, she must behave as a good girl.

Now, Ralph saw himself as a liberal and was not the kind of man to set detectives on her trail. But apparently there had been teasing in school and John had given a boy a bloody nose. Now, Hull House was a good place for her to stay. Naturally, it would be hard for her and Andrew to keep from seeing each other . . . Laura flushed. "I'm the last man," Clarence said, "to advise going against human nature." The weariness lifted for a moment; he had that look of boyish guilt. Everyone knew, doubtless even Ruby, that he had a new love. Still, he had to caution her, until the actual divorce . . .

Laura controlled her inward shudder. All those scenes in novels. Court trials, with the private detective taking the stand, opening his notebooks to recite hours and places.

Clarence sighed. Now, he had had several talks with

Ralph's attorney. Ralph agreed to long visits, even to the children practically staying with her all summer. He would not deprive the children of contact with their mother; he agreed they needed to love and respect her.

As he had written, though the courts normally in the case of young children went with the mother, in this case there was no chance. He believed he had extracted the best conditions. If she would accept, Mr. Masters would get it done.

At least, her life at Hull House was full. Almost all her meals Laura took in the commons, usually at the big table with Jane, Florence Kelly, Julia Lathorp, and the guests—a great variety, always lively.

On Saturdays, the children came, Maida to her dance group, John took to making animals in clay, fired them and carried them home.

Only, it all seemed provisional. Not her real life. Once, twice a week, Laura slipped out to Andrew. With the early spring, he was indeed starting construction in River Valley, but the thought of moving away to Wisconsin—the train took six hours . . . And would Ralph really let the children come for the summer?

Mr. Masters was not perturbed. At first she had been put off by his manner, scowly, hunched within himself, almost disagreeable. Yes, Mr. Darrow had had some conferences, but the legal work remained to be done. His plan was simply to allow the lawsuit for desertion; she would not appear. It would all go off in a routine manner, quietly. The understanding about the children would depend somewhat on which judge was sitting; they might have to wait, to make sure of the right one.

Then, touching on her sojourn in Europe, there came a mention of the lectures on Goethe, and the man changed. Ah, and she could read Goethe in the original! And the story of the poem that she and Andrew had found and translated. He must see it! "Hymn to Nature!" And presently she was speaking of the new poets, of Rilke. And were they like the free-verse people here? he wanted to know. Did she like the free-verse people here? Amy Lowell? He was not really opposed, oh no. Though some, like Vachel Lindsay, were beyond him. Too much howling. Now, even Harriet Monroe was turning altogether modernist. Talking about starting a new poetry magazine, and now she had charged off on a trip around the world! . . . And Laura wrote? Only for herself? Oh, there were indeed some things of his own that he put away, only for himself.

And suddenly, with a curious, impish glimmer, Mr. Masters pulled open the bottom drawer of his desk, fingered among some papers, drew one out, and handed it to her. The poem was written in a prim, indeed legal-looking hand. What she read was like an epitaph, a life. Yes, yes, that was just what he meant! She had grasped the irony of it all! He had a whole cemeteryful, in that drawer!

If you in the village think that my work was a good one,
Who closed the saloons and stopped all playing at cards,
And haled Old Daisy Fraser before Justice Arnett
In many a crusade to purge the people of sin;
Why do you let the milliner's daughter Dora,
And the worthless son of Benjamin Pantier
Nightly make my grave their unholy pillow?

There was something in its direct tone that reminded Laura of a younger poet, who had been coming around to Hull House. While this elegy of Masters' was somber, and young Sandburg's work was charged with energy, there was in both of them a kind of American quality, she told herself. Like Andrew with his American architecture, unencumbered and direct. Masters showed her a few more. — He ought to publish them, she said. The lawyer seemed even to blush. —She didn't think they were too modern?

YOUNG SANDBURG—another Swede! had lately come from Milwaukee, and was a reporter on Chicago's socialist daily, the *Herald*, the paper that carried no advertising and could say what it pleased. At labor rallies at Hull House, he'd end up singing Wobbly songs, twanging a guitar and leading the crowd, "There'll be pie in the sky when you die!" Yet he didn't din politics at you; he told his own variety of yarns, he had bummed around riding the rails. And he might pull out his latest poem and read it. There was a new one about Chicago, in free verse, that Laura had copied out for Andrew. "Hog Butcher for the World, / Tool Maker, Stacker of Wheat, / Player with Railroads and the Nation's Freight Handler; / Stormy, husky, brawling City of the Big Shoulders . . ." Andrew thought it was tremendous, as great as Walt Whitman.

26

THE SAN Francisco people were excited. Daring, original. They had commissioned a set of plans, the first stage. With the entire office working on it, himself tackling the foundation problems—deep in solid rock; he had in mind the earthquake of 1906—Andrew sent off the preliminary layout. Meanwhile, awaiting their go-ahead, he started building the house in River Valley.

Helena knew, how could she not know? Naturally Aunt Nora wrote of it to Marta. A summer home?

Through these months, Helena had managed appearances, somehow. Only now she confronted him—"You're building, out there."

"Why not?"

"It's not for your mother." What was he building, then?

A house.

"You mean to live there. With her."

"I mean to have a house there."

Oh, she saw his intention. After the Garnetts' divorce, he would leave this sham life. He would go to River Valley to live. Laura with him.

This time it would really be over.

Perhaps best. What sort of life was this? Perhaps best for him to go. But as for her giving Andrew a divorce, never. No need to say it again. They knew.

Yet, week to week, month to month—when? If you knew the day of doom, you could count off your remaining days. Or should she simply ask him to go, as his mother had, with his father, and be done with it!

Yet, like the knowing-doomed, Helena could not bring herself to make shorter whatever time remained to her. She could not send him out to his mistress, and be done. She was the wife of Andrew Lane.

The house was up, walls, roof. Laura must see it. She could even decide with him on certain furniture he was building in.

"Decide? You mean agree with you!"

They laughed.

A young Italian that Jane Addams had sent him, Pete, who was staying on the job as supervisor, met them with the Ford at the station; not even Aunt Nora need know of Laura's presence.

Like reading a work while the author hovers over you, Laura walked through the structure. She had indeed seen each detail in the plans, yet this was hearing the music. Andrew followed her, his ease increasing as she appreciated every subtlety.

Yes! She saw. The Prairie House was a primer, to this. In those Oak Park houses the walls could be brick, wood, even stucco, but here nothing but the stone of the hill. One hardly knew where the hill stopped, the walls began. The flow of space that Andrew had talked and written about—only, now she fully felt it. There was a continuity of enclosures, sometimes even burrowing into the hillside, cavelike. Then flowing across little gardens, and through the living room, around its vast stone fireplace, and out to the veranda daringly projected over the treetops. There you felt yourself indeed as in a treehouse, and a thought came to Laura: Of all man's habitations, there were two principles, almost Hegelian in their dialectic. Inward and outward. The cave and the treehouse. It was all here in this one habitation. Wedded. Andrew had created this, surely not to a thesis, but this was the genius of Andrew's understanding.

"Did you mean it?" she said to him. "The cave and the treehouse?"

Not in so many words. Yet Laura had seen right into the nature of his work.

There was already a large drafting room, reached across an inner courtyard, with his own private drafting room tucked between. And for herself, behind the bedroom—*their* bedroom, she corrected herself—a small study. A writing nook by a low stone fireplace. Then, as in the crook of an arm, behind the fireplace, two children's rooms. For Maida and John. Even this coming summer? Could it be? At last to live with Andrew normally, as in those months in Fiesole. And with her children.

27

RALPH HAVING high business connections, Masters pointed out, the papers reported the divorce without flamboyance, alluding only as though for identification to the famous "hegira" case of last year.

The ex-Mrs. Garnett, active in the women's movement, had been granted the right to resume her maiden name, Bendersohn.

They had not yet moved out there, Helena knew. He had the children's theater to finish for the Eastmans. And another house here in Oak Park. Andrew still kept a draftsman in the studio, still even kept up the pretense of the paterfamilias.

But in the late fall, his draftsman no longer came, and when she looked into the studio, it had a half-deserted appearance, drawing boards cleared, rolls of blueprints gone.

For appearances—last appearance, Helena bitterly told herself—they together attended the Eastmans' grand opening of the children's playschool theater. And she even accepted, as a wife, people's compliments at the masterful structure. The beautiful stained-glass windows with their motif of colored balloons, reminding her of the decoration he had done years ago for the children's playroom upstairs.

In the morning after the children were off to school, Andrew appeared carrying a last roll of blueprints. "I can't go on with this sham any longer. I'll be living in River Valley."

"Is she going with you?" Her same words as two years ago.

He was silent.

"Perhaps you imagine her divorce changed things, Andrew. I haven't changed. I don't intend to change."

He said, "The household expenses here, for you and the children, I'll manage, but it would help just now if the studio could be rented. For offices, or even for living. I could easily remodel it." She stared at him. "I spoke to Whaley to try to rent it."

"Have you told your mother you are going?" she said stonily.

Just now he had stopped over and told Marta that the house in River Valley was ready and he was moving his headquarters there.

Headquarters. A family, a home, here for twenty-two years. And out there, on the land Marta had bought for him. Could Marta even have foreseen—? No, Helena stopped herself; she would not blame Marta.

"Helena—"

She said, out of a strength she was not sure she possessed, "Just go. Find peace. Fulfill the gift God gave you." And she could not hold back the last, "I'll explain to our children, their father is a genius, and that genius lives by its own rules."

When she went around later, Helena saw that he had hung a "For Rent" sign in the studio window, facing Chicago Avenue.

An enormous quiet settled around Helena. The house that had always thrusted with immediate needs, coffee for Andrew and the draftsmen, lunches, wanted nothing of her. Just as he who had been her man, whose needs, desires, irritations, even once love, she had felt within her organism, wanted nothing of her. She went to the telephone, sat on the chair-and-telephone unit he had designed, with the pad-rest measured to her arm, just as everything in the kitchen had fitted her reach. But she could not bring herself to raise the receiver. To tell her mother, "He's gone, this time for good." What a word to utter, "good." Nor could she say "forever."

The other time, two years already, she had still had little Richard in the house, tugging, demanding. Now also in school.

No, not her mother. And not his mother; Marta's kindergarten kids were coming in right now. But Marta would leave them with her helper and hurry over, fetching sympathy and . . . and, like a woman to a half-bewildered girl at her first bleeding, bringing advice, and the sense of being admitted to the eternal fate of womankind, the true curse of Eve. For even at this bad moment the thought struck Helena: had there not been Lilith?

Almost, it felt better to sit alone for a while, brood.

The other time, the hegira, she had known in advance. But so had she now. These months. For whom else could he have been building that house?

Yet, the other time there had been a boundary, a year. Leaving at least a hope. And she had grandly, magnanimously waited it out, even discussing with his mother how Andrew had known nothing of women, had never sown his wild oats.

But if now those two were decided to go and live together in a kind of seclusion, in River Valley, it was not a passing lust.

Then, seizing the receiver, she called Hull House, in the last moment asking not for Mrs. Garnett but, as had been in the papers, for Miss Bendersohn. And this was again the difference between them: never, even if by some strange circumstance there *should* come a divorce, which there could not, never would she think of herself or want again to be known as Miss Hewlett. In marriage she had become for the rest of her life Mrs. Lane. That was the difference between them. Even in their conception of women's rights. Some women did not really know what it was to be a woman. If someone now was even to call her Miss Hewlett, she would not at once recognize that it was she who was meant. Miss Who?

Miss Bendersohn was no longer a resident, the Hull House operator responded. So now it was certain. Helena hung up, her hand still staying on the receiver.

And her mind kept repeating, I'll never give him a divorce. She can die first.

Part Five

Truth
Before
The
World

28

FROM THE Elm Street apartment, before going to the train, Andrew telephoned the house in River Valley; the hired couple was there, from the village. August, said Mrs. Strom, was out cindering the approach drive, as there had been snow last night and the road was skiddy. The house was good and warm, oh yes the heat from under the floor was a wonderful idea. It worked fine. —Were there icicles hanging from the eaves? he wanted to know. She went to look. Yes, long icicles! Andrew smiled to himself. Exactly as he had envisioned! By omitting the gutter, he had a curtain of icicles.

In luminous streaks, in all lengths, as the car approached, the icicles glittered. "Andrew, you planned it!" she cried.

"Even planned the snow last night!" he replied. And Laura quoted, " 'When icicles by the barnyard wall doth hang.' "

The Stroms had emerged, the two of them in lumber-jackets, to help with the unloading. He had explained his situation. Refused a divorce. He was coming with the woman he regarded as his wife.

337

August Strom had even once been a Wobbly, riding the rails, working the harvests. And after working hereabouts one summer, and getting fond of Amy, a farmer's daughter, the old story, he would say, with his old lady joining in the joke, except her father didn't need a shotgun.

Amy was still fresh-faced, nice-looking. Their older son, Jasper, already thirteen, in the eighth grade, the other boy, Gil, was six, just started school. Good people, but with bad luck. August had labored and got his own farm, had an accident with a McCormick reaper, laid up for half a year, lost the farm, nearly lost the leg—still, better the farm than the leg, limped a bit, became a hired hand again. Worked sometimes for Gus's dairy. It was Cousin Susan who had thought of August and Amy for Andrew.

By late twilight the house was in order, supper on the stove. The Stroms, not yet installed in the cottage being built for them, hitched their wagon and took their way home.

Gazing out over the frosted treetops, Andrew identified for Laura the house of Uncle Matt, by a series of four glimmers on the other side of the river. And on this side of the river, the house of Aunt Nora. By now Marta surely had spoken to her from Oak Park. Surely, indeed, the whole clan was aware of his arrival.

The telephone remained silent, and Laura came out with what Andrew too was thinking: in the circumstances it was better for them to wait for a first sign, rather than to take the initiative, even with his Aunt Nora.

On her hill, above her school, there stood outlined against the wintry sky an accusation: the Love Tower of Andrew's honeymoon with Helena.

Wavering up their approach road, pale headlights, like Halloween lanterns, came closer. Andrew went to the door. Arriving, the pickup sputtered into silence; hoisting themselves down, there came Susan and Gus, Susan carrying a basket covered with a napkin which she removed on entering the house, even before embraces were exchanged, and with laughing half-formality she made the presentation of a loaf of home-baked bread, with a little cup of salt. Gus, beaming on Laura, pulled out a bottle from the basket. Hard cider. "Good luck in your new house!"

They were both now rather thick, large people looking much alike, parents of five: three sons, two daughters, one already married to a boy right here in the valley. To Laura they seemed even to talk in unison. But what good people, what a sense of relief they brought her! And with a touch of applejack in their tea, all of them settled into the hollow-log seats that Andrew had had built in a semicircle before the fireplace; Susan was soon discussing things quite openly and frankly.

At the start, Susan said, everyone had supposed Andrew was building this house so that Marta in her old age could live near her sister. Then as the size of the place became clear, it was concluded that it would be a summer home for his whole family now that he and Helena were reconciled after that notorious hegira of his in Europe. Then when that drafting room was going up, people decided, though at first puzzled, that in the summers he might be conducting a good deal of his work out here.

But today, all afternoon, Susan had heard the party line ringing. Counting the rings, it was mostly to Aunt Nora. No, Susan hadn't picked up her receiver to listen, though never had the temptation been greater! But she hadn't: Gus was her witness! —Couldn't vouch for it, Gus chortled—been in the barn most of the day.

Gazing directly at Laura, Susan gave her a serious opinion. It wouldn't be easy, or quick.

But now that she knew Laura, Susan was convinced the situation would be accepted in the end. All that she herself could do she would do. They were welcome to her house, and must come Sunday to dinner. Her thought was, maybe Andrew and Laura shouldn't be the ones to take the first step, not even to Aunt Nora, as she had not yet given any sign. And not even Sunday to the chapel, maybe they ought to wait. She would talk to Aunt Nora—perhaps try inviting Nora as well, for Sunday.

Standing on the veranda, watching the lights of the small truck curving downward, then dipping out of sight, standing close side to side with Laura, Andrew recalled the time, the first time he had felt a unity with a woman. With Susan and himself it had been as they stood on the cave ledge, on this same hill, a late Sunday afternoon, and gazed outward. And though he was still just a boy and she was older and engaged to be married, he had felt this man-and-woman unity, a harbinger of this completeness that he felt now.

And to Laura looking down on the dark river, this was like their time against the steamer rail, watching the dark flow of the ocean, as they sailed out on their adventure.

His arm around her waist, they went into their house.

Through the bedroom window the tips of the tallest trees were in silhouette; this room seemed indeed to nest up among them.

She came from the bathroom, her face suddenly shining in a childlike pleasure at a new sensation as her bare feet felt the warmth of the heated flagstone floor.

How nice she looked, the fresh, scrubbed skin, her hair in braids.

This was a night like that first night cradled by the ocean. Only, tonight, not the fierce tension of uncertainty and discovery, but a cleaving to each other, a man and a woman in primordial union against the elements, the unknown wild beasts, even human ones, a man and woman in union in their sheltering cave, against the rising howling outer windstorm, against the menace of primal cruelty. But above this, joined in a mutual pride. They had done this. They were joined, into their inner selves.

Early every Saturday morning the *River Valley Weekly Clarion* was delivered on virtually every doorstep in the town. The Stroms brought the paper with them when they arrived in their wagon. Taking care that it should not first be seen by the Lady, August sought out Andrew; "Expect you haven't seen this yet."

The paper was folded to the editorial page, with its photographs of children already making Christmas decorations, and its standard column of Sunday-service announcements. Then the heading over the editorial caught Andrew's eye: NOT WELCOME

This week there had moved into the River Valley area a notorious pair who had until now confined their illicit relationship to Europe and Chicago. Plainly and emphatically the editor here declared that their presence was a menace to the morals of the community. . . . It was as though Andrew knew each coming nauseous word in advance. . . . The tragedy was that Mr. Andrew Lane came from a noble and high-minded pioneer family, settlers who had, like the Pilgrims of America's earliest days, brought to America the highest Christian ideals. More than any other family, it was the Danielses who had established River Valley. And, as unfortunately to almost every great family, there came the black sheep . . . True, Mr. Andrew Lane was an architect of world renown, ironically he was even renowned for a place of worship that he had built, but . . . On it went: The woman, who had deserted her two small children to go cavorting off to Europe on a brazenly announced "hegira" of free love . . . Then came the whole miserable litany, Andrew's return home, his apparent or pretended reconciliation with his wife. The hegira woman's husband had of course divorced her, and here was the second hegira, fallen upon River Valley! The philandering architect had built himself a house, and moved here with his paramour, to live! These immoral intruders, flaunting themselves before a community of decent, churchgoing people and their children, were an insult to every family in River Valley, and a danger particularly to young people approaching manhood and womanhood. Soulmates! They were either insane or degenerate! Andrew Lane, with his habit of making a spectacle of himself in his knee panties and long hair, flaunting his bohemian ways, was even the more guilty, as he came from a noble family of teachers and preachers. Well, then, "Andrew Lane, you and your 'consort' are not welcome! This is a decent Christian community in the heartland of America. . . ."

He crumpled the damn rag. But she'd see it soon enough. Then better directly from him.

August Strom was looking at him, plainly waiting to know what Andrew Lane might do.

What could a man do? Except go up there to that editor's office with a horsewhip?

She was sorting her books, arranging her desk for work.

"Laura, I thought you had best see this now."

Not until this had she felt so totally the impulse, a bodily impulse, to crumble into tears. Though her mind told her outrage, to be scorned, there came only this inner crumbling.

It was the sense of total failure. And she had brought this on Andrew. In his own home place. And after all the months he had labored here, this utterly beautiful house, his most perfect achievement. And such foul righteousness, such small-minded, brutal . . . Yes, it was this that made you want to weep, not for yourself, but at the hating, the hating.

She gazed up at Andrew; his face was a mixture of contempt, anger, even shame—for, after all, this was his own community, his own family's place, that he had brought her into.

"In the old days," he half shrugged, half blustered, "a man would just go and horsewhip the fellow." But what use? A doddering old fool.

Her weeping impulse had become submerged.

Andrew knew this Editor Pringle. Old pouter pigeon. Past sixty. "I suppose I wasn't prepared for anything so filthy, so soon."

They discussed, yet knowing that no action would be useful. Libel? Everything would then only be repeated, the press all over the country would pounce on it. And they might even lose.

It was surely not the editor alone, but what all the people here were saying. Perhaps even some of Andrew's own family.

She ventured: Might not some of the younger generation even find it ludicrous? The best was to ignore it.

"No, I'll answer it."

"Andrew. Not in anger."

He shook his head.

Then she wondered, should they—if to reply—reply to it together?

No. This was *his* community. For him to answer. Show it to her before he sent it off.

He wrote most easily standing at the drafting board, this gave him a better sense of being in control. Now—not in anger, not in scorn. He would explain their presence here, in his home, even as though that screed had not appeared. He was, after all, not an ordinary person come to live here in ordinary circumstances, and the community ought to have his explanation.

Having built his home on his own portion of the ancestral family acres here in River Valley, and now come home in the hope of finding peace in which to continue his work, and neighborliness in the community that he knew from boyhood, having indeed come home, he felt he owed his neighbors an explanation of certain circumstances in his life which had received notoriety.

Like many persons, he had in the middle of his life experienced a certain crisis. A crisis in his work, a crisis in his marriage. He had married quite young, he had raised a large family, but, as happens perhaps more widely than is known, in twenty years, as their natures developed, a man and his wife could find themselves grown apart. He and his wife had made every effort to keep their marriage intact. But as has happened all though the history of love between men and women, so it had happened to him that he had formed another attachment. To this woman, as to himself, there had also come an estrangement in her marriage. Yet, they had tested their feelings for each other through a year of separation. At last convinced that their emotions were genuine and mature, each had sought a divorce so that they then might wed. Divorce was not unknown, not disallowed, in the faith of his forefathers who had settled this community. Indeed, had not the right to divorce been a basic tenet, long ago in England, in the very formation of their church?

Surely in itself a marital change was not sinful. Rather did he believe it sinful to continue a failing marriage by coercion. No one person owned another person. A husband did not own his wife, nor a wife her husband. At last, on one side, the woman's, in the history of this man and this woman, a divorce had been granted. The woman was freed from a marriage no longer a true marriage. But in the case of the man, of himself, a divorce continued to be refused.

In the circumstance, he had had to decide to take his freedom. He did not put aside his responsibility to his family; they were and would be provided for. He and his companion had come here to reconstruct their lives. He had, as a man does, built a home in the place he considered home, and to this house he had now come with his chosen companion. As their relationship could not yet be formalized, he had hoped to find understanding and tolerance in the community that knew him since childhood. He indeed deeply hoped that he would prove of some use to the community. He trusted that he and his companion would be judged and in time accepted for their own selves, their personal qualities, rather than subjected to prejudice.

True, as some observed, his appearance was not always conventional. Architecture was an art, and artists often wore their hair long—this was not found objectionable in painters, concert pianists, poets, and even in certain noted political orators and statesmen. He had always felt more natural this way. He hated sham, and this way he looked like what he was. And in his attire, too, just as a carpenter wore an apron, and a surgeon a gown, he, as an architect, had found knee trousers most adaptable for clambering about on building sites—

Andrew hesitated. Was he becoming too trivial? No, they had picked on this. And maybe it was well to introduce a lighter note. He'd ask Laura.

Finally, he hoped in living here to bring to his life an organic harmony, to farm his land as well as to create his architecture; he hoped to remove himself from notoriety and to live a private and productive life. He hoped not to be prejudged by the press, not to be misunderstood through hasty conclusions based on distortions, but in time indeed to be welcomed home.

Laura thought it good, excellent; yes, he ought to send it.

Then Andrew had a further idea: in Madison, he had a good friend in the editor of the *Times*, Zacharia Sorenson. After all, an early triumph, the winning of the Boat Club design, had been in Madison. People here in River Valley all read the *Madison Times*; support from the big daily in the capital could even turn them against their pouter-pigeon village editor for making rubes out of them!

"Here you go! Off and flying!" Laura laughed.

No; it would be good to have his friend in Madison aware of the situation. Perhaps Zach Sorenson would simply print something about his coming to live and work in Wisconsin. But Laura was still doubtful. If the big-city paper made fun of the rural attitudes in River Valley, wouldn't the local people feel even more offended? Perhaps, if they simply quietly went about their life here, people would come to know and in time to accept them.

Indeed the very virulence of the attack, as Laura had surmised, brought a degree of counterreaction. Aunt Nora was the first. Susan telephoned. "She's furious over the article! She's coming tomorrow to dinner."

Already present when they arrived, wearing her perennial blue visiting gown of his mother's weaving, with the black velvet band around her throat, Nora gave Laura the all-seeing gaze that she had for new pupils, with her lips pursed as though eternal judgment were about to issue forth. And then it was the acceptance smile. "I hope you haven't permitted our village idiot to upset you."

Naturally, Laura replied, she could not deny that the editorial had been unpleasant, but she hoped that as she lived here opinions would change.

"They will!" Aunt Nora declared.

Susan's youngest, the sixteen-year-old Merry, was gazing at Laura. Andrew teased her. Wasn't she afraid of being corrupted?

"You didn't corrupt me when you were up here building all summer, Uncle Andrew, so I feel pretty safe, alas!"

Laura took the moment of laughter to present to both Susan and Aunt Nora copies of her translation of Ellen May, just come off the press. Ah! Aunt Nora appreciated finely made books, and she had heard of Ellen May, the Jane Addams of Sweden, wasn't she? For a few moments the conversation was diverted as Laura told about visiting Ellen May, but then Merry remarked that this morning every member of the Daniels clan had been at the chapel, even she herself had for once gone to church! Uncle Andrew had really got Uncle Matt a big audience! But—not a single thunderbolt! Uncle Matt hadn't even preached. Matt's son William had taken over, as he did at times, and William hadn't even mentioned the scandal.

Matt had doubtless instructed his son, Aunt Nora surmised. So, as nothing had been said at chapel, the policy would be silence. She turned to Laura. "They'll ignore you. My advice is, you ignore them. They'll come around." Of Uncle Matt's daughters, Dorothy might be the first to thaw out, just because she was nosy. Now, Susan's sister-in-law Alberta was active in the women's movement, not too active, but she let her views be known. She might even take up the cudgels.

Gus, carving the roast, advised, "Just you live your own life. They'll all come around sooner or later."

It was a great farm dinner in the old style, innumerable preserves, vegetables, pitchers of milk, cider, pumpkin pie. At one moment Laura realized she had stopped thinking of that awful newspaper screed altogether.

But the town had not. If the editorial had been ignored in the family chapel, it had nevertheless been the subject of at least two sermons in River Valley churches. By midweek, three anonymous letters had arrived: "Get out!" And one letter, in ostensibly "reasonable" terms, signed by some sort of Chamber of Commerce fellow whose name was vaguely familiar to Andrew, suggested with a show of reason that as he sought peace of mind, surely he and his "consort" would be more likely to find it elsewhere, as for example in a large city where they could choose anonymity, or even perhaps find a few others who held views similar to their own.

Andrew went to Madison. Bulky, overflowing his swivel chair, Zach Sorenson wheezed he had already heard about the fuss, seen that slimy editorial. Reading through Andrew's reply with professional speed, as though swallowing the text in one gulp, he declared he'd be glad to print it, but was Andrew sure he wanted that? Maybe best let the flare-up die out.

It wasn't going to die out unless stamped out, Andrew said. He had already had a call from Pringle informing him that his reply would be printed, but that puffy old hen had added a remark. Had not Mr. Lane's . . . . uh . . . consort recently published a translation of a book by a Swedish woman writer named Ellen May? Wasn't she the one who openly advocated unmarried women having children, if they so desired, just by using some male, like a stud horse?

Andrew had sputtered, and started to explain Ellen May's views, only to hear a wheezy chuckle and a goodbye. He hadn't told this to Laura but had got into his automobile; here he was.

Sorenson had one of those swivel chairs that tilted back on a spring. And as sometimes incongruously happened to Andrew when he was keyed up, he had a sudden totally unrelated idea: why not adapt such a swiveling, tilting chair for living-room comfort?

What, then, was in this Swedish woman's book? Sorenson was asking. With all the Swedes in Wisconsin, Ellen May was of course not unknown here, and a review of this translation might even sell some copies.

"It's about young people facing world problems. Pacifism, war, social ideas."

The editor wobbled his chair upright, made a note on his desk. "Don't worry too much, Andrew. You're a valuable person, and, I see, so is your lady. If that old fart keeps jumping on you, we'll take him apart. Hell, this isn't the Middle Ages!"

The next issue of the *River Valley Weekly Clarion* carried Andrew's letter. Nothing else. Nothing about the views of Ellen May as translated by Laura Bendersohn.

Christmas was already in the air; until now Amy Strom had picked up their groceries; now Aunt Nora took Laura on the rounds of the shops and introduced her to the merchants: Laura Bendersohn, of the new house on the hill. The grocer, the butcher, each managed a smile, or perhaps it was genuine. Put out a hand. "Pleased to meet you, Mrs. —uh—"

"Miss Bendersohn," Nora repeated. Did the smile fade a trifle? Yet inevitably, though covertly, the male look-over. "Hope to be of service to you!" With that, the normal business smile.

It hadn't been too bad, Laura told Andrew.

29

IN A large frame house with a belvedere, off the Main Street of River Valley, there lived an elderly but active widow named Helga Vogel, who had inherited the town's central business block. She lived with seven cats and her son Albert, a lawyer, who had an office in the building that had the name Vogel chiseled on the lintel, and whose practice consisted mostly of leases on family holdings. His mother busied herself as president of the River Valley Humane Society, and had her son prosecute teamsters whom she had seen cruelly whipping their horses.

The society met at the Vogel home, and a few of the ladies had given out interesting little details. For example, every door along the hallway was locked with a padlock. Perhaps to keep out the seven kitties.

Indeed, Helga Vogel, though respected, was at times spoken of with a discreet smile; everyone has their little eccentricities.

When the *River Valley Weekly Clarion* printed a paragraph about Mr. Lane's companion, Miss Laura Bendersohn, being the translator of a book about pacifism by the Swedish writer Ellen May, who in another book advocated unmarried women bearing children, Helga Vogel at once got that other book from Milwaukee's German library. She read German fluently.

If the whole affair had seemed to be dying down, it was, with that item in the *Clarion*, once more aflame. As Andrew bent over his board he found whole sentences of pleadings for decency taking over his mind. Again, he would appeal as though he were reasoning humanly with fair-minded people. Eliminate the personal. Not he, not she, not Helena, not Ralph. Simply a man and a woman. His first letter to the paper had been too personal. He must ask for the privacy to which every person has a right, instead of having their hearts publicly pried at and pecked over. The man and the woman had withdrawn to the country hoping to do their work and live their lives, instead of living a lie. This right to live in privacy, due to anyone, was all they asked.

Laura read it and knew it would not help.

Yet Andrew decided he would hold an open conference. In the spirit of Christmas. He would invite the press to his home, to see for themselves his plan of life here, a private life of decency and work.

From Madison, two came. They also represented Chicago papers, and the Associated Press. Laura served hot rum punch. Each received a copy of the "man and woman" statement; folding it so as to scribble interview notes on the back, they took more words from Andrew. Laura simply offered refreshments and said yes, she had studied literature and philosophy, and had lived and worked at Hull House. She had translated two books by Ellen May, the world-famous Swedish writer. Oh, not only on women's rights, but on great human problems, on teaching the young, on peace.

The reporters were most respectful. Together, Laura and Andrew showed the house, though not the bedroom. The drafting room, the barns with the cattle munching their fodder. The men appreciated the beauty of the structures, the planned way of life, the view from among the treetops, the icicles that hung, Andrew couldn't help pointing out, exactly as he had planned. "Merry Christmas, ma'am, merry christmas, sir!"

And a few days before Christmas, the plea appeared, with descriptions of Andrew Lane's magnificent "retreat." Architect and Soulmate.

One Chicago paper headlined: NEW HEGIRA IN HIDE-AWAY LOVENEST

Yet, with Christmas goodwill, cards began arriving. Nice, warmhearted notes from Jane and others at Hull House, from the Darrows and the young poet Carl Sandburg. And indeed from Andrew's children and hers. And a surprisingly understanding letter from sister Tess, in New York.

By taking the early Chicago train they would still have time for some final Christmas shopping. They'd stay at the Palmer House, have the children brought there. —Her children and his, together? Well, why not? The youngest were the same age, in the same grade.

Almost at once, Christina arrived with John and Maida. Andrew had brought his own little gifts. For her boy, a combination tool with hammer, screwdriver, chisel, awl. Johnny at once began to change around the parts. For the girl, a beaded Indian headband, just now a schoolgirl fad. Her eyes widened with the pleased look that Laura had, she started as though to kiss his cheek, held back, and made a curtsy. Then ran to a mirror to put it on. So far, excellent.

Now his own arrived, Ellen in charge. Ned and Wally were not yet in from college. Ellen was more than ever a twin of her mother when he first had met her, so much so that Andrew could feel an instant of hesitancy in Laura. They exchanged womanly cheekpecks, and Laura presented to Ellen a leather reticule designed by Andrew himself. For Richard, the combination tool. "Starter" gifts for all. Before uneasiness could set in, Laura and Christina led the whole pack off to Marshall Field's. Andrew had a small errand—to Sato's. To pay for the Christmas spree, one Hokusai had to be sacrificed. But soon, surely, the approval from San Francisco would arrive, and he could buy it back.

Exclaiming at the providential coincidence of his arrival, Sato said that the Consul only yesterday had been discussing Andrew Lane. Surely Andrew would recall from his voyage a few years ago—ah, already six years? but in Japan nothing was forgotten, only left to its proper time. The project of a hotel had been mentioned by the honored Baron Okira; much thought had since been given to this project, for commerce between the two nations was happily increasing, and the need for a Western-style hotel was greater than before. As Andrew knew, there were great problems, but even so—Sato smiled, with many creases now, and as though quoting ancient Japanese wisdom said that the best cure was to prevent the cause.

Prevent earthquakes?

Sato's smile broadened, appreciating Andrew's humor. But, as Andrew had long ago explained, even if a structure was fireproof, if it split open would not the flames rush up? Thus, in these years, a way to prevent collapse had been sought. But, alas, not yet found.

Andrew had already caught the real problem. Rigidity. A building possibly tilting in a severe quake, and breaking up. Perhaps, then, a question of foundation? In the mushy, muddy soil of Tokyo? And suddenly he had the connection. Chicago's muddy soil; the floating foundation. If a structure—like the Auditorium building next door, he explained to Sato—rested on an enormous slab of concrete, as on a raft, it could balance itself on shifting mud. Sato nodded, nodded. He himself recalled the Auditorium foundation being laid. Would Andrew be willing to develop his idea, to present a design? Naturally this would be compensated, the first stage, in advance. In fairness, Mr. Lane should know that two other architects, Europeans, were also commissioned to submit ideas.

So all this time they had been scouring the world for ideas.

And as he now did not even have to sell the Hokusai, Andrew bought a lovely statuette, a gift for Laura, and hurried back to the Palmer House. A change of fortunes! Merry Christmas!

The children's mob had returned loaded with gift parcels, and there was still enough time—his Richard and her Johnny seemed to have conspired—to see a nickelshow! On State Street, one was playing the cowboy William S. Hart, and John's father did not object to pictures with William S. Hart. William S. Hart, Andrew's favorite! Why not all go together!

Andrew and Laura, in the spirit of nickelshows, held hands.

Together with Aunt Nora, they attended Uncle Matt's Christmas services, and while some people stared a bit, there were also squeezy smiles, tinged with Christmas-love tolerance.

In the *Madison Times*, Mrs. Helga Vogel's eye was caught by the shocking story of a person offering college girls automobile rides to Chicago, at Christmas vacation time, and trying to induce them into white slavery! He was charged under the Mann Act with taking a woman across a state border for immoral purposes.

The news story gave her an inspiration. Albert Vogel agreed with his mother. The Mann Act certainly ought to apply.

In the later afternoon, in a white silence, a large car with sidepieces buttoned all around churned up the driveway. Through his drafting-room window, Andrew saw two men emerge shielding themselves from the snowfall—looked like police! He hurried into the house.

Laura was coming forward questioningly. "What is it, officers?"

The older one, first to take off his hat, held a document. With a certain respect in his voice for the surroundings, he declared, just as Andrew reached the group, "I have a warrant here for the apprehension of Mr. Andrew Lane." And, turning to him, "That's you, I suppose?"

The rigmarole began. In violation of the Mann Act the said Andrew Lane was charged with transporting across the borders of the state of Illinois and the state of Wisconsin . . . The phrase "for immoral purposes" flicked out. Somebody's bad joke? They had traveled across all the borders of Europe! Laura's glance restrained Andrew's fury. The man had his piece of paper and his job.

"Sorry, sir, but there has been a legal complaint to the state's attorney's office."

"But who on earth—"

August Strom had come up from wherever he was working, on his face the barely suppressed old I.W.W. glare.

Though it was all too absurd, incredible, Laura said, "We must call our lawyer. That is permitted, isn't it?" Andrew was at the telephone. "Our attorney is in Chicago," she told the police. "It may take some time for the connection." And after a moment, as the men shifted on their feet, "Won't you sit down? Would you like some coffee?"

They hesitated, the second man eying the first. It was a long drive back to Milwaukee and in the snowstorm the motor might even go dead. He'd advise Mr. Lane to bring along overnight clothes.

In a prison cell, could he mean!

The constable advanced toward the fireplace, noticing the hollowed-log seats, sat, said, "Nice place you have here." Amy brought coffee.

The Chicago line seemed to be down. "Don't you know some lawyer around these parts?"

Couldn't they post bail, a bond?

Have to go before a judge in Milwaukee to have the bail set.

Laura suppressed a desperate thought—to call Governor La Follette, who had visited Hillhouse.

In the end, finishing their coffee, the officers arose.

Nothing for it. The lady, they said, could meanwhile reach their attorney.

Laura went to pack him some clothing. She would demand the right to go along; from Milwaukee the connection would be easier. Meanwhile Amy Strom kept trying.

They were all standing, waiting by the door. Andrew with his expression of bitter irony as though seeing this in history. Just then, Amy reached Darrow's office. He was expected soon. Laura decided to wait here, follow in their own car; August could drive.

And so, well into the growing dark, with snow coming down on the canvas roof, Andrew rode with the police to Milwaukee. He felt a bleakness such as he had known only a few times in his life. Once, an article attributing all his ideas to "borrowings"; even tracing his own house to a New England "precedent." The feeling that humanity, society, could be so needlessly hostile, that for no reason, no need, people could act with such mean spirit. One felt simply hated. By people unknown, to whom one had done no possible harm. What was the word—gratuitous. Hated gratuitously. Oddly, the search for the word broke his depressive feeling, and his mind rose back to an overview. WORLD-FAMOUS ARCHITECT JAILED FOR MANN ACT. Maybe bigamy too? Not so funny. The Mann Act, as he recalled, was considered quite a dangerous accusation, a Federal offense. Who, then, could hate him so? That was perhaps the most horrifying realization. That while thinking of himself as a decent man, a man who followed the truth in himself, no sham, whose whole thought and energy was toward creating, constructing, finding the beautiful, that such a man was nevertheless hated so much that someone could do this, go this far to hurt him. Surely not Helena, even in the worst shock. Not Ralph Garnett. Even if such a revenge were suggested to him, Ralph would see himself as too decent to use it. Nor would he want to re-arouse the scandal. Maybe that copying scum, Robert Mann. Andrew's instinct said "no." Then who on earth?

"Am I permitted to know who made the complaint?"

he asked the officer, dryly. In a workmanlike tone, not without respect for the owner of such a fine house, and in the easier way of a man once a job is basically accomplished, the officer replied, "Well, the complainant is the State, but a citizen, someone, has to start it. Well, a lady hereabouts— You know Mrs. Vogel?"

"Vogel?"

"She gets in the papers. President of the Humane Society."

To Andrew's involuntary high-pitched laugh the front-seat constable turned around.

"The Society for the Prevention of Cruelty to Animals!" Andrew repeated.

"That's the one!" The officer didn't seem to get the humor of it, but, as happens, laughter made everyone a bit amiable. And the mutual experience of the snow, the danger of the slippery road, created a feeling, too, of men thrown together by some sort of chance, on a journey against nasty weather. They arrived at the station house talking casually about the construction trade, the policeman's trade, the weather.

Several reporters awaited them. A flashlight went off. Andrew retained his composure, the Humane Society joke somehow still sustained him and he managed to get it into his first reply. He was not aware, he said, that his behavior in his private life could have proven cruel to stray dogs, cats, and birds protected by a certain Mrs. Vogel, president of the local Humane Society. . . . He was always gratified to visit Milwaukee, where he had been honored for his public-library design and had built a number of homes, some of them included in the portfolio of his works published in Berlin, and since many of the citizens of Milwaukee were originally from Germany, he hoped they would acquire this book. . . .

"All right, you boys, you got your story"—the desk sergeant was not amused. And now to the routine. No, no word from any Chicago lawyer. Well, maybe Mr. Darrow was on his way, but in the meantime the regulations. Andrew gave name, address, profession, etc. Born, etc. As his thumb was grasped, pressed on the ink pad and then on the sheet, the stockyard image, the roping of an animal's hind leg, flicked through his mind. He was handed an ink-smeared half-towel. Wipe. Oh, he was used to inky fingers, he might have remarked, but by now he was feeling dulled; why entertain them any further.

And presently, just as in the movies, a corridor of iron-barred doors. One opened, he was inside a whitewashed space, interior of a cube. The classic small window aperture, iron-barred, high in one wall. Even a fleeting impression of snow still coming down. As he heard the lock, the word "turnkey" came to him from its precise derivation, and now Andrew Lane looked around the space: an open toilet, two iron bunks, on the lower a man sitting, his cell-mate—that was the label. A lighted bulb on a cord. Professionally his mind shuffled a kaleidoscope of cells through the ages, dungeons, men chained to stone walls, holes where the prisoner could not stand erect or stretch out. And this a kind of standardized present-day model. With its odor: a combination of institutional disinfectants, with an underlayer of toilet stench, piss. While already his professional self was introducing a ventilating system, there came over him, rising from toes to head, the physical sense of being caged, almost to the feeling of being roped up, trussed. A passing impression, but within it the hallucination of a finality. Nonsense. Yet an awareness that this must be some basic sensation that every inmate experienced on the closing, the lock-sound of the iron door. Of course for him this might even set him to designing a model place of detention! . . . White slavery!

The other man in the cement space was sitting on the edge of his bunk, appraising him. The man looked Italian, curly black locks, heavy forearms—a laborer in his forties. His smile showed uneven teeth, a few gaps. Could have been any of scores of laborers on one of Andrew's own construction jobs.

"You first time?"

Andrew nodded.

"This jail okay, clean. Eat not so bad." Andrew was put in mind of August Strom, his ex-Wobbly, who had in his time seen the inside of many a hoosegow. "Me—too much *vino*." A child's look of readiness to join in a little laughter at something silly he had done. Like Wally, when a kid, over some prank. "I'm hit my old lady. You?"

Suddenly Andrew felt he was himself again. "Maybe same thing," he said. For after all, going back far enough, this situation could be traced to the pain he had caused Helena.

His cellmate held up four fingers. "Four times, in here. This time, thirty day."

Andrew nodded, comradely.

Then off and on Emilio fell into telling of his life. Hard life in Chicago, America. But to go back, Italy no good. Even more poor. Yet when Andrew spoke of having not so long ago stayed in Fiesole, the Italian became eager, nice place, yes? His village was not far, half a day on a donkey, his wife's family from the same village. A good woman. Six bambinos, four alive. He no wanted to hurt his woman. But in a man's life he does things, he no like himself for having done them. Especially if he is feeling good from wine, and a woman takes away the bottle. Santa Maria! . . . And pieces and chunks from the immigrant's life; again and again Andrew found himself remembering that book, such a sensation, was it ten years ago, Upton Sinclair, *The Jungle*, the Polish family in the stockyards. Emilio had not worked there in the yards, the Irish and the Polish, they had the jobs there. But pick and shovel, hod carrier, sometimes no job. Two rooms in alley back of Sholto Street. Toilet outside. The scarlet fever, all the children. The youngest died, one year old, a girl.

Yes, Andrew knew those alleys there. Had ladies come to help, from the Hull House? Hull? Hull House? Emilio didn't know such a name. Only Italians, Sholto Street. — Halstead Street? Keep away. Saloons. For him—vino in the house. Have some job, street cleaning, buy the grappa, make it, in the basement. All the time, Emilio said, all the time he is thinking, a little piece of land, only have a pig, a few chickens, garden, even some grapevine, from small piece of land a man could live. After Chicago, no work, Emilio said, a cousin in Milwaukee here, a job, load out from ships. . . . But sometime, one day—Emilio had his utopian dream—every man, how much you need, even one acre! Every man one acre, come bad times, no starve. Every man—like Henry Ford says—even every working-man have cheap automobile! Work on his job, go home, one acre, goats, chickens, even one cow. Children grow up, they know what is grass. Not always the city, Don't Step on the Grass. As a boy in Italy, no shoes, too poor, but your feet in the grass. Emilio smiled.

Later, Andrew even with eyelids closed felt himself staring into the lighted electric bulb, beautiful color circles pulsing under his lids, purples with yellow edges. But also he saw an entire layout, on a twenty-five-foot module, forming into larger squares, rectangles, with main roads, offshoot lanes, industrial areas, administrative areas, rail-road sidings, shopping clusters, schools, picture shows, even a theater, churches, unit dwellings with connecting barns; population—optimum say twenty thousand for a basic unit, suitable-size industry in each population center, the factory located along the railway feeder. Some of the old Henry George ideas. A householder, using his acre. Ideas were now coming, wave on wave, the plan developing from within itself, like one-celled units proliferating. He had no paper. A soft pencil was still in his coat pocket. On the whitewashed wall Andrew sketched reminder lines, so he wouldn't lose the concept. Even sketches for unit homes, Prairie style, prefabricated, interchangeable sec-tions for variety. Small barns, one cow, one horse. How was it he had never set himself to work on really cheap housing?

Even that simple five-thousand-dollar design for Theo-dore Dreiser's magazine—not for the masses! An entire semirural community, schools, meeting halls, one acre— one family, instead of the megalopolis; twenty interlocked ruralities, each area with one or two basic industries to provide local employment, this net spread out over all America, human contacts restored, contact with nature restored. Why, this could become his life's creation! Entire planned communities. Instead of some steel mill set down at random, with clusters of shanties spreading under its fumes and smudge as the immigrants came. Houses for workmen, George Pullman had thought of, but with feudalism, and all exactly alike. Still, Andrew reflected, even here in what he was sketching, where was each man's own will? All must remain open, optional, with a great variety of design. Roads, schools, power supplies, all things used in common—this surely should be the nucleus of the master plan. A courthouse. A hospital. Even a jail, with narrow bands of windows, no bars.

The American Plan. Join it if you will. And a humorous thought came: there ought to be totally unplanned areas left to anarchists!

Andrew slept.

The serving hole opened. Coffee and bread.

What he had sketched on the wall—even in sleep his mind had added ideas. Heat piped to every home from a central plant. . . . How many great works had been written in prison? He'd get it on paper, go on with it. And there came an amused idea: this jail wall preserved for history—

There was Darrow.

"How's life in the hoosegow?"

So early, he must have come up on the dawn train. As the turnkey let the lawyer into the cell, Andrew, through a peculiar kind of embarrassment, though one knew one should treat being in jail with outrage, or humor, still noticed that, aside from his usual rumpled shabbiness, Darrow had a somewhat changed look: the weariness in his face was different from that of early waking and a tiresome ride, it was the settled-in weariness of a man who has been through an exhausting sickness, or some profound disillusionment.

"I never meant to drag you up here at the crack of dawn," Andrew apologized. "You shouldn't have come yourself. I thought maybe you could phone some lawyer in Milwaukee."

Clarence made a brushing-aside gesture. "Least I owe you, young man," going back to the old appellation with an effort at his old smile. "Maybe I'll still build that lakeshore house someday. If I'm not in jail myself!"

Something from recent headlines came back to Andrew. That hullabaloo last month in the papers—the dynamiters case in Los Angeles. Again, Clarence Darrow had saved his clients' necks, they had finally confessed to blowing up the *Los Angeles Times* but he had got a life term instead of hanging for the actual dynamiter, and fifteen years for his brother, the union leader.

"Well, you saved their necks," he said, but Darrow shook his head heavily. "May cost me mine!" With a try at his old chuckle.

Now there came back to Andrew some newspaper rot that he had taken for absurd legalistic hocus pocus. An accusation of jury bribing. Some sort of detective had worked for Darrow to check out information on prospective jurors, a common practice, it seemed, of lawyers before a case, to ward against prejudice. But this Los Angeles detective had admitted bribing a few men on the list, supposedly with money from the union. And he claimed that Clarence Darrow knew about the bribing. What mudslinging. Aside from Clarence's simply being incapable of such a thing, he certainly wasn't stupid enough to try it!

Indeed, Andrew sought for a jesting way to put it, the whole story was like his own being here for the Mann Act!

Darrow also tried to make light of both. "Why, Andrew, you could have stopped the car at the border and had her walk across. Are you sure she didn't!" He shot

Andrew his under-brow glance, as in a courtroom, and laughed.

Oh, for himself, he wasn't worried about the rantings of that Los Angeles stoolpigeon, a known perjurer. But still it might mean going back there to stand a hearing. Could cost a lot of money too. Just out of revenge there were powerful people out there who'd like to get him disbarred. And for jury tampering you could also go to jail.

"Hell, I didn't take that dawnlight train out here to discuss my troubles, but yours!" He handed Andrew a clump of newspapers.

Headlines again. Andrew Lane jailed. Amorous Architect. And all the usual filth. Morals charge. The Mann Act. And here in the *Trib*, that same sob sister, Genevieve Wynn, had already spoken to Helena. Exclusive interview. Helena indeed was indignant over the arrest. Andrew Lane, whatever her own tribulations, was a great artist, and artists could not live their lives by conventional standards. She could not approve of his new life, could never give him a divorce, but could not understand why he should be persecuted. This life of his in his own house in Wisconsin was his private personal life.

Ralph Garnett, the industrialist who had divorced Andrew Lane's free-love soulmate, Laura Bendersohn, had refused to comment on the arrest.

Clarence had even picked up the *Madison Times*. Already with courtroom irony, he quoted the headline, KINDNESS TO ANIMALS. While Andrew read, Darrow, his eye caught, was scrutinizing the penciled-over wall. "See you've been busy." Andrew began to explain. Presently they were back to the old days of Henry George, all those utopian ideas. "Have to get this wall preserved!" Darrow chuckled.

"The Great American Plan!" Andrew agreed, feeling lighter, as though they had come back to the real world. Darrow was becoming more and more intrigued, examining even the little detail sketches, unit houses, factories. "I see you've at last come down from your ivory tower!"

Now back to work. In an hour or so, as soon as he could get hold of a judge, he would doubtless have Andrew out on bond. "Got any money?" Oh, shoot, Andrew ought to be let out on his own recognizance.

The Mann Act! What a vermin-ridden world! Why, any man who drove a woman friend from Chicago to the Indiana dunes, or to a North Shore beach that happened to cross the Michigan state line, would be liable to charges under the Mann Act! Then, with a pass of his long fingers, Clarence wiped all this away—somehow, Andrew felt, as though he were wiping his own troubles away, he was really troubled about that thing in Los Angeles, and what a friend Darrow was to have dragged himself here at dawn, even while under such a serious threat himself.

This stupid mess should never come before a court, Clarence declared. He'd call Carl Sandburg; as Andrew knew, Carl had been secretary to the mayor here until a few years ago. This case reflected on a civilized, advanced community. Persecuting a world-famous architect! Meanwhile, he'd maybe have a talk with the Federal office here to get the charges dropped altogether, this kind of vicious use of the Mann Act would weaken its serious purpose. Hell, Governor La Follette could make a call and ask the Federal authorities to drop it. Yes. And gazing at Andrew, he mockingly shook his head. The last thing Andrew Lane needed was a courtroom circus with a humanitarian plea by Clarence Darrow, notorious defender of dynamiters, murderers and anarchists. Jury briber to boot!

The turnkey appeared, Laura behind him. Court had convened. As they left the cell, Darrow glanced back at Andrew's cellmate. "Need any help?" "No, thanks," Emilio smiled. "Just thirty day."

Before the judge, Darrow mumbled a few words. Mr. Lane was released on his own recognizance, pending Federal instructions.

In the car, Andrew talked to her about his cellmate, Emilio, the wife beater. —Sholto Street Laura knew; she might even have been in that back-lot shanty, disinfecting. But what was that wall she had glimpsed, covered with sketches? Andrew was off on his whole idea, his American Plan. —"And you left it all there!" "I couldn't very well take the wall with me! . . . But I have it all here"—he tapped his head. Anyway, perhaps he would still wind up in jail and could continue his American Design at leisure!

And so they came home.

30

ON HIS drawing board lay a sheet of paper. Sometimes, though not often, Laura, in her elusive way, would leave lines for him to read.

Into the downpulling reptilian slime
Our underpinnings reach and hold,
Belief in a Purpose perfecting itself,
Wisdom of prophets and sages of old,
A book once read,
A teacher once said,
Mother's admonitions, father's look,
—A decent person doesn't—
—An honest person should—
Maxims, sermons, and childhood's testing,
Each self resting on its own-learned truths, these
Its underpinnings, its myriad supports.

In subterranean attack
One pillar may crack.
What then? A myriad remain.
And truths, and love that cannot change maintain.

Unseen, anonymous, those who understand
Upbear, sustain us.
Good friends reach out a hand
And we stand.

Andrew took it to her. She was in her writing nook; the door slightly ajar meant she wasn't really working; Laura sat reading.

Superb, he said. This one really must be published. Maybe send it to Harriet Monroe for that poetry magazine she was starting?

Laura flushed. She didn't want to embarrass Harriet in case Harriet might feel she ought to print it because of friendship. Besides—this poem was for him.

Then Andrew sat with her, teasing a bit: if this poem was now his, her gift, he might just have it published.

"Oh, no!"

Well, all right, then, he would put it safely away. He slid it into his drawer of print masterpieces.

Still the flood of letters, some with press clippings, some obscene, but also, this time, more with serious sympathy. And in these weeks the tide seemed to be turning. First, in the press, Darrow's barbed remarks about the lady of the Humane Society. Even the "Line O'Type" in the *Trib* had quips proposing a new society, for the prevention of cruelty to human beings. Eugene Field wrote one of his wise little poems, "I love cats and people too." Alfred Eastman sent a copy of a letter he had written to Governor La Follette. *La Follette's Weekly* published an editorial about the misuse of the Mann Act.

Yet the hullabaloo was slow in subsiding. In the midst came a package from San Francisco. Andrew's structural plans.

A daring, revolutionary concept, the letter said, but the engineers who had given it attentive study were concerned by a major difficulty particular to the region. As

Mr. Lane doubtless knew, San Francisco, with its cata-
strophic earthquakes . . .

The engineers feared that in a quake, this structure,
with its rigid single-stem foundation, would be susceptible.
And the very appearance of the building, with its elements
projected out into open space—while this was the dramatic
essence of the design, it could frighten prospective tenants.
Therefore, with true regret . . .

Andrew filed the sheets away. The preliminary design
fee was long used up.

Money problems again. The bank threatening mortgage foreclosure on house and farm. The nagging suspi-
cion that maybe it was the headlines about Andrew Lane
that had brought the San Francisco rejection, with the
engineer stuff as the excuse.

Earthquakes. He threw himself into the sample design
for the Tokyo hotel. Already, an overall concept had been
forming. Not a "modernistic" structure, despite the flap-
doodle about the Japanese influence on his Prairie House.
What was forming began with the interior, a long, rather
open lobby floor, with several fireplaces, for small groups
talking things over, thus making first meetings easier, soft-
ening the Japanese formality.

Various ceiling levels, manipulating the space around
stairs and balconies, alcoves, corridors. Small and larger
banquet rooms; entertainment chambers, oh, he knew
what the Japanese believed must be offered to American
businessmen. . . . And two floors of bedrooms with American bathrooms. There he could get away from the standard box; give each room, each suite in its own form.

Overall—the material? Partly, a special brick he had
seen combined with their common stone, Oya stone, even
used in Tokyo pavements, whitish in color, and soft, easily
carved. But not with obvious idiograms; something with an
archaic feel, perhaps Mayan? A feel, an atmosphere of a
timelessly persisting civilization. Something of that. The
building enveloping pools, gardens, pergolas, latticework,

strolling paths, screened corners, the pools even useful for bucket brigades in case surrounding flimsy houses caught fire. For still Andrew was troubled, and even more—since that San Francisco rejection—by that basic problem, earthquakes.

And hadn't he had enough earthquakes in his own life?

The rigid foundation he had tried for San Francisco didn't appeal to him. Tokyo soil was like mud. That was why he had thought of an Auditoriumlike massive floating foundation.

Like a raft, the Master had said of the floating foundation, a raft equalizing itself. Yet in a powerful tremor couldn't the enormously overweighted superstructure tilt it over?

Into his mind came a word, a phrase: "underpinning." A pier on sunken logs? Multiple underpinnings. How had she written it? Our multiple underpinnings—or was it myriad? Our myriad underpinnings? Andrew slipped out of the drawer the poem Laura had given him. "In subterranean attack one pillar may crack. What then? A myriad remain." And he saw his foundation. Not the conventional massive pilings. But a myriad of tentacles underneath—like some primordial sea creature. A forest of concrete pins sticking downward, an upside-down pincushion of concrete. The earth-muck pressing around each pin, holding it firm. Thus, a variation on the floating foundation. And the foundation floor itself, not rigid, perhaps in sections? Segmented, giving a degree of play, in a tremor? Instead of rigidity, a constant flexibility. That was the need. Flexibility. That was the answer to earthquake.

But here at home, the very ground was about to be sold from under him. Hillhouse and all! Foreclosures. Again in the papers. With all the past raked up, of course.

Jack Slater called. He had an idea. "Andrew, you've got one asset they can't foreclose." Talent, he said. Good old friend. Compliments were fine for the ego but paid no mortgages, Andrew said.

Wait. Jack meant business. Have lunch?

This last thing with that insane woman was too much, too dirty, Jack said. Hurting bad? Andrew had to admit a few cancellations. Even more nasty: Aunt Nora had had pupils withdrawn from her Home School. Now the bank was setting up an auction, house and farm. Andrew couldn't tell if that came from plain financial considerations or still the local hostility. Maybe Jack and his friends would give him a loan? He had hopes for something big. In Japan. They got to talking of that old trip, the fun in Tokyo, and, say, Jack said, he himself had made money, those prints Andrew had got him to buy were now up to ten times the price! Damn, Jack said, Andrew's ideas were okay, it was just all the trouble he got himself into. —Or trouble that others made for him, Andrew said.

Now Jack came out with his thought. A way to take over all his troubles, pay his debts, his running expenses, Helena's stipend, and leave Andrew free to do his work. Suppose a group of friends were to form a corporation— the Andrew Lane Corporation. Andrew's talent, the main asset. And he would own fifty-one percent of the stock so as to remain independent. But the corporation would take care of all the finances—pay the bills, collect the fees, keep him in household and working funds. Fact was, Jack had already sounded out a few people. Whaley, and Alf East-man, and Arthur Kaiser, Andrew's Rookery landlord, were ready to come in, also the owner of that masterpiece house on Woodlawn Avenue. Andrew found he had to lower his eyes attentive to his food. "Man, I'm in this for profit!" Jack declared. "Andrew Lane, Inc.! We intend to make money on you!"

Though the "incorporation of Andrew Lane" by a consortium of substantial people, almost all of them owners of homes he had built, received an excellent press, the "Mann Act episode" never failed to be included, with the "hegira," and even to the last day before the summer vacation Laura feared Ralph might refuse to send the children. Andrew reassured her; Ralph was a man of his word. But he had already remarried. A quite young girl, twenty-two, who was trying to win them over.

The children arrived. In a few days, constraint had worn away. Oh, their new mother was nice but not really a mummy, Maida said, hugging close.

Carl and Lillian Sandburg were visiting; the whole gang would go out gathering strawberries, then a picnic lunch, Carl would sit on a rock and tell absurd whimsical stories he made up as he went along. Laura got Maida to put off her Marshall Field ladylike frock and try a pair of jumpers. They rode. Soon, John tried riding bareback, then Maida had to do it, too.

Monday, Johnny wandered into the drafting room. Andrew didn't turn his head. The boy began to fiddle with pieces of a model for a house in Kankakee; he put some together. When he had the house assembled, Andrew showed him how to read the blueprint for it. When Andrew explained that the dotted lines were for what was behind that you did not see, the boy nodded, "Oh, I see," and at this they chuckled together. The boy had Laura's very white skin and her elusive smile. Andrew could not help thinking of his own youngest, Richard.

After supper, on the treetop veranda, Carl would strum away, and they'd join in as he sang. The favorite was "I've Been Working on the Railroad." There were fireflies and mosquitoes. They lighted punks to keep off the mosquitoes, and the kids waved them in the dark, like more fireflies.

After the Sandburgs had left, mornings the boy went farming with August, learned to harness a horse, and to yell "Gee haw!"

Passing from the drafting room into the house, Andrew would see two great wide sunhats, Laura and Maida in Laura's garden enclosure, where she had her flower jungle, as she called it, no primly laid beds but of Impressionist wildness, yellow, red, pink roses in profusion, blots of white carnations, purples, blues, greens.

Idyllic. And a new atmosphere was beginning to be felt in the area, as distinguished—looking men in foreign-looking suits came to inspect Hillhouse, a touch of homage in their voices as they asked their way. German architects, for the folio was much written about there; a new printing had been ordered.

Laura's second translation of Ellen May was announced and now a New York publisher inquired about a third. When even the *River Valley Weekly Clarion* began to print social notes about the distinguished visitors to Hillhouse, they had their laugh. Andrew proposed sending one in: "Jailbird Andrew Lane on Saturday had ex-convict Eugene Debs, Presidential aspirant, to tea." "Don't forget—Mistress Laura Bendersohn poured," Laura added.

And then, just after the children had returned home, Marta came. Ostensibly, it was for a stay with Nora. But almost at once Nora brought her over for a tour of the house, and encountering Laura was like a perfectly natural reencounter of former Oak Park neighbors. Though mention of Oak Park was avoided. And on succeeding days when Marta was in and out of the house at all hours, Andrew's children were freely spoken about. Laura was careful not to offer opinions, and also to be in her garden when Marta might want to talk to Andrew alone.

It was well.

Andrew was even collecting again. Indeed, as Alf Eastman in his art series published a deluxe little book of Andrew's Japanese prints, he was becoming known as an expert; people sent him prints for evaluation.

Even Sato would ask his opinion on some doubtful attribution, while Andrew declared himself about to go into competition as a dealer. It took the humorless Sato some time to catch on before he broke into laughter.

The Andrew Lane Corporation was solvent. A few commissions had come along, and the Chicago office expenses were lightened, for Gladys Beam and Gene Tillit, who had surprisingly got married, had won the world contest for a plan for the capital of Australia, and were off to build Canberra. That left Wallace to hold the fort.

And Clarence Darrow was acquitted. NOT GUILTY! the papers headlined, over entire columns of his plea to the jury, the greatest, all said, that he had ever made.

At the end of the summer, Sato conveyed news from Japan. Andrew's hotel plan had found favor. Important developments might be expected. When? Perhaps soon. —Soon, that meant in another decade? Andrew responded. Most seriously, Sato assured him: very soon. Well, Andrew said, the first time he had heard of that hotel project was when he visited Japan in 1905. Seven years ago. So—1919 then? Now his old friend smiled. Soon maybe this year.

Now came the annual show of the Architects Club at the Art Institute. Somehow, Andrew suspected, Harriet Monroe's connections at the Institute had something to do with it, for though he had never become a member—he was no joiner—Andrew was offered an entire wall! Fine, maybe he would bring in that wall from the Milwaukee jail where he had laid out his Great American Plan!

What most tempted him was to show the rejected San Francisco skyscraper—except that Robert Mann would be sure to adapt the central idea, changing the pattern of the cantilevers, thus convincing himself that the whole revolutionary concept was his own. No, it had best stay in its drawer. Instead, Andrew decided to put up the Tokyo hotel elevations. That would show he was going strong again.

And presently, a call came from old Sato's son-in-law the Consul. Would Mr. Lane kindly consider extending an invitation to a cousin—the young man, sent by Baron Okira, had completed a year of architectural studies at Stanford University and was coming for a visit to Chicago with his wife, an American Japanese.

This would be the decision, Andrew scented.

The couple arrived at Hillhouse, charming, the young

man a combination of American collegiate and formal Japanese, the girl as beautiful as Sato's daughters. Laura murmured to Andrew, "Go ahead, fall in love with her, only don't devour her completely every time you look!"

Young Okira presented an inscribed invitation from His Divine Majesty, the Emperor himself, for the distinguished Andrew Lane to honor Japan with a visit.

Then it must be on! Over the competition, whatever that had been! Probably this lad would be his liaison. He seemed all right—at once had caught the fine points of Hillhouse. Spoke enthusiastically of the Andrew Lane section in the Art Institute exhibit, including the elevations for the hotel. They drank a toast. The girl's eyes had that look of American joy in life, touched with Oriental decorum. Andrew remembered not to stare too long.

Early in the year Andrew and Laura arrived in Tokyo. This time Andrew counted off forty tatami mats in their abode. Housekeeping servants, and personal servants for Lane-san and his lady.

The conferences. Baron Okira this time used his Japanese office, as for an old familiar. Subtly, an elderly engineer reminded Andrew—having studied his magnificent portfolio published in Berlin—that his experience was with dwellings of a far smaller size than this project. Delicately, Andrew reminded the engineer of the large Stover Building in Buffalo, and his part in the construction of the vast, renowned Auditorium in Chicago. The Baron's consultants smiled the smile that was like a formal bow. They hoped the Imperial Hotel would become just as renowned. —So did he! Yet his estimate for the structure made it a costly venture. Didn't they want the best? Andrew said.

And the unusual foundation plan, the underpinnings, as he called them—didn't these sunken concrete piles, or "pins," as Andrew had explained, seem rather thin for bearing the mighty structure? Andrew cited the example of an Indian fakir borne up on his bed of many, close-placed nails. After a puzzled moment, they formally laughed.

One chamber of their dwelling was now his drafting room. Laura had taken to learning Japanese, and each day recognized more ideographs. Somehow she had made contact with an educated aristocratic lady eager to further the feminist movement, who was undertaking a Japanese translation of Ellen May.

One day the walls trembled. Like cheeks trembling. Nothing—the servants laughed, greatly amused, for this was only the sort of mild tremor that came often enough to keep the greater threat always in mind. Yet it brought Andrew a thought.

Below, his sectional pinioned foundation would have a certain flexibility. But what of the upper structure? Hadn't rigidity been the fear in San Francisco?

In quakes, one usually imagined the opening of the earth, but the effect was more like earth waves. His flexible foundation could receive the flow of force, balance on it, but should not a degree of flexibility be continued in the superstructure? Andrew did not want to raise this added problem—better first to receive the commission.

They still seemed dubious about his foundation idea. Why not conduct a test? he suggested. Cast a number of his narrow concrete "pins." Sink them into the muddy ground. Rest a platform atop them, and load it with sandbags, up to the estimated bearing load for the building. Agreed.

Behind a high bamboo fence they gathered one day, when he had all in readiness. There stood the Baron with his aides and advisors and several of his co-investors, some in frock coats, some in traditional gowns. Presently arrived a most impressive personality, in top hat and cutaway, to whom all bowed. An emissary of the Celestial Emperor himself?

A simple pile driver, with ropes dangling all around it, stood like a Maypole on the test site, each rope end held by a squat, sturdy female laborer. Was this the machinery he would have at his disposal, Andrew whispered to Laura, if it ever came to construction?

At a signal, the female coolies tugged in unison, hauling up the pile driver to a raucous chant; now one of Andrew's concrete pinions was set below the weight. With a merry grunt the women let go; the weight slid down, driving the pinion into the mud soil. A few more hoistings to their grunting chant, and the pile driver had driven the pinion flush with the surface. Every two feet Andrew placed his piles, until they became an inverted little concrete forest in the soil. Now all was set for the test.

A thick concrete floor-slab sample lay ready on a huge tarpaulin. Scores of laborers, male for this job, took hold around the edges of the tarp, lifting the slab and setting it atop the pilings. Next, they lined up before a heap of sandbags, and, each bent double under his load—reminding Andrew oddly of that picture, way back in Madison, in Professor Gamsey's office, of Egyptians building the Pyramids—each coolie skillfully unloaded his sack atop the test slab, neatly alongside the last. On his bead-counter, a tallyman kept track.

As the peak load was called out, there came hand-clapping from the frock-coated, a murmur of marvel, augmented by a loud exhalation from the laborers, topped with a wave of laughter from the women. The emissary of the Imperial House doffed his top hat, bowing to Andrew and Laura, then to the Baron and his entourage. These now turned to one another with felicitations. The Baron extended his hand to Andrew. All ventured closer, and peered around the sack-piled slab. The concrete had not cracked, nor had all that weight pressed it into the ground, not a sliver of an inch. As Andrew had reasoned, the pressure of the surrounding mud on each pinion kept the whole from sinking.

He signaled to the foreman—continue. More sandbags, to increasing exclamations. He kept them going until the stockpile of sandbags was exhausted. A fifty percent overweight, at least. From all assembled, the observers, the coolies, men and women, came a great *Banzai!*

With contracts signed, he could go home and get the detail drawings started. There was no hurry, the Baron assured him. A special quarry must be opened for Andrew's building stones. Could he return perhaps in a year?

The last days before sailing, their house was besieged —every print dealer in Tokyo had heard. The American was buying without stint.

Yet, even on the ship, one structural problem—on Andrew's mind ever since that day of the tremor—still nagged him.

31

LEANING TOGETHER over the rail, watching the phosphorescence in the water, Andrew felt a compelling need to tell her about the source of the idea for the myriad underpinnings. Why hadn't he? And suddenly he brought it out, into their musing quietness—"You know, that idea, for the concrete pilings in the mud . . ."

"One-track mind! Don't you ever stop!" She laughed her warm-throated laugh. He said, "That idea came from you."

Laura's face turned upward from the glitter in the sea. " 'Into the downpulling reptilian slime,' " Andrew quoted, " 'our myriad underpinnings hold . . .' "

The luminescence was within Laura's face, like the phosphorescence in the sea. Their hands clasped on the rail. It was, Andrew thought, perhaps their moment of greatest beauty. He felt glad of himself, that he had said it to her. As though he had overcome something. A selfishness, even with Laura?

They were in the dining room when the ship began to roll, pitch, even shudder. The waiter came toward them with his loaded tray, how deftly the fellow balanced the tray on his spread fingers, keeping its equilibrium, even as he set the dishes on their table. Laura praised him. A Japanese, with his broad, large-toothed smile. Oh—he held up his spread-fingered hand, and gestured, his whole body fluidly balancing—"I learn in Tokyo." The shaking earth, like this rolling sea.

And this was the way to do it! Floor slabs like the waiter's tray, supported across central uprights instead of by the outer walls. Thus, a certain flexibility, in case the walls were affected in a tremblor. The slabs, cantilevered —his favorite form of construction—would be balanced and upheld as by the waiter's arm. They could even extend out past the walls to form balconies.

Now he had his flexibility, not only in the foundation but throughout the edifice! Quake and shake!

At the station, Wally waited, glowing, handsome, the image of his father in youth. No longer the slightest restraint toward Laura—a nice hug. "You got it!" to Andrew. No, no announcement had appeared, but everybody knew. The office was all set to plunge in. But something more, right here! Impatient of porters, seizing the heaviest bags —he had his car right outside—Wally imparted his news. Hank Eastman—it took Andrew a moment to recall those Oak Park days when they were hand-printing on Eastman's home press, and his little son who helped, and wouldn't go to bed—young Hank Eastman, now a real-estate operator, was all fired up with a big idea, couldn't wait for Andrew Lane to get home, as Andrew was the only architect he'd trust to fulfill his dream. And as Wally twisted recklessly through Chicago traffic which seemed in these few months to have thickened double, he expatiated: Hank Eastman's dream was to revive the excitement of the great Columbian Exposition—yes, he'd been just old enough to be taken there, he remembered it—the excitement of the Midway, and . . . no, not another fair! What Hank had in mind was a vast but high-class pleasure garden, just where the entrance to the Midway had been, a summer-and-winter, indoor-and-outdoor place with a concert stage, a restaurant, they'd have ballet, symphony, even opera, they'd even bring back Isadora Duncan, the sensation of Europe. A kind of elegant gathering place like in Vienna, Copenhagen, Munich, also dance floors, outdoors and indoors— "Just your kind of idea, Dad, bring the outdoors in and the inside out." "Whoa, hold on!" But Andrew knew he was caught, they had him. Already his mind had leapfrogged the Tokyo Hotel—after all, that was solved, what remained was detail work. Hank Eastman had got a few money men interested in his project, Wally rattled on, yelling above the traffic, honking, swerving madly around streetcars. Pop— it was Pop now—what Hank wanted was something sensational, original, young! The big new university campus was just a few blocks up the Midway. All Chicago, every Chicago visitor would flock there. And, unknowingly, Wally had touched a point. That fake-Gothic university! To Andrew, this brought back the old fury at the fake white Greek and Roman columns, their goddam Renaissance exposition. To fling something in their eclectic faces, even this late! Right opposite their Rockefeller Gothic university!

It had taken appreciation from both ends of the world —Europe and Japan—to make him wanted at home. And he was pleased, enormously pleased. A new atmosphere! From the jailbird who had left without a commission in sight, his San Francisco tower canceled! Andrew could feel the glow from Laura, in the rumble seat. Chicago's welcome home.

They'd get on to River Valley, get settled in, Monday he'd be at the Chicago office— "But, Dad, can't you stop for an hour and see Hank now? He's bursting!"

Meanwhile, properly, Andrew asked Wally how were things at home, with the brood, with his mother? All fine. Ellen had a new beau. Law student. Serious? "Well," Wally yelled, over a horn blast, "you really care?"

Scarcely had they settled in, at Hillhouse, when there came a call from Chicago, and as though there had been no interval, Andrew recognized the voice he had not heard for eighteen years. "This is Louis Sullivan."

"Well. It's good to hear from you." He was trying to feel, through the voice. There was the same assurance, yet . . . ? "Say, Andrew, I'm glad you're back. I—" as though he were straightening his shoulders—"I'd like to see you."

"I'd be only too glad to."

The old bitterness had already dropped away. That the Master was in difficulties he knew as everyone knew. Not a single commission all last year, what a waste, what a pitiful waste.

First thing in the morning, soon as he got to town, he'd be there, he said.

Hadn't he himself badly needed help, not so long ago? And been pulled out by his friends?

The two rooms—really a single, partitioned room— reverberated so badly when the El passed, that you had to pause in what you were saying. Already, during the hand-shake. But their hands remained grasped. It was still the same Louis Sullivan, his eyes clear, his stance straight, and that was a relief right away to Andrew. Only, in the move-ment to the chair, Andrew saw the wavering as in some image partly out of focus.

Been following Andrew's work. Damn proud of him!

"I got it all from you."

The Master's old dry laugh. "They're saying that the little I've done lately I got from you!"

Andrew joked off the reference. It was about a resi-dence done a few years ago, in Riverside, in the Prairie House manner. After all, Sullivan wasn't used to doing homes.

He hadn't been out there in several years, Andrew said, so hadn't had a chance to look at it.

Sure, Sullivan said with the old twinkle, "Women." Too bad about Andrew's marital troubles. He'd had his own, too. Oh, she had gone her own way. He'd been alone now for some time.

Andrew had heard, vaguely, from Frank Whitaker, of the way the old man lived. Lonely hotel rooms. Cheaper and cheaper.

Soon the immediate trouble became clear. They were even trying to push him out of here; this miserable little office.

Well, there was no need to worry about that! Andrew reassured him. He'd get someone to talk to the management. Say, Sullivan ought to do what he had done himself—get some friends to incorporate him!

Yeah, he had heard about that, said the Master. And while there was no self-pitying, something in the voice was changed, as though to comment, who the hell would do it for this old wreck.

But then it got cheerier: Some things he had been writing. After those "Kindergarten Chats" in the *Builder*, a few years ago—"Ever see them?"

"Read every one!" But it was ten years ago, Andrew recalled.

Well, he hoped to get them out in a book. And now he was starting on his life story. Writing it at the Cliff Dwellers, the club was really decent to him, kept his own corner for him, with his chair. Every afternoon, he went up there to write. Did Andrew remember that old story about his grandfather getting him out at dawn, in the snow . . . ?

The way they used to vie, about whose grandfather had been tougher, on the farm. They got to laughing together. Sure, Andrew would come around. Often.

He would, too. It had gone off fine. Andrew went up to the building office and paid the back rent.

Then came better than a year of apogee, a life as it should be, a peaceful rhythm at home, the full thrust of ideas, fruitful work, with two big commissions in execution, so it should be! So man should create! Why all the hideous hate-born waste and torment, envy, strife, bitterness, duplicity? Was it only luck that brought the bad years and the good, or could man find a way of behavior, a wisdom, a control? Laura teased him in his sententious ponderings. They were like Clarence Darrow's philosophical lectures that had started again, after he was clear of his second trial, on that jury-fixing charge: "Is Human Nature Evil?"

Even in River Valley, there were now postcards of Andrew's world-famous Hillhouse on sale in the drugstore!

A rhythm of life, something like a large family, formed; Laura gathered them all for lunch, some days out in the courtyard, sometimes on the veranda, or by the pond; the two or three young draftsmen, Andrew—when he wasn't in Chicago—her children now in summer, a few other children from the farm . . . Often she simply wore overalls and a big straw hat. How easy and pleasant it was, that summer!

The young impresario, Hank Eastman, had turned out a mesmerizer, one of the new young breed of enthusiasts, no more the rough-riding Chicago pioneers, but well-bred, cultured. Hank was quick, like a bright schoolboy who had an instant answer for every problem. What of the somewhat far-out location, for a place that needed such a big clientele? Why, had the distance stopped the mobs from coming to the Columbian Exposition? And that had been nearly twenty years ago, before automobiles. And the university a few blocks away, a youthful, dancing crowd. And the whole neighborhood now populated. Open-air gardens in winter? Exactly why he had waited for Andrew Lane! Andrew's inventiveness could surely solve that little problem. Huge glass sliding walls? But—with a young man's urgency—the entire shebang must be built and must open the following summer. Why "must"? Must!

At first, though intrigued, Andrew found no overall idea for what they wanted. Couldn't detach his mind from the Tokyo hotel; new details, patterns for the stone-carving kept coming to him. Yet one thought grew: the hotel would be standing far away, remote—in Japan.

Each time he came in to his Chicago office, the Loop throbbed around him. The old firms, Holabird and Roche, new firms, even Bob Mann downtown now, hurling up structures. What did he have, to show of his work in his own Chicago? The Prairie Houses? A phase long behind him. And what of now? What structures of his would stamp him on Chicago—"That's Andrew Lane's!"

But first the Tokyo job had to be smoothly on the rails. Luckily, Andrew had found an extra man for the detailing —a young Texan had turned up, eager for the experience with the Chicago master, whom he had heard of not in Texas but in Berlin, where he had just completed his architectural schooling. While sitting there in a favorite *Bierstube* with a young German who was starting a place called the Bauhaus, this Texan, Lionel Hanser, no cowboy with a sombrero, but round-faced, pink-cheeked, wearing a heavy gold-set scarab ring, an aesthete if you wanted, even wearing Andrew's flowing artist tie (but not, Andrew sensed, in imitation of himself, for suddenly it came to him: more like that poor miserable Oscar Wilde)—there in the Berlin *Bierstube*, Lionel had been told by young Walter Gropius that he *must* go to Chicago, to Andrew Lane. Shown the rough layouts, this pink-cheeked Texan put his finger on every area that needed working out; he was easy, self-possessed, and entered instantly into the plan, comprehending, but not intruding, not taking over. It was as though the much-missed Gladys had suddenly come back from Australia, in this other form. As far as staying out in River Valley to do the work, "You mean I'd be living in Hillhouse?" he repeated like a child granted a fairy wish.

And he fitted at once, conversing with Laura in poetry quotations, her favorite Rilke.

While one or two draftsmen had left, feeling lonely in the country, Lionel was at once adjusted, like a perfect long-staying house guest. And in the drafting room turning out an amazing amount of work. Perfect.

Thus, as Tokyo rapidly got under way, Andrew awoke early one morning with the Chicago Gardens structure standing complete within his mind's eye. Once more, it had happened! There stood the new structure, gay pennants atop high pillars of light. Brick piers bearing abstracted forms of slender sprites, a touch futuristic, but upward songs of linear joy. A great courtyard with plantings, dance platforms, the vast orchestral shell. There echoed to him, "A pleasure dome did he decree." The stage projecting right out amidst the banks of dining tables, with runways for ballet dancers—yet the gaiety of American burlesque!

He'd design tables, chairs, lamps, dishware, even the napery!

Ranks of tables, continuing beyond high glass sliding doors for winter. A great central kitchen serving outside and inside. Dance-band stands, secluded corners, walks half screened by foliage, intimate balconies, a bar to rival the Auditorium.

The entire structure enlivened with murals, sculptures, all the arts embracing; a place of beauty and gladness. Bright colored lights like rising balloons!

So it detailed itself in his mind, all the way on the train to Chicago, and, walking into the offices, Andrew went straight to his drawing board, and in an hour the Gardens lay there. Wally hovered, and as Andrew lifted his arm from the sheet, his son took in the design, complete, and let out a whistle. Andrew glanced up. Wally's eyes were alight, he was beaming. One thing with Wally—never the atmosphere of tormented uncertainty in a son following his genius father. Yes, admit that word—what else was it when a vision appeared complete? Been generating itself, within him. But from where? Andrew didn't brag of it to himself. Something given. But he had treated his creative gift honestly, never twisted or choked. Worked damn hard to give it all the skills it needed. Here once again the vision had come through. No greater feeling in life. Like consummated love. Joy! Joy in life!

Young Eastman was in ecstasy. "That's it! That's exactly it! I knew what I wanted, but I couldn't see it! Mr. Lane—I knew you were the only man who could show it to me! Perfect!" His enthusiasm would have been embarrassing were it not so spontaneous—a child's. Hank seized the telephone, got his father's office, commanded Alfred to drop everything and come see. In half an hour Alfred was there, delighted, praising, recalling the old days with the handpress, did Andrew know those copies were now worth five hundred dollars apiece! Well, and what did Andrew think of Hank here! Some promoter! "He even sold me! I put in five thousand even before I saw this!"

"You'll put in more before he's through," Andrew predicted wryly. They laughed. "The boys make a good team," Eastman glowed.

Then it was full steam ahead double speed. The ground was being prepared, the foundations were dug, before the drawings and blueprints were completed. Even before an all-over contractor was set. Every builder shook his head. Impossible to give a firm price. Heavy plate glass on runners, statuary, experimental electric fixtures, walls that projected into space—and, atop it all, a fixed opening date. At last Andrew got hold of Lonergan from Oak Park, who was a bit skittish, understandably, considering his losses on that Woodlawn Avenue masterpiece—but what a magnificent job it was! Graying now, Lonergan gave a groan-laugh on arrival. "Oh, I'll lose my shirt." Then joked a bit, with Andrew—did he remember that day Old Man Sullivan caught onto that foundation on Dorchester! "He roars at me—'Andrew Lane!' And I pretend I never heard the name!" Say, he had heard the old Master really was having it rough. And, sighing, the contractor set himself to examining the plans. "I'll lose on it. I'm sure to lose my shirt on this." Andrew too was sure of it. But still . . . The contractor shrugged and smiled, like a man deciding on one more drink. Not every day a man got a chance to build something different. Lonergan shook his head, no use resisting temptation. "Nobody wanted to take it on, huh? You want it done, Andrew, I'll do it." He sighed his bottom sigh, and put out his hand. They drove at once to the site.

Everything had to be started simultaneously, even the sprites. Behind stockpiles of bricks, a studio shed was set up for the sculptor, a young Chicago-Italian Futurist. While riveters worked on the orchestra shell, the sculptor was chiseling on the sprites; Wally found for him the skinniest model on the near-North Side, all angles.

You could hardly thread your way between piles of lumber, sacks of cement, wheelbarrows banging at your ankles, electricians unwinding heavy cable, coal braziers in November, fire inspectors to bribe. Through it all, to Andrew's pride, Wally moved with ease, patience, and the gift of quick solutions, taking the whole load on himself. Don't worry, Pater.

Fortunately there was no pressure from Japan. Each progression on the detail drawings meant more than two months of back-and-forth mail, and perhaps an extra few months of deliberations in Tokyo before they sent their suggestions, usually minor, accompanied by florid apologies.

Before the year was out, Hank was behind in payments, but even as he scurried for new investments—everybody, Marshall Field II, Cudahy, Potter Palmer, was escorted over the layout—he kept announcing more and more grandiose plans for the opening. The full Theodore Thomas Orchestra. The corps de ballet of the opera. He was negotiating to bring Isadora Duncan back from Europe—he would sail over himself to persuade her! What a triumphant return it would be for Isadora Duncan, to Chicago, where she had failed in her first recital!

And then one morning at breakfast Laura uttered a small gasp, and passed Andrew the *Madison Times*. A tragedy. The American dancer's two children, from her love life with the Russian poet Esenin, had died in a car accident in Paris. Miss Duncan had survived.

Andrew was startled at Laura's face, ghostly. A tragedy, yes, yet why should she be so utterly shaken?

Two children about the same age as hers.

He had to leave for the train. "I'll be all right." Her pale smile. "I don't know what came over me. Poor children. Oh, poor Isadora Duncan."

In the brazen July heat, with double crews, carpenters, decorators, overtime, Lonergan meeting payrolls out of his own pocket, Hank even borrowing from usurers, Wally, in shirtsleeves, trowel in hand—after a bribe to the union delegate—cementing sprites into place. Photographers letting off flashlights, Hank giving smiling interviews, the opening would definitely be on time, it had to be—boyishly—as all Chicago society had parties planned, he was sold out, the Armours, Mrs. Potter Palmer, the fabled opening of the Auditorium would be outdone. Ah, no—to a knowing elderly reporter—Miss Harriet Monroe was not composing a special ode, though he would be delighted, but the greatest French chef had been engaged. Beauty and joy, that would be the theme of the Gardens, *savoir vivre*, Futurism, originality, the masterpiece of America's world-renowned architect, Andrew Lane, modernity, gastronomy, sophistication!

Chicago not only the hog butcher, Chicago in the avant garde!

In the last weeks the form of the Gardens gleamed behind the stretches of scaffolding like the gleam of some half-dressed, or half-undressed, hussy. There was no leaving the job, no desire to, Wally and young Eastman slept on sacks of cement, Andrew betook himself to the Elm Street apartment. Laura came from River Valley, bringing her children to see Chicago's Fourth of July parade, but stayed over a few days in the apartment, as keeping house in the country was a problem at the moment, since their young couple, Walter the houseman and Kate the cook, had suddenly taken themselves up and gone home to the fatherland, lederhosen and all. Laura had to engage another couple. Meanwhile Texas Lionel and Pete, who had stayed on to work on the Tokyo job, could manage for these few days, the Texan loved to cook, and Mrs. Strom would take care of the house.

With the newspaper stories about Europe a caldron and Germany militarizing and worrisome articles in *The Statesman*, and Lionel receiving letters from a poet chum in London who was convinced that the Kaiser had plans to conquer the world, Laura was sure war was near. Nonsense, said Andrew, the Germans liked pomp and parades, after all didn't we too, on the Fourth? The Germans were too intelligent a people. But Laura was worried about their Wotan spirit, and the *Statesman* article spoke of the ghastliness of machine-age warfare, every country was building airplanes that could rain explosives, set entire cities ablaze, and it was reported that the Germans were preparing a diabolic deadly gas. Andrew hardly had time to read the papers these days. Just glanced at the headlines.

Here was the heir to the Austrian throne assassinated, with his wife. In their carriage, visiting some city in Serbia. Anarchists, again.

Not anarchists, it turned out. Some secret society of Serbian patriots. What difference?

They'd have dinner at Rector's; Andrew could then go back to the Gardens site and check up on a few things.

Nor did Andrew forget her problem with household help. Rector himself came to the table, and he knew of a couple, from Barbados, he'd had them both working in the kitchen, the man was a good second cook, good worker, serious, but—Rector's fat jowls shook and he smirked at Laura—the fellow was terribly jealous of his wife, which was why they worked in the same place, so he could keep an eye on her. All it had taken was a wink at her from another nigger in the kitchen, and William was after him with a cleaver! No, nothing serious, just the nigger way, but he had let the couple go. Peace in his kitchen. But he'd like to help the couple out, very clean, good workers, and since nothing like that incident was likely to happen out in their country household . . . A serious churchgoing couple. One of the kitchen boys was a neighbor of theirs, so Rector would send word for them to get in touch. He noted down the Elm Street address and telephone, always glad to help out, oblige a friend.

Under arc lights, carpenters were putting down the floor of the great outdoor stage. Hank Eastman was in high spirits—he had the enormous seating chart spread over sawhorses. Tables for the gala opening dinner were being scalped for a thousand dollars each! He'd held a few in reserve, and was being importuned by every Gold Coast parvenu! Now, at his own table, next to his parents, he was keeping places for Andrew and his lady . . .

There was just a touch of question in his voice.

Andrew could visualize it. Laura under the stares. Flashlight powder going off, and all heads turning. Next day the white-glare faces in the papers—Architect Andrew Lane accompanied by the ex-Mrs. Laura Garnett, with whom . . .

True, they had not permitted themselves to be intimidated, they had gone to plays, concerts, restaurants. Yet he could visualize in the lists of guests: Architect Andrew Lane—with consort? companion? mistress? The whole stupid hegira talk all over again; it had never really stopped. But young Hank Eastman only laughed. A new generation. All different. And for Andrew Lane's great Chicago creation!

Laura was in her peignoir, brushing her hair, a movement that never failed to give him the sense of the beautiful —a caught breath. And desire.

Andrew began by growling about having to wear soup-and-fish for the big occasion, and in the August heat, and then—didn't Laura want a new gown? Perhaps a kind of Lake Michigan blue, what did she think?

She wasn't going to the opening, Laura said, in her

whispery voice that meant it was firm. Then she added in her faintest voice, "Why hurt Helena?" Even though Helena was still refusing a divorce. "Take your mother," Laura said. "Your Chicago triumph at last!" She was in earnest, there was no irony. —Well, and why not? Marta would have her glory.

Laura's way of finding the appropriate.

The day came up another sizzler; Andrew with his ferocious work discipline had gone off early to the Gardens. That servant couple telephoned, and would come at ten. Laura took the children to the beach at the end of Oak Street; even here, the city's heat engulfed them, awful; she wanted only to get them home.

The housekeeping couple arrived in their Sunday best, the man wearing a full suit in this heat, preacher-black cloth, stiff as sheet iron. The young woman Laura at once took to, perhaps because of eyes that had surely seen trouble, but peeped into yours, hopefully. Already on the telephone Laura had heard the Caribbean lilt. Oh, yes, she wanted the country. The dirty city air was bad for her husband. They came from the country, but the land there was so poor, too poor.

The man's eyes seemed restless. He was tall, long-armed, and Laura would not let herself think ape. She explained the isolation of River Valley, they might feel lonesome, as there were very few of their people in the area. Of course, on their days off they could visit Chicago to see their friends, but it was a long train ride, she had to warn them.

The woman asked if there was a church they could go to. Of theirs? Negroes in River Valley? In the city of Madison, Laura said. And there was a bus.

The woman was so eager. The country. And her man kept nodding in assent. Laura explained about the household, her two children were with her now but only for the summer, she was divorced. Mr. Lane was an architect and usually had two or three people working for him there, making drawings for buildings, everybody had their meals together, and guests came and stayed, so it was a place with sometimes eight, even a dozen people at the table. . . . The couple kept nodding, they had worked in big homes, they had worked in restaurants. The young woman offered some creased pieces of paper, references. Laura glanced, the usual thing, honest, satisfactory. The young woman, Lucy, was so eager. She'd take them on trial, she told Lucy, if Mr. Lane said it was all right. Then reassuringly she added, he usually said that if it was all right with her, it was all right with him. Lucy beamed.

Another professor had come from abroad in search of American architecture—an Italian this time, and he *must* see the noted Hillhouse at River Valley. The household was back in order, every object rubbed, the kitchen running smoothly. Lucy was a ceaseless worker, laundering, ironing, helping William; she had not yet ceased exclaiming with awe at each beautiful thing. And a cottage for themselves! Along the curve of the hill, two rooms with their own garden that William dug in.

Only, each day Laura was more uncertain about William. He had proven indeed a competent cook, restaurant-taught but with a Caribbean chicken gumbo that was a delight, Johnny couldn't stop being greedy about helpings. Yet—Laura couldn't define her uneasiness. The man's eyes? Sometimes, a flare of yellow like an electric-bulb filament flaring up before going dead. Generally the eyes seemed never to see you but only to include you among other objects before him. He was polite, he served correctly, but seemed absent. He scarcely spoke to anyone; but his wife didn't have this distantness, and chattered.

Maida said he gave her the creeps. That was no reason to dismiss a person, there was no fault in his work and Lucy was a jewel.

WILLIAM KNEW now who they were. In the town of
River Valley were a few black people after all, doing the
nigger work. Old black man, Charles, been there twenty
years stoking furnaces before sunup in winter, shoeshine
in the barbershop, odd jobs and garbage all the year, lived
by himself in a shed in Mrs. Vogel's backyard, picked up
stray dogs for her before they bit people, oh she was all het
up about stray dogs and cats, Mrs. Vogel, she was the
Animal Care Society, you'd be surprised the number of
stray dogs could turn up in a town like this, and Charles
was the dogcatcher too, his job with mangy stray dogs was
to put them away, he had a special place by the garbage
dump, incinerated them with kerosene, too, so as to be no
chance of disease. Now, as to Mr. Andrew Lane and his
paramour, Charles savored the word, learned from the talk
around here, those two sinners, come out here from Chicago a couple of years ago, that architect run away from
his wife and the woman run away from her husband, first
they traipsed all over Europe together. Why, that man had
six children at home, and she had these two children, her
husband threw her out, divorced her, but the law even let

her see her children in the summer. Why, Mr. Andrew Lane, he was even put in jail in Milwaukee, by Mrs. Vogel's son the lawyer, and Mr. Lane had to get himself a big lawyer from Chicago to come and get him out of jail. The paper out here was full of it—Charles had his wheezy laugh, telling William how all the white preachers hereabouts roasted them in hell and damnation, and half the town wouldn't speak to them yet. Why, all along the valley —Mr. Lane's uncles owned a big stretch of the valley—his own uncles still wouldn't have that woman in their homes.

After a few weeks Laura gave them an extra day off, for the trip to Chicago to see their friends. Laura herself drove them to the train, they were all spiffed up in their fine clothes they had worn when they came to apply for the job.

Saturday night was poker in the next-door flat, King Kelly and their friends, and Lucy didn't stop William from a few drinks, he had behaved out there, been an angel. Came a big pot, and she saw that William held a pair of deuces and a queen, and King Kelly was pushing up the stakes, raise a whole dollar now, it was over thirty dollars in the pot before Kelly stopped raising, just called, and put down three jacks. William slapped down his two queens and the deuce, triumphantly reaching for the pot, shouting, "Three queens! Deuces wild!" "Who said deuces wild!" King yelled. Not a soul had heard it said, Lucy neither. William leaped for King Kelly, howling, "I heard it! I goddam heard that deuces wild!" Took every man around the table to grab William and hold him down.

SLEPT HEAVY, ate heavy, Sunday breakfast, and heavy-headed let her lead him to her preacher on Wentworth, the store door was open for air, stove-hot inside, every black face glowing with sweat, the hot words blazing out from the furnace mouth, *"Lucifer!"* the mouth was calling out and to William the name was a connection, a secret call to him, Lucy his wife always leading him in the righteous way, the way of the Lord. *Lucifer the devil is the hand of the Lord, yes, he is the punishing hand! Now Lucifer is abroad in the world, the Lord has loosed his devil's chains and Lucifer is the hand of vengeance, the punishment of the Lord for the sins of man, oh yes, the fires of hell are raging on earth, oh yes, the conflagration oh yes, for the wages of sin is death, yes Lord! and the flames are spreading, the whirlwind, the great conflagration, the wrath of the Lord is loosed upon all sinners! Across the ocean, the great conflagration, spreading, consuming the continent of sin, the flames leaping to the city of sin, Paris, that is the meaning of this war that has only begun, for the fire will devour all evil, the flames will leap the ocean, all the seas of the ocean cannot put out the Lord's avenging fire, and it will reach all sinners, here in America too, here in Chicago too, for the time has come to purify with fire and flame . . .*

In the eyes of the preacher William saw, like match flares, red flickers, Lucy's preacher talking to him, black suit, and the shrieks arose, "Fire! Oh yes!" *Hellfire!* The flaming sword arm of Lucifer, William could feel the fire-power coming into his own arm, an arm with a flaming sword—sin everywhere around them out there in that country place, sin in the master, the woman of sin that they served, sin from the land of sin, always talking Europe, Paris, when he served them, bent to serve them at their table, Paris, was their talk, they and all who came to them out there, bringing sin, spreading sin, the house was a house of sin, *oh Lord I am the flaming arm the flaming sword . . .*

The preacher shouting. Had not the Lord given man every opportunity to repent? Yet evil was piled on evil, gambling, drinking—and worst, he shouted, was lechery, the worst of sins! A stench in the nostrils of the Almighty! The Lord's vengeance was coming! The flaming swords in the hands of the Four Horsemen, who would scourge the earth of sin! Already the Four Horsemen rode across Europe, hunger, pestilence, fire, death, from Europe they would leap the ocean, only the cleansing, the purification with fire and sword, only repentance would save the remnant! Repent!

And he had Lucy and all weeping and shouting, Save us! . . . Save us! Lord Lord save us!

Choked with the fiery words, the early August heat, the airless crowded store, William had a paroxysm, gasping, and Lucy led him out, to breathe.

On the train back Lucy read the paper, William saw the big war headline—IN FLAMES . . .

Assassins, Laura read. A French Socialist leader shot to death through a restaurant window in Paris, because his party was antimilitarist. . . .

Russia invading Austria, Laura read. Germany marching into France. England mobilized against Germany. Warplanes in battle.

William was working in the garden when Johnny came by. William raised himself tall. His eyes were yellow, "This is a house of sin!" he shouted at the boy.

Johnny didn't scare. But, going into the house, he remarked to his mother that the nigger—Negro, she said —that the cook was loony. It took Laura a while to get him to tell just what William had shouted. —It was, she explained to Johnny, because William had been to Chicago, and their people got all worked up by their special kind of preacher, everybody was a sinner, it was called Bible-shouting, she told Johnny.

Already in his boiled shirt though he was keeping the artist tie, Andrew arrived to find last-minute trouble over the electrical wiring for the table lamps, but just as the first limousines began to arrive the lamps switched on, like early stars brought down into the garden, with the white napery a trailing garment of the departing day. The sprites floated above the walls; parties entering, his entire construction glistened, the patterned black-and-white of the males counterpointing the tinted tulles, the bright silks, with the sprinkled jewels in the hair like an overflow from the Milky Way that was just becoming discernible in the sky. From the string ensemble, a bare-armed harpist included, there came Mozart's *Don Giovanni* overture, and everywhere the accompanying twitter of ahs and exclamations. More and more wealth flowed into his created perimeter, glittering female eyes, the splendor of Chicago.

There came his mother on the arm of handsome Wally her grandson!

Because it was in the open, with a sky canopy, it seemed to Andrew that here even the inauguration of the Auditorium was eclipsed. Twenty-five years. Chicago's "society" was more worldly.

The Eastmans had pressed him into the receiving line. It crossed his mind that while in Europe royalty stood reviewing their troops—if Laura had come she'd have appreciated this—here the royalty of Chicago celebrated pleasure! The ball before the Battle of Waterloo. One heard snatches of conversation—the Germans now inside France—like news of a distant relative in trouble. No, America would never go in . . . Then—Hank Eastman's idea, Andrew had let it go through—a page blew a fanfare announcing the gala dinner.

The children were asleep. She felt on her cheek Johnny's good night like a brushed damp petal, and from Maida's lips a slight lingering, and her child reached up an arm around Mama's neck.

Now, these last few summers, it was well: there was not that fright in Laura as when they were very little and she had the constant fear—because she knew she would have to leave their father—the fear of losing them. Or stifle her life, the way so many women in their passion for their children would bind themselves for their continuing years to the wrong man. And now at last she even felt that her children were losing their blame for her.

How lovely, how lovely they both grew. She had such

joy in them; even if limited to these few months of the year, still, with her Chicago excursions all year around, the bond held. It was still she who was Mummy, despite the young new Mrs. Garnett.

In a loose robe of light India cotton, Laura sat reading, the French windows open to the inner garden. What a perfect, soft, luminous night for Andrew. How right that she had not gone.

She was immersed in Dreiser's new tome, *The Financier*, the continuation of the saga of that amazing Yerkes, whom he called Cowperwood. What detail, what power! And here—quite amusingly, though she didn't suppose Dreiser meant it so—was the story Andrew had once told her, about the penniless would-be newspaper reporter, surely young Dreiser himself, and that young actress in the Ibsen play at Hull House, whatever had become of her? That financier Yerkes had set her up in the Michigan Avenue Studio Building, and become suspicious, and planted a spy across the hall, who had spotted poor Dreiser, of course fictionized here, slipping in. The spy at once called Yerkes, who had come roaring and thrown the fellow out, and even got his editor to fire him and chase him out of town! Well, now Dreiser had his revenge! And hadn't Yerkes himself been driven out of Chicago some years ago, by some banker with whose wife he was having an affair? Surely Dreiser would come to it. Oh, he really was amazing. What energy! Oh, she could never bring herself to write of things so intimate in her own life. But so much of novel-writing was like that, nowadays. Perhaps this way of the new novel, this public display of oneself, this fashion of a total lack of reticence, was what had really impeded her, all these years, in her own writing.

She could just imagine Mr. Yerkes-Cowperwood and his redhead, had they remained in Chicago, making their grand entry at Andrew's opening, right now! How quiet, how well, she felt here. Not only to be away from all those ostentatious people, from the artificiality that people had on all those big "pleasurable" occasions, the display of wealth, how did Professor Veblen at the university put it, "conspicuous consumption." Not only that in general she was shy and uneasy in crowds—except in the anonymity of populous crowds, parades like the Fourth which she enjoyed as much as the children. But society. Although Laura suspected that in a certain way, despite his disclaimers, Andrew liked it. When he was the center of attention. Oh, a touch of vanity that he well deserved, it was even endearing. But tonight—even without the whispering and side glances and behind-the-fan remarks that would have been inevitable had she appeared with him— No! The wisdom of negative choice.

And there was something about this night's event that was even more alienating to her than her dislike of crowds and ostentation. Granted that just because a war had broken out in Europe, people could not be expected to abstain from a long-planned festival in Chicago. But this war was so ominous, the ghastly new weapons that were being described, the predictions of bombardments from zeppelins —striking not only the enemy army but ordinary people, children! Already, humanity's ever-dreamed-of achievement, the ability to fly, was being turned into horror, destruction. Oh, she knew that she was being unrealistic, that nothing was served by her mourning for mankind. But Laura felt relieved not to be taking part in festivities. Even though her appearance with Andrew in his triumph would have shown she had not destroyed him. And even though it might have taken her mind off the bad moment here, of this day, that kept weighing on her. She had had to speak to Lucy, tell the poor young woman that she and her husband must leave. No, there was no complaint as to their work, never had the house been so well kept, Lucy was perfect and her husband was a good cook, especially with his delicious Caribbean dishes, but . . . And Laura had seen the haunted expression in the poor woman's eyes, a dread "again."

But after the black man had shouted at the child, terrified John—and shamed him! True, Laura agreed with the pleading young woman that it could be a fit of temper that came and passed. They had had trouble with it before? Lucy burst into tears. William was a good man, a church-going man, yes, sometimes he burst out like that, but he had never hurt anybody—if only they could have another chance . . .

The black face showed such womanly suffering, Laura all but yielded, except that there came an instant's intuition —when the woman swore he never hurt anybody—a sense of perhaps a desperate, accustomed lie? And there was her own fright, an unreasonable reaction that William's mere presence sometimes unaccountably engendered— she had even mentioned this to Andrew. But worst were the words that he had cried out, that she had finally got Johnny to repeat, her boy's training for truth overcoming his shame. Not shame of her, but of what came out of people, even out of a servant. "He said this is a house of sin."

So Laura had the firmness to insist, they must leave. She was giving them two weeks' notice. If they wanted to go to Chicago to look for another place, she would mean-while manage.

He still had things to finish, Andrew said on the tele-phone. They'd got by with the opening, the concert had been magnificent, and people hadn't noticed the covered-up incompleted murals. But he couldn't leave until things were right. Even with Wally on the job. He had had some sleep. . . . No, hadn't gone to the flat, but had managed right here. In the conductor's retiring room there was a couch.

Lionel drove to town and returned with the Chicago papers, which he had already folded over to pictures of the society gala. The gleaming jewels on the gleaming bosoms. The triumphant young originator and entrepreneur, Henry Eastman. There with him stood Chicago's interna-tionally famed architect Andrew Lane. Laura could imagine how Andrew must have maneuvered to get them into a position where the Gardens' striking entrance would show in the photo, though, alas, the head of the sprite was cut off. Still, there was the panoramic picture across the bottom of the page that gave some feel of the design. Laura refolded the paper. On the front page: FRENCH CLAIM VICTORY. An eyewitness dispatch, havoc, flames, people fleeing homes.

Johnny was fascinated by the idea of machine guns. She tried to explain the war to him, and he was solemnly comprehending: of course war was bad. It was not like knights on steeds in the old days, and of course even in those days any kind of killing was bad. Maida declared the war was because of kings, the age of kings was past, though those kings and kaisers in Europe didn't seem to know it. That was why such awful things could never happen in America, because we had no king. Then Maida turned the paper and exclaimed over the beautiful women and their gowns. —Yes, Laura felt, she must be pleased that Maida's reaction was so natural.

John ran off, no doubt to play at machine guns with the Strom boy. She called after him to bring Gilbert to lunch. She and Maida went into her garden; Maida was beginning to hint at womanly questions. Oh, if she could have her daughter with her all year! Perhaps Ralph would consider, surely he would not deny that at this age particularly a girl had constant need of her mother. Perhaps if she suggested Aunt Nora's Home School?

The marigolds were so thick they were choking out everything. Cutting masses of them, Laura and her daughter brought the flowers into the house, Maida carefully placing a large Japanese vase for them on the dining table.

Lucy helped get ready the lunch: a farmer's chop suey, fresh cucumbers and radishes, fresh cream from Mr. Strom's, and William's specially good cornbread. Pitchers of cold milk and lemonade.

Then she went to their cottage to dress for the city. Mrs. Lane had said she could go and get registered with the agency for another job. Mr. Strom would drive her to Madison to catch the express train, right after they ate.

Often they had lunch on the treetop terrace, but the sun was so fierce today that Laura decided to have it in the dining room, which was fairly cool. Almost ashamed of the touch of aversion that rose in her—she was really being oversensitive about William—Laura stepped into the kitchen to tell him. He hardly raised his eyes. Yes'm. She made a smile, but he didn't see it. Well, no doubt he had reason to be surly, having been given the sack. Had she after all been unjust? But the man did give her the shivers. And that outcry—house of sin! To her son!

The noon gathering around the big table was always lively. Johnny had indeed made himself a machine gun, out of a round stick that swiveled on a nail stuck into a block of wood, and Gil Strom had a similar contraption. Each kept ducking down from the table while the other yelled, "You're hit!" until Laura quieted them, play was fun but after all war was no fun. "I know," Johnny said, looking her calmly in the eye. She felt a kind of hopeless distress. There were things in man that one could not stop. Maida made a grand entry wearing an enormous cardboard tiara à la Mrs. Potter Palmer; it was studded with raspberries!

The huge bowl of farmer's chop suey was already on the table. William brought in a large plate piled with warm cornbread; Johnny loudly sniffed the delicious aroma and called out his appreciation, but William had already gone back to the kitchen, closing the door behind him.

With their loudness in there, he was sure no one heard as he carefully turned the key in the door lock. Picking up the pail of kerosene that he had placed, ready, he moved swiftly. Beneath each window he poured from the pail. Then, turning back, flung the lighted match as he passed, and as the flames spurted he was back by the dining-room door; seizing the hatchet he had placed ready against the wall. With the first shrieks of "Fire!" he unlocked the door.

A surge of joy in him as they followed exactly as in his vision, rushing to the door—to him! Avenging Lucifer! The sin woman and her spawn, the hatchet arm swung, swift, cane-chopping, a grand exultance surged through him like the surging flames, he raised higher his strong arm for the big one, that Texas man, he felt his blade imbedded, in meat, he heard his own voice howling above the howls, pulled loose his feet from bodies, hot blood, lifted high his legs from clutching hands, the task was done. Ran, saw one leaping through a flaming window, axed him as he rolled on the ground, ran on.

Keeping farmwork hours, the Stroms had already finished their meal; August was resting when his wife shrieked, "Fire!" He ran toward the conflagration, Amy behind him, calling, "Gil!"

William heard, saw them, if he went across the open to the woods he'd be seen, he tumbled into the brick furnace hut. The Angel of Vengeance was gone out of him, he was he now, with what he had just done. Hound dogs would tear his flesh. Still alive he'd be strung up, the hounds leaping at his tattered legs.

On a shelf was cleaning stuff, he saw a bottle with skull and crossbones, seized it, shook it. Half full.

The furnace door hung open, black inside. He fitted himself in, one hand holding that bottle, closed the iron door on himself, waited.

August Strom, snatching the garden hose, cried out to his wife to turn on the water, kept shouting, "Gil!" The futile stream, like his shouts, was lost in the roar; handing Amy the hose, he ran around to the rear, the fire hadn't yet jumped the back patio, he ran into Mr. Lane's private drawing office and seized the telephone, cranking, crying, "Fire!" The operator girl, it was Roberta Cass, stayed steady. "How big? Hold on!" First gave the alarm, came back to him. She must reach Mr. Lane in Chicago. August heard himself telling her, all dead in there, all at the table having lunch, his own boy in there, too. Dead. "Oh, God,

August, are you sure?" "No one came out. I can't get in."
He waited, heard her calling the Chicago operator, emergency, Mr. Lane must be at the Chicago Gardens, that
new place just opened, it was in the papers yesterday, one
minute, I know the number, they call it all the time from
Hillhouse. He heard the ringing, at last a man's voice, hang
on. They called Mr. Lane.

"You say all, all?"

"I didn't see one come out. My boy is in there, Mr.
Lane."

"I'm coming at once," Mr. Lane said, and August
heard him hang up.

There was only the two o'clock, that was a local, six
hours, but still by automobile it would take longer. And
Wally was on an errand with the car. Andrew got a cab to
the station, ten minutes to wait for the train, tried to put
through a call, useless, and then saw Ralph Garnett. Saw
in his face. "All," Ralph said. She and the children. Others.

The two men stood before each other. Andrew half
started to speak, what words would come out he didn't
know—"I—"

"It wasn't you," Ralph said. They walked silently together to the train.

The car was half empty. To sit apart? Ralph waited for
Andrew to sit first, then took the place beside him.

The whole long way, every halt, every resumption,
what would be said? Each was in his own life with her;
neither could speak, share. Andrew again and again sought
to form words. The children. But what could he say that
was not an intrusion?

Perhaps an hour had passed, when Ralph uttered a
few words: "I tell myself . . . disasters . . . in the war over
there in Europe . . ."

Andrew said, "I was thinking, in an earthquake . . ."

They fell silent again. Thus, at long intervals, a few
words.

The dining-car waiter came through announcing dinner service was available. Only partly their eyes moved, each to the other, no.

At the station before River Valley, Andrew said, "Next one."

The police chief, Quincy, waited. Spoke sorrowfully to Andrew, looked at the other man. Andrew introduced them. It took the police chief a moment to realize. "It was the nigger," he said. "Went berserk. Set the fire with kerosene." And driving them in his car, trying to prepare them. The sight. "Locked the door first, and stood behind it with a hatchet, then unlocked it and killed them when they tried to escape. One draftsman may be surviving in the hospital in Madison, the young Italian.

"We haven't found the nigger yet. Couldn't have got very far. We caught the woman, running away, two miles down the road. She had nothing to do with it. Said he had fits before, never this bad, never killed. We just brought the bloodhounds from Madison. We'll get him." There were already newspaper people, he said, but he'd keep them at a distance if . . . Neither man answered.

Driving up the access lane, rear lights from standing cars, for an instant, oddly, Andrew expected house lights, then realized. Already the acrid smell. Spotlight from a state trooper's car, as they parked. And then the ruins, half-walls in the flashlight beams.

Several young men, reporters, photographers, were gathered. His Aunt Nora came to him, with Susan and Gus. Susan took his hand, pressed it strongly. Nora said she had called Marta. August Strom came forward, Andrew sought his hand, spoke of his boy—the damn reporters with their pads trying to catch his words. A flash-gun went off and the police chief held up his arm remonstrating.

Quincy led them, only the two of them, Andrew and Ralph, along the tumbled walls, the fallen half-burned roof timbers; Andrew could make out the distorted debris inside, blackened stone, contorted iron. Even the great stone fireplace fallen in on its hearth, the bedroom gaping, he would not look inside, then across the rear terrace to his workroom. And there—his drawing board pushed back—on the floor there lay the bodies wrapped in sheets, a row of white forms. Hers, it must be, between the two smaller ones, her children.

The police chief said, "I don't know if you gentlemen want to—" Ralph made a small hand gesture and Quincy knelt and folded back the edge of the sheet from her head.

Hairless, a head of black stone, of archaic eternity, the features not distorted in agony but reduced, contracted to the expressionless elemental form.

Andrew beheld, fixedly saw, all sensation absent in him. Ralph after a glance turned away his eyes. A repressed sound. He again made the slight hand motion, and the police chief uncovered the heads of the two children. The same carved basalt, unexpectedly small. Shrunken into stone. And, in their elemental form, duplicates of their mother.

The boy's head had fallen sidewise, and the gash could be seen at the base of the skull. Ralph bent over them; he was weeping, his head swaying from side to side, his hand making the sign, cover them, cover them.

As the viewers emerged from where the bodies lay, the reporters waited. In a tone respectful of sorrow, one called to Andrew—Andrew recognized him, he was from Madison—"Anything for us, Mr. Lane?" He wanted to say, ought to say, what she was, as one should say for history. But he shook his head. "Not now." Before Ralph Garnett, they remained silent.

Captain Quincy said to the reporters, "Why don't you give them a rest. Maybe in the morning."

Aunt Nora waited. Andrew ought to come now to her house, for the night. There was room for Mr. Garnett too. Ralph thanked her, but she would understand, he would go to the town hotel, Captain Quincy had already made arrangements. He wished to bury his children at home. With a quiet good night, he went to the police chief's car.

Hearing the bloodhounds in the yard, raging, those police must be giving them his clothes to smell, William could already feel their teeth in his throat; he lifted the poison bottle, gulped, contorting with the fire inside him. His brief choked gagging sounds were muffled by the furnace walls, the iron door, the thick stone, thus unheard across the yard as the searchers headed for the woods, the river. In his agony, sweat in his eyes, his hands clawing at his searing abdomen, he lost hold. "Be dead, be dead," a last flickering wish, was all.

Aunt Nora kept everyone away. Andrew sat in the room where he had stayed when building Hillhouse. After some time, from just outside the door she spoke his name, and brought in a cup of hot chocolate, a sandwich, an apple. She said, "Try to sleep, Andrew," and left him. Before the cocoa was quite cold, his lips parched, he sipped. Then he lay on the bed. It was as though he heard a din, a clamor of words. A marketplace. The wages of sin! . . . And what of the innocents that had died, not only her two children, but the Stroms' boy, and what of Tex, what evil had he done, to whom? What of old Stan Klaus, his whole life a hired farmhand, proud of the simple joke of his name, until with enough years he could live into it, grow the white beard, "Santa Klaus, that's me!"

Somewhere in the night Andrew must have fallen off, but when the predawn light came into the room he was awake.

In the morning Wally arrived. "A pine box," Andrew said, "a plain pine box." That wouldn't take long. Bring it soon as he could.

Ralph Garnett had come with the town hearse, for the bodies of his two children. No, he said to Andrew, he would not wait and take part in her burial. For a moment the two men stood together. There was in Andrew a question, an anxiety, for Ralph perhaps to reach out his hand —but how could that be? "Well, goodbye." Ralph mounted the hearse.

Wally took care of all that needed to be done; there were the other dead; August and Amy Strom had already taken their own boy's body to their house; the Texan's family had been telegraphed by the police, but Wally reached them by telephone. The surviving draftsman, Pete Genna, had family in Chicago; they already were at the hospital in Madison.

Late in the morning old Neil Hagedorn arrived with the pine box on his Ford.

With Wally, Andrew got ready the farm wagon, the one they had all gone on for picnics. The whole bottom of it Wally helped him fill with flowers from her garden. On this bed of green and rose and golden yellow and all colors they placed her casket, then heaping the box high with her marigolds, sunflowers, daisies, and white lilies.

Just himself and Wally, only the two of them. Wally took the bridle and walked ahead; Andrew walked alongside. Up to the top of the hill, by a boulder where she used to come to sit and read. Susan's Gus had already come, with a helper, and dug the grave. They had brought ropes, and after lowering the box they went away.

All the wagon's flowers Andrew and Wally heaped over the casket in the earth. Then Wally removed a distance, leaving his father alone.

What Andrew had to say to her, he said within himself.

After a time he turned, and with his eldest son, the one who had accepted her, he led back the horse and the empty wagon.

That morning, giving the hounds the scent again and starting out from the servants' cottage, the police were startled when, on passing a squat structure—the furnace house—the dogs tugged and growled.

Inside, the hounds leaped at the furnace door.

So there they found him, still with a pulse. Later, in the hospital, though he had opened his eyes once and mumbled something incoherently, the madman was dead.

Once again Andrew wandered through the burned-out ruins. Her writing nook where she had kept her poetry was in a mud of ashes. In his workroom, empty of the bodies, he sat in his chair. Only to hear no more talk, and be alone.

They came with Wally and told him of the black man's capture and death. The woman had been caught, fleeing. Did he have any— Shaking his head, he asked Wally to have them leave him by himself now. To tell Aunt Nora he had decided he would stay here, in what was left; he would manage.

At nightfall, Susan appeared. She had brought food. She didn't want to disturb him but would sit a while if he didn't mind.

He swallowed some of what she had brought.

They sat, without talking, and to have her there was not as with others. His thoughts went to the boyhood time when they had stood alongside each other in the cave, just inside the mouth of the cave, with the uncles and aunts below in the valley, his mother and sister down there, just after his father had left home.

And again now, as at that time, her presence was natural to him.

Susan didn't remain long. After a while she gathered the dishes and said she would come by in the morning. If he wanted, any time, to come to the house . . . She touched his hand, and he grasped hers and said, "Thank you, Susan."

Several days, Andrew remained where he was. She brought food. On Sunday he knew what was being declaimed, preached all over the land. Down there in River Valley and in Oak Park and in Chicago and all over the land. The Hand of God. The punishment of the Lord. The wages of sin! . . . And in the papers. He had already seen. Susan had brought the Madison editorial. A tragedy; let us hope that fiery coals will not be heaped on the head that sits bowed in ashes. . . . But also she had brought one or two of the other kind, perhaps imagining to rouse him with bitterness, even anger.

That insane woman Mrs. Vogel in River Valley had got herself quoted in the Milwaukee press, a tirade. Sinners! Lust! Divine Justice!

From all of them, dinning, dinning, into his cave. He handed Susan back the cuttings. What did it matter? None of it existed.

Sunday she came again. In the family chapel Uncle Matt had asked, without speaking any names, that there be no recriminations. Only bowed heads and silent prayers, each to his own thoughts, but remembering the mercy of the Lord.

That night Andrew wrote down a few lines. Seven innocent souls had died in a madman's outbreak of murder, among them a lovely woman whose grace and intelligence had illuminated the lives of all who knew her. Now slander besmirched that being, "with whom I have lived these several years in the fulfillment of the true relationship of a man and a woman. Must human society be so cruel—"

He didn't continue. Perhaps in a few more days he would find himself able to say it all. He'd ask Sue to give it to Zacharia Sorenson at the *Madison Times.*

But even after the little he had written, he felt as though he were perhaps now halted in the downward way he had been going. Though he was still as if he did not exist.

Her own lines came into his mind:

> *Into the downdrawing reptilian slime*
> *Our underpinnings reach and hold . . .*

As they had stood together at the rail, above the vast Pacific ocean.

And then a line she had translated from the poem by Goethe that she had found, the "Hymn to Nature"—

Life is her most beautiful invention, and
Death her ruse that she may have much life . . .

Andrew stood in the room as though becoming oriented to a strange place. His eyes fell on his drafting table that had been pushed against the wall, and he thought, to her, It was better where it stood before. We ought to move it back.

Then he moved it back alone.

Author's Note

As THIS work is a novel drawn from the life of Frank Lloyd Wright, I have through the use of the fictional name Andrew Lane indicated that the work does not pretend to biographic accuracy. However, I trust I have not violated the essential truth of the man, his ideas, his genius.

In the novelization, particularly of the experiences leading to the tragedy of 1914, there had to be an imaginative creation of persons who have remained virtually unknown.

Certain events have been moved in time and place; those familiar with Mr. Wright's life will recognize such fictional accommodations and I trust will agree that the significance is not altered.

Yet, in portraying the period, I have kept the actual names of various of Mr. Wright's contemporaries who enter his story, among them Clarence Darrow, Louis Sullivan, Jane Addams, Theodore Dreiser, all part of that remarkable world of Chicago at the turn of the century. This was the world of Frank Lloyd Wright, the determinedly American architect, whose inspirations and prodigious innovations have left us so many structures of great beauty, and whose aesthetic and practical genius have affected the way we live in virtually every dwelling designed since his time.

My LAST meeting with Frank Lloyd Wright was in the fifties, a few years before his death. But already, as he neared ninety, his face seemed translucent, the spirit shining through.

I had spent some months filming his structures: the Prairie House series in Oak Park, culminating in the Robie House in Chicago, the Taliesin masterpiece, the Usonian houses, the Johnson administration building, and perhaps the most celebrated modern house in all the world, Fallingwater. I had filmed the Master himself, sketching and explaining the construction principles of Tokyo's Imperial Hotel. The filmed material was uncut, but he wanted so much to have a look at it, and he appeared so frail that I thought perhaps there was no time to wait, so he had his wish, and viewed what he had wrought. Inexplicably, the material was then lost, and thus, perhaps, I continued for years to feel that my work on Frank Lloyd Wright was still to be done.

I have halted my story at the time of his great tragedy, in 1914. As is known through his own classic autobiography and other accounts, Mr. Wright not long afterward met Miriam Noel, a sculptress, who accompanied him when he went to Tokyo to build the Imperial Hotel. Their relationship deteriorated; unfortunately he again became a headline scandal-subject, then there ensued more than a decade of neglect. During this time Mr. Wright elaborated his planned community, Usonia, whose conception I have prefigured in *The Architect*. Mr. Wright had at last been granted a divorce by his first wife, who remarried. Separated from Miriam Noel, he met the woman who became his third wife, Olgivanna, with whose help he entered his greatest creative period.

It was my friend Edgar Tafel, one of the first apprentices in the fellowship established at Taliesin, who brought me there, and in 1938 I published an article about Frank Lloyd Wright in *Coronet* magazine. From then on my fascination with the man and his works continued to grow, for he achieved, many believe, the greatest individual architectural creativity of all history.

Meyer Levin